ANTI-HERO BLUES

ANTI-HERO BLUES

CHRISTOPHER LEE RIPPEE

BALANCE OF SEVEN
Newport, VT

Anti-Hero Blues

For information, contact:
Balance of Seven
www.balanceofseven.com
info@balanceofseven.com

Cover Design by Natalie Diaz, The Artistic Geeks
natalievdiaz@gmail.com

Lettering by Nicole E. Harrer

Developmental Editing and Copyediting by Leo Otherland

Formatting and Proofreading by TNT Editing
www.theodorentinker.com/TNTEditing

Publisher's Cataloging-in-Publication Data

Names: Rippee, Christopher Lee.
Title: Anti-hero blues / Christopher Lee Rippee.
Description: Dallas, TX : Balance of Seven, 2024.
Identifiers: LCCN 2024938952 | ISBN 9781947012677 (pbk.) | ISBN
     9781947012684 (ebook)
Subjects: LCSH: Superheroes – Fiction. | Life change events – Fiction. |
     Trust – Fiction. | Good and evil – Fiction. | Ambiguity – Fiction. |
     BISAC: FICTION / Superheroes. | FICTION / Science Fiction /
     Action & Adventure. | FICTION / Science Fiction / General.
Classification: LCC PS3618.I67 A58 2024 (print) | PS3618.I67 (ebook) |
     DDC 813 R57--dc23
LC record available at https://lccn.loc.gov/2024938952

28 27 26 25 24   1 2 3 4 5

To those who choose
kindness and empathy
over cruelty and self-interest.

CONTENTS

Contents

ONE

FAILED EXPERIMENT

*Y*ou want to know about the explosion and the pillar of fire in the sky at the Resistance Day celebration? What happened to Vincent Vaydan? Sure, we'll get there, but we need to start at the beginning.

It all went off the rails the day we turned MICSy on.

"Ladies and gentlemen, on behalf of Union City University and the Vaydan Institute for Experimental Physics, welcome!" Claire's South London accent colored her greeting as she smiled at the research review committee. She was really turning on the charm, which made sense given that the committee could pull the plug on our project with an email.

That worried me, but not as much as the possibility of blowing us all up in the next few minutes. My heart pounded against my rib cage as I raced through the pre-ignition checklist for the twentieth time, trying to focus.

With my hands shaking and a tangled snarl of

anxiety, excitement, and dread roiling in my stomach, I glanced at the clock.

9:57 a.m.

Three minutes until the moment of truth.

On the dubious bright side, if the test went badly, I wouldn't have a lot of time for regrets.

"We have what will undoubtedly be an exciting morning in store!"

Dr. Claire Wright was the head of our research team, my mentor, and basically a member of my family. She was in her fifties, having spent her life climbing to the top of her field. Despite her professional stature, Claire was only five foot five in two-inch heels, and slim. Short, iron-gray hair framed a face that seemed cheery despite her aura of cool professionalism. As usual, she wore an elegantly conservative blazer and matching skirt.

For our test run, she'd gone with navy blue.

A few members of the research oversight committee were clumped by the door. Most were watching remotely. We'd expected a better turnout, but I suspected the desire to be present for a scientific breakthrough was outweighed by an aversion to the possibility of sudden energetic events—explosions, for the nonscientific.

Two representatives from the physics department chatted with the Vaydan Industries contingent, a suit in his late twenties named Ashcroft and a tall woman I hadn't met, while Dr. Clifford from the Department of Energy, a grumpy-looking bureaucrat in a tweed jacket older than I was, glowered at everyone from behind an impressive mustache.

The lab used to be a bomb shelter, so it wasn't exactly spacious. Despite taking every safety precaution imaginable, the chance of us causing a massive explosion in a couple of minutes was slightly greater than zero, so it was good we were wrapped in concrete and steel a dozen feet underground. Unfortunately, it also meant the lab was a cramped maze of fabrication machines, workstations, and bundles of wiring taped to the floor. Most of the equipment was impressive, but none of it compared to the machine in the middle of the room.

Claire turned to me and the rest of the team standing awkwardly in front of the machine that dominated the lab. "These individuals represent some of the brightest young minds in our field, and they deserve the real accolades. Despite my title, all I did was approve purchase orders." Claire's smile turned mischievous. "Rarely in a scientist's career does one have the opportunity to take so much credit for doing so little."

The observers chuckled.

She gestured to Harvey, who nodded curtly before looking away.

"Dr. Zhang comes to us from the University of Toronto and specializes in the computational modeling of energetic systems."

Harvey was pale and thin, with a mop of stylishly unkempt black hair. Dressed in a tight, black button-down and fitted jeans, Harvey looked more like a model than a mathematician. He'd seemed like an asshole when we first met, but he just wasn't great with people. I wouldn't have called us friends, but we weren't far from it.

He didn't smile as the observation group shifted their collective gaze to him. He made most stoics seem emotionally unhinged.

"Next is Dr. Itzel Rodriguez," Claire continued. "Dr. Rodriguez is a mechanical engineer from the University of Mexico, by way of MIT. She specializes in exotic-matter containment and applied xenotechnology."

Itzel was short, with an olive complexion and a mane of wavy brown hair, streaked with blue, that surrounded a face with round cheeks. She was in one of her many science-pun T-shirts, battered jeans, and Chuck Taylors. Her shirt of the day had a smiling proton telling an electron to be positive.

Itzel's endless enthusiasm almost made up for her tendency to sing when she was excited. Nothing helped complex engineering problems like lab karaoke. Still, I'd put money on her winning a Nobel Prize.

Vibrating with excitement, Itzel beamed when Claire said her name. "It's great to meet everyone," she said, with a hint of a Mexican accent.

Claire pointed to our third team member. "Many of you already know Dr. Nathan Chambers."

I resisted the urge to roll my eyes.

Barely.

Nate was blandly handsome, with sandy-blond hair, blue eyes, and the muscle tone of someone who worked out for looks. Straightening his salmon polo, he smiled with the casually smug air of a guy used to being showered with praise. I guess it came with being the child of a billionaire.

Nate was the son and heir apparent of tech mogul Jeremiah Chambers. His PhD was just part of preparing for his legacy.

As much as I disliked the rich, though, Nate's money wasn't why I couldn't stand him.

The guy was just awful.

He ignored Harvey and treated Itzel like a waitress, but he reserved his real contempt for me. I was the only one in the lab without a PhD, but that didn't bother him as much as the fact I'd grown up *poor.*

The first time we met, Nate had asked Claire if she'd given all her *strays* research projects. I'd asked him if he was planning to be buried in his father's shadow or just live his whole life in it.

It went downhill from there.

As much as I hated the guy, though, Nate was good at computational physics. It was why Claire had brought him in on the project, even if his presence was a needle in the heart of my chill.

"And of course, I want to introduce Brandon Carter." Claire gestured to me, her smile expanding with pride. "Brandon came to my attention years ago, thanks to his high-school physics teacher."

Someone snickered. Maybe they'd been born with an advanced degree.

"While research is a team effort, Brandon's equations—his revolutionary way of visualizing and modeling gravitational waves in tandem with highly energetic systems—are this project's foundation. The first time I read the paper that launched all this,"—Claire gestured around the lab—"a paper Brandon wrote as a second-year undergrad, I might add—I thought it was rubbish, mostly because I didn't think what he was suggesting was possible." Claire chuckled. "When Brandon explained his work to me, I realized I was holding something extraordinary."

The observers looked at me. Some seemed impressed; others, dubious or dismissive.

I managed not to glare.

Whatever they saw, I doubted *physicist* was the first word that came to mind. *Musician,* maybe, if they were being generous. *Armed robber* if they weren't.

I was twenty-three and nearly six foot four, with a wiry build and the colorless complexion of my Irish roots. My hair was dark, a product of the Korean side of my dad's family, chopped short and shaved on the sides. I wasn't what people called handsome. Striking, maybe, with deep-set hazel eyes under a heavy brow, a large nose, prominent cheekbones, and a strong chin.

My uniform—a hoodie, band shirt, jeans, and a pair of boots, all black—didn't exactly scream *scientist*. Neither did the tattoos that peeked out from beneath my sleeves and spread across my hands.

If asked, almost anyone who knew me growing up would've said the only way I'd end up in a physics lab was by robbing it. Before fifteen, I would have agreed. The trajectory of my life hadn't been aimed anywhere good.

Why?

Because a *superhero* killed my dad when I was eight. If it hadn't been for that high-school science teacher sending a paper I'd written to Claire, I probably would've ended up in a jail cell instead of a lab.

Claire smiled again. "Collectively, this team has accomplished something monumental: the first step in bridging the gulf between our world and the infinite other worlds beyond."

She waved at the device behind us. "Our machine uses alien matter to shape a gravitational distortion and generate a microscopic breach in the membrane separating our reality from others, allowing us to receive electromagnetic radiation from a nearby multiversal strand. To put it another way, we'll be capturing radio signals from parallel Earths."

The size of a cargo van, our machine might have looked like a haphazard tangle of wires, cables, and components grafted at random to a metal frame, but every module, field generator, and dedicated processor had been custom built for this experiment. Collectively, it represented three years of my life and more than $9 million of funding.

The machine's official name was the Multiversal Intermembrane Communication System. We called her MICSy.

MICSy wasn't pretty, but she didn't need to be. At her heart, straining against a xibrantium containment bottle, was a piece of voidrium the size of a fingertip, capable of generating enough gravity to punch a hole through the fabric of space-time.

Assuming the test didn't kill us all in the next few minutes.

"That's right. Some of you traveled two thousand miles to watch us turn on the world's most expensive radio," Claire said, eliciting more chuckles. "But if we're successful, the technology will pave the way for full matter transference."

The multiverse wasn't a theory. It was a fact made hard to ignore by the occasional monster attacks and invaders from alternate timelines. Masks had been known to travel to other multiversal threads, or parallel worlds, and tread on strange and "undreamed shores," to borrow a phrase from Shakespeare. They did it in ways not easily replicated, however: Magical portals. Falling through black holes.

If successful, we'd take a step toward making the trip easier.

"Now, ladies and gentlemen, shall we make history?" Claire turned to the team and raised an eyebrow.

I looked at the clock, my stomach churning.

It was 10:01 a.m.

Breaking apart, we headed to our workstations. Harvey and I were on one side of the room, monitoring the control system and the voidrium to ensure the exotic material's energy output remained within the containment fields' tolerances. On the other side, Itzel monitored MICSy's power system, while Nate watched CPU usage on the control-software servers to make sure they didn't crash.

I glanced at the team. They seemed as nervous as I felt, even Nate, who had the least to lose, outside his life.

Taking a breath, I pulled up the ignition sequence. "Everyone ready?"

Harvey nodded.

"Make it so!" Itzel chirped.

"Get on with it, Carter," Nate groused.

"Here we go." I took another deep breath and clicked the initialize button.

The refrigerator-sized xenotech power block began to vibrate, and MICSy hummed as she generated a series of overlapping containment fields. The smell of ozone filled the air, but the diagnostics showed everything as nominal.

"Containment fields on, control system running," I breathed. "How are we looking on your end, Itzel?"

"Stable. MICSy's purring like a kitten."

"Opening the containment bottle and bringing the voidrium online." Hoping I wasn't about to kill us all, I started the activation sequence.

The power block's hum deepened as the xibrantium bottle at MICSy's heart opened. The voidrium inside glimmered with violet light as energy flowed through it.

A stillness filled the room. This was the real test. If

it went well, we'd change the world. If it went poorly . . . well, we might still change the world, at least on local topographic maps.

"Uh, Brandon, you should look at this," Harvey murmured, a ripple of tension in his tone.

"What?" I asked, hoping my voice wouldn't carry to the observers. Harvey's calm demeanor was a joke in the lab, which meant the worry in his tone amounted to hysterics for anyone else.

"We're getting some instability in the voidrium modulation field."

A chill ran through me. *Shit.*

Voidrium was *highly* unstable. Investigators had discovered it among the wreckage of the Rakkari ships that assaulted Earth nearly three decades ago. The Rakkari had used it for faster-than-light travel, but research so far had produced no results other than fatal accidents. Our project was one of a handful authorized to work with the exotic matter, and only for a brief window of time.

Sliding out of my seat, I made my way to Harvey as quickly as I could without running, weaving around equipment and through wires. Harvey slid to the side as I stepped in front of his terminal. The screen was covered in graphs and other monitoring tools that would have been incomprehensible to most people, but we had designed the system. I saw what he meant instantly.

An alert message flashed in the field control system. *Uh-oh.*

Voidrium's energy production rate was unstable. Previous attempts to harness it had failed due to unpredictable power spikes, almost as if the voidrium were fighting to break free. To compensate, Harvey and I had created an algorithm to predict energy fluctuations and modulate the overlapping containment fields in real time. Without it, we couldn't have put enough power into the voidrium to penetrate the membrane separating our reality from other multiversal strands without it exploding.

Some of the best computational physicists at the university—and by extension, the world—had reviewed our algorithm. We'd run thousands of simulations, using data models constructed from other experiments.

It should have been *working*.

Instead, the algorithm was failing to predict nearly a third of the energy spikes, pushing the field generators to the limit of their tolerances. Unless we could get the spikes under control, the generators would burn out. If we lost one, failure would cascade through the rest, which would be very, *very* bad.

Our theoretical modeling predicted that an explosion *probably* wouldn't generate an ever-expanding singularity that would engulf the solar system, but it *would* destroy the lab, along with a significant portion of the building, not to mention kill everyone inside.

No pressure, I thought, breaking into a cold sweat.

I racked my brain, ignoring the voice telling me to shut MICSy off. If I hit the emergency shutoff, I could check the field generators and debug the algorithm. I could blame a faulty power relay and use the incident to demonstrate our rigorous safety protocols. But our research review was at the end of the month, and there was no guarantee the Department of Energy would let us keep the voidrium long enough for a second test run.

This needed to work.

Suddenly, the solution hit me. My fingers flew across the keyboard as I threw commands into different windows.

"Is there a problem, gentlemen?" Claire asked from behind me, her normally unflappable cool unable to keep the tension from her voice.

"It looks like the algorithm isn't modulating the fields properly," Harvey whispered. "It's failing to prevent roughly thirty percent of the energy fluctuations."

"Shut it down," Claire ordered. "Immediately."

Harvey reached for the emergency shutoff.

I grabbed his wrist. "Don't." We locked eyes. His were wide with fear. "I've got this."

We looked to Claire.

"We're still within tolerances," I said. "I need sixty seconds."

Claire's eyes narrowed, and she glanced at the committee. "One minute. If the power fluctuations aren't under control in *one minute*, shut it down."

I was typing before she'd finished speaking.

Our energy growth model wasn't the issue. It had to be a software bug. The night before, Nate had "fixed" a syntax error I'd supposedly overlooked. I was guessing whatever he'd done had broken something.

I initialized the previous version of the control software on a backup server. MICSy sent data to both primary and secondary control systems as a failsafe. I could compare the readings on the secondary server to the primary and, if there were no errors in the earlier version, switch to it. The two control systems ran concurrently, so there shouldn't be any interruptions. If I was right, the switch would stabilize the process.

The program was system intensive, so it took time to synchronize. Each second felt like an hour as the diagnostics flashed alarms.

I tried not to think about the consequences of being

wrong as MICSy's smooth purr shifted into a rumbling growl, drawing concerned murmurs from our observers.

"Apologies, gentlemen!" Claire flashed them a practiced smile. "It wouldn't be science without a little excitement."

Nearly there. Five seconds until the backup came online.

The lights flickered.

Four seconds. My pulse pounded in my ears.

Three.

The grumbling increased. Harsh, violet light radiated from the containment bottle. The field generators' output levels began to redline.

Two.

The acrid stench of overheating electronics filled the room. Electricity crackled, and a blue flash, followed by a spray of sparks, erupted from MICSy. It was only the secondary power relay burning out. We were still good.

One.

A field generator blew, sparks erupting from the side of the machine, but the other generators still worked.

The fix was going to *work*. I was sure of it.

The prior version of the control system finished initializing. Immediately, I could see I was right. The energy curve began to smooth out. I switched control systems, and the levels started to stabilize.

"I've got it—"

Claire hit the emergency override. MICSy sputtered and went silent as the diagnostic panel flatlined.

The stench of smoldering electronics intensified, and a haze filled the room.

People coughed behind me.

Shit.

TWO

DOWN UNDER

I slumped in a chair outside Claire's office, Aus-Rotten's *Rotten Agenda* pouring through my headphones. Punk rock might not be most people's choice when trying to unwind, but it was one of my comfort albums, even if it wasn't much comfort right then.

Like the rest of the Vaydan Institute, the reception area had a vaguely futuristic aesthetic. Everything was minimalist white, with clean lines and too much glass. A holographic representation of the institute's logo, a stylized *V*, spun slowly above a podium near the door.

Itzel, Harvey, and Nate had already left, leaving me alone with Lilly, the office manager. If the circumstances had been different, Lilly would have been showing me new pictures of her grandchildren or videos of her French bulldog, Tesla. Instead, she glanced at me over her monitor periodically, her expression a demoralizing blend of pity and sympathy.

I checked the time on my phone, trying to ignore the anxiety and disappointment churning my stomach.

It was 2:02 p.m.

Only two minutes had passed since the last time I'd checked, but it felt like twenty, dread and tedium dilating time. Claire had been in her office with Dr. Clifford, the Department of Energy's observer, and Jason Ashcroft, the Vaydan Foundation's representative, for more than an hour, leaving me to ruminate on my failures.

After the experiment, the review board had scattered as quickly as dignity would allow. Most had seemed a little dazed, probably unsettled by the realization they'd just come close to a disaster. Only Dr. Clifford had remained behind, tweed sleeves crossed over his ample belly and mousy-brown mustache trembling with rage, as he watched us cycle everything down and return the voidrium to cold storage. After that, he'd asked for a "word" with Claire and the Vaydan representatives.

That word had turned into many, most of which Dr. Clifford shouted during the ebb and flow of his tirade. It was hard to glean details from the muffled conversation, but words like "reckless" and "catastrophe" were audible despite my music and came up more than once, usually with my name attached.

I tried not to panic as a knot of stress formed between my shoulder blades.

Part of me knew this wasn't the end of my career. We'd achieved more than we'd expected, even if we hadn't hit our ultimate goal. The data alone would give other researchers something to pour over for years, and the field generators had a lot of potential in both scientific and commercial circles, even if I didn't love selling out to soulless corporations.

Still, I couldn't quite shake a bone-deep sense of shame or the demoralizing knowledge that I'd failed so visibly. I'd invested so much of myself. I made sacrifices. The project had consumed my life.

And we'd been so *close*. If I'd had another few seconds, we would have changed the world.

The proximity of success made failure all the more bitter.

I tried to focus on other things, but that didn't help much. I had a missed call from Mom, and my best friend, Vee, had sent me a text at eleven asking if I'd blown up the world yet.

Abby, my ex-girlfriend, had reached out before the experiment for the first time in weeks: *Hey, big day. I know it means a lot. Hope all goes well.*

Her name on my phone's screen conjured a familiar ache in my chest. I thought about replying, but I couldn't find the words.

Or the courage.

I sent Vee a text instead: *Nope, the world is still intact. Beer later?*

She responded with a GIF of a robot puking into a toilet, which meant she was in.

After that, I made the mistake of checking the news. The headlines were the usual mix of banal gossip and existential horror.

"Hero Red Streak and Influencer Kaiden James Have Fallout on the Red Carpet"

"Demonic Invasion Narrowly Avoided in Des Moine"

"VPhone 7 Ultra Promises More Processing Power than 2000s Supercomputer"

"Outbreak of Mutation in Bristol Linked to Popular New Fast Food Chicken Sandwich"

Christopher Lee Rippee

Most of the day's headlines were about an army of fishmen invading Sydney, Australia. It wasn't even the first aquatic assault in the last month. A league of undersea civilizations had declared war on their terrestrial neighbors after their demands to curb water pollution had been ignored.

A familiar mixture of numb horror, helplessness, and boredom gripped me as I watched another disaster unfold on various news channels.

The invaders were supported by gigantic war crustaceans mounted with the fishy equivalent of field artillery and flying manta rays that spat lightning. The centerpiece of their assault was a cerulean-blue crab twelve stories tall. A whimsical castle bristling with cannons and warriors perched on top of the creature's shell, while gun emplacements and assault troops clung to its underbelly.

Thanks to a last-minute warning from the Atlantean League, the Australian army had been able to start an evacuation and muster a defense. After being mauled for two hours, the Australians had retreated entirely, making way for a combined force of mask teams, including luminaries like Vanguard, Last Watch, and Omega Force, along with hundreds of independents from Australia and beyond.

When the masks had shown up, whether by flight, teleportation, super speed, or invisible aircraft, they'd blunted the furious fishman assault with their own ferocious violence, breaking the conflict into melees in the streets and the skies above Sydney.

Most people called masks "superheroes" or "supervillains"—easy labels that put sorcerers, mutants, demigods, aliens, and rogue inventors into neat boxes. But someone covering their face didn't make them a hero—

or a villain, for that matter—so some people used the term "mask" instead.

A few of the masks repelling the Sydney assault tried to avoid collateral damage, but most didn't bother, as terrifying and destructive as the undersea invaders. A news drone live-streamed a twelve-foot-tall werewolf in fuzzy blue knee boots and a matching speedo as he hurled a city bus at a fishy invader with enough force to punch through an apartment building in an eruption of masonry. The werewolf howled victoriously while the building collapsed.

Another stream caught a pimply-face teenager in a cape waving a wand over his top hat. Tucking his wand under his arm, the teen reached into the hat, pulled out a quivering ball of flesh, and threw it at a company of Myctophian infantry. The fleshy orb grew explosively into a writhing nightmare of tentacles and teeth, and the young magician watched with a smile as his summoned horror devoured those too slow to escape.

Not all of Sydney's dubious saviors did so well, though. One drone captured an older mask with a retro-futuristic jet pack and a rifle get plucked out of the sky by a massive claw and torn apart. A teleporting ninja appeared in front of a blast from a fishman weapon and burned like a star from the inside, before his ashes drifted away on the breeze.

Another live stream showed the massive crab fortress crashing through the Sydney Opera House, breaking the structure's clamshell domes into chunks of white stone that tumbled into the bay. At the edge of the frame, a figure appeared in the air. The shaky camera focused on it, revealing a muscular young woman with a mane of dark hair and golden-brown skin. Her sleeveless smart-weave suit was patterned to resemble crashing waves and clung to her like a second skin, while her exposed arms were covered in traditional Maori tattoos. I'd seen her in the news before, but I couldn't recall her name.

Ngaru, maybe? There were too many superhumans to remember.

The young woman wove her hands in front of her, and the ocean churned below the gargantuan crustacean. Roaring torrents of water as thick as buses erupted beneath the living fortress, piercing a shell that had shrugged off tank rounds and air-to-ground missiles. The crustacean screamed, its mouthparts trilling an agonized death song, before it exploded in a rain of meat, shell fragments, and coral.

The sight was a terrifying display of power, but it wasn't even the most impressive thing I'd seen that week.

Despite the Atlantean warning, a banner at the bottom of the news feeds put civilian casualty figures in the hundreds. No doubt they would climb into the thousands by the end of the day.

Not for the first time, I wondered how anyone managed a sense of normalcy in a world where mad scientists, supervillains, aliens, gods, and fishmen armies could terrorize cities, particularly when their motives were often as inscrutable as the assailants themselves.

The truth was, even the horrifying and astonishing became depressingly commonplace after long enough, especially when ignorance or numbness were the only defense.

Claire's door opened, jarring me back to the reception area. Pulling my headphones out, I stuffed my phone in my pocket as Dr. Clifford stormed through the room. He paused to glare at me and straighten his jacket before he left. I hadn't expected anything else, but his withering disdain did nothing to abate my crushing sense of failure.

"Are you sure you don't want some tea, hon?" Lilly asked. "I've got a whole bunch of different types. Black, green, maybe some chamomile?"

"No, thanks." I tried to smile. "I'm good."

The look Lilly gave me seemed to disagree, but she nodded. "It'll be here if you change your mind."

The volume of the conversation dropped after Dr. Clifford left. Ashcroft, the Vaydan representative, lingered in Claire's office for a few more minutes before he stepped out with the tall blonde woman from the test. He turned my way as soon as he saw me, his eyes lighting up.

Ashcroft was in his late twenties and irritatingly handsome. Tall, dark, and perfectly put together, he oozed confident professionalism. His tailored suit, charcoal with black patterning, had probably cost more than I spent on rent each month.

I'd disliked him the moment we'd met.

The woman behind him was stunning, too, lean and statuesque, with cheekbones that could have cut glass.

"Brandon, I'm glad you're here." Ashcroft flashed a polished smile. "I was hoping for a quick word. This is Cara. She works for Mr. Vaydan as well."

Cara regarded me unblinkingly and smiled. "It's a pleasure to meet you, Brandon."

"Yeah, you too." Sighing inwardly, I started to apologize, but Ashcroft lifted a hand to silence me.

He glanced back at Cara. "We wanted to reassure you that the Vaydan Foundation is *very* pleased with your results."

I opened my mouth again, but nothing came out.

After a couple of speechless seconds, I finally managed, "I'm sorry?"

Ashcroft's smile became comforting, and he leaned close, his volume dropping. "Between the three of us, I spoke to Mr. Vaydan right after the test. He was pleased with the outcome. He's planning to attend the gala tonight, assuming he can wrap up the unpleasantness in Australia, and he'd like to meet you."

I nodded numbly.

Vincent Vaydan.

Genius. Billionaire. Philanthropist.

Superhero.

Vincent Vaydan was a founding member of Vanguard, the team that had saved the world when the Rakkari attacked. His alter ego—assuming you could apply the term to an identity he'd publicly acknowledged decades ago—was Aegis. Like Empyrean, Polaris, Hecate, Knightblade, and the rest of Vanguard, Vaydan was known by everyone on the planet. All of Vanguard's stories had been told and retold thousands of times.

Biographies had been written about them.

Hollywood had made movies based on those biographies.

There were even musicals.

One article I'd read had said that nearly ten percent of all porn traffic was Vanguard related.

Vaydan was an icon, an example of how a baseline human could use intellect, perseverance, and will to create order from chaos. He was something like a normal person in a pantheon of super soldiers, aliens, and gods.

Unlike most of Vanguard, who were metahumans with inherent abilities, Vaydan's powers came from his high-tech exosuit, hence the name Aegis. He had developed the suit himself using his father's research after soviet agents kidnapped his parents. Depending on how family friendly the story was, tweenage Vincent had killed or incapacitated the kidnappers and rescued his family using a prototype his father kept in his home lab.

When the military found out Vaydan's father had a prototype at home, they'd arrested him and seized his work. Vincent Vaydan then reverse engineered the prototype and built his own suit, a later iteration of which he'd used to fend off the Rakkari invasion alongside the rest of his Vanguard buddies.

Vaydan Industries, the company Vaydan had built, had revolutionized industry after industry as it grew. Breakthroughs in robotics and artificial intelligence had transformed automation and data analytics. Breakthroughs in nanotech had established new paradigms for medical care and manufacturing. His work in applied physics had changed the world's power infrastructure. His telecom satellites had become the backbone of the globally distributed internet, capable of speeds undreamed of even a decade ago.

Vaydan's space agency was mining the asteroid belt.

His detractors pointed to piles of profit and unprecedented influence, as well as the military hardware that Vaydan's company developed, weapons sold around the world.

I agreed with the detractors, but the majority of the world didn't.

Nearly *everyone* had benefited from Vaydan. He was a superhero who regularly donated billions to charity. He'd contributed massively to the reconstruction of Union City after the Rakkari attack, helping to build "a city of the future." Vaydan had created funds that offset the damage caused by metahuman conflicts and educational programs that helped kids enter tech fields. One of his subsidiaries had built the free virtual learning platform used by schools around the world.

His philanthropy had also benefited my mom and me. The money from his foundation had changed our lives, and I worked in a research institution with his name on the door.

I owed Vaydan. A part of me even admired him. But the kid in me, who still mourned his father's death at the hands of a mask, couldn't help bristling at the man's accolades, statues, and hero-worship.

Regardless of my feelings about the guy, I'd never *dreamed* of meeting him.

"You've had a challenging morning, Brandon," Cara said, snapping me out of my thoughts. The hint of a smile played at the corners of her lips. "Just make sure you're at the party tonight. We look forward to seeing you there."

They said their goodbyes and left me stunned in the reception area.

Claire called me into her office a few minutes later.

THREE

PROJECT CANCELED

'm sorry, Brandon, there's nothing to be done." Claire sighed, sagging into her chair. She'd taken off her jacket and hung it on a door hook—a shocking breach of decorum for her—and she turned her wedding ring as she considered me, a touch of fatigue in her ice-blue eyes. "The Department of Energy is pulling the voidrium. They have a team coming tomorrow at nine a.m."

Claire's office was large and well-appointed, with windows that overlooked a green expanse of trees filled with undergrads enjoying the last bit of nice weather before fall buried them in gloom.

Unlike the rest of the institute, the room was filled with dark wood furnishings that matched an immaculately ordered, handcrafted desk with only a computer and a picture of Claire's wife on top. Her shelves were full of books, many of which she'd written, and her walls were dotted with framed awards and photos of her with other prominent physicists, like Hawking and Higgs.

"I don't understand," I replied, fighting to keep my

frustration in check. "We've hit *all* of our benchmarks. It was just a bug in the code, which we *fixed*."

"And I told them that." Opening a drawer, Claire pulled out a bottle of scotch and two glasses. "For what it's worth, the Department of Energy was going to pull the voidrium no matter how the experiment turned out. They've already pulled the samples from every other research team across the country. We were the last. The department has a new director, and she doesn't believe the benefits are worth the risks. Every piece of voidrium is going into deep storage."

"*Damn* it!" I growled. "If you'd waited a second longer, it—"

"If I'd waited a second longer, you might have killed us all," Claire cut in, but there was no heat in her voice. She poured a glass of scotch for herself, then one for me—both filled nearly to the rim—and slid mine across the desk.

I looked away, frustration and shame burning in my stomach. A photo of Claire at the White House caught my eye.

Following my gaze, she smiled, tired, wistful. "It's hard to imagine so much work—so many years—reduced to a display on a wall." She snorted softly. "The awards feel almost tacky at this point."

"They shouldn't," I said after a moment, picking up my glass with a sigh. "You earned them all."

"You'll earn your own shelf of awards, I suspect." Claire turned back to me, her smile widening.

I grunted, looking away. The lead weight in my chest didn't feel like a beginning. It felt like failure.

"Did you know Imani thought you'd plagiarized the paper she sent me?" Claire finally asked.

I shrugged. "Can you blame her?"

"I suppose not." Claire sighed, the hint of a smirk on her lips. "Most ninth-grade science teachers don't get students proposing a new model of gravitational computation accounting for quantum pressure near black holes. I didn't think you'd written it either."

I hadn't been trying to show off. Electromagnetism, Newtonian motion, energy, and especially gravity—they were all like languages my brain was wired to speak. The math too. I could visualize equations and what they described, see the beauty hidden within the numbers.

Curiosity clashed with the failure that sat like a weight on my shoulders, pulling my eyes back to Claire. "Then why'd you come to New York?"

"Because Imani was one of my favorite students," she said after a moment, "and it was an excuse to visit her. And because there was a chance, however small, that you *had* written that paper, which would mean Imani had discovered someone truly remarkable. So she took me to your tiny apartment, and we spent hours at your kitchen table while you answered questions and solved problems my PhD students couldn't manage."

"All while Uncle Mike drank and yelled at the television in the next room." I leaned back in my chair, looking at the ceiling as memories momentarily pierced the pall of frustration and disappointment. "And then you got me a scholarship to Isabella Ruiz High School, the best science high school in the country, and a grant from the Vaydan Foundation that gave Mom and me more to live on in a year than Mom could've made at the diner in five."

"And you did *brilliantly*." A wry expression crossed Claire's face. "There were rough patches, obviously, particularly all the fighting. I'm sometimes amazed your brain is still in good working order given how often you were hit in the head. Still, you made it through."

"Thanks to you," I acknowledged. "They'd have expelled me if you hadn't stopped them."

"I'm glad I stopped them. Not only did you graduate, you went on to finish undergrad in three years, with degrees in physics, computer science, and engineering. And you chose to do your PhD with me."

I smirked sourly. "I'm sure you had nothing to do with me getting into the Vaydan Institute."

"You earned your place here, Brandon." Claire picked up her glass. "You've proven that to me and everyone else. You and your team achieved more than we ever expected. From every perspective, your work is an astonishing success."

Pausing, she looked down at my glass. After a moment's hesitation, I picked it up, sighing as I held it out. She gently touched the rim of her glass to mine, and we both drank, the scotch a blend of smoke and peat that burned pleasantly on the way down.

Claire closed her eyes for a second. When she reopened them, she leaned across her desk, resting her hand on my arm.

"This may be an end, but it's also a beginning. Try to look past your disappointment. You're a brilliant young man, and people have *noticed.*

"On a personal note, I also wanted to tell you how terribly *proud* of you I am. When I walked into your apartment and found you, a wary, serious young man, I never could have imagined what you'd accomplish, or what you would come to mean to me." Claire smiled warmly. "You're like a nephew to me and Gracie."

The fog of dread and shame, the palpable sense of failure, receded a little. "Mom and I think of you both as family too." I paused for a second. "Can we convince the Department of Energy to—"

"No." Pinning me with her gaze, Claire removed her hand from my arm and leaned back in her chair. "Listen to me, Brandon." Her expression hardened. "You've already accomplished more than most people do in a lifetime. You have a *future.*"

I looked away. She was right. A few seconds later, I nodded.

"Look forward, soon-to-be-Dr. Carter. Not behind."

We sat in silence, drinking scotch.

"Gracie and I are leaving for London tonight, after the gala," Claire said eventually, "but we'll be back in early October. I'm throwing a birthday party for Gracie the week after we return. You and Laura should come. It'll be a good chance for you to network."

I nodded. "Absolutely. Mom would really enjoy it."

"How's Laura doing?"

Sighing, I looked out the window. "She has good days and bad days."

Like hundreds of thousands of others, Mom had been diagnosed with Harden-Klein syndrome. No one knew what caused the debilitating, and ultimately fatal, neurodegenerative disease. The prevailing theory was that it resulted from exposure to unknown substances released by Rakkari ships when they were blown up above cities across the world.

Claire's expression became sympathetic. "Laura's a strong woman, and many of the treatments on the horizon show real promise. Are you still helping her?"

Mom had done okay for a while, but her health had

declined over the last year. She was only able to work part-time, so she was having trouble making ends meet. I wasn't going to let illness rob her of the home she'd worked so hard for, so I gave her as much as I could every month. However, I was paying rent alone now, and things were tight.

My struggle must have shown in my expression. "Don't lose hope," Claire said, smiling comfortingly. "I know the lead researchers on a couple of trials. I'll make some calls."

Nodding, I closed my eyes as I fought a sudden wave of emotion and took a ragged breath. "I'd really appreciate that."

Claire refilled our glasses, and we drank again.

"I was waiting for you to broach the topic," Claire said after a minute of companionable silence, "but I couldn't help noticing that Abby hasn't been around. Is something amiss?"

"We had a fight." I sighed. "She wanted some time."

"Oh, no." Claire leaned forward, her expression shifting to concern. "What happened?"

"Do you remember the field-stability test we ran last month?" She nodded. "I came in the Sunday before to do some last-minute calibrations and lost track of time." I slumped in my chair and swirled the scotch in my glass. "I missed her brother's birthday. It was a *big* deal."

"Oh, Brandon," Claire said, her tone sympathetic.

"Abby was furious. She called me self-absorbed. Told me she was tired of always coming last. She packed a bag and went to stay with a friend. She's been there for a few weeks." I sagged in my chair a little more, suddenly weighed down by the memory.

"Have you spoken since?"

"A couple of times. We've been texting."

Standing, Claire moved around her desk and put her hand on my shoulder. "Go talk to her. Apologize. *Fix* things. Take it from someone much older than you: this is *not* the sort of regret you want to carry for the rest of your life."

I nodded, but I didn't think there was anything left to fix.

Claire squeezed my shoulder. "I have work I need to finish, but I'll see you at the party tonight."

"See you tonight." I attempted a smile.

Claire returned it encouragingly as I shut the door behind me.

I said goodbye to Lilly and left the building, avoiding eye contact whenever possible.

Pulling out my phone, I checked the emergency alert app. It was a slow day, especially for Union City. Some low-level villains were robbing a jewelry store near the waterfront, and a couple of masks were fighting a small horde of what looked like mutant mole rats west of the institute, but the area around the university was clear.

Lost in thought, I drifted off campus and found myself on the Boulevard of Heroes. It was a popular artery, full of theaters, restaurants, and bars. Despite being early, the sidewalks were already filled with street performers, hawkers selling memorabilia, and crowds of people.

I eventually ended up in Vanguard Square, the park commemorating Vanguard's victory over the Rakkari. Trees and benches surrounded a circular clearing dominated by a fountain that contained statues of Vanguard's founding members.

Resistance Day, the global holiday marking the Rakkari defeat, was coming up, so the Square was packed with even more people than usual. Musicians, street vendors, and food carts mingled with tourists being accosted by costumed performers. The performers were poor copies of the bronze demigods above them, though, taking pictures with tourists for tips instead of saving the world. A few D-list masks were mixed in as well, but no one paid them much attention.

I guess it was better to get your picture taken with a fake Knightblade than a real nobody.

Above the crowd, the greatest of Union City's resident pantheon, cast in bronze, surveyed their charges.

I knew their names and stories. Everyone did. All of Vanguard's founding members—not just Vincent Vaydan—had been the focus of decades of collective obsession and worship.

Knightblade, or Claudia Winston, stood at the left end of the semicircle of statues. A scientist, she had worked on the Allied super-soldier program during World War II. According to her biography, she couldn't stand to watch others sacrifice their lives, so she'd taken the first dose of the super-soldier serum, transforming herself into the Allies' first uniformed metahuman.

The bronze statue depicted Knightblade in her first costume, holding Queensguard, her xibrantium longsword, face molded into an expression of fierce resolve.

Hecate, or Elena Lambros, stood to Knightblade's right. Hecate claimed to be—and probably was—a literal goddess of magic, right out of Greek mythology. She was one of the most powerful sorcerers on the planet and had once turned an army of frost giants attacking a Swedish soccer match into butterflies.

The sculptor had captured Hecate in her classic peplos, a mysterious expression on her too-perfect face, which was framed by wavy locks that fell to the ground from under a crown of flowers.

Empyrean, or Jor'An, humanity's alien savior, stood in the middle, looming over his comrades. Raised to be the greatest warrior of his people, Empyrean had arrived right before the Rakkari attack, bringing a warning that had allowed the world's metahumans to unite against the alien invasion.

Inarguably one of the most powerful beings on the planet, Empyrean's strength defied reason, and he'd proven impossible to kill, despite *many* attempts. For many, he was *the* symbol of strength, duty, and sacrifice, depicted as a tireless defender of his adopted planet. For others, he was an icon of our dependence on meta-humans beholden to no authority. The sculptor had done their best to capture Empyrean, making him tall, improbably muscled, and impossibly perfect.

Polaris, or Isaiah Freeman, stood to Empyrean's right. Polaris had been an engineering student at Howard University in the 1940s, until he was chosen by alien sentinels to bear the Everspark—a mote of the cosmic fire that had birthed the universe—and protect the world.

Fennec, or Isabella Ruiz, stood on the far right. Known as the world's greatest detective, Fennec had been the only baseline-human, or unaugmented, member of the team aside from Vaydan. She'd been a master of hand-to-hand combat, supplementing her abilities with gadgets she built herself.

Fennec had been dead for almost three years now, murdered in her Union City apartment. It was the greatest unsolved murder of all time, and the world still mourned her, though nowhere more deeply than here in Union City. She'd been born and raised here, and she'd touched it in a multitude of ways. Even my high school had her name on the door.

The platform below her sculpture was covered in tokens of appreciation, flowers, and candles.

The sculptor had depicted Fennec in her original costume, a slim armored suit with a half mask topped by fox ears. The statue was smirking, as if she were thinking about a joke she wasn't going to share.

Above them all soared Aegis, or Vincent Vaydan, sculpted in the original iteration of his armor. I shook my head, unable to believe I was going to meet the guy.

"Hey, man." A scruffy kid in a hoodie was standing behind me when I turned around. "Have you heard about Vanguard's proposed expansion?"

I nodded. "Yeah, why?"

"Dr. Catastrophe's attack on New York was a tragedy, but that doesn't mean Vanguard should be handed unprecedented authority." The kid shoved a pamphlet into my hand. "They're building towers across the country and bringing in new teams and even baseline personnel augmented with tech, which they're calling Sentinels. No superhero team in history has attempted what they're doing. More than that, some of the new 'heroes' they're inducting—the Union City Defenders, for one—have a *lot* of excessive-force complaints. This talks about how expanding Vanguard's authority could be dangerous. There's a website on the back."

I wasn't thrilled, either, with the idea of Vanguard's expansion, and we weren't alone. Some lawmakers, along with the Bureau of Metahuman Affairs, opposed the moves being made, but governmental authority over metahumans had ended with the dissolution of the Initiative, the organization that had once policed metahumans.

I put the pamphlet in my backpack. "Thanks, man." The kid nodded and made his way over to a man and woman sitting with a little girl on a nearby bench. After a few seconds, the two scowled. "Get the fuck out of here," the guy snapped at the budding activist, who scurried away.

I sighed, my shoulders tensing with familiar frustration. Most people basically worshipped masks, Vanguard in particular, and couldn't imagine why anyone *wouldn't*. They wanted black and white, heroes and villains, a world that fit neatly into categories, instead of the seething chaos and uncertainty they actually lived in.

To those people, suggesting that criminal-justice reform and safety-net programs might be a better way to fight crime than guys in spandex was almost as bad as putting on a cape and robbing a bank oneself.

And if a *hero* had killed my dad, then my dad had probably deserved it.

Don't get me wrong; I appreciated that Vanguard had saved the world more than once. I lived here. But even if Vanguard *were* the paragons people wanted them to be, it didn't mean they'd stay that way forever. Besides, people's blind spot toward the institution made it easier for other masks to get away with flagrant abuses of power, something I knew better than most.

Looking around, I sat on an empty bench, pulled out my phone, and opened Abby's text message.

Hey, I typed. *Thanks. Didn't go as planned.* I took a deep breath. *Want me to tell you about it at the Vaydan institute party tonight?*

A text notification went off a few minutes later.

I would like that.

FOUR

THE OLD APARTMENT

For the first time in months, I had a free afternoon. I thought about going back to the lab, to look over event logs, but I was oscillating between lethargic despair, jittery anxiety, and frustrated anger. There was no way I'd be able to focus.

My stomach rumbled. The hunger that had been kept at bay by stress finally crashed over me, so I went back to campus, jumped on my motorcycle, and rode to my apartment. The growl of the engine, and the electric thrill of adrenaline that came from weaving in and out of traffic, helped my mood a little.

Growing up, Dad had worked on bikes, so when I turned sixteen, I bought one at a scrapyard and taught myself how to fix it up with a little help from Uncle Mike.

My place was in Brackenridge, one of the wildly overpriced neighborhoods in the ever-expanding shadow of academia a few blocks from the lab. The building was "historic," which meant it was falling apart. The university owned it, renting apartments to researchers at a steep discount. With the neighborhood's sky-high rents, I couldn't have afforded a box in an alley otherwise.

I stopped in the bodega on the ground floor on my way up from the garage. The store usually had a good selection of premade food from a local deli, but the pickings were slim today. I grabbed a salad and a protein bar, the late lunch of champions, and said hi to Ali, the owner, on my way out.

A young couple was fighting in the lobby about how to get their overstuffed couch into the single working elevator, so I took the stairs up to the seventh floor. The old building's hallways were narrow, and I had to squeeze around one of my neighbors and her dog as I made my way to my door.

The apartment was a cramped one-bedroom, but it was a palace compared to some of the places I'd lived in growing up. Abby had taken her stuff, leaving my collection of concert bills, band posters, and art, as well as the mismatched crap we'd accumulated from curbs and secondhand stores. She'd left the pictures of us, though. I tried not to look at them, wondering when I'd work up the resolve to take them down.

Not that I was home much.

I flicked on the lights and kicked my boots off in the general direction of the battered shoe rack Abby had pulled off a curb. Flopping onto the couch, I pulled out my phone and dialed Mom. I'd promised her a call after the experiment.

"Hey," I said when she picked up.

"Hey, kiddo." She managed to sound excited.

"How are you doing?" I asked, dreading her answer.

Mom was one of the toughest women I knew, but Harden-Klein syndrome was a brutal disease, and slowly losing her fine motor skills had taken its toll on her resolve. Constant pain and fatigue weren't doing her any favors either, and the last few months since her diagnosis had been rough.

I'd offered to take some time away from the lab to help, but she wouldn't hear of it. Mom had known the test run was coming, and she'd said the last thing she wanted was for her illness to get in the way of my future.

"Oh, I'm tired but okay." Her tone was light, but exhaustion bled through. "I had to leave work a little early."

I winced. Money was already tight. The pain must have been bad.

"Get some rest and try not to worry. One of the trials we applied for will come through. They're doing some amazing work." I tried to sound optimistic, but there were thousands of applicants and only a handful of slots.

"I wouldn't bet on it, kiddo." A heavy sigh echoed through the phone. "I got a couple of rejection emails yesterday."

The news hit me like a fist in the gut. "Hey, we still have some grant applications out for nanotherapy trials. Claire said she knows a couple of the people running them and offered to put in a call. Stay positive."

"I'll do my best. How did the big day go?" she asked, changing the subject.

"Pretty well. A couple of small glitches, but we'll get it sorted out." It wasn't quite the truth, but Mom had already heard enough bad news for one week.

"You can tell me all about it on Sunday. You're still coming, right? Vee will be there. She said the two of you had plans this week, but you ditched her."

My shoulders slumped. *Shit.* Vee and I were supposed to have seen a band. "I was getting ready for the test, but I'll apologize tonight. We're meeting up."

"What about Sunday?"

"Wouldn't miss it."

"Hey." Mom's tone changed, becoming deceptively casual. "Have you talked to Abby lately?"

I groaned inwardly. "Yeah. She's coming with me to the institute party tonight."

"You know, honey. Sometimes relationships don't work, and that's okay. Who knows? Maybe there's someone you were meant to be with."

Vee and I had dated a couple of times, and Mom was convinced we'd end up together—an idea she brought up constantly. Subtlety was not her strong suit.

Sighing, I rolled my eyes. "On that note, I've got to run. Love you. Tell Uncle Mike I said hello, if you talk to him. I called him earlier this week, but you know how he is."

"I love you too, honey. See you Friday." Just as I was about to hang up, she added, "Oh, and Brandon?"

"Yeah?"

"Your uncle and I are proud of you, sweetie." Her voice cracked. "Your dad would have been too."

My chest tightened. "Thanks," I whispered before hanging up.

Most of what I knew about my dad came from the times Mom could bring herself to talk about him. I only had a few hazy memories of my own. A scruffy smile. Him holding me on his shoulders so I could see Empyrean flying at the head of a Resistance Day parade. A couple of motorcycle rides.

Growing up, Dad had wanted to be an electrical engineer. He'd been smart, the first person in his blended immigrant family to make it into college, but he dropped out to take care of his mom after she was diagnosed with cancer. He'd never made it back, bouncing between shit jobs until someone offered him more money in a night than he otherwise made in a month.

That was how he became a thief.

The neighborhood in Brooklyn where my parents grew up was the kind of place where criminality was a part of life. Everyone had an uncle who drove trucks for the mob or a cousin who ran numbers, or maybe their parents paid protection for their shop or got a loan from a "family friend" when the assholes at the bank wouldn't help.

Mom had tended bar in a pub owned by the McGraths, the mob family Uncle Mike worked for. It was where my parents met.

By the time they married, Dad had been pulling jobs for half a decade. One of those jobs got him killed a few weeks before my ninth birthday.

The official cause of death had been blunt trauma resulting from "resisting detainment by an authorized agent." In Dad's case, the "authorized agent" was a mask called Nightfang. He didn't even have *powers*, just a trust fund and a raging case of undiagnosed narcissism. He was still on the street in a costume, putting nonviolent criminals into comas while people called him a *hero*, which was almost enough to make me root for the other side.

Dad had worked for dangerous people, and Mom had worried they'd see us as loose ends. Normally, she'd have gone to Uncle Mike, but he'd been doing time for insurance fraud, which had left us with no one to turn to.

So the night Dad had died, she packed us up, and we ran with the clothes on our backs and a couple of suitcases. We used fake names. Sometimes we'd manage a month-to-month lease on a shitty apartment or mobile home, but we were homeless a lot of the time, living out of hotels or cars or camping in the woods.

I'd bounced from school to school, sometimes five or six a year, while Mom got crappy jobs at diners, truck stops, and bars, but we always had our eye on the door.

We didn't stop running until Uncle Mike got out of state pen almost four years later and convinced Mom his friends in the McGrath family—the same ones he used to find us—could keep us safe.

We moved back to New York City after that. It gave us something like stability after years of chaos. Mom got a job at a diner and reenrolled in school.

Meanwhile, I spread my miscreant wings, starting with all the usual hits. I smoked and stole and got into trouble. I skipped school, snuck out, and trespassed. I vandalized and stole cars. I even stole a boat once.

It sank.

What can I say? I had a gift.

Mostly, though, I fought. Winning or losing didn't matter.

Fighting was a chance to vent, to burn others with the anger roiling inside me. As the perennial new kid with a dead dad and no friends, I'd had *plenty* of opportunities, but I stuck up for other outcasts, too, mostly as an excuse to hit someone.

Eventually, I'd started to enjoy it, finding a savage serenity in the dance of black eyes, bloody knuckles, and broken noses.

The cops didn't give a shit.

Who cared about kids knocking each other around when an army of robots from the future could show up and assault the mayor's office on any given Tuesday? Who gave a damn about a few kids stealing a boat when a giant squid was attacking cargo ships in the harbor?

My schools didn't care, either, until my freshman year at Isabella Ruiz High School. They had different standards, I guess, and Claire had had to step in when they threatened to pull my scholarship for "disciplinary issues."

As part of the deal to keep me in school, I'd started therapy. I'd also found a Muay Thai gym, thanks to Uncle Mike. He'd boxed in the army and figured hitting people would help me manage my anger. He'd been right. Therapy helped, but Muay Thai helped more. I still came home with bruises, but I stopped fighting in school.

I had trained hard in high school and undergrad before MICSy and the project devoured my life. After that, I was lucky to make it to the gym a couple of times a week. Work meant I was always in my head, thinking about theoretical models, equations, code, or technical solutions for MICSy. It was stimulating, but it didn't do wonders for my health.

With Muay Thai, I could shut off my brain, and when I left the gym exhausted, bruised, and bleeding, I felt better than when I had walked in.

I called it kinetic therapy.

Given how the day had gone, I needed some kinetic therapy now. But by the time I finished eating, glancing through a journal while listening to a Restarts album, it was nearly five, and the gala started at seven.

I had a party to prepare for and a superhero to meet.

FIVE

PARTY

The University Center, a massive stone building with a dash of gothic flair, was the heart of Union City University. Somehow, UCU had been spared the worst of the Rakkari attack, so unlike a lot of the buildings put up afterward, the University Center felt solid, like it had history.

I liked it.

The main entrance was located on a tree-and-statue-lined drive that ended in a roundabout within a stone portico. For the night, crimson banners hung beside the door, announcing the Fiftieth Annual Science Gala. Spotlights hidden throughout the lawn projected images onto the building's façade, shifting between formulas and representations of helium atoms undergoing fusion. A line of cars stretched down the drive, depositing guests at the entrance, and I recognized physicists and engineers from some of the world's leading institutions.

Given the concentration of scientists, a who's who of the experimental physics community, the gala was a target

41

for all sorts of metahuman and technologically enhanced criminals. Probably to spare themselves from having to hunt down kidnapped scientists later, Vanguard had offered to provide security.

As a result, imposing figures in cobalt-blue hard-shell armor, with the Vanguard *V* on their shoulder plates and energy rifles slung across their chests, loomed among the guests and event staff. Two guards were stationed by the door, while others patrolled the grounds.

I still couldn't believe the US government had signed off on the Sentinel program, effectively green-lighting the creation of a private army, but the men and women in blue armor were proof it had.

One of the Sentinels looked over when I sat down on a bench near the entrance. I glowered, pointing to my employee badge, and he looked away.

Less than a minute later, Abby pulled up in the back of a driverless taxi, smiling at me as she stepped out. Standing, I made my way over to the entrance to meet her.

Abby was short but athletic, with muscle tone visible beneath her golden-brown skin, which seemed to glow in the light of the entrance. A waterfall of dark curls, tamed by hairclips, surrounded a round face with rich brown eyes, a small nose, full lips, and a dusting of freckles. For the gala, she wore a strapless, form-fitting peach dress that accentuated her curves.

"Hey, you," she said with a tentative smile, a hint of nervousness in her voice.

I was nervous too.

The silence dragged out for an awkward second.

"Hey," I eventually managed. "You look amazing."

Her eyes twinkled, and she gestured at the dress.

"This old thing? You look pretty great yourself, Mr. Carter. Who knew it was possible to get you into a tux?"

I wore the tuxedo Claire had bought me when she'd come to the horrified realization that I didn't have anything in my closet that approximated formal wear. The tux was the nicest thing I owned by a wide margin.

"What, this old thing?" I mirrored Abby's body language and tone, and her smile widened. I offered her my arm. "Shall we?"

Abby hesitated for a moment, before threading her arm through mine.

"How's work?" I asked as we started the long walk to the ballroom. It was a boring question, but I wanted to avoid any landmines.

She smiled, rolling her eyes. "Glamorous as always." She was a social worker at Youth House in Washington Heights, which provided services to unhoused kids.

"This week was exciting. We've had some problems with the W9s, a gang that cropped up after Nightwalker took down the Eighty-Eights. They jumped Marquis, a fourteen-year-old Tara was working with. After we got him back, banged up but safe, a group of them showed up armed and demanded we turn Marquis over."

I stiffened in surprise. "Holy shit. What happened?"

"Dr. Davis called Polaris—*the* Polaris—and he *showed up*, all on fire and shit." Abby shook her head, her expression bordering on awe.

My eyes widened. "Damn."

"Crazy, right? He scared off the W9s and then took pictures with the kids."

"He and Dr. Davis go way back, yeah?"

"Yeah. They met when Dr. Davis was a kid. Polaris saved his life."

I had a lot of reservations about anyone arrogant enough to call themselves a superhero. But Dr. Davis had a ton of respect for Polaris, so the mask couldn't be *all* bad.

"Oh!" Abby brightened. "You probably haven't heard. We got the Nelis Grant. It'll fund us for the next five years."

"That's great! Dr. Davis must have been ecstatic!"

"He was." Abby glanced up at me, her brown eyes sparkling. "He asks about you, you know. Some of the kids do too. They miss you."

Abby and I had met when I was volunteering with an after-school science program at Youth House. A lot of the kids there had it harder than I ever had, and I felt obligated to do what little I could.

Grimacing, I looked away. "I figured you'd probably want some space."

"I appreciate that, but I think it would be good for you to come back. Good for the kids. Good for you."

"I'd like that." I nodded. "Do you think it could be good for us too?"

Abby glanced away. "Today was a big day, right?" she deflected.

Great.

Abby always changed the subject when something was uncomfortable.

I struggled to keep a smile on my face as we turned a corner and saw the entrance to the ballroom. The line was stalled at the name-tag table.

"Yeah . . . the experiment, uh, didn't go so well."

Her expression became concerned. "Oh, no. How bad?"

"Nothing was on fire. Well, nothing *stayed* on fire."

"Ouch."

"It wasn't great," I admitted. "The oversight committee was there too. The timing couldn't have been better."

"What happened?"

I told her as the line wound slowly toward the registration table: about the generators, the control software bug, everything.

"Vaydan Industries was okay with the outcome," I said when we finally reached the table. "Apparently, Vincent Vaydan is coming tonight and wants to talk to me."

Abby's eyes widened in surprise, and she stood up straight, punching me in the chest just as the event staffer looked up to ask us for our names. "Shut up!"

I grinned. Abby looked embarrassed for a moment, before laughing. "Sorry," she said to the staffer, who handed us our name tags. We had to present them to two more Vanguard Sentinels at the door to the ballroom. The guards stared at them through the smoked glass of their visors for long seconds before waving us through.

Union City University was one of the most prestigious universities in North America, and our experimental physics department was second to none. As a result, UCU had a *lot* of funding, and the gala was grand in a way that most universities couldn't afford.

By the time we walked into the massive, opulently appointed ballroom, it was filled with people and thrumming with conversation as hundreds of scientists, industry leaders, members of various governments, and university representatives chatted, laughed, and debated.

I paused in the entryway, my shoulders tensing. I'd been coming to these things for years, mostly under protest, but every time still felt like I was slipping on a mask and costume that didn't quite fit.

Abby glanced at me and smiled encouragingly. She knew I didn't love these things. "Want a drink?" She gestured to the open bar.

I took a breath. "Definitely."

As we slipped through the crowd, I caught sight of Claire entertaining a group of laughing academics. I'd seen her work a crowd before, but it was difficult to reconcile the reserved professional with the energetic entertainer she became in these sorts of scenarios. Noticing Abby and me, Claire smiled at us and excused herself from the group, making her way over.

"Abby!" Claire's face lit up. "It's lovely to see you!"

Returning Claire's smile, Abby hugged her. "Claire, I missed you, girl! You look divine!" She gestured at Claire's outfit, which was a couple of shades lighter than her previous suit. "Those earrings are great!"

"Thank you!" Claire's smile grew wider. "Gracie got them for me."

"I thought so. She's got great taste." Abby motioned to the room around us. "This is impressive. I feel like there are even more people here than last time. I can't wait to see your recap presentation. You've done some amazing work this year."

Claire's smile made the skin around her eyes crinkle. "How's Youth House?"

"Really good! I was just telling Brandon that we got a grant from the Nelis Foundation."

The two of them continued to chat, catching up. Abby and Claire got along well, and I suspected they'd be friends even if I wasn't in the picture.

I caught sight of Harvey and his wife, Xia, out of the corner of my eye. Dressed in a black sequined dress, Xia was a willowy woman in her early thirties with straight black hair. Harvey wore a tuxedo and had somehow beaten his hair into submission. They were quite the sophisticated couple, particularly surrounded by physicists.

The tweed quotient was increasing by the minute.

Harvey saw me at the same time I noticed him and Xia, and he made his way over with Xia. "Hey, Abby. Claire." He seemed more uncomfortable than usual. Something was wrong.

"Hey!" Xia hugged Abby. The four of us had gone out a few times, mostly due to Abby and Xia. They'd become friends.

"Abby, can I steal Brandon for a second?" Harvey asked, his eyes flickering to Claire.

"Of course!" Abby smiled at me. "Ladies, why don't we go get some drinks? Brandon, come find me at the bar?"

"Absolutely," I said, not wanting her to go. Abby led Claire and Xia away, and I turned to Harvey. His eyes darted around as he hugged himself, rubbing his arms.

"Hey, man. What's going on?" I asked.

Harvey looked around warily. "Let's talk outside."

What the hell?

He led me to the balcony and out into the night air. Turning to face me, he started to speak, only to stop as he glanced past me, his eyes widening.

"Don't tell me you just left that beautiful woman alone in there," said a baritone voice I almost recognized. "Better watch out. Some awkward scientist might sweep her off her feet with a twenty-minute monologue on particle physics."

I turned. For a second, I couldn't believe my eyes.

Vincent Vaydan.

SIX

CONFRONTATION

*V*incent *Vaydan.*
     Aegis.

The legend was in his late forties and shorter than I'd expected, with a compact build packed into a tuxedo understated enough to ooze money. His chestnut hair was just a little unkempt, framing a face with a prominent brow, a square jaw, and a goatee. He strode quickly toward Harvey and me, a couple of bodyguards following in his wake.

Something about his expression instantly rubbed me the wrong way, and a spike of surly resentment roiled in my chest.

Vaydan glanced at Harvey, eyeing his name tag. "Dr. . . . Zhang, is it? Would you give Brandon and me a minute?"

Harvey blinked and glanced at me. "Mr. Vaydan, uh, of course. Brandon, I'll be just inside." He lingered for a second, eyes nervously shifting between Vaydan and me, before slipping back through the balcony doors.

"Mr. Vaydan," I started, "thank you for—"

"Look, I get it. You're grateful, I'm an inspiration, et cetera, et cetera." He waved his fingers in a circle impatiently. "Can we skip the fanboy stuff and get right to the real talk?"

"Uh, yeah. Absolutely," I said, irritation creeping into my tone.

"Good!" He patted the balcony's stone rail invitingly. "We're just two guys. The only things that separate us are a few years and a few patents. And billions of dollars, of course." He flashed me a quick smile, barely more than a twitch that never quite touched his eyes.

"So, I looked you up." Vaydan turned and leaned back against the railing, ignoring the fact that I hadn't moved. "Well, *I* didn't. I had one of my people look you up and write a summary, but I liked what I saw. You're a smart kid. Not as smart as I am, but still, a lot of potential. Your paper on using Dameran radiation to breach Colville membranes? Really good stuff. The equations were elegant, beautiful even."

Glancing at my empty hands, Vaydan snapped his fingers. A bodyguard materialized out of a corner of the balcony, where he'd stationed himself without my noticing. "Sir?"

"John, get us a couple of drinks. I'll take another glass of the scotch we brought." Vaydan turned to me. "Tell me you like scotch. I always bring a bottle of Macallan 26 to these things so I have something worth drinking.

"You know what?" Vaydan said to the guard, not giving me the chance to answer. "Bring the kid a glass of that too."

"Sir." Nodding, the guard went into the ballroom.

Vaydan crossed his arms and looked me up and down. "You don't like me much, do you?"

I guess I wasn't hiding it well.

"Is it weird that I find that refreshing? I dig your whole 'outsider science genius from the wrong side of the tracks' thing, by the way. It works for me. I can sympathize with it, even. I'm a bit of an outsider myself.

"You're one of mine, right?"

The question confused me, which must have shown on my face.

"One of mine," he repeated. "My educational program. Financial support for gifted students with barriers—tuition, room, board, a leg up in the application process for schools with Vaydan research grants." Rolling his eyes, he gestured to the ballroom. "Occasional parties."

"Uh, yeah." I straightened up a little, a dissonant note of gratitude clashing with my growing dislike. To distract myself, I turned toward the railing. The sun had nearly set, bathing the campus in an orange glow. Beyond it, the skyline of Union City dominated the view, some of the world's tallest buildings, covered in holographic halos, shining in the evening light.

A caped figure landed on a roof in the distance.

Finally, I nodded. "I won a Vaydan Foundation scholarship when I was fourteen, after writing a paper proposing a new model of gravitational computations that took into account the fluctuations in quantum pressure near black holes. The money really helped. My dad—he, uh . . . it was just my mom and me most of the time."

I had a feeling I couldn't discuss my dad's murder by a mask with one of the world's most recognizable superheroes without screaming, so I didn't elaborate.

Vaydan chuckled humorlessly, shaking his head.

"Like I said, I can sympathize. My father was arrested when I was around that age." He glanced at me. "You were wrong then, you know."

"Yeah, well, I was fourteen."

"What about today?"

I frowned. "I'm sorry?"

"You were wrong *today*." Vaydan studied me. "Your experiment. The centerpiece of the whole event. You had the time, the funding, the resources, but it didn't work. What happened?"

I looked away, irritation and embarrassment making my jaw work. A knot of tension formed between my shoulders. "There was a syntax error in the field stabilization algorithm's code. A stupid mistake. I triple-checked the algorithm myself and had another researcher go over it too. The failure *shouldn't* have happened."

"But it did." He peered at me. "Whose fault was it?"

His guard returned before I could answer, slipping up unobtrusively. Accepting the drink he offered me, I took a sip to give myself another beat. The scotch was fire and smoke, with touches of clove, ginger, and cinnamon.

"Mr. Carter," Vaydan said, voice sharp. "I asked you a question. Whose fault was it?"

I thought about blaming Nate or a power surge, but I couldn't. The code had been my responsibility. "Mine. It was on me."

"That's a good answer." Vaydan nodded and took a sip of his drink. "Not an easy answer, but the right one."

Vaydan fell silent for a moment, gazing into the quiet twilight of the evening. Finally, he glanced back at me, swirling his drink.

"So, what's your plan?" Vaydan gestured at the building behind us. "For what it's worth, I looked over everything. The work was solid. If it weren't for the bug, the test would have succeeded."

"I was hoping for a second chance. Once I show the committee what caused the error, they should understand that the *concept* is still sound."

Vaydan winced. "The Department of Energy is pulling the voidrium. It was a big ask to get a sample in the first place, and after a near accident like today, the voidrium will sit in storage for a century before they let anyone touch it again."

I sighed.

"But that's not what I mean." Vaydan looked out over the balcony. "Union City University seems *cozy*. You've got a nice little life here, maybe a future wife in there. If you wanted to, you could probably get tenure, crank out some patents. Maybe a couple of kids. Not a bad life, all things considered. Especially for someone with your history."

I didn't know what to say, so I sipped my scotch.

"You know, there could be other options for a smart young man like you." He walked from the railing to the center of the balcony and then turned back to me.

"I'm not sure what you mean." I tried to keep my voice steady. I sensed the shape of what he was saying, but the implication was too big.

Vaydan frowned, stepping close. "I'm saying, I want to offer you a job." He half turned, gesturing at the party, the whole building behind him. "All this? It's nothing. It's a tax break, a budgetary rounding error. I could use someone with your gifts. If you come work for me, you'll have access to *everything*, stuff you could never get here. Stuff these people couldn't even *dream* of."

I held onto the rail, fighting the wave of shock that

crashed over me. For someone else, the offer might have been a dream come true. For me, it felt like selling out, yoking myself to something I hated.

Vaydan took another sip of his drink, his gaze never leaving me. "I'm offering you access to the best labs and a chance to work with the smartest people in the world. The absolute best of the best. You'll create things that change the *world*, Brandon. No reins. Just total freedom and unlimited resources."

I stared, speechless.

Vaydan smirked, gesturing back to the crowd in the ballroom. "It doesn't hurt that you'll make more in a year than any of your colleagues would make in ten. Twenty maybe. Not to mention stock options and a percentage on any patents you generate."

"Can I have some time to think about it?" I finally managed.

He sighed. "I get it, okay? I'm 'the man,' but I'd remind you that my work has changed *billions* of lives. The profits from that work have rebuilt cities, created infrastructure where it previously didn't exist, brought people fresh water, and put talented kids with records and chips on their shoulders through school."

Vaydan glanced at me pointedly.

"We also have *great* healthcare. Real cutting-edge stuff. I hear someone in your life could probably use it. Say yes, and I'll make some calls."

I thought about Mom and saw two scenarios. In one, she got the care she needed and lived the long, happy life she deserved, and all it cost me were my principles. In the other, she wasted away, losing the use of her hands and feet, then her limbs, until eventually she was trapped inside herself, waiting for her neurons to disintegrate.

It was no choice at all.

I nearly said yes on the spot, but Vaydan patted me on the shoulder before I could answer, making eye contact for a second before looking away. "John, give him a card."

The guard who had brought us our drinks stepped forward again and pulled a metal card out of his pocket, handing it to me. I took it, my fingers numb.

"If you decide to take me up on my offer, call that number. But don't take too long. There are other people on my list."

As Vaydan finished his drink, Cara—the woman from Vaydan Industries whom I'd met earlier—appeared in the balcony doorway, stunning in a black floor-length formal dress. She glanced at me and nodded, smiling. "Hello, Brandon."

"Hey, Cara," I managed. "Good to see you again."

"You too." Cara glanced back at Vaydan. "Mr. Vaydan, you should finish making your rounds. You have other engagements this evening."

"Duty calls," Vaydan said, an ironic twist flashing across his face. He turned, walked to the entrance to the ballroom, and then glanced back. "Think it over. You've got twenty-four hours."

I stood on the balcony for a minute, staring out at the city. My eyes were drawn to the two tallest buildings, massive spires of glass and steel bathed in holographic light. On the first, the Vaydan Industries logo glowed blue in the twilight, and the Vanguard *V* was emblazoned on the second.

I barely had time to think before I heard footsteps again, and I glanced back as Harvey slipped back out onto the balcony. I turned to him. He looked tense, troubled. He may as well have been shouting, and he glanced over his shoulder a couple of times as he walked over.

Something was *definitely* wrong.

"Hey, I'm sorry about—"

"What?" Harvey shook his head. "Oh, no, don't worry about it. Look, I don't know how to say this."

He paused, took a deep breath, and let it out explosively. "I was taking a walk about half an hour after the experiment. Trying to clear my head, I guess. I saw Nate behind the building."

"Nate Chambers?" I grimaced and rolled my eyes.

Harvey nodded. "He was on his phone, talking about how he'd deleted the 'code and the documentation,' and that there was no way 'they would find out.'"

Taking another deep breath, he looked away. "After that, I went back over the control system code. The modulation parameters looked fine, other than the syntax error I was expecting, but when I checked the version documentation notes, there was nothing there. The changelog was also empty, but I was able to restore it on the primary backup. Nate changed the parameters and then changed them back after the experiment was over."

I frowned. "What are you telling me?"

"Brandon." Harvey caught my gaze and held it. "He sabotaged us."

It took a second for the words to penetrate my shock and confusion. Anger welled up, pressure and heat that burned away rational thought. *Why?* Why would someone born with so much ruin something we'd all worked so hard for?

"That motherfucker," I growled, turning toward the ballroom door.

Harvey reached out. "Brandon, wait! Let's talk about this."

I was beyond listening. I stormed into the ballroom with Harvey trailing after me, the pressure behind my eyes building with each step. Pushing my way through the crowd, I found Nate at the bar, standing between Xia and Abby, both of whom looked uncomfortable.

He was standing close to Abby—too close—leaning in to say something with an expression somewhere between a smirk and a leer as she leaned back, putting a hand on his chest to keep him away.

The background noise of the gala faded. Something roared in my ears.

Nate must have caught a glimpse of me striding toward him. Turning, he smirked. "Hey Carter, I was just telling Abby about how you nearly blew up the—"

I hit him, a straight left that rocked his head back with a spray of spit and bloody snot. He started to fall, but I grabbed his arm and smashed my forearm into his throat, bending him back over the bar. Drinks spilled and glass shattered. Xia shouted in surprise, but it was distant.

"Harvey found the changelogs!" I snarled, my face inches from Nate's. He tried to speak but couldn't, as my weight pushed my forearm into his neck, cutting off his airway. "You *sabotaged* us?"

He sputtered and spat as he flailed, trying to push me off and get his feet under him, but he couldn't get any leverage. His thousand-dollar shoes slipped uselessly across the carpet.

"Brandon!" Abby's voice cracked like a whip. "Get off him!"

With an effort of will, I took a step back. "We're not done, asshole," I spat.

Nate slipped to the floor and then dragged himself up. His hair was a mess. Blood, snot, and spit covered his face, and his tuxedo jacket was soaked from the spilled drinks. He started coughing.

"What the *hell* is this?" Claire was suddenly behind me. I looked back. People had stepped away, forming a ring, as more heads turned toward us, murmurs of alarm growing.

"Can I have your attention, ladies and gents?" Vaydan's voice unexpectedly cut in through the speakers. I caught him on the stage out of the corner of my eye. "You know what they say about experimental physics: We throw some *energetic* parties!" There was a bit of uncomfortable laughter, but people began turning away. I might have imagined it, but I thought Vaydan winked at me.

"Brandon." Claire's eyes were hard. "Out. *Now.*"

"You don't understand! He—"

"Get. Out," Claire snapped. "We'll talk tomorrow."

Abby was beside me. Grabbing my arm, she started pulling, gentle but insistent.

Nate had stopped coughing. "You're fucking *crazy*, Carter!" he rasped. "You're done. Do you hear me? Done!"

Claire moved over and started speaking quietly into his ear, but he waved her off and staggered away, blundering through a couple of servers by the door. Seething, I tried to follow, but Abby's fingers dug into my arm like iron spikes.

"Brandon, come on," she hissed. Maneuvering me toward a different exit, she led me out of the ballroom and then the building, out into the chill of the fall night beyond.

We walked for a couple of minutes, stopping near a

fountain with a statue of Poseidon. By the time we got there, my fury was the only thing keeping at bay the realization of how enormously I'd just fucked up.

Abby whirled on me. "What was *that*?" She glared up at me. Despite her heels, I was still significantly taller. "Do you think I need you to come swooping in to *save* me from Nathan Chambers? Get out of here with that alpha-male bullshit."

I shook my head. "It wasn't that—at least, not just that. Harvey heard Nate talking to someone after the test this morning. Harvey did some digging, and he found some deleted changelogs. Nate sabotaged our code."

Abby's anger ebbed, partially replaced with shock. "Wait, really? That asshole sabotaged your work? Is Harvey sure? Are you?"

I nodded. "Yeah."

Abby shook her head. "Still, Brandon, what were you thinking, attacking him in a room *full* of people, including your *boss*?"

She was right. I'd just assaulted the son of one of the richest men in the world, and one of the university's biggest financial supporters, in front of a crowd of people—not to mention Vincent Vaydan. If my career hadn't been over before, I'd just ended it. I wouldn't have been surprised if Vaydan rescinded his job offer.

Hell, I wouldn't have been surprised if the cops were waiting at my apartment when I got home.

I'd been so stupid.

So much for anger management.

"I wasn't. Thinking, I mean."

Abby sighed again. "You need to tell Claire and whoever else handles stuff like this inside the university." She paused. "You might want to talk to a lawyer."

I nodded. She took a few steps toward the fountain and watched the water flow out of Poseidon's seashell.

We stood quietly for a moment, surrounded by the muffled noise of the city and the burbling fountain. The air had grown cooler since sundown.

I finally broke the silence. "Hey, do you think that maybe we could get dinner? Talk?"

"Brandon, look. Tonight was a lot." Wrapping her arms around herself, Abby lifted her gaze to the city beyond the garden. "I need some time. You need to think through some stuff."

"I'm sorry," I said. "For everything."

"I know." Abby's tone softened. "But my brother's birthday was just the last straw. You spent fourteen hours a day at the lab most of the time. You didn't exist for months. I was lucky if I saw you twice a *week*, and we *lived together.* That's not what I want from a partner."

The world unraveled, turning to ashes in my hands. The ground between us seemed to stretch without either of us moving.

"Look, that won't happen again. I promise—"

She waved her hand dismissively. "*Don't.* You've said that before, but you got pulled back in. You always do. It's just who you are."

"I don't understand." Anger and frustration crept into my voice. "Why would you come with me to the gala if you didn't want to get back together?"

Abby turned back to me, her nostrils flaring. "I came with you tonight because I care about you. I knew today must have been awful, and I wanted to *support* you."

"Is there someone else?" I felt like an idiot as soon as I said it.

"Are you for real right now?" Her eyes widened

incredulously, but there was something in her expression that said I was right.

Looking away, she shook her head. "This was a mistake." Abby turned and walked toward the street, pulling out her phone and opening the autocab app to call a ride. "I'm going to go. I'll let you know when I'm ready to talk."

She paused at the edge of the walkway that led out to the road. "Take care of yourself." She turned and vanished from view.

SEVEN

DRINKS WITH A FRIEND

The Downlow was a dingy, hole-in-the-wall punk bar Vee and I had discovered in high school. It sat off Epiphany Square, a bohemian art community that was gradually gentrifying, filling with college bars, upscale restaurants, and a bunch of other bougie crap masquerading as authentic city culture. As the rent went up, most of the places that had given the neighborhood its identity were driven out, but the Downlow carried on as one of the last holdouts, a local fixture too surly and stubborn to let go.

It was small, just a narrow front room with a bar dominating the right wall and a back area with a tiny stage. The walls were covered with old show flyers, band stickers, and random graffiti. The Downlow was also loud, unapologetically crass, and a little dangerous, making it my kind of place.

The usual atmosphere of cigarette smoke, shouted conversation, and music crashed over me as I walked in. For a Monday, the place was busy, filled to bursting with the normal mixture of aging punks, college kids, and hipsters. Grody, the Downlow's surly owner, was tending bar in a Crimson Specter T-shirt. His spiked mohawk bobbed up and down while he poured drinks and glared at the clientele.

I nodded to him and pushed my way through the crowd toward the back room, anger and frustration boiling in my chest.

I was angry at the Department of Energy. At Abby.

At myself, most of all.

The noise diminished as I turned the corner into the back room, scanning the tables. All four were filled. Vee had a corner booth tucked in behind the stage.

Vee and I had met on my first day at Ruiz High School. We'd clicked immediately, both outcast misanthropes from broken homes who didn't fit in with the rest of the well-adjusted baby geniuses. We had become friends, and more, since.

Vee was skinny, thanks more to her metabolism than because she worked out. The left side of her head was shaved, and the right had streaks of red among the black chin-length hair that fell across her thin, sepia-brown face, large, heavy-lidded eyes, full lips, and prominent nose. Small hoops pierced the lengths of her ears and the left side of her lower lip.

As usual, Vee wore black jeans and combat boots paired with a battered T-shirt she'd cut the sleeves off, exposing the tattoos that covered her arms, some of which matched tattoos on my own arms.

When I closed in on the booth, she looked up and gave me a lopsided grin, closing her laptop and sliding it back into her bag. "Hey."

I grinned back despite my mood. "Hey."

Vee gestured to an open beer sitting on the other

side of the table. Sliding into the booth, I picked it up and took a swig.

"How are you?" I asked.

"Better than you, probably." She raised an eyebrow. "Rough day?"

I shrugged. "It could be worse. I'm not on fire."

Vee's eyes glimmered wickedly as she sat forward. "Want some help with that?"

I nodded. "Seems like a fitting end to a shitty day. Let me get a few beers in first?"

Vee touched the top of her bottle to her forehead in a mock salute. "Cheers." We both took sips and grinned.

I'd missed Vee. The lump of anger and disappointment smoldering in my chest was already receding, making one of the worst days of my adult life a little better.

"How's work?" I motioned to her bag.

"The usual blend of corporate douchebags."

Despite having a full ride, Vee had dropped out of Union City University's computer science program our sophomore year and started making a living helping activist organizations uncover compromising data on shady corporations and their executives. It was dangerous and more than a little illegal, but Vee was *very* good.

She also had plenty of motivation.

When Vee was twelve, her mom, Dharshi, blew the whistle on her employer, Raxxil Pharmaceuticals, for concealing the harmful side effects of a new drug. Instead of receiving the medal she deserved, Dharshi had been put in jail on bullshit industrial espionage charges. Vee had been working to expose the executives responsible since she'd dropped out of college.

"How's"—I tried to remember the name of Vee's latest fling—"Dianna?"

"Please." Vee rolled her eyes. "Dianna's ancient history."

"Ancient history? I met her two weeks ago."

Shrugging, Vee took another sip of her beer. "Keep up. I haven't seen her since the Despoiled Youth show. The show you and I were supposed to go to together?" She kicked me under the table. "Dick."

"I'm sorry. The ignition test kind of consumed my life. How was the show?"

Vee's eyes lit up. "It was *chaos*. A guy threw a full beer at the vocalist from the opening act but also hit the drummer, who then dove off the stage and attacked the *wrong guy*! Some of *that* guy's friends got involved, and then the rest of the band jumped in. The best part? Everyone in the band was wearing one of those sexy-mask Halloween costumes." She shifted in the booth, putting her back against the wall so she could stretch her legs out. "So much body hair."

I laughed and shook my head. "I'm sorry I missed it."

We both took a drink.

Music was a huge part of my life. When Mom and I were on the run, music had been a place to hide, a drop of stability in a sea of uncertainty. I'd learned early on that I liked my music angry and loud, and punk rock spoke to me. It spoke to Vee too, and much of our misspent youth had been involved punk shows in shitty bars and seedy venues across the city.

We'd even started our own band in high school: Anti-Hero Blues. We'd played a few shows around the city and gone on one glorious tour in a battered cargo van, before life had gotten too busy. We'd gotten the band logo—an upside-down anarchy symbol next to a stylized *H* and *B*, which Vee had designed on the back of a diner placemat at three in the morning—as our first tattoos. My old bass was still in a closet at home.

I took another sip of beer, settling in. "Hey, I talked to Mom today. She mentioned we were on for Sunday. Thanks for being around."

"Laura let me live with you for most of middle school and all of high school after Dad broke down." Vee nursed her beer, her expression shifting to concern. "Did she talk to you about her last doctor's appointment?"

"Not yet." I sighed. "How was it?"

"The meds aren't doing as much as the doctors hoped. They said there are procedures that use nano-surgery to repair some of the nerve damage, but the surgeries are still 'experimental,' so Laura's insurance won't cover them."

I nodded, sighing again.

"If you need cash . . ."

I shook my head. "Without insurance, those procedures are north of a million dollars. I checked. We've applied for a couple of grants from the Vaydan Relief Fund, but it's not a sure thing."

Vee raised an eyebrow and took a swig of her beer. "If that doesn't work, we could rob a bank. I always said we'd look good on wanted posters."

"There . . . might be another option."

"What?"

"I met Vincent Vaydan tonight at the party."

Surprise crossed Vee's face, quickly giving way to disgust. "What did that asshole want?"

"He offered me a job."

Vee blinked. "And you told him to shove it up his armored sphincter?"

"I'm thinking about it." I rolled the neck of my beer bottle between my fingers.

Her eyes widened. "You're *thinking* about it? Vaydan's a billionaire industrialist living out some messiah complex. What the hell is there to think about?"

I nodded, setting the bottle on the table. "I know. But Vaydan Medical is the company that developed the nanosurgery for Harden-Klein syndrome. He implied he might be able to get my mom into a trial or something."

Her anger drained away. "Shit."

"Yeah."

We sat in silence for a minute or so. I hated the idea of working for Vaydan as much as Vee did. It felt like a betrayal of everything I believed in, but it was also more than that.

Taking the position felt like a betrayal of Dad's memory.

"Fuck that guy." Vee leaned forward. "We'll find a way to deal with this. Let's see how the grant goes."

"Sure." That would have been great if I had had more than twenty-four hours, but Vaydan had given me a deadline.

"Hey, that photographer I introduced you to, Leila, has a gallery opening next week. We should go," Vee said, changing the subject.

I looked up and did my best to smile. "That sounds great."

"You have zero excuses, given that you flipped the switch on MICSy today. How'd the test go, anyway? Why aren't you showing me interdimensional porn?"

My shoulders slumped. "Not great. The modulation control system failed to compensate for low-range energy spikes, and it burned out some of the generators."

"At least you didn't blow up the city, so thanks for that. How's MICSy?"

"A little worse for wear, but nothing we can't fix. Not that we'll have a chance to turn her on again."

"Oh, shit." Vee's eyes widened. "The Department of Energy is pulling the voidrium?"

I nodded, picking up my bottle and tipping it toward her. "Tomorrow at nine a.m."

"Dude, I'm sorry." Vee shook her head. "I told you to let me look at your code."

"I asked Claire. She didn't think it was a good idea."

What Claire had actually said was closer to "over my dead body." She didn't find Vee's pathological need to be an asshole to people in positions of authority as endearing as I did.

"I wish you had, though. Nate Chambers screwed us." I took a long gulp of beer, my mood souring.

Vee nodded sagely, taking a drink as well. "What did he mess up?"

"Nate didn't make any *mistakes*. Harvey found evidence of him sabotaging the test."

She stared at me, her nostrils flaring. "That *prick*. Let's light *him* on fire."

The memory of Nate staggering out of the party hit me, and I grimaced.

"Wait, what are you doing with your face?" Vee asked. "What happened?"

"Harvey told me about it at the party, and I went looking for Nate. I wasn't thinking; I was just so fucking furious. When I found him, Nate was creeping on Abby, and I lost it."

"Abby? *Your* Abby? What was she doing there?"

"I invited her." I shrugged. "That was a big mistake

too. Anyway, I hit Nate, pinned him to the bar, and threatened to kill him in front of five hundred people."

"I wish I had been there." Vee's eyes flashed with sympathetic fury. "I'd have held his arms."

She would have, and I loved her for it.

Vee held out her beer for a toast. "To bad decisions."

I glowered at her for a moment before clinking my bottle to hers. "Helpful."

She shrugged and took another sip. "If you want helpful, see a therapist."

"I tried that."

Vee's expression turned mock serious. "You should ask for your money back."

"I should," I agreed. "I'll need it for a lawyer. I wouldn't be surprised if there was a warrant out for me by tomorrow morning."

Vee's look of pretend seriousness switched to real concern. "Hey, if you need anything—*anything*—I've got you." She put her hand on mine and squeezed, leaving her hand there for a couple of moments before she pulled it back.

"I know," I replied, and I did.

There was *no one* I trusted more.

Vee was my best friend, and unsurprisingly, we'd tried to be . . . *more* a couple of times. On both occasions, it was an absolute shitshow, mostly because we were too young and dealing with too much. After the second time, we didn't speak for months. Only when she showed up at my house, drunk and sobbing, after her mom was denied parole, did we started fixing things.

"So, circling back for a second, what was Abby doing there?" Vee asked.

I grimaced. "She reached out and asked about the test, and I offered to tell her about it at the party. I hoped maybe we could talk."

"How'd that go?"

"About as well as the rest of the day. Abby wasn't happy about me trying to kill Nate in front of a room full of people. I told her what happened, apologized, and asked her if we could get dinner or something and talk. She told me I'd been completely absent for months and that she wanted more from her partner. That she had to think some things through, and she'd call me when she was ready. I think she's seeing someone."

Vee winced. "Brutal."

"Yeah."

"Want me to talk to her?"

"I don't think it would make any difference. Besides, Abby thinks you're kind of an asshole."

"Brandon, I *am* kind of an asshole. It's part of my charm."

"Charm," I said with air quotes.

Vee grinned and pulled out a cigarette, before gesturing at the empty bottles between us. "Hey, we're both out. Next round's on you."

I dragged myself out of the booth and made my way to the bar, pushing through the swollen crowd. A couple of big groups had piled in, and the front room was starting to feel like a mosh pit. It wouldn't have been a great time for the building inspector to show up.

While I waited, I caught a glimpse of five hedge-fund types at the end of the bar. All in their late twenties, they were dressed like they'd just left work and loud enough to be disruptive—which said a lot given how noisy the Downlow already was. Three of the future white-collar criminals were catcalling Celia, one of the waitresses, while the others harassed Grody as he served other customers.

Blatantly ignoring the two trying to order, Grody turned to me, grunted a greeting, and brought me a couple of beers.

"Hey, bro!" one of the guys yelled over the noise. He was tall, just a little shorter than me, and broad, with blond hair pushed back from a wide, profoundly punchable face already flushed with alcohol. "What are you? Stupid?" he slurred, swaying slightly on his feet.

Grody slowly turned toward the group, his eyes narrowing. "What do you want?"

The guy rolled his eyes and gestured to one of the taps. "A beer?"

Grody grabbed a glass and poured a beer from the tap, glaring at the pair of dude-bros, who snickered to each other. They were muttering about shitty bars as Grody finished the beer and set it in front of them.

When the drunk—who I mentally dubbed Wall Street—reached for the glass, Grody picked it back up. "Almost forgot." Hawking up a massive wad of saliva and mucus, he spat it right into the beer, before slamming the glass onto the bar in front of the duo. The glass's contents sloshed all over their slacks, and they recoiled. "There you go."

"What's your fucking *problem*?" roared the guy with the punchable face.

"He has a low tolerance for douchebags," I snapped, unable not to. "Why don't you find another bar?"

Looking at me, Wall Street stuck out his chest, his expression turning ugly. "Why don't you mind your own business before you get hurt?"

Though the bastard looked a little like Nate, I didn't think another assault charge would be a good way to end my evening. *Time for a little diplomacy.* "Why don't you and your buddies do everyone a favor and piss off?"

Conflict de-escalation had never been my strong suit. Wall Street's face purpled, and as he cursed and stepped toward me, I sighed. It had been a while since I'd been in a bar fight, but I was pretty sure it would come back to me.

Predictably, Wall Street stepped in to bump chests, a timeless dude-bro prefight tradition.

Deciding to skip the foreplay, I drove my forehead into his nose, breaking it with a rewarding crunch.

Wall Street collapsed to the barroom floor, moaning, as blood oozed from his nose. *Sorry, bro.* I didn't fight the twinge of satisfaction that pulled my lips into a smirk as I looked at the rest of the future white-collar criminals. They were moving in on me, but a familiar warmth flowed through me as I balled my hands into fists.

Grody pulled out the bat he kept under the bar, the old oak stained brown, and glared down at the four of them. "Fuck off," he growled.

Wall Street's friends stopped, either not drunk enough or not stupid enough to escalate things any further. Instead of jumping me, they dragged their friend up and carried him out, shouting insults and screaming about the cops.

I'd always found it funny how people became law-abiding citizens as soon as the trouble they'd started became too much for them to handle.

Grody picked up the beer he'd spat in, shrugged, and downed it in one gulp, loogie and all. He shook his head, disgusted. "What a bunch of cunts."

"You were gone a while," Vee said when I finally returned to the table, her tone suspicious.

I shrugged. "Just making friends. We might want to get out of here, though." Grody had told me he'd cover the cops and to use the back door, as the fire alarm still wasn't fixed. "Hungry?"

Vee narrowed her eyes. "Oh, something *definitely* happened. Do we need to settle up?"

"I took care of it. Let's bounce."

Vee studied my expression, then grabbed her bag, and we slipped out into the alley behind the bar. I caught a glimpse of police lights flashing in front of the building as we came out onto a side street. My new friend was yelling about being assaulted, his voice distorted by his broken nose.

Vee looked at me sideways, raising an eyebrow. "Making friends?"

We turned away from the cops and walked in the other direction, putting a couple of blocks between us. It was a busy night, and we blended into the masses of people making their way into or out of bars, restaurants, and nightspots.

Eventually, I shrugged. "More like performing a public service."

"Brandon!" Vee grabbed my arm and stopped, turning to me. "Should I be worried about you?"

My instinct was to say I was fine, but the concern in Vee's eyes stopped me.

I sighed, my shoulders slumping. "Honestly? I don't know. I poured everything I had into MICSy, for *years*. It made me a bad friend. A bad boyfriend. I figured it would all be worth it when the trial run was a success, but it wasn't. And *then* to find out the test was *sabotaged?*" I looked away. "And Mom?" The weight of her illness hit me like a speeding truck. My hands started to tremble, and something gave in my chest.

Vee pulled me into a hug as people flowed around us, laughing and chattering, busy with their own lives.

"Hey." She squeezed. "It's been a rough day, but it's not like your life is over. One way or the other, Mom will be *fine.* We'll handle it. And sure, you put a lot of time into MICSy, but you're still a *grad* student. Things are going to work out."

I squeezed back.

"But, man, you're spiraling. You need to get a grip, okay?"

I nodded.

Vee pulled back without letting go so we could look at each other. She sniffled, and I could see tears in the corners of her eyes. "Now, can we eat? Neither of us likes having emotional moments on the street."

We ended up at Bangkok Palace, a Thai place on the second floor of a building on Ellis Street near the edge of Epiphany Square. We ordered a couple more beers and some food and chatted, enjoying each other's company.

After ordering another drink, Vee looked at me, pausing in a way that meant she wanted to say something.

"What's up?" I asked between bites of curry.

"You know, we could get out of here for a while. It's been forever since the two of us took a trip." I nodded. Abby hadn't loved the idea of me traveling alone with Vee, given our history. "It might also be good to get you out of town, what with the multiple pending assault charges. We've always wanted to go to London. Let me get us some tickets. Mom will be fine for the next week. Hell, we can bring her. She'd love it."

Vee stared at me, hopeful and nervous and trying to hide it. I felt like we were standing on the edge of something—something vast and scary but maybe wonderful. It was reckless, for both of us, but I couldn't not jump.

I smiled. "I'd love that."

EIGHT

POINT OF NO RETURN

Vee left after dinner. Neither of us wanted her to go, but a lot of her work happened at odd hours, so we went our separate ways and made plans to meet the next day.

I finished my beer and started meandering back to my apartment on foot. I'd left my bike back at the Downlow, but even if I hadn't, I was drunk and didn't feel like making the day even worse by crashing it.

The walk home from Epiphany Square was only about ten minutes. It was a nice night, and the cool air helped me calm down. I was in a better place after spending time with Vee, but I was in no hurry to follow that by spending a sleepless night replaying one of the worst days of my adult life.

On a side street I passed, a guy was cleaning gooey clumps of webbing off a building. They were the handiwork of the Huntsman, a mask with spider powers. He was being sued by the chamber of commerce, as well as businesses and landlords tired of paying to have his goo cleaned off their buildings' facades.

Despite the hour, when I finally made it back to Brackenridge, the neighborhood was bustling with small groups of locals and students out for a late meal or drink. Turning down a side street, I saw a familiar figure reclining on a bench, using a backpack as a pillow as he sketched in a battered journal.

Marcus was a big man in his late fifties bundled in an old, worn coat and a pair of baggy jeans tucked into a pair of battered boots. His mane of gray hair surrounded a weathered face mostly covered by a long beard.

"Brandon, my boy!" Marcus's outward wariness gave way to an easy grin when he caught sight of me. He dragged himself to a seated position and slid over on the bench to make room for me.

"Hey, Marcus." I smiled as I sat down beside him. "What are you doing out this late?"

"I got locked out of the shelter." Marcus snorted and rolled his eyes. "I was two minutes late—*two*—and this new guy locked me out. He saw me walking up and locked the door. Stared right at me." Marcus shook his head. "Can you believe that?"

I shook my head, too, silently commiserating.

Marcus sighed. "How do you lock a guy out when you're looking right at him?"

"Do you want some help looking for another place to stay?" I pulled out my phone. "I heard there's a new place with private rooms on Fifth. Abby might even know someone there."

"Nah." He waved me off. "Will you be around tomorrow, though?"

"I can be." I snorted, fighting the sudden hollowness in my chest. "I suddenly find myself with a lot of free time. We can grab lunch. My treat. How's noon?"

Marcus smiled, a flicker of appreciation in his eyes. "Noon's good."

"Are you sure you're good for tonight?"

"Yeah. I've got a friend that gets off at two. He lets me stay with him sometimes. I figured I'd come out here and do some drawing until he gets off. I found a coffee shop that might put some of my stuff up on the walls for people to look at, even buy, maybe."

Marcus had gone to school for art but ended up in a factory, where he'd injured his hand on an unsafe machine after almost twenty years of service. Like thousands of others, he'd become addicted to his pain meds, graduating to heroin when his prescription ran out. It cost him his job, his home, and his family—all because he'd taken his medicine as prescribed.

He had picked up art again a few years ago while going through rehab. Rediscovering art had given him back something he loved, something he could take pride in and use to connect with people.

"That's great, man. Which coffee shop?"

"The Nook, over on Seventh." Marcus nodded in the general direction. "You know it?"

"Yeah. It gets a lot of traffic. What are you working on now?"

Marcus turned the sketch toward me, gesturing down at the pad. He'd drawn a woman sitting on a porch swing. She looked to be in her forties and wore a shawl that framed warm eyes and a tired smile. It was beautiful and tinged with melancholy.

"Who's that?"

"That's my mom." His smile grew wistful. "Or at least, that's how I remember her, anyway. She loved her porch, especially in the spring. She'd sit out there and just watch the birds and drink her tea." He looked away for a moment.

"It's beautiful," I said.

When he looked back at me, his eyes glimmered with amusement. "You still have that picture I drew of you and your girl?"

I nodded, trying not to wince. "It's still up on the wall."

"Speaking of," Marcus said, changing the subject, "You two back together yet?" He closed the drawing pad and put it back in his bag before turning toward me.

"Not yet," I replied, looking down. "Maybe not ever. I think she's done with me."

Marcus shook his head, grinning as he rolled his eyes. "For someone so smart, you sure are stupid sometimes, you know that?" He sighed, leaning back on the bench.

"You're not wrong, but I saw her tonight. I think maybe she's found someone else."

We sat in silence for a moment. Pulling a stubbed cigarette from behind his ear, Marcus relit it.

"So, what happened with your big experiment, anyway? Wasn't that what you two were fighting about in the first place?"

"It went," I replied with a sardonic smile. "Something was wrong with the software that controlled the containment fields. They nearly burned out. I fixed it, but not in time."

"I'm sorry to hear that." Marcus took another puff. "Are they going to let you try again?"

"Probably not." I shook my head. "There's a team coming to pick up the voidrium sample in the morning."

"Huh." Marcus took a long drag. He was quiet for a

second after exhaling, crossing his arms contemplatively. Then he glanced back at me, a speculative expression spreading across his bearded face. "Can't you just try again before they take the voidrium sample?"

I sat up with a quick intake of breath and stared stupidly at Marcus.

"I'm just saying, if they haven't taken it yet, why can't you give the experiment another shot?"

I checked the time on my phone. It was 12:15 a.m. The voidrium wasn't going anywhere until morning. I had nine hours, give or take.

My mind spun. I'd have to replace some parts and run some diagnostics, but I'd built that machine. I could fix MICSy in my sleep.

I took in a sharp breath as a wave of nerves mingled with a sudden rush of excitement, leaving me jittery. Re-running the test was ridiculous to even contemplate. I'd be breaking a *lot* of rules—probably some laws too—but I'd never much cared for rules in the first place. This was my last chance.

The idea was reckless and stupid, and maybe it was the alcohol talking, but if I was already going to jail, at least I could do so having changed the world.

"Marcus, man," I said, "thank you. I've got to go."

Marcus chuckled as I stood up. "Happy to help."

I buzzed with alcohol and excitement as I rushed back to my apartment, compiling a list in my head of what I'd need to do, what parts MICSy would need replaced, and what diagnostics I'd need to run. None of it would take all night.

By the time I got into my apartment, it was 12:30

a.m., which gave me plenty of time. I gulped down a coffee and went to jump on my motorcycle, only to remember I'd left it at the Downlow.

Frustrated and beginning to panic, I tried to head through the park on foot, but I forgot to check the emergency app. The road was blocked off by the corpse of a mole monster the size of a bus that lay partway out of a pit of churned earth and broken asphalt. Its eyes were stuck open, in agony or fear, and a pink tongue lolled out between its jagged teeth and onto the road. The back of the monster's head was missing, the bone, skin, and fur replaced by a cracked glass braincase that oozed cerebrospinal fluid or some other liquid. A woman dressed in an electric-blue mask, cape, and unitard was having a conversation with some cops nearby.

This city, I thought as I took a detour.

By the time 1:00 a.m. rolled around, I was back on campus and making my way to the Vaydan Institute. The campus buzzed with activity during the day—between undergrads chatting or playing and staff and faculty making their way from one class or appointment to the next—but at night, the dark stillness gave it a surreal, otherworldly vibe.

Barely pausing to consider what I was about to do, I slipped up to a side door. A lot of scientists and researchers, some of whom could easily be called eccentric, kept whatever hours they liked, so the building was never really closed. I could have walked through the front, but there would be a guard on duty, and I didn't feel like having a conversation.

I made my way toward the lab, still hoping I wouldn't encounter another person, though I knew I was being monitored by the security system. Because of the Vaydan

Institute's research, we were a target for enhanced criminals looking to access exotic materials and prototypes. As a result, Vaydan Industries had covered the cost of an advanced automated security system. The actual specifications of said system were a secret, but I'd heard the small sensor pods in the walls, floor, and ceiling were capable of producing force fields to protect parts of the building or block a potential thief's escape.

Thankfully, I arrived at my lab without having to talk to anyone. I paused at the door, wavering as doubts roiled up.

My mouth was dry. I was at the point of no return.

My badge had been logged at the side entrance and would be by the lab door as well if I went in, but I hadn't broken any rules yet. If anyone asked, I could say I'd left something in the lab. There wouldn't be any questions. I could take Vaydan up on his offer, assuming I hadn't ruined it by punching Nate, or try to market some of the intellectual property we'd developed.

All I needed to do was turn around. But I couldn't.

If I went through with my unapproved test, I'd be breaking dozens of university rules and violating ethical research codes.

Still, there were literal new worlds waiting to be discovered. Once I had the data, once I'd proven I was right, none of the rules I'd broken would matter. How could policies and safety protocols stand up in the face of a scientific revolution?

Safety wasn't a concern either. We'd already proven that MICSy *worked.* If it weren't for Nate, we'd still be celebrating.

They wouldn't be able to fire or discharge me. The project would be too visible. At worst, I'd get formally

Christopher Lee Rippee

reprimanded. Claire would be angry, but she'd understand, especially when she learned we'd been sabotaged. Besides, this would be a major success for her as well.

I also couldn't shake the thought that I might be going to jail anyway. What did it matter if I added one more charge to the list?

Taking a breath, I used my badge to open the door, slipped in, and quietly shut the door behind me.

NINE

UNINVITED GUEST

The lab was cool and quiet, the silence broken only by the hum of idling equipment. The overhead lights were off, but flashing displays, monitors, and power indicators shed enough light for me to see.

I made my way through the gloom to a workstation next to MICSy and brought up the diagnostic suite. The glitch in the field modulation algorithm had burned out several circuits and power relays, and we hadn't seen much point in fixing any of it, given the circumstances. It took me an hour to go over the power system and replace parts, and then another hour to check the field generators, run some diagnostic tests, and replace emitters. When all of that was done, I ran diagnostics on the hardware and software systems.

I even checked the cabling.

By 3:30 a.m., all the diagnostic indicators were green and MICSy was ready for another test. The only thing left to do was to get the voidrium from storage and plug it in.

I'd been up for almost twenty-four hours and should

have been exhausted, but any fatigue I might have felt was washed away by the electric thrill of excitement flooding my veins.

Hoping I still had access, I made my way to the voidrium containment room. I doubted they would have revoked my clearance. Why would they? They couldn't have conceived of someone being so reckless. If nothing else, I'd be responsible for changing the Vaydan Institute's exotic materials storage protocols.

Pulling out my badge, I tapped it on the sensor near the containment room door, which unlocked with a pneumatic hiss. I slipped inside. The room was small and chilly, even cooler than the lab. Soft, blue light emanated from the floor and ceiling where they met the walls. The containment room had redundant dampening fields designed to render the voidrium inert, and the containment unit itself was only about the size of an industrial fridge.

A touch screen lit up with a tap of my badge, asking for additional verification, and I entered my personal code. For a split second, an irrational part of my brain expected the code to be rejected and an alarm to sound, but the containment unit popped open with another hiss.

The containment bottle, a silvery xibrantium cylinder about nine inches long, floated in a suspension field inside.

Here we go.

Taking a deep breath, I reached in and pulled out the containment bottle. I'd never seen our voidrium sample firsthand, but I knew from data analyses and scans that it was a violet crystalline substance so dark, the fragment seemed to drink in light. Maybe it was my imagination, but I thought I felt a faint tingle of energy course through my fingers when I touched the bottle.

Huh.

The xibrantium from which the containment bottle was made was a marvel in itself—nearly impossible to fabricate, unbreakable, and capable of absorbing and dissipating energy. The bottle had been provided by Vaydan Industries and likely cost as much as the Vaydan Institute's annual operating budget. It was worth it, though; xibrantium was one of the only substances able to contain voidrium.

I made my way back to MICSy, carrying the bottle gently. With as much care as I could muster, I placed the containment bottle into MICSy's heart.

That done, I walked back to the primary control terminal, cracked my knuckles, and started playing Bad Religion's "Generator" through the lab's sound system.

Moment of truth.

Taking a deep breath, I pulled up the activation protocols and initialized MICSy, making sure to run the iteration of the control software that Nate hadn't messed with. The pitch of the generators' hum changed as MICSy began to draw power. Workstation screens flickered. With a command, the containment bottle slid open and the modulation fields took over.

Glancing at the diagnostics, I started feeding power to the voidrium. It began generating energy in excess of what it was being fed, and the sensors detected gravitational distortions.

Too nervous to breathe, I checked the diagnostics again, terrified that I'd see uncontrollable energy spikes threatening to burn out the field generators. The control system was working, though, predicting energy fluctuations and smoothing out the spikes.

I was smiling so wide, my face felt like it might split.

Using our meticulous calculations, I entered the frequency of one of the directly adjacent multiversal strings. Taking one last breath, I pressed a button and tore a hole through space-time to a parallel universe.

The containment bottle glowed brighter, violet light filling the room. Something like a static charge began building in the lab around me. The lights flickered, and the small hairs on my arms and the back of my neck stood up.

I held my breath as the multiversal breach formed in a secondary containment field inside MICSy. It was too small to see—too small for anything other than electromagnetic signals to pass through—but violet radiance, the hues shifting and dancing, erupted from MICSy, filling the entirety of the lab. Squinting, I glanced at the display. After a moment, the machine began to register and record a transmission.

"Yes!" Exaltation roared through me. We'd done it! All the work. All the pain. All the sacrifices. Suddenly, it seemed like they might be worth the cost.

The music stopped abruptly, "Generator" cutting off midline.

"Congratulations, Mr. Carter," purred a voice from behind me—female but heavily distorted. Her tone was pleasant but undercut by an almost palpable menace. I stiffened in surprise for a heartbeat, jolted by the suddenness of the intrusion, then spun around, backing up against the workbench as I scanned the shadows.

At first, I couldn't see anything. Then I noticed a distortion in the air about ten feet in front of me, a vaguely humanoid refraction of light.

"What the hell?" I muttered.

The distortion rippled and flickered off, revealing a

female figure. She was tall and lithe, her form covered entirely by a suit of high-tech armor composed of flexible black weave and thin matte-gray plates molded to the contours of her body. Her helmet, a solid piece of the same gray material, swept behind her head into two points, reminiscent of cat or fox ears, covering her face with a solid plate that had no visible sensors or lenses.

She stood perfectly still, one foot slightly in front of the other, with her head tilted. Like a predator regarding her prey. The whole impression was feline and threatening.

Shit.

"My office hours are Wednesdays at ten a.m," I babbled, pinned in place by her eyeless gaze. "Do you, uh, want to make an appointment?"

Adrenaline pumped through me. The intruder's armor had small containers built into it, but I didn't see any obvious weapons. Not that she needed any.

Hell, she'd been *invisible* just a few moments before.

A chill rippled down my spine and out through my limbs, making my fingers twitch.

The voidrium.

Materials like it carried the risk of criminal attention. That was why our security system was supposed to be nearly unbreachable. I guessed the emphasis should have been on *nearly*.

I looked at my phone, which sat at the end of the workbench behind me. The faceless woman's gaze followed mine and then turned back on me. We stared at each other for a beat, then I lunged, hoping I could get to the phone before she covered the distance between us.

Grabbing the device, I smashed the emergency call button. Instead of lighting up, the phone sputtered and shut off. I stared at it, dumbfounded, before looking up at the masked woman.

The intruder tilted her head, giving the impression she was looking at the dead phone in my hand, then turned her faceplate back to me. "I'm afraid you won't be making any calls. I've also disabled the cameras and microphones." She languidly rotated her head. "It's just us."

Dread churned in my stomach as she started walking the perimeter of the lab, studying the equipment as she moved with fluid grace in absolute silence. She could've been a hologram. Or a ghost. Even without whatever tech or inhuman power made her invisible, it was hard to make her out in the shadows at the edge of the room.

"Who are you?" I asked, racking my brain for a way out.

She paused, glancing at me over her shoulder. "You can call me Lynx."

I swallowed. As far as supervillain names went, Lynx wasn't the *most* terrifying thing I'd ever heard, but it didn't exactly fill me with rainbows either. "I don't suppose you have a last name?"

"Please," Lynx replied, a note of reproach in her tone as she resumed her circling.

"Why are you here? Is it the voidrium? It's too dangerous to stea—"

"I'm not here for the voidrium." She paused to look at a fabrication machine in the corner of the lab. "What you've accomplished here is extraordinary. It's a pity no one will ever know."

A chill shot down my spine, and I made a break for the exit, leaping over bundles of wire at a dead sprint. Crashing into the door, I smashed my badge against the security sensor and pawed at the handle, but it wouldn't open. I glanced at the sensor, and my heart sank; the light was flashing an angry red. I tried again, my hands shaking with adrenaline, but nothing happened.

"You won't be going anywhere," Lynx purred while I fumbled with the door. I shot a look back at her, but she hadn't bothered to turn around.

A quick glance at the door across the room was enough for me to know it was locked, too, its sensor flashing the same warning red, and there were no other exits. No other way to call for help.

If the mask didn't want the voidrium or the data, then she must have been there for me. My heart hammered against my ribs. "What do you want?"

Lynx shifted on her feet to face MICSy, tilting her head as if contemplating it. "There are some doors you shouldn't knock on, some keyholes you shouldn't peak through. You've stumbled onto one of them, Mr. Carter. You should have left well enough alone."

Lynx turned and began walking toward me, stopping just outside arm's reach. "For what little it's worth, I had hoped this would go another way. You seemed useful." She rolled her neck and then her shoulders. "Let's make things interesting."

The door on the other side of the room clicked, the light on its sensor switching to green. "There's your way out," she purred. "All you have to do is get through me."

When I was growing up, Uncle Mike had told me that if I had to fight, to hit first and hit hard. With no windup, I threw a cross with as much force as I could put behind it, terror giving me strength.

As if she had known the punch was coming, Lynx slipped to the side.

I kept swinging, throwing a lead hook and another cross. Lynx flowed under the hook and around the cross, not even bothering to put her hands up.

Then her lead hand flickered. The side of my face erupted in pain, and I was blasted sideways, crashing into a server stack that kept me from ending up on the floor.

My mouth filled with blood as I righted myself and raised my hands again. My ears rang, and my vision darkened around the edges. I'd *never* been hit that hard, and I hadn't even seen her move. Lynx, or whoever she was, wasn't in another league; she was on another planet. She hit like a heavyweight boxer, and she was *fast.* Superhuman fast. I couldn't even follow her movements.

She was toying with me, drawing this out.

Enjoying it, probably.

The profound realization that I was well and truly fucked settled over me like a weighted blanket. With terrible certainty, I understood she'd kill me as soon as she got bored.

Staggering like a drunk, I caught sight of one of the power mains behind her. The generator in the near corner of the lab pushed out a huge amount of power. *Maybe enough to hurt her? If I can disable the safety sys—*

Her lead leg flickered. My face exploded in agony, and her kick lifted me off the ground. Crashing down on an instrument panel, I tumbled off it next to MICSy, landing hard on my shoulder and the side of my face.

I dragged myself up, using the panel for leverage, then stumbled and spit blood. The power main was a couple of feet from me. I turned and staggered toward it, the world tilting with every step.

A ring of metal sang out, and something punched me in the back.

My legs stopped working.

I looked down, but I couldn't process the blade sticking out of my stomach, just below my ribs. I tried to say something, but blood was all that came out, spilling down my chest.

"That's all the fun we have time for, I'm afraid." Lynx wrenched her blade out of me with a twist.

Heat and agony radiated from the wound. I attempted to take a step, but my legs gave out, sending me to the tile.

I struggled to get up, I think, but I couldn't. Blood—my blood—pooled around my face and into my mouth, flowing toward the eye pressed against the tile. I spasmed and coughed, choking and spitting up more crimson.

Lynx stepped around me and over to the control console, where she began typing rapidly. "Voidrium is notoriously unstable. If the safety protocols are off by even a hair . . ."

Her typing stopped, and MICSy got louder, the hum of the generators shifting to an angry growl as the light emanating from the containment bottle became erratic.

"Well, the results are often quite explosive, I hear."

I was nearly unconscious, making the horror distant and abstract. I tried to speak, to reason with her, but I couldn't. All I could do was die.

The burning agony in my gut receded, replaced by a bone-deep numbness.

As if from the other side of a tunnel, I heard Lynx speaking. "He's dead. I'll handle it; don't worry."

I thought about Vee, the way her lopsided smile spread across her face when I woke her up. How much I'd let her down.

Mom.

Tears spilled from my eyes and mixed with my blood.

Lynx walked soundlessly to the door but paused for a second. "Goodbye, Brandon." She sounded far away, and then she was gone.

I was alone.

The voidrium containment bottle was too bright to look at, even as my vision faded. The generator was vibrating so much, lab tables and chairs were shaking, but I barely felt it.

Before my eyes, droplets of my blood began to float *up*. In the haze at the edge of my receding vision, other things began floating too: Pencils vibrated and rose off tables. Papers slipped over one another and whirled upward as if in unseen air currents. Computers levitated.

Then the world went white.

And then nothing.

TEN

RUDE AWAKENING

I dreamed of floating through seas of radiant energy, my body a length of sinuous light. Thoughts that weren't my own stretched my mind into incomprehensible shapes, but there were emotions I recognized among the alien concepts. Joy, as I swam through space-time with others of my kind. Terror and rage, as I was dragged into the muck at the bottom of reality and crushed into crude, physical matter.

Coughing and gasping for air, I tumbled back to consciousness, overcome by animal panic and the over-powering pain from my dream. For a while—maybe a minute, maybe an hour—I wasn't sure where, or even *who*, I was, the foreign memories overwhelming my sense of self.

Eventually, my breathing slowed and something like higher brain function returned. It was night, and I was outside, face down on the cold ground and surrounded by rusted beer cans, old food wrappers, and other trash. The stench of damp earth and fall rot filled my nostrils.

Christopher Lee Rippee

Exhaustion battled with jittery energy as I took stock of my body. A deep ache throbbed in my chest, and I trembled uncontrollably, a mixture of adrenaline and the fall chill, but I didn't notice any other pain.

Shock, probably.

Shivering, I pushed myself to my knees and looked around, my eyes adjusting to the gloom. I was in a copse of overgrown bushes, the kind that grew wild and tall in untended lots, in fields, and along roadsides around Union City. Their spindly branches were bare, but they were dense enough to make it impossible to see beyond them.

I struggled through the disorientation to figure out how I'd ended up dumped in a lot like trash.

Suddenly, memories came crashing in.

The attack!

The sense memory of a blade impaling me through the gut hit like a blow. Sour bile filled my mouth, and I vomited, trembling with terror. Frantic, I looked down at myself. My clothes were soaked and sticky with congealing blood.

My congealing blood.

Pawing at my shirt with shaking hands, I looked for the wound, expecting to see a gaping hole in my stomach, but there was nothing. Just unbroken skin. Fumbling, I wiped some of the blood away, but I only found a scar, glimmering with a metallic sheen in the faint moonlight.

What the fuck? My head started to hurt, a dull ache radiating from my temples.

Dimly, I realized my earlier thought of being in shock must have been right. I should have been dead. *Had* died, maybe, yet I was alive. For a moment, I couldn't comprehend the two conflicting realities.

Schrödinger's sucking chest wound. I chuckled, or sobbed, as I started to unravel.

No, focus.

With conscious effort, I wrestled with my amygdala, forcing my ragged breathing to slow.

Someone had tried to kill me. I had a scar where Lynx had stabbed me, and the blood was still wet, which meant I hadn't been out long.

Great.

For better or worse, I hadn't lost my mind.

In shock and traumatized? Hell, yes. But not crazy, which left a lot of questions I couldn't answer.

I had no idea who'd attacked me or how I'd ended up wherever the hell I was. I couldn't even begin to guess how I'd survived, let alone healed.

Reflexively, I reached into my pocket. It was sticky with blood. And empty. A fleeting memory of my phone on the lab bench drifted up, along with how it had gone dead when I tried calling for help, and I took my hand back out of my pocket.

A breeze rustled the branches around me, carrying woodsmoke and hushed voices. I dragged myself to my feet, fighting a wave of vertigo, and turned around. Orange firelight flickered through the brush not far away.

I swayed. Instinct told me to head toward the light, but a sense of being observed was slowly settling over me. I had the profound feeling that someone was standing at my shoulder. Peering through the darkness, I didn't see anyone, but that didn't dispel the bone-deep certainty I wasn't alone.

"Who's there?" I croaked, my voice a harsh whisper as my heart rate spiked again.

The pain in my skull intensified as mental static filled

my head. Suddenly, I could feel a presence, as if I shared my brain with someone—or *something*—else. Through the noise, alien thoughts distinct from my own pushed against the edge of my awareness.

A burst of surprise flowed from whatever was inside my head, as it seemed to notice *me* for the first time, accompanied by a flood of strange impressions, incomprehensible thoughts, and indecipherable images. What I was seeing felt familiar, like the dream I'd woken from, and for a second, I wasn't sure I'd woken up at all.

I stumbled, barely catching myself on a tree, as the consciousness nearly overwhelmed me, battering my mind with frustration and rage—as if my psyche were trying to break out of the confines of my skull. A few intense heartbeats later, the feeling receded, as if the other consciousness was exhausted, but I could still feel it in a corner of my head, radiating distrust and hostility.

What the hell? Was I having a psychotic break? With an effort of will, I held myself together and tried pushing the alien consciousness away like I would an intrusive thought. Yet still it lingered, crouched at the edge of my mental awareness.

Dread roiled in my chest as I considered possible explanations, everything from psychosis or traumatic brain injury to—

The voidrium!

As the explosive realization hit, a wave of numbness rushed through me. Voidrium was exotic alien matter that the best scientific minds barely understood, and I'd been right next to it when it went critical. Hell, I shouldn't have even been alive. Who knew what it might have done to my brain!

Something was *deeply* wrong, but having a nervous

breakdown in the middle of the woods wouldn't help. One problem at a time.

I didn't have a phone and I needed help, which meant I needed people, even if I didn't feel especially trusting. I glanced toward the flickering orange firelight and muffled conversation, logic again telling me to head that way.

As if sensing my intent, the presence crouching in my mind radiated fear and wariness, but I ignored it, trying to move quietly, without much luck. I was unsteady on my feet and barely able to see. Branches snared my clothes and tripped me as I crashed through the brush.

Eventually, I made it to the edge of a clearing, still aware of being watched from the inside out by whatever was in my head. Tents were set up in a ring around an inner circle of lawn chairs and old plastic patio furniture, with a fire in the middle. There were a dozen people in the camp, maybe more, including some children, and a couple of dogs lying near the fire. Most wore worn, mismatched clothes in more layers than they needed.

An unhoused encampment. The realization tore through my shock.

Mom and I had lived in a camp like the one in front of me after we'd fled New York. It hadn't been too bad, until some guys from a nearby town showed up with rifles. They'd kicked the shit out of Sam, the camp leader, and then drove us all out in the middle of the night, laughing as they trashed what little we had.

I'd stared at their guns, wondering if I was going to die.

In the clearing, everyone was on their feet, staring in my direction. The dogs had jumped up and begun to bark, and a girl shouted, pointing. A couple of adults called out in alarm that shifted to horror when they got a good look at me. Given my appearance, I couldn't exactly blame them. Gasps and curses spread through the group when I stepped into the firelight, raised my hands, and stopped.

"Oh god, is that *blood?*" one woman muttered, her voice choked.

I gestured at the blood. "Would it help if I said it was mine?" From their expressions of horror, it *didn't* help.

Two women and three men stepped forward, putting themselves between me and the rest of the group. They were armed, mostly with knives and baseball bats, but my eyes were drawn, as if by gravity, to the pistol in the hands of the woman in the middle. She was in her forties, with medium-dark skin and tight braids running along her scalp.

The woman's eyes narrowed as she aimed at me with a curse, looking me over. "I don't know who you are or what happened to you, but we don't want any of it," she growled, her voice as steady as her aim.

Time seemed to slow as I stared into the dark abyss of the gun barrel. Sensing danger, the presence inside my head thrashed with alarm, fear, and less intelligible emotions as the throbbing pain in my head increased. Despite the alien fear, though, a strange calm settled over me. *These people don't want to hurt me. They're scared too.*

As if it heard, the presence in my head relaxed slightly, receding warily to the edge of my awareness.

I kept my hands up, forcing myself to breathe. "Look, I don't mean anyone any harm," I croaked, breaking into a cough at the end. "I was attacked."

"That's a lot of blood," said the woman with the gun, gesturing at me with the muzzle. "Sure it's yours?"

"Uh, yeah. I'm not exactly sure what's going on. I—"

"Anyone after you?" the woman interrupted, glancing behind me into the tree line.

Given that the only people I thought had a reason to be after me had just left me for dead, I guessed probably not.

"Uh, no, I don't think so." I shook my head, keeping my hands up.

She studied me for a moment. "You a meta?"

"No."

The woman narrowed her eyes again. "Then why are your eyes glowing?"

I blinked. *Huh?*

"I don't want to cause any trouble. My name is—"

"Don't," the woman cut me off again. "I'm guessing trouble's following you. I don't want to know who you are. Or anything about you. Get out of here."

I glanced behind her. A couple of kids, younger teens maybe, huddled together, while a woman around my age did her best to comfort a little girl.

Swallowing hard, I nodded. "Sure." Whatever was happening with me, these people had enough troubles of their own. "Can you at least tell me where I am?"

Cocking her head slightly, the woman sighed. "This city . . ." She lowered her weapon, and the other defenders relaxed slightly. One of them drifted back to the huddled group in the clearing, whispering quietly.

I sagged when the gun barrel dropped, lowering my trembling hands.

"You're on the edge of Union City. Route 622 is a couple hundred yards north of us." The woman gestured through the trees. "Brooksburgh is on the other side of that. You know it?"

I nodded. Brooksburgh was a rough part of town just south of Washington Island, but I could catch a bus or a cab there. Not that I knew where I was going.

"Cross 622. Turn left on Lawrence. A couple blocks up, you'll see a diner named Dellah's. It's open twenty-four hours, and they've got a phone. Tell the guy behind the counter, Jonah, that Tamara sent you, and he might let you use it."

"Thank you."

Tamara nodded, and I turned to leave.

"Hey," she called after I'd taken a few steps.

I looked back to see her stuffing a few bottles of water, a packet of wipes, and two protein bars into a battered backpack. Glancing at me, she untied the ragged gray thermal shirt from around her waist, stuffing it in as well, before tossing the backpack my way.

"People won't respond well to you walking out of the woods covered in blood, and I don't want anyone asking questions. Clean yourself off. Get rid of that shirt."

"Thank you, Tamara," I managed. "I'll pay—"

"Just go and take your problems with you."

I nodded again, not quite stumbling in the direction she'd pointed. The diner was as good a spot as any to start figuring things out. I didn't know what I was going to do, but I'd eventually need to call someone, and something like food probably wouldn't hurt.

I was frayed to the point of breaking and felt like I was floating, untethered from my own body.

I followed the path from the camp toward the road until I saw the ruddy-orange illumination of highway lights. I went a little farther, wanting enough light by which to clean myself off, while taking care not to be visible from the road.

Reaching into the backpack Tamara had given me, I pulled out a bottle of water. Hands still trembling, I took a sip, swished it around, and spat—trying, and failing, to get the taste of blood out of my mouth—before drinking the rest of the water in a few deep gulps. It was pure relief. I followed the bottle with a protein bar, wolfing the food down so fast, I nearly choked. I washed it down with another bottle of water.

After that, I stripped off my shirt, threw it into the woods, and broke out the pack of wipes, cleaning my hair, face, arms, and chest. By the time I was finished, I was reasonably sure people wouldn't immediately call the police if they saw me. After dragging on the thermal shirt, I stuffed the rest of the wipes in the backpack and made my way toward the road.

The unwanted passenger in my head continued observing me, confusion and wary hostility pouring through the psychic noise of its alien thoughts.

"Yeah, well, I'm not too thrilled with you either," I mumbled, wondering what the hell it was. "Feel free to leave any time." The thing in my head bristled as if it understood my intent, if not my words, and gave the mental equivalent of a growl.

When I reached the tree line, I had a good view of Route 622, just like Tamara had said. It ran east to west, roughly following the coast, and formed the southern boundary of Union City. It was a desolate stretch. Warehouses, vacant lots, and abandoned buildings huddled on either side of the pavement for as far as I could see, punctuated occasionally by out-of-date billboards covered in graffiti. Ahead, the specters of more buildings stretched north.

I followed the tree line, keeping to the shadows until

I caught sight of an unmarked road to my left that ran between an abandoned car dealership and a boarded-up plumbing store.

Unlike a lot of other American cities that transitioned quickly into suburbs, Union City was surrounded by a no man's land. A lot of masks attempted to avoid property damage by taking their fights beyond the city limits, and demigods raining death didn't mesh well with 1.8 kids, a two-car garage, and a white picket fence.

A silvery wingless craft appeared in the sky overhead and shot across the horizon, ablaze and pursued by an elfin figure with fairy wings firing shimmering arrows from a bow spun from moonlight. The craft streaked over the city and crashed into a lake beyond.

Business as usual for Union City.

I shook my head, wondering if that's what someone would have said if they saw me.

Trying to force away the image of a blade sticking out of my chest, I crossed the last couple hundred yards to Lawrence Avenue. It wasn't any livelier than Route 622 had been, but at least some of the businesses looked like they might still be in operation. Up ahead was the diner.

A car passed me, blaring music. Tucking my hands in my pockets, I hurried along, making my way toward the diner sign flickering in the distance.

ELEVEN

COFFEE

The diner wasn't big, just a red brick box with a door and windows, but I was anxious for whatever oasis I could find on the city's bleak outskirts. *Dellah's* flickered above the door in neon, but the *a* and *h* were out. The parking lot was deserted except for a battered hatchback.

I peered through the glass as I approached. The diner was even smaller on the inside than it looked from a distance. It was also empty. Booths lined the windows and curved around the exterior walls, four on each side. Everything seemed clean but worn, as if the place were quietly struggling on with as much dignity as it could muster.

Confusion and distrust emanated from the presence in my head, along with more indecipherable thoughts.

"Got a better idea?" I grunted under my breath. If my unwanted guest *was* the result of a psychotic episode, I was taking the concept of cognitive dissonance to a whole new level. And if it was the byproduct of the voidrium going critical . . .

I didn't have the bandwidth to ponder that just yet.

A bell jingled when I pushed through the door. "One minute!" a woman yelled from the back. The smell of coffee and fried food hit me as I made my way to the counter, and my stomach clenched with hunger.

I tucked my hands into my pockets, trying to ignore the fact my jeans were still damp with blood. At least they were black, and I'd wiped the worst of the blood off. I hoped whoever was here wouldn't notice.

A sinewy woman in her late fifties with chemical-blonde curls, scarlet lipstick, and a faded blue uniform that smelled of cigarette smoke walked out of the kitchen. Her smile curdled when she saw me.

"Are you from that camp?" She looked me up and down, frowning sourly. "I told the last one, you can't use the bathroom unless you buy something."

Some people treated poverty like a character defect. Mom and I had been on the receiving end of that attitude plenty of times.

"I've got money, lady," I growled, pulling out my wallet and slamming it on the counter. "Is Jonah around?"

The waitress rolled her eyes. "He ran out. Don't know when he'll be back. What do you want?"

"I need to use the phone."

"Up to him." Disgust crinkled her nose. "He'll probably be a while. If you order something, you can wait inside."

"Coffee," I grunted, stuffing my wallet back into my pocket. I dragged myself over to the corner booth to the right of the door and slumped onto the worn upholstery.

She filled a cup from the carafe behind the counter and set it roughly in front of me, spilling coffee on the table before wordlessly stalking away.

"Hey," I said, stopping her in her tracks. She sighed and glanced over her shoulder, not bothering to turn around. "What time is it?"

"Seriously?" She pulled her phone out. "It's 5:03 a.m.," she muttered, before vanishing into the back again.

Still shaking, I picked up the cup and let the warmth spread through my hands. I took a sip, hoping the caffeine would take the edge off the pain spreading between my temples while I considered my circumstances.

I had no idea who Lynx was or why she wanted me dead, but there was no way around the terrifying fact that she was metahuman. A mask. Her comment about doors and keyholes came back to me, but I was still too shell-shocked to puzzle my way through her cryptic bullshit.

She'd called someone, which meant there was at least one other person involved, and she'd slipped through the Vaydan security system like a ghost. Either she was skilled enough to bypass the system on her own or she'd had help from the inside.

Both options were *very* bad.

At least she probably thought I was dead. *What a silver lining.* I snorted and then choked back a sob. There was no explanation for my survival, let alone for me waking up miles and miles away from my lab. It had to have something to do with the voidrium.

The voidrium. I stiffened and jolted upright, spilling more coffee from the cup in my hands. *The lab.*

Lynx had done something to MICSy that caused her to overload. The memory of the explosion came crashing back. People could have been hurt. Killed. A ball of cold dread solidified in my stomach.

I needed to find out what had happened, and there was only one person I could think of to call. Vee. After that, I didn't know. The cops? Head to the Vanguard Watchtower and tell them what had happened?

One way or the other, Vee and I would figure it out.

My unwanted passenger must've heard my thoughts, even if it couldn't fully understand them. Its frustration and annoyance lapped at the edge of my awareness.

"I haven't forgotten you either," I muttered. Closing my eyes, I focused on the presence that had invaded my head. It felt *tangible*, as if someone stood beside me just out of view. As if my consciousness had fused with another's just at the edge of my perception. I could *feel* its thoughts and emotions, even if I couldn't interpret all of them. It felt alien, complex, and multifaceted, a nuanced consciousness with layers and depth. If the presence *was* a hallucination, it was a damn good one, but the more it lingered, the more it felt like my passenger was something *else*, which was even more terrifying.

The presence bristled, as if sensing my attention, and regarded me warily. Another burst of incomprehensible thoughts and images flickered through my head, followed by more frustration, fear, and profound weariness.

Whether or not my unwanted guest was a hallucination, I felt a sudden pang of sympathy for it. Its emotions and exhaustion mirrored my own.

We considered each other in silence until a burst of alarm and psychic noise erupted from the presence as an old SUV pulled into the parking lot and shuddered to a halt. The driver slipped out of the vehicle and hurried inside the diner, turning to lock the door behind him. He was in his sixties, the deep-brown skin of his face heavily lined under a Union City Liberties ballcap. Despite his age, the man had broad shoulders, big arms, and a thick neck under a plain white T-shirt.

A moment later, a battered cargo van sped into the parking lot, one tire bouncing over the berm. It squealed to a stop behind the SUV, blocking it in, and the occupants jumped out as metal blasted from a bad stereo.

The van driver was in his early twenties, skinny and pale, with a shaved head and rawboned features covered in acne scars and enveloped in a black bomber jacket. He giggled and glanced back at the passenger, whose beady eyes were bright with malevolent anticipation as they both swaggered toward the diner.

The passenger was in his late forties and heavily built, with broad features and a light dusting of freckles. Two thunderbolts were tattooed on the side of his head, visible beneath shaved ginger hair that didn't touch the top of his bald head. He cracked his neck, revealing another tattoo just above his shirt collar: a stylized *4* combined with an *R*.

Fourth Reich. Disgust and anger cut through the fog of my shock and fatigue. *Nazi skinheads.*

"Maggie." The SUV driver's deep voice was loud enough to carry into the back. "Lock yourself in the kitchen and call the police."

Despite what was happening outside, the man was surprisingly calm.

"What the hell, Jonah?" The waitress stuck her head out from the back, and the confused irritation on her face shifted to horror.

Moving behind the counter, Jonah glanced at me. "Son, if I were you, I'd get on out of here."

I tried to reply, but my headache spiked and all I managed was a grunt.

The van squealed as the last occupant emerged from the rear. He was massive, easily seven feet tall, and impossibly bulky. His craggy features were a bust rendered by a brutalist sculptor. He was shirtless, displaying pale skin that was stony, angular, and covered in small rocky growths that burst through old nazi tattoos.

Splicer, I thought, new dread twisting my gut.

Everyone knew about splicers—people desperate, or stupid, enough to inject themselves with retroviral cocktails derived from metahuman and alien DNA, hoping for a taste of what most masks took for granted. Beyond the fact the cocktails were *highly* illegal, the risks of using them far outweighed the benefits. The people who used them were as likely to die or develop debilitating genetic disorders as they were to get powers.

There were a lot of splicers in neo-Nazi groups around Union City, though. Despite their bullshit purity rhetoric, they only cared about power. The Fourth Reich was the worst, supposedly tied to Nazi metahuman masks and mad scientists from the 1930s and '40s.

My pulse quickened, suddenly pounding in my ears, as my headache expanded into a crushing pain behind my eyes that threatened to white out my vision.

The youngest skinhead started pounding on the door, making the bell jangle against the glass. "Open up," he tittered.

The older skinhead moved up beside him. "Hey, Jonah!" he called in a raspy voice with a hint of a Southern accent.

"Will." Jonah crossed his arms. "Is there something I can do for you?"

"I hear you kicked Ethan out on Tuesday." Will jerked his thumb at the younger skinhead beside him.

"Your boy was harassing customers. I couldn't allow that."

Will shrugged. "We need to have us a conversation, then."

"I don't think we have anything to talk about," Jonah replied, his voice firm. "Now why don't you get off my property before the police get here?"

Will looked at the younger guy beside him as their hulking partner loomed up behind them.

The younger guy giggled again, his voice almost cracking. "They ain't coming to help your old ass."

Will shook his head, clicking his tongue. "Now, I've let you operate for years, Jonah, because you knew my daddy. Can't we have us a conversation?"

Jonah pulled himself up, his expression hardening. "You haven't ever *let* me do shit, Will, and I knew your father well enough to know he'd be disgusted with the man you've become."

The skinhead's expression turned ugly. "Hank, get us in there."

The splicer, presumably Hank, punched the glass of the door, shattering it in a spray of shards. He wiped his hand around the frame to clear out the few jagged pieces that remained, breaking them on his stony hide.

The presence snarled and surged forward in my mind, rage pouring through the link connecting us.

My head *hurt* so bad, my skull felt like it was cracking open. But through the pain, I noticed an electric thrill in my chest that bloomed into a crackling charge of energy. My vision shimmered with strange patterns as everything around me seemed to glow.

Dragging a shotgun out from under the counter, Jonah fired, pumped, fired again, pumped, and fired a third time. The shotgun roared, deafening in the cramped diner, which filled with the stench of gunpowder.

The first shot grazed the splicer's shoulder, while the following shots caught him in the chest and neck. None of the pellets penetrated his rocky hide, but a ricochet caught the younger skinhead in the gut, sending him tumbling to the ground with a squeal. His expression shifted from bloodlust to agony by way of surprise.

Shaking his head in annoyance, the splicer stepped into the diner. He walked toward Jonah with the same unhurried pace that had carried him from the van to the door, and floor tiles cracked under his weight.

Jonah fired again, but like before, the shots failed to pierce the splicer's stony hide.

With another step, the splicer was at the counter. Grabbing Jonah by the throat with a massive hand, he hauled him into the air as if he weighed nothing.

"You shouldn't have done that, Jonah." Will shook his head. "Now things are gonna get messy."

"Where do you want to do it?" the splicer asked, his voice the guttural rumble of grinding stone, while Jonah struggled in his grip.

"Around back, I reckon." Will examined the young skinhead still mewling outside the door, before leaning down to drag him back to his feet. "Ethan can do it if he can stop blubbering. He needs to earn his laces."

The splicer grunted an affirmative. "What about the waitress and the kid?"

The lead skinhead sighed. "We'd better do them too. Uncle Jack don't like witnesses."

The presence seemed to be screaming, battering my mind with a deluge of alien thoughts and images. I moaned, my head lolling.

The splicer glanced at me. "What's wrong with him?" he rumbled, but I could barely hear any longer.

A shifting, multitone sound reverberated inside my head, flowing from the presence as it desperately tried to communicate. Concepts, almost like mathematical formulae, appeared in my mind, and suddenly, like in my math class years ago, I understood.

I looked up at the splicer. The hammering headache vanished as I reached inward and found crackling power. With the alien presence guiding me, I channeled the energy. It expanded until every fiber of my being was ablaze. The table, and then all the booths, started shaking. Coffee sloshed and spilled over the edge of my cup, then flowed upward, pooling on the ceiling. My vision was tinged violet as crackling arcs of energy in the same purple hue erupted from me, burning the table and walls.

I stood.

Light bulbs shattered, and windows burst. Broken shards of glass sparkled as they rotated in the air.

I felt like I was floating. Distantly, I realized I *was*, my feet dangling a foot off the ground.

The splicer's jaw dropped.

Driven by instinct that wasn't my own, I raised my hand and made a fist. I **squeezed** the monstrous nazi with a thought, unleashing the roaring torrent of energy that had built under my skin.

With an abrupt whomp of air, the splicer collapsed inward, too quick for him to scream, and then exploded outward in a shower of gore that spattered the entire diner. Jonah fell out of the air, landing back behind the counter; the splicer's stony fist, severed at the wrist, still clutched his neck. Everything that had been floating toppled to the ground. As glass shattered into smaller pieces on the diner's tiles and the concrete outside, my feet hit the floor.

Swaths of red and brown painted the room, interspersed with chunks of rocky skin embedded in the walls, filling the diner with the stench of blood and shit. The lead skinhead was covered from the top of his bald head to the bottom of his red-laced combat boots.

Everything was still for a second. Then a chunk of the splicer dropped from the ceiling and splattered atop Will's head.

The lead skinhead slowly turned to me, his shock and horror visible through a mask of blood and viscera. His mouth opened and closed and opened again. He staggered back, tripping and falling onto glass, before pulling himself up again and lurching toward the van. Scrambling into the driver's seat, he threw the van into reverse and floored it.

"Wait!" wailed his remaining confederate, stumbling after the fleeing skinhead, one hand on his gut wound. Will was already speeding away by the time the younger skinhead reached the curb, but he halted the van long enough for the kid to drag himself into the back before hitting the gas again.

The waitress peered through the kitchen door and let out a choked scream, just as Jonah stood up, gasping, revealing that he, too, was covered from head to toe in gore. He looked around, eyes wide behind the red veil that dripped from the brim of his hat and onto the floor.

"What . . . what . . . ?" he managed.

"Hey." I stepped forward, my shoes crunching over glass. Waves of exhaustion and dizziness engulfed me, and my vision blurred around the edges. Yet despite everything, I was strangely calm. Detached. Shock compounding on shock. "Do you happen to have a phone?"

TWELVE

CAB RIDE

When I came to again, I was moving.

Must have passed out.

Rummaging through disjointed memories, I dimly remembered calling Vee and then falling into the back of an autocab, where I'd probably blacked out.

The alien presence was still in my skull. I could feel it crouching at the edge of my awareness, exhausted from what had happened at the diner. I might have imagined it, but the presence seemed relieved I was awake. After a moment, it faded into the background noise of my mind, as if my uninvited guest had taken my waking up as an opportunity to rest.

With effort, I managed to peel my eyes open. Sure enough, I was in the back of a self-driving taxi, and the city drifted by outside the windows. Most of Union City was filled with light, the signs, screens, and holographic displays bathing the streets in bright color. The neighborhood currently on the other side of the glass, though, was dark, with aging brick facades, suggesting it was one of the

113

few that had survived the Rakkari attack mostly intact. *Washington Island, maybe?*

A worm of fear burrowed through the fog of exhaustion and shock. My vision was filled with a violet haze, as if I were looking through a purple film—except the glow was still there when I closed my eyes.

Shit.

It was *extremely* disorienting. For a minute, I thought I was going to puke in the back of the cab, but I managed to keep my coffee and protein bars down.

Fighting a wave of dizziness, I reached into the backpack Tamara had given me and pulled out another bottle of water. I guzzled it and then flopped back down on the seat.

"Cab, what's our destination?"

"I'm sorry," announced the cheery feminine voice of the cab's AI. "I can't provide that information. Would you like to hear about the exciting new Pumpkin Bomb Latte available at Nora's locations near you?"

That's weird. "Cab, where are we now?"

"I'm *so* sorry! I can't provide that information either, but I can tell you all about *Crimson Specter: Twilight of Terror*, opening in theaters on October third. Would you like to hear more about it or purchase tickets?"

"Ugh, no." I struggled to sit up again. "Who booked this ride?"

"I'm *very* sorry! I don't know the answer to that."

"Great," I sighed. "What can you tell me?"

"Would you like to know some facts about the city?" the cab asked, annoyingly chipper. "I can also recommend destinations or fine-dining options. Would you like to hear more?"

"No."

Autotaxis were required to disclose information to their passengers. The fact the cab wasn't talking meant someone had tampered with it. I had a guess as to who was responsible: Vee. Not that I'd be able to do much about it if I was wrong.

"Please let me know if you change your mind. Would you like to listen to 'Slippin' Wet,' the last track from Jal Fresh, available on VTunes?"

The person who'd had the idea to upsell people during cab rides needed to be flogged. "No."

I dropped my head back to the seat, and replayed the last few hours yet again.

The skinheads.

The splicer threatening the owner and then spattering all over the diner.

The energy roiling up from inside me. It was still there. Waiting.

To my surprise, I wasn't immediately overwhelmed by horror. Maybe I was still riding the waves of shock and disassociation. Maybe I was just too tired. Humans had a finite capacity for extreme emotions. Eventually, everyone hit a wall and went numb.

I'd hit mine.

Hard.

Numb or not, I couldn't shake the thought that I'd killed someone. My stomach clenched, and I nearly vomited as the memory of the splicer imploding and then exploding played on a loop in my mind. I hadn't meant to do it, and I didn't know *how* I'd done it, but that didn't change the outcome.

The splicer had been seconds away from murdering me, Jonah, and the waitress, and he'd seemed *bored* by the whole thing, as if executing a diner full of people was so mundane, he couldn't work up the energy to be excited. Who knew how many other people he had hurt or would have hurt.

As if sensing my thoughts, the alien presence emerged from the background of my mind and unleashed a burst of psychic noise tinged with what seemed to be savage pleasure.

He got what he deserved, I thought in response, even as remorse crashed against my resolve. I wondered what Dad might have said if he were around.

Eventually, the autocab pulled into an alley. "You have arrived at your destination!" the AI announced. "Would you like to rate your trip?"

Before I could think to respond, a door at the back of a nearby building opened and Vee rushed out, barely visible through the violet haze still covering my vision. She threw the taxi door open and dragged me out, crushing me against her, tears spilling down her cheeks.

"Brandon!" Her voice was a tangle of anger, grief, and relief as she buried her face in my shoulder.

"I'm okay," I managed. We clung to each other, battered by a storm of emotion and circumstance. My hands shook as a tremor ran through me, and my eyes started to water, but I held myself together.

At the edge of my consciousness, the alien presence watched us, its thoughts and feelings a snarl of static.

"Do you require further assistance?" the cab asked eventually.

"No!" we both said.

As the cab pulled away, we pulled apart, sniffling and wiping our eyes. I staggered and fell against Vee, clumsy and off-balance, so she slipped herself under my arm and held me up. My body refused to listen to me, and my vision was worse than it had been in the cab. Everything radiated violet light of varying brightness and intensity, turning the world into an indistinguishable mess.

A distant part of me registered the fact and piled it on top of all the other horrors of the last twenty-four hours. I pitied my future therapist, assuming I lived long enough to see one.

"What the hell, Brandon? You smell like literal shit. What are you wearing?" Vee looked me up and down, her concern shifting to horror.

I looked down at myself. The shirt Tamara had given me was spattered with blood and other fluids. "*Who* is probably a better question," I mumbled, following the words up with a choked sound that was somewhere between a laugh and sob.

"What's wrong with your eyes? Are you wearing contacts—is that *blood*?"

"Among other things, yeah," I slurred, looking away. "Most of it's probably mine, but at this point, I can't be sure."

Vee's eyes widened. "We need to get you to a hospital!"

"I can't. It's not safe." When Vee pursed her lips, I added, "I'm not hurt. At least not anymore." I sounded insane. I was pretty sure I looked even worse.

"Okay." Vee took a quick breath. "Let's get you inside."

We staggered to a heavy-duty security door set into the brick of a three-story building. "When did you get so heavy?" she grunted as she punched a code into a pad. The door opened with a soft beep.

On the other side, a small vestibule, barely large enough for four people to stand in, led to an elevator. She helped me into the elevator, punched another code into a keypad, and then hit the only button.

"Where are we?" I mumbled.

"A safe house," she said as the elevator rose.

The doors opened directly into a large apartment I assumed was on the top floor of the building, though it was barely visible through the violet haze filling my vision. What little I could see felt austere, like a display room. The only thing with any personality was Vee's sticker-covered laptop, which sat open on a table.

"Who owns this?" I muttered, looking around.

"I do."

I grunted, too tired to ask follow-up questions.

Vee helped me into the bathroom and sat me down on the toilet. "I'll be right back,'" she said, disappearing. Cabinets opened and shut in another room, punctuated by curses, before she returned with a garbage bag.

"Strip," she ordered.

Too exhausted to argue, I struggled to pull my shirt off and nearly slipped off the toilet lid in the process.

Vee steadied me and then helped, her eyes widening in shock when she saw the silvery scar just below my sternum. I couldn't blame her. Shimmering in the light, the line was nearly three inches long and almost half an inch wide, and it was still covered in congealed blood.

Part of me had hoped it wouldn't be there—just a fever dream nestled within a larger psychotic episode—but Vee clearly saw it too.

"What the . . . ?" Forcing herself to breathe, she looked for other injuries. There were more scars on my face, arms, hands, and back—injuries I'd probably acquired during the beating Lynx had given me. All had the same silvery sheen as the scar left by Lynx's sword.

Opening the garbage bag, Vee tossed my shirt in. "Pants." She helped me get those off too, making sure to retrieve my wallet before dropping them into the plastic bag. They were caked in blood, as were my socks and shoes. Those, too, went into the garbage bag, along with everything else I'd been wearing.

That done, she turned on the shower, stripped off her own clothes, and helped me into the stall, before stepping in as well. The water turned Vee's hair into a curtain of red and black. Running down her skin, it traced the lines of her face as she helped me wash away the horrors of the evening. She was gentle, as if I might break if she pressed too hard.

Something in Vee's expression—a mixture of love, concern, and fierce determination—cracked the veneer of resolve holding back the panic, fear, and guilt. I trembled and then shook uncontrollably, racked by sobs that tore their way out of my throat. Vee eased me to the floor of the shower and settled beside me, pulling my head to her chest so she could run her fingers through my hair.

When I'd finished, Vee dried me off and helped me into the bedroom. Like the rest of the apartment, it felt more like a tableau than a living space, but the bed was comfortable.

Vee tucked me under the covers and then crawled in with me.

I rolled toward her, and she pressed herself closer. Taking my hand, she held it to her chest, and we lay with our faces a few inches apart. Vee was a smudge of violet unlight, but her features were carved into my memory.

"The lab?" I croaked.

"There was an explosion." Vee turned away briefly. "I thought you'd gone back."

"I did." I concentrated, trying not to slur. "I was there." A knife of worry, dulled by exhaustion and emotional fatigue, slipped into my chest. There had been people at the Vaydan Institute. People I knew.

Vee's confusion was palpable. "What happened?"

I told her everything I could remember, stuttering, stopping, and digressing as I tried to order my thoughts. I told her about my conversation with Marcus. About rerunning the test and succeeding. About the attack.

About the voidrium exploding and me waking up miles and miles away and staggering into an unhoused camp. About the presence hitchhiking in my head. The diner and the skinheads—the splicer. About the crackling power inside me and what I'd done with it.

I was worried she wouldn't believe me or that she'd think I was losing my mind, but she took it all in stride.

The presence seemed to be listening, too, concentrating intently on the shape and texture of my thoughts and memories, as if trying to learn a language by hearing it. Maybe it was.

"Someone tried to kill me," I reiterated as I finished. "I don't know how I survived. Don't know what's happening to me."

"Whatever it is, we'll figure it out, okay?" Vee rested her forehead against mine. "I've got you."

"I know," I said, asleep before I finished speaking.

In the dreams that followed, stars and solar systems—whole galaxies—came into existence and died and revived anew before my timeless gaze. Alien thoughts and concepts, so clear in the dreams, became fuzzy when I woke, but they lingered nonetheless.

THIRTEEN

SAFE HOUSE

Panic constricted my chest when my eyes opened, but I relaxed as I registered Vee's muffled voice coming from what was probably the living room. The bedroom door was ajar, and the scent of coffee and toast wafted in through the crack. My stomach clenched. It had been awhile since I'd eaten anything other than a protein bar.

The clock on the nightstand next to the bed said it was nearly one in the afternoon, which was corroborated by the afternoon light drifting through the blinds.

Slowly, I sat up. My headache was gone, and whatever had been going on with my vision had receded. *Something* was still there—a faint violet shimmer that covered everything I looked at—but I could *see*. Given everything that had happened, that felt like a win.

The alien presence was hunched at the edge of my awareness, its attention focused on the city beyond the window, as if studying the skyline. It seemed lost and alone.

I guess you're still here, I thought. *Don't take this*

the wrong way, but I was kind of hoping you'd be gone when I woke up.

I could feel its attention shift to me, regarding me distrustfully. More concepts and impressions poured through whatever link we shared, followed by what felt like frustrated annoyance.

Yeah, well, you're not exactly making a lot of sense yourself. Feel free to find another skull to squat in. I tried to ignore the fact that I was bickering with what might have been a hallucination.

Another barrage of alien thoughts followed, along with something like irritation. It might have been my imagination, but the impressions seemed more intelligible than the night before. Whether or not that was true, my unwanted passenger shifted its attention away from me again, as if I'd offended it. I got the distinct impression it was ignoring me.

"Great," I muttered, shaking my head.

Not feeling any of last night's clumsiness, I gingerly stood up. I was a little wobbly, but the vertigo was gone. Whatever had robbed me of my coordination seemed to have faded along with the headache.

Vee had set out some clothes—a black T-shirt, black jeans, boxer briefs, and socks—which was good, because everything I'd been wearing had vanished into a garbage bag. There were even new boots waiting. I slipped everything on and made my way out into the living room.

The apartment was nice, with exposed brick, hardwood floors, and picture windows that overlooked the street, but it didn't look any more lived in during the day than it had the night before. The space was sparsely furnished, with only a couple of fake plants passing as decorations in several corners.

Vee stood in the kitchen in a battered Public Enemy T-shirt and a pair of underwear, David Bowie's "Life on Mars?" playing in the background. She set her phone down when I walked in, relief washing over her face before she broke into a crooked smile. "Hey."

I smiled back. "Hey."

"You were out for more than twenty-four hours," she said, a tremor in her voice. "I'm glad you finally decided to get up."

"I had to," I replied, keeping my tone light. "I realized you were cooking and didn't want you to burn your *safe house* down."

Vee gestured to the table. "I only caught the stove on fire once."

"More like three times." I sat down. "You managed it twice in one week when we were living in the apartment on Elm."

Plates clattered. "Communist propaganda."

I grinned, comforted by the familiarity of our banter.

A few seconds later, Vee came to the table juggling two heaping plates of pancakes, fruit, a carafe of coffee, and a couple of mugs. The coffee smelled like comfort with notes of chocolate and orange. I poured mugs for both of us, putting some sugar and a bit of soy milk in hers.

Vee slid into the chair across from me as I picked up my fork and started shoveling food into my mouth. I couldn't remember the last time I'd been so hungry.

I didn't have long to enjoy the food uninterrupted, though. The alien presence emerged from the recesses of my mind, emanating revulsion as it watched me eat.

What, don't you like pancakes? I shrugged mentally. *More for me, then.*

This time, I ignored *it*, prompting more waves of annoyance to flow through our link, along with incomprehensible thoughts and what felt a little like a mental *Go fuck yourself.*

"So, can we talk about the safe house?" I asked Vee between bites, continuing to ignore the consciousness pouting in my skull.

One of Vee's eyebrows shot up. "*That's* the first thing you want to talk about?"

I shrugged. "It would be nice to know where I am."

"We're in Arlington Court on Washington Island. I got some leads on my mom's case that made having a place to hide out a good idea." Vee grabbed her laptop off the end of the table, flipped it open, turned it around, and opened a window that contained a collection of video streams. Most of the cameras were positioned so they covered the street and rooftops outside, but one also showed the alley I'd arrived in the night before.

"There are motion sensors too, all tied into the security system. Oh, and the glass in the windows is bulletproof." Vee leaned over, pulled a second phone out of her computer bag, and slid it my way. "This is for you. It's a burner, but it's also tied into the security system here. You can check the feeds."

"Thanks." I gestured around. "Is all this about Raxxil?"

Vee nodded. "Yeah. I hooked up with an organization that has, uh, some similar goals. They connected me to a source inside the company, a board member's assistant. Her husband had some gambling issues, and they needed money, and she was willing to talk. She mentioned she'd heard some of Raxxil's board talking about a payout ledger. One of the names the assistant mentioned was the judge that declined to charge the Raxxil executives after my mom blew the whistle on them."

"Fucking hell." I leaned in. "Do you think one of the execs were stupid enough to keep records?"

Vee's jaw tightened, and she nodded. "Someone almost always is. The trick is finding it. If they get wind of what I'm doing, though . . ."

I reached across the table and squeezed her hand. "You're going to get those assholes."

"If they don't kill me first." She smiled sardonically. "Speaking of attempted murder . . ."

I sighed, slumping back in my chair. "I was thinking about going to Vanguard HQ. I mean, I met Aegis a couple of *days* ago, and with what happened . . ." I trailed off. "Vee, I killed someone."

Vee's expression hardened. "That nazi asshole was going to kill a guy for refusing service, along with two other innocent people. You did *nothing* wrong." Her eyes bored into me until I nodded. "But Vanguard might not see it like that. Other people have been put away for defending themselves with powers, and you'll end up in Blackstone over my dead body."

I nodded again. The thought of spending the rest of my life in a maximum-security prison for metas didn't exactly appeal to me.

Apparently, the concept of captivity didn't appeal to my new roommate either. The alien presence snarled mentally, fury and fear pouring through the link strong enough to drown out my own thoughts for a moment.

Hey, it's okay, I thought to it. *No one's going to lock us up.* I felt another flicker of sympathy for whatever was trapped in my head as it battered me with more anger-tinged psychic noise. Eventually it quieted, as if it understood my meaning, if not my words, and receded to the back of my mind.

When I was able to focus again, I looked back at Vee. She closed her eyes and took a breath. "We need to figure out who *Lynx* is, why she tried to kill you, and what happened to you when the voidrium went critical. After that, we can talk about our next steps."

My pulse quickened and my hands started to shake as I forced myself to think about the woman who'd almost killed me. And who would almost certainly try again if she found out I was still sucking air. I took a long, slow breath.

"Lynx knew enough about MICSy's interface to modify the safety protocols. It's not exactly an intuitive system. I've seen more user-friendly control systems on nuclear reactors. To someone who didn't know how to navigate the system, it would be a mess. She had to have been familiar with it before she walked in."

Vee's brow furrowed, and she pulled a leg up onto the chair with her. "I'm guessing the list of people who can use that system isn't a big one, then. Who's on it?"

"Outside our team? A couple of the research reviewers. Maybe?"

Vee chewed her bottom lip, thinking. "Did Lynx need a password to modify the control settings?"

I shook my head. "The terminal was open under my login. But Lynx also had to have a way to access the lab itself, not to mention the building. Security was supposed to be top-notch. The Department of Energy had some insane requirements before they would even release the voidrium to us. Claire made a call to Vaydan himself and had his people overhaul the whole security system."

"Do you know anything about the system's specs?" Vee took another sip of her coffee.

"I don't." I sighed. "I should've paid more attention. I know there were containment fields and full-spectrum sensors. The system was supposed to be impenetrable."

"No such thing," she said around a bite of pancake. "Humans are always a weak link."

I took another gulp of coffee. "I can think of a human who sabotaged the test and has knowledge of the building and the resources to hire someone like Lynx."

Vee met my gaze and narrowed her eyes. "You think Nate Chambers was behind this?"

I nodded grimly. "Nate, his dad, or someone working for them."

"Isn't sending a metahuman assassin dressed like an animal to murder you and blow up the lab a little extreme, even for that entitled prick?"

"I'm not saying it was revenge. What if they didn't want the test to succeed for some reason? Nate already sabotaged us once. Besides, Lynx made a call; someone sent her."

"What about motive?" Vee finished her coffee and poured herself another cup.

"Nate's dad owns Nextech. They're one of Vaydan's few competitors. Maybe Nate was feeding his dad and Nextech our progress the whole time and then tried to scuttle the project at the end."

"What's the payoff? I'm sure there was some great tech in the lab, but nothing they'd want to destroy."

"Maybe Jeremiah Chambers just wanted to kick some dirt on Vaydan's reputation. The Vaydan Institute's pretty visible, and Vaydan's closely involved."

Vee nodded but didn't look convinced.

"What?" I asked.

"It's stupid. Putting your own kid in a project that you plan to wreck? And pulling the trigger after your *very* public fight with his son? Seems like a rookie move, and Jeremiah Chambers is no rookie."

"You said yourself, someone's always stupid."

She nodded, her expression still skeptical. "There's also the timing." Vee grunted, chewing her lip in thought as she pushed potatoes around on her plate.

"The timing?"

"It can't be a coincidence. I think Lynx was watching you or at least the lab. She moved in after you restarted MICSy, which means they thought you might succeed."

"That points to Nate again," I countered. "He knew the test wasn't actually a failure."

"Maybe, and if it is him, I'll help you nail him to a wall, but let's be careful, okay? Whoever's behind this already tried to kill you once."

I snorted, frustrated, but nodded. I wanted to find Nate and beat him like a piñata until the truth fell out, but I could see how that might be less than helpful in my current predicament.

"I'll do some digging, okay? In the meantime, whatever happened when the lab exploded did something to you. I know a guy. His name's Rictor. He's a little, uh, *eccentric*, but he's good people. I think he can help figure out what happened to you. He works with some dangerous types as a, uh, consultant, I guess. Metas and fringe scientists—masks mostly—but he's made some time to see you."

"If you trust him, I trust him," I said. "Is there any way we can get word to a few people? I want them to know I'm okay. Warn them."

"Brandon." Vee's voice was gentle but firm. "We need to be extremely careful right now, okay? Whoever we're up against, they probably think you're dead, and we need to keep it that way. These people might be surveilling everyone you know. Abby, your mom. Claire."

My throat tightened, but I nodded. The thought of putting people I cared about in danger was worse than letting them think I was dead, but I didn't like it.

Vee took a breath. "Look, your mom, Clarie, Abby—they don't *know* anything. Killing them would just attract attention. So long as we don't reach out, they're probably safe."

"Okay." My panic receded slightly. "What about Mom?"

Vee frowned, a flicker of worry in her eyes. "I was on the phone with her when you called from the diner. Right now, she's surrounded by reporters, but I'm going to get her somewhere safe."

"When?"

"Don't worry." Vee held my gaze. "When we get through this, the three of us are going to London. Hell, Claire can come too."

A lump formed in my throat. "I love you."

A lopsided smile spread across Vee's face, lighting up the room. "I love you too."

After a moment, her expression shifted to curiosity. "So . . . is your, uh, *friend* still around?"

As if the presence sensed it was the topic of conversation, it flowed to the forefront of my mind, studying Vee.

"Yeah." I sighed, shrugging slightly and pouring myself another cup of coffee. "I was hoping maybe it would be gone when I woke up."

The thing in my head gave me the mental equivalent of a grunt, as if to say it had hoped the same about me. *No such luck, pal. This is my head.*

Vee leaned forward. "What does it feel like?"

I paused, considering the alien presence squatting in a corner of my mind. It seemed to regard me as well, wary and distrustful.

"Like I'm sharing my brain with another consciousness. We're distinct from each other, if that makes any sense. Like, I can feel where my mind ends and it begins, but I can hear its thoughts—*feel* them almost—even if it's hard to understand them. They're too . . . I don't know, *alien.* Its emotions are too. It's afraid and confused, though. And angry. It doesn't seem to like me much either."

Vee nodded and reached across the table, resting her hand on mine. "What do you think it is?"

"I was experimenting with extraterrestrial exotic matter that manipulates space-time." I shrugged. "Who knows? It could be a hallucination. It could be something . . . else."

Vee straightened. "The Rakkari are telepathic, right? It was how they interacted with a lot of their tech. Didn't some of the initial research suggest that voidrium was psychoactive?"

I nodded. "Yeah. A couple of the research teams brought in masks with psychic abilities to assess samples. A few claimed to feel *something,* but nothing conclusive."

As I thought about the Rakkari, the alien presence unleashed a burst of psychic noise tinged with loathing, nearly drowning out my own thoughts again.

I stopped, mentally recoiling from the intensity of its emotions, until it withdrew, coiling in on itself. Psychic agony radiated from it like an open wound, and an ache of sympathy for my uninvited guest bloomed in my chest. Vee's expression became thoughtful. "Does it have a name?"

I blinked. *Huh.* Shifting my attention to the alien presence, I concentrated, trying to convey the concept of names as simply as possible. I fixed an image of myself in my head and thought, *Brandon.* Then looked at Vee. *Vee. Do you have a name? Something for me to call you?*

The consciousness seemed to rouse itself, mentally turning back to me. I caught a flicker of understanding in its thoughts, followed by a dizzyingly complex tangle of impressions, memories, and images, more than I could handle. The sense memory of speed, coupled with the exhilaration of discovery, merged with the flickering image of the light of a stellar nursery. All of it fused into a distinct sense of self.

Woah, I thought as a wave of dizziness washed over me. *Too much. I need something a little easier.*

Just then, the chorus of Bowie's "Starman" kicked in, making me blink. *What about Bowie?* I tried to distill the core concept of the song: an alien too fantastic for the planet-bound humans it had hoped to enlighten.

The presence seemed to consider the idea before shrugging mentally and settling back into the recesses of my head.

I looked back at Vee. "Either we just had a breakthrough or I'm even more lost than I thought. I'm pretty sure it just said I can call it Bowie." I took a deep breath. "I don't know what the hell this thing is, but it feels too complex—too real—to be some part of my own mind."

She squeezed my hand. "One way or another, my friend will help us figure it out. Now, eat your pancakes."

We lapsed into silence as we finished our food. Once we were done, Vee started to clean up, but I waved her off, grabbing the dishes myself. I took them to the sink and washed everything, while she got dressed.

I was just getting the last dish in the drying rack when Vee returned from the bedroom and threw herself into the chair in front of her computer. "I'm going to start digging, okay?"

"Sure."

Wandering into the living room, I turned on the television and dropped onto the couch, still worried about the other researchers and staff members that had been at the Vaydan Institute. I flipped through channels, hoping to find some news coverage about the lab. When I did, I stopped, unable to comprehend what I was seeing for a moment.

A news drone was live streaming aerial footage of the university on a national news channel. The entire southern half of the Vaydan Center was just *gone*. The rest of it was a charred ruin. The surrounding buildings were also damaged, windows blown out and huge rents torn into their stone facades. The lawn was scorched and strewn with rubble, massive hunks of blackened concrete and stone.

My eyes were drawn to the massive pit that had been blown open in the ground just south of the ruin that was the Vaydan Institute. Black smoke still billowed out. It might have been my imagination, but I thought there was a flicker of violet light in the depths.

The lab . . .

FOURTEEN

NEWS FLASH

The area around the crater that used to be my lab was blocked off by Vanguard personnel in azure-blue hard-shell hazard suits with *HSE* on the front and back. The Hazardous Scientific Event teams handled the aftermath of *really* awful stuff: extreme radiation, temporal disturbances, tears in space-time, psychic viruses.

Explosions caused by alien exotic matter that generated gravity capable of warping space-time.

Dread gnawing at my gut, I checked the runner at the bottom of the screen. *A hundred presumed dead.* I rocked back, concussed by the enormity of the loss. Casualty statistics were easy to handle when they were from half a world away, but these weren't numbers; they were people I knew. My mind spun as I considered who all had likely been in the building when MICSy exploded.

Dr. Haruka had shown me a picture of her niece the week before. Bernard had been teaching me Congolese phrases, and Jasmine, one of the night guards, had invited me to see her band.

I could see their faces and hear their voices, but they were all gone, just ash and memory, along with dozens of others.

A pit of grief and loss opened in my stomach, threatening to swallow me whole. An erratic crackle of energy surged up from the wellspring of power I'd drawn on at the diner. When a tremor shook the floor, Vee looked up, her eyes widening with alarm. Slipping out of her chair, she rushed over to me.

The coffee table between me and the TV started to shake. Dishes rattled. A glass fell to the floor and shattered, and an ominous groan echoed from the walls. Even Bowie seemed alarmed, unleashing a burst of indecipherable thoughts.

"This is my fau—"

"Hey!" Vee stepped in close, her eyes still wide, and put her hands on my face. "*You* didn't do that. It was done *to* you, and to them." Vee pointed at the runner. "Fuck the guilt. Get angry."

I swallowed the lump of grief in my throat, struggling to stem the flood of emotion trying to drown me. Vee was right. Nate Chambers, or someone else, had sabotaged MICSy and nearly killed me. Had killed to cover it up.

I forced myself to take one breath after another and push down the guilt. Cold rage welled up in its place, smothering it. Slowly, the tremors subsided.

"Now, what was *tha—*"

As Vee glanced at the previously shaking coffee table, something on the TV caught her eye.

I looked over. In the bottom corner of the footage, a picture appeared.

It was the photo from my lab ID.

Vee and I turned to each other, her look of shock

mirroring my own. "Shit," we muttered at the same time, and I turned on the audio.

The commentator was a woman in her midthirties with a practiced smile and platinum-blonde hair. "—still don't have a clear picture of what happened, but we do know that Brandon Carter, a graduate student with a troubled past, entered the lab late at night, just before the explosion occurred. Reports suggest he was involved in an altercation at a university function earlier that evening and may have been intoxicated. Mr. Carter is missing and presumed dead, but anyone with information is encouraged to share it with the authorities."

Vee muted the TV again before turning back to me, unable to hide the worry in her eyes. "Your face is going to be on the news a lot, okay? I'm going to get back to work. I've got to meet someone later, an informant, but it shouldn't take long. I'll pick up a clean laptop. Until then, uh . . . maybe try not watching the news?" I nodded. "Remember,"—Vee's gaze pierced me—"you are *not* responsible for that."

What-if scenarios flashed through my head. What if I'd caught Nate's sabotage? What if I hadn't rerun the experiment? What if I'd never accepted the scholarship? Intellectually, I knew Vee was right. Viscerally, it was hard to accept, and acceptance didn't do anything to numb the horror and loss that clawed at my chest, barely held back by a wall of smoldering anger.

Something like fear radiated from Bowie when another tremor rippled through the room.

"Hey!" Vee snapped, catching my wandering gaze. "Let me hear you say it."

I closed my eyes and took a deep breath. "It's not my fault."

"Good enough." Vee glanced at the coffee table again. "Now, was that you?"

"I think so. I'm sorry. I don't know—"

"It's okay." She gently put her hands on my shoulders. "Try not to let yourself spiral, okay? Whatever's going on, Rictor should be able to help us figure it out. We just need you to hold it together until we can get you to him."

Nodding, I forced myself to take slow, measured breaths as Vee went back to her laptop, shooting me the occasional concerned glance. Whatever had just happened was uncomfortably close to what I'd done at the diner. I couldn't prevent the idea that I might be a danger to others from taking root in the fertile soil of my anxiety.

I don't suppose you have any ideas. Bowie just continued regarding me warily. *Didn't think so.*

Hoping to distract myself, I changed the channel and found a marathon of *D-List*, a show about street-level masks with minor or no powers. In one segment, a mask got stuck changing in a porta-potty, his force field pinning him inside while the teenage vandals he was trying to catch tipped the portable toilet over and sent it tumbling down a hill. In another, some guy dressed like Baron Samedi was being chased around by his own haunted hybrid sedan.

Bowie seemed to watch too, bewilderment flowing through the link.

I shrugged mentally. *I don't get it either.*

Eventually, I muted the television and turned to watch Vee work. She'd pulled both her feet up onto the chair and sat chewing her lower lip. It was something I'd seen a thousand times before, but now, the sight sent a rush of wonder and gratitude through me. I couldn't imagine facing this situation without her. She had probably saved my life.

Not for the first time either.

When I was sixteen, Mom had tried dating again. The second guy, a biker named Bill, had been a real winner. He'd shown up drunk for their date, and when she wouldn't let him in, he had forced himself inside and hit her, breaking her nose and knocking her senseless.

I'd thrown myself at him, but Bill had had three inches and a hundred pounds on me. He'd knocked me down and started kicking me in the stomach, over and over again, spittle falling from his lips.

Looking into his eyes, I'd been sure he was going to kill me. He probably would have if Vee hadn't been there. She'd jumped on Bill's back, stabbing him with the knife she'd carried with her until he'd staggered outside and collapsed on the curb.

Bill had survived, but he'd broken my left orbital, cracked my jaw, and given me a concussion, along with broken ribs. I'd needed surgery and had been in the hospital for more than a month.

Vee had been there with me every day.

Friends didn't even begin to cover what we were. It was Vee and me against the world. She was the rock I leaned on. The first person I called, good news or bad.

Even when I'd been with Abby.

Suddenly, the truth of it was right there, staring me in the face. As it had been the whole time. *I'm still in love with her.*

Vee caught me watching out of the corner of her eye, and her mouth twitched into a lopsided smile. "What are you staring at?"

"Just you."

Her smile widened. "Well, your eyes are screaming at me. Watch some more *D-List* or something."

"Hey," I said quietly. "You saved my ass. My life, probably."

Vee glanced out the window. "Do you remember the Minks show at the Limelight back in high school?"

I nodded. "Yeah. You got so drunk, you let that shitty opening band from Milwaukee give you a ride home, but they took you back to their hotel room instead. You locked yourself in the bathroom and texted me."

"And you stole a car, kicked in the door with a baseball bat in hand, and took on all four of them to get me out of there." Vee's tone softened as she looked back at me, tears forming in the corners of her eyes. "When Dad tried to kill himself, you were at the hospital with me *every day*."

I nodded, my eyes stinging.

"You went to all my mom's hearings with me, and when she lost her appeal, you stole *another* car and drove me to the lake she took me to when I was kid." Vee sniffled, wiping her eyes.

My throat tightened. "I guess grand theft auto is kind of my love language."

"We take care of each other. No matter what." She smiled crookedly, wiping her eyes. "Now let me figure out who's trying to kill you."

Vee worked for a few more hours. The sun slipped below the skyline while I watched random nonsense to fill the time before making dinner. After we ate, Vee got ready to meet her informant.

She paused by the door. "I don't need to go."

I smiled with more confidence than I felt. "I'll be

fine. It's a safe house, right? Besides, it's not like I'm alone."

Bowie grunted mentally, as if he understood. He seemed as thrilled with the situation as I was.

Vee nodded reluctantly. Slipping on a black hoodie and pulling the hood up, she grabbed her backpack. "All right. Remember, there are cameras and motion sensors on the surrounding rooftops. I'll get pinged if something larger than a pigeon shows up. Keep the burner phone on you, okay?"

"When do you think you'll be back?"

"I shouldn't be long. An hour, maybe two. My informant and I are meeting at a coffee shop nearby, and then I'm going to see a guy I know to get you a clean laptop."

Reaching out, I cupped the side of her face and leaned in slowly, giving her plenty of time to pull away. Instead, Vee stepped closer, her lips coming up to meet mine. She kissed me slowly but pulled away after a moment, resting her head on my chest with a sigh.

"The fifteen minutes I thought you were dead were the worst of my entire life." She looked up at me, brushing strands of black and crimson hair from her large eyes. "And when I heard your voice?" Her voice cracked. She wiped her eyes, leaving a streak of eyeliner. "Look, things are crazy right now. Can we wait until we get through this to figure us out? I want us to get it right this time."

I nodded, shaking off a twinge of disappointment. She wasn't wrong. "Yeah, of course." I managed a smile. "See you soon."

I couldn't help but wonder how many people at the lab had said something similar to their loved ones before the explosion.

FIFTEEN

EXPERIMENTATION

I lingered in the entryway after Vee left, trying to ignore the scenarios that bubbled up in my imagination, of Vee being caught or killed. *She'll be fine,* I assured myself. *She knows what she's doing.*

I did my best to believe it.

Trying to distract myself, I turned my attention to Bowie, who'd been observing Vee and me with a mixture of what felt like bewilderment and annoyance. *I guess it's just you and me.*

He grunted mentally, something like resignation flowing through our link.

Sighing, I made my way to the bathroom. I'd been in shock when I arrived, and I wanted another look at my injuries. It was dark, but in the gloom, I could see the murky, violet shimmer that had nearly blinded me, as if I were looking through a glowing film. Concentrating, I tried to make sense of what I was seeing. The violet glimmer blazed, filling my vision, as a wave of vertigo sent me stumbling.

I put a hand on the wall to steady myself. Bowie radiated smug amusement, but I ignored him. Unease wormed through me, fear that whatever I was experiencing was the result of damage to my eyes, optic nerves, or brain.

I didn't love any of those options.

However, there was another possibility. I might, instead, be seeing *something*.

In undergrad, I'd read an article about a guy whose sight had been restored by a prosthesis after he'd lost his vision as a child. After the surgery, it took months for his brain to decipher the new information. Maybe I was experiencing something similar. Maybe I was seeing into the ultraviolet spectrum or detecting some other form of electromagnetic radiation. To be sure, though, I would have needed a lab, a way to run tests, and someone with the expertise to help.

"Here goes," I muttered and turned on the light.

Shock washed over me as I took in my reflection. *My eyes.* They were filled with violet flecks, nearly replacing my natural hazel, and they were too bright, as if they were glowing. Vee had said something when I got to the safe house, and Tamara had asked why my eyes were glowing back at the unhoused camp, but their comments had slipped my mind.

As if my eyes shifting color weren't unsettling enough, my skin had a subtle metallic sheen that looked strikingly like the xibrantium from MICSy's containment bottle. My hair too.

Those weren't the only changes.

Dozens of small scars covered my face, hands, and arms. One stretched from above my right eye, across the bridge of my nose, to just above my jaw on the left side of my face. A trio of them drew lines from my cheekbone to the bottom of my jaw on the right side. They'd all healed with the same silvery hue, as if someone had used metal to mend flesh.

I gawked at myself in the mirror, fascinated and afraid. It was a good thing I'd never wanted to be a model.

Bowie seemed to be staring at my reflection as well, a mixture of what felt like morbid fascination and disgust flowing through our bond.

You can complain when you've got a body of your own, I groused internally. Taking a deep breath, I peeled my shirt off and tossed it onto a towel rack.

Three inches long and half an inch wide, the scar just below my ribs was even more prominent than it had been two nights before. I could see in the mirror that the entry wound on my back was the same.

I touched the exit scar, expecting it to be rigid, but it was as supple as the rest of my skin.

I didn't need a doctor to realize a normal human couldn't have survived the kind of injury I'd sustained. *Metahuman.* The word reverberated in my mind.

The first documented metahuman, at least in the modern era, was a jewelry thief from London at the end of the nineteenth century. He wore a top hat, a mask, and a *monocle* and called himself the Handler. The name didn't age well, but it was a different time.

The Handler's power?

He could lift things with his mind, up to about ten pounds, and move them around within twenty feet or so. Barely worth mentioning by current standards, even as a joke, given how much the power curve had increased, but at the time, his power made him a criminal celebrity.

Until the late 1930s, metahumans cropped up infrequently. They were novelties with near-joke powers, lurid tales that existed in newspapers and penny dreadfuls, too strange to be believed.

That changed with World War II. The Axis powers went all in on metahuman research: super-soldier serums, alien technology, magic. Attempting to counter them, the Allies followed suit. Shit got *weird.* Nazi demonologists and brains in jars. Zombie Bolsheviks. Most metahuman activity during the war was clandestine, but Knightblade and a few others ended up famous.

After the war, the first crop of superheroes and villains appeared, putting on capes as they attempted to save, or conquer, the world. Polaris protected the Earth from an exiled Alien Warlord. Crimson Specter started his reign of terror. Baron Von Skull built a lair on the moon and declared it his dread dominion; it was still visible with a telescope.

The Rakkari invasion changed *everything* in 1991, though. Hundreds of thousands died around the world. Empyrean arrived, and Vanguard formed. Other mask teams, on both sides of the line, followed. Masks battled aliens in the streets, in the skies, and aboard massive alien warships in orbit. Not only did metahumans—heroes *and* villains—come swarming out of the woodwork to put on masks, the frequency at which metahumans were created increased exponentially. No one knew why.

The attack also wove masks into the fabric of society. They became the icons of a new and terrifying world of demigods, divas, demons, and celebrities, birthed from the ashes of the old.

At present, as much as 0.1 percent of the population met the *extremely* loose criteria for being metahuman. Lots of people had powers as lame as the Handler and did their best to keep their heads down and go about their normal lives, but that still left a *lot* of would-be masks.

It wasn't exactly easy to put people who could warp reality with a thought into boxes. Over time, though, a few categories emerged, along with different power scales—even if a lot of metahumans blurred, crossed, or ignored such distinctions entirely.

Most metahumans were normal people who'd been transformed by an external power: Imbued by a god or given a spark of cosmic fire. Infected with a nanovirus. Turned into a vampire. Others were gods, aliens, or mythological creatures that had *never* been human. Some wielded magical artifacts or technology: A power suit. A rocket pack and blaster. The actual Excalibur.

Wizards, sorcerers, and shamans used magic to give the laws of reality the middle finger and move through the universe at oblique angles. Psychics did the same thing with their minds.

Some particularly dedicated or disturbed individuals trained so hard, they bordered on superhuman. World-class athletes, martial artists, detectives. The would-be heroes and villains in that category didn't have a great shelf life. A boxer with talent and a lifetime of training still couldn't do much against an underachiever made of living magma. Those who survived usually picked up tricks or augmentations along the way.

Metahumans with power woven into their very DNA were the least common, and the least understood. A few were born with powers. Some had their abilities awoken later in life when exposed to the wrong mix of pollutants or alien radiation.

The rarest of the rare developed powers in response to danger, but that was a roll of the dice. For every soaring hero, two poor bastards were mutated, often in life-shattering ways. I'd watched a documentary about a woman whose respiratory system transformed while she was being drowned, forcing her to live underwater. Since, she'd lived in a special tank in her family room.

In another instance, a kid had transformed into living ooze after a lab accident at his internship. He'd started a podcast, gone to prom in a bucket, and dropped a hip-hop album.

I was more likely to have been struck by lightning while winning the lottery than to have developed powers from the explosion. Besides, I'd been nearly killed before and nothing had happened. Yet as impossible as it seemed, I'd survived having a sword shoved through my guts before being blown up. I'd been *transformed* and given abilities.

I concentrated again, this time looking inward. The power I'd felt in the diner was still there, waiting, along with my psychic hitchhiker.

A wave of guilt hit me. Whatever I'd gained wasn't worth the cost paid in lives. But there was no going back, and like Vee had said, it wasn't my guilt. It belonged to whoever was responsible for sending Lynx. I hadn't had the power to stop them before, but maybe things had changed.

It was time for a little experimentation.

Turning the bathroom light off, I went back to the living room, where I turned off the lights and pulled the curtains. Once again, everything glimmered with murky violet unlight. Sitting down on the rug beside the coffee table, I pulled my legs in and closed my eyes. I could still see the violet unlight on the inside of my eyelids.

As I sat in the dark, my brain began to sort through

what I was sensing. I didn't press as I had before, allowing myself to observe.

At first, it was hard to differentiate one fuzzy shape from another, but as time passed, they became more distinct, gradually resolving into discrete violet shapes. The coffee table came first, followed by the rest of the room. Everything was still hazy, as if I'd opened my eyes underwater, but I started to recognize individual objects.

The couch. A lamp.

A potted plant.

Still, I sat with my eyes closed while the room and its contents grew clearer. I thought back to the experiment. Voidrium was the X factor. I remembered the violet radiance, nearly too bright to look at. Like the light that had poured out of *me* in the diner.

Like my eyes.

Gravity!

Somehow, the xibrantium had merged with my body. Maybe the voidrium had too. If so, it was possible I wasn't seeing ultraviolet light or any other electromagnetic radiation. It could be *gravity*, and my brain was just trying to interpret a new sense.

That line of logic caused other puzzle pieces to fall into place. In the diner, the instinct to **crush** the spliced skinhead had nearly overwhelmed me, and I *had*. He'd imploded. If my guess was right, then I wasn't just sensing gravity, I was manipulating it.

Every object with mass produced gravitons that distorted the fabric of space-time. Practically speaking, the microgravity of small bodies was undetectable, imperceptible ripples drowned out by the waves of celestial objects.

Since encountering extraterrestrial life, humanity's

collective understanding of gravity had increased exponentially, but most of that knowledge was still theoretical. The Rakkari had had tech that could manipulate gravity, and they and other advanced civilizations used gravitational drives for faster-than-light travel. Humanity, however, was still centuries away from understanding those technologies, let alone using them.

My theory explained the power, but not the alien consciousness squatting in my head. Unless . . .

The realization hit me like a thunderbolt. The Rakkari were conquerors; they'd come to Earth to enslave the entire planet. They'd almost certainly done the same to others.

What if something was inhabiting the voidrium?

When I'd first woken up after the attack, I'd considered that what was happening to my brain could be because of the voidrium. Not in my wildest imaginings, though, would I have considered that the alien matter had been housing a consciousness.

As if he understood, Bowie seemed to give me the equivalent of an eye roll through the noise of his alien thoughts, as if to say, *Took you long enough.*

"Fucking hell," I breathed, nearly dizzy with the idea. It fit with what limited evidence I had, but more than that, it felt right. I turned my attention inward. *If you're not a hallucination, then who, or what, are you?*

Bowie crackled with frustration, as if he wanted to tell me but didn't know how.

Unsettled, I went back to experimenting, hoping to calm myself. To my shock, I realized my sixth sense was more than just sight. As I studied the coffee table, I felt a strange prickle, as if the sense had a tactile quality.

With my eyes still closed, I slowly reached out to a

potted plant in the corner of the room. It grew more distinct as I focused; the leaves, the shape and texture of the bark, and the granules of fake soil in the pot all became clearer and clearer. I could feel the shape and weight of it, as if my sense of touch had been rewired. A sort of metahuman synesthesia.

Guided by instinct and my new kinesthetic awareness, I took hold of the plant and gently **pulled**. Power crackled up from within me, and the fake plant shot toward me as if it had been launched out of a cannon. I threw myself to the side, and the plant shot past me, smashing against the brick wall. The pot shattered.

Smug amusement radiated from Bowie.

You're welcome to help, I thought, remembering how he'd guided me at the diner, but Bowie seemed happy to watch me destroy Vee's limited decor.

I needed something a little less fragile. There were throw pillows on the couch—another sign Vee hadn't decorated the place. Grabbing them, I set them on the floor and sat back down.

Looking at them with my eyes open, I could still see the faint violet shimmer overlying my vision. When I closed my eyes, the violet unlight image of the pillow, and the rest of the room, remained. I opened my eyes again and focused on my new sense. The unlight image grew brighter.

Concentrating, I **felt** the pillow's mass and density. With as much finesse as I could muster, I **lifted** it with only a thought and a flicker of power. It staggered and sputtered upward with starts and stops, but it moved. I boggled at the implications.

Despite years of study, my understanding of the concepts and equations that underpinned the generation and interactions of gravitational fields didn't matter. Only the part of my brain that just *got* physics on a subconscious level seemed to help, along with flashes of insight from the alien dreams I'd been having since the accident. Using my new power was more like learning to walk than solving a new, complex equation.

And it was beautiful, a delicate symphony of gravitational ripples that expanded across the entirety of the multiverse, creating a web that held everything together.

I'd been like a chemist explaining the chemical composition of paint without an understanding of the beauty of the painting their interactions created, or a physicist who could solve the equations for motion without ever comprehending the dance they described.

Everything that had happened, the violence and the horror, couldn't stop a sense of wonder from coalescing in my chest.

Concentrating, I eventually managed to move the pillow in a circle parallel to the floor, before rotating it along its axis. Then it exploded in a shower of fluff, much to Bowie's amusement, obvious despite the alien shape of his thoughts.

Uh-oh.

Gradually, I constructed a working theory. I was able to generate new gravity fields while simultaneously hijacking, severing, or increasing an object's—or area's—connection to other gravity fields. The possibilities were endless.

I practiced more, clumsy and fumbling. The process reminded me of learning to use chopsticks. The evening waned and night settled in, and it started to rain. My new sensory range increased, and the vertigo lessened as I gained more control.

This is you, isn't it? I thought to Bowie in awe. *How*

you see and interact with the world. After a moment, he mentally nodded.

Despite the progress, there were setbacks. Erratic spikes of power resulted in broken dishes, a shattered coffee table, and a crack running up one wall. The more power I drew, the more dangerous the spikes became. I cracked the wall when I tried to **lift** the couch with a thought and a small surge of power.

Over the course of my experimentation, I realized I was using the smallest amount of energy from the well of power inside me, a giant pushing a feather with its breath. I shuddered to think of what more force might do.

The whole time, I could feel Bowie observing intently, listening to my thoughts and watching me fumble.

I'd just managed to **lift** two pillows and a coffee mug without anything exploding when the cell phone I'd lost track of vibrated. With my eyes closed, I used my new sense to locate the phone on the floor. Opening my eyes, I stood and picked it up. I couldn't wait to tell Vee what I was learning. Unlocking the phone, I looked at the screen.

Alerts from the sensors around the apartment were flashing red warning messages, and Vee had sent a text. It was a single word.

Run.

SIXTEEN

MIDNIGHT ATTACK

The power died.

I shivered as a nearly subaudible hum, thrumming like an engine, emerged through the sound of traffic outside. It seemed to be coming from above.

Uh-oh.

Glancing out the windows, I noticed blurry forms moving through the rain on the rooftops across the street, only visible within the faint violet unlight that overlay my vision. *They're invisible,* I realized, sharp fear churning in my stomach.

I focused with my new sense, and the forms became more distinct, revealing armed figures in hard-shell combat armor moving into cover with practiced ease. *Mercenaries?* The pit of dread deepened when four more figures, also visible only to my gravity sight, rappelled onto the balcony from above, their visors swiveling toward me.

Bowie's thoughts turned jagged, something like a growl surfacing from his psychic noise.

151

Maybe they're well-armed delivery guys?

One of the armed figures raised a high-tech assault rifle, and the others dragged batons from their belts.

Guess not.

The armored figure with the rifle pressed a button on their gauntlet. There was a whining sound that clawed at my ears, followed by a pulse of energy that shattered the armored glass in the windows and balcony door.

Shit. Raising my hands, I scrambled backward. "Wait, we can—"

The mercenaries with batons rushed in. My vision tunneled as the first one attacked, weapon crackling. I threw myself back, nearly tripping as the weapon connected. The baton unleashed a blue-white blast of electricity that coursed through me.

It stung, but not with the crippling pain I'd expected.

The mercenary paused, glancing at the baton as if surprised. Gripping it tighter, he surged forward.

"Wait, wait, wai—"

He lashed out again as the others moved in.

Bowie snarled, and energy crackled up from within me. The mercenary's movements slowed, along with the rest of the world, time dilating like a video suddenly played back at half speed. Even the sound changed.

Simultaneously, a sense of where the blow was going to land brushed my mind. It was slight but enough, and my forearm smashed into my attacker's, cracking armor.

Huh.

Adrenaline pumping, I threw a clumsy hook. My assailant tried to block but still seemed to be moving in slow motion. To my utter shock, my punch slipped through his guard and shattered his helmet, launching him across the room.

What the . . . ?

Stunned, I didn't react when the second attacker drove his baton into my ribs. Ozone filled my nostrils as it discharged another lightning-bright jolt of stinging pain. He pressed in as I lurched back.

The third mercenary used my stumbling retreat as an opportunity to press in from the side. He lunged at me, but his movements were still slowed, and I still had a sense of where the strike was going to land. At the last minute, I threw myself to the side, and the tip of his baton sparked as it missed me by an inch.

As the guy retracted his hand, I caught his wrist and squeezed, wrenching it to the side. Armor and bone splintered, and he collapsed, gurgling in agony and clutching his mangled arm.

Seeing what had just happened to his friends, the second mercenary cursed. He took an unsteady step back, dropping his baton and ripping a gun from its holster. The black void of the barrel seemed to expand as he aimed it at my head.

Bowie snarled again, and a rush of instinct, jagged and alien, took over. Channeling energy, I made a fist, **squeezing** the man in front of me with a thought. Like the splicer in the diner, he imploded with a whomp, and then exploded, showering the interior of the apartment with gore and armor fragments.

The urge to vomit hit me, and I nearly blacked out again as a wave of exhaustion made my legs wobble. Whatever that was, it took a *lot* out of me.

A flash of warning hit a fraction of a second before the mercenary with the rifle, who'd stayed on the balcony, opened fire. With no time to move, I covered my face with my arms, certain I was dead.

The rifle shrieked, unleashing hypervelocity rounds that hit me dozens of times, each impact a burst of stinging pain that somehow didn't kill me. Throwing myself out of the line of fire, I fell into the elevator alcove, smashing the call button as soon as I reached it.

Nothing happened. The elevator was dead, along with the power.

Panic replaced pain as I looked down at myself. My clothes were shredded, but I didn't see any blood. *How the hell . . . ?*

Glass crunched in the living room as someone came my way. *The mercenary with the rifle!* I staggered to my feet. *Gotta move.*

Lungs heaving, I stumbled down the adjoining hallway and dove into the bedroom, throwing myself against the wall beside the door.

Trapped. Animal panic rushed up.

A second passed. And then another.

Bowie growled as more glass crunched in the hall.

Dropping my chin, I threw an arm in front of my eyes and charged out of the bedroom toward my last attacker.

The guy stood in the middle of the hallway in front of the elevator with his rifle up. He opened fire as soon as I emerged, weapon shrieking again as another spray of bullets stopped me in my tracks. Each round was a burst of agony, but none of them penetrated, instead shattering or ricocheting off me.

Guided again by Bowie's instinct, I **grabbed** the rifleman with a thought and a flicker of energy and **pulled**. The mercenary seemed to fall toward me with a shout, accelerating beyond terminal velocity in less than ten feet.

I threw myself flat against a wall, letting the armored

assassin shoot past me. He hit the wall at the end of the hall hard enough to shatter brick and bone.

Hallway empty of people trying to kill me, I glanced at the elevator alcove. I moved toward it in a daze before remembering it was dead.

I stopped, panting, and made a decision. *No way out but through.*

Heart crashing against my ribs, I went down the hall toward the living room. A warning screamed in my head just before I caught the glimmer of four new figures on the balcony, each carrying a rifle. I covered my face with my arms as the mercenaries opened fire, rifles screaming.

My skin rang as rounds shattered against me or deflected away. Anger burned away my terror, melding with the alien rage flowing from Bowie. I turned into the fusillade, and every impact stoked the blaze of our fury.

Violet light crackled around me as every cell in my body became saturated with power. With a ragged shout, **I pushed**, unleashing a burst of energy. A rippling distortion erupted from my outstretched hands in a wave, blowing out the roof, walls, and floor and tearing the mercenaries apart, too quick for them to scream. The blast struck the building across the street, shearing off the top third.

Screams and car alarms echoed up from the street as glass and masonry rained down.

Aghast, I stared at the wreckage before remembering a comment Vee had made about the building across the street being abandoned.

Not that I had long to think about it. A thrill of warning filled me, just before a flash winked in the corner of my vision.

The world went white.

I came to face down in a pile of broken glass against the rear wall of the apartment, almost a dozen feet from where I'd been standing. Bowie's desperation and fear battered at my consciousness, my head rang like I'd been hit with a sledgehammer, and my vision swam. I tried to push myself to my knees, but the ground seemed to tilt precariously, and I was driven back to the floor.

Blood dripped down from my temple.

So much for being invulnerable. I vomited what was left of my dinner.

"Well, well, Mr. Carter." The distorted female voice that spoke from nearby was familiar. "Aren't you full of surprises?"

Turning my head, I saw Lynx flicker into visibility in the middle of what was left of the living room. She wore the same armored suit she'd worn the first time she'd tried to kill me, but unlike then, she was *very* visibly armed. A matte-black rifle more than six feet long—some sort of railgun probably—was pressed against Lynx's shoulder. Her eyeless faceplate peered down the barrel at me.

She just shot me with that thing, I thought groggily, struggling to focus as the world did cartwheels.

Shaking my head, I dragged myself into a seated position. I tried to reach out with my power, but as with my body, I could barely control it.

Lynx stalked noiselessly toward me, stopping about ten feet away, the rifle trained on me the whole time.

"Why are you doing this?" I slurred.

Lynx cocked her head slightly. "Again, you don't expect me to answer that, do you?"

I grunted, shifting minutely. My head was clearing. I needed to keep the woman talking, give me time to recover. She'd toyed with me before. She probably got off on fear. Maybe I could use that.

"How did you find me?" Anything to buy time.

Lynx paused, considering me down the sight of her rifle. "Our threat assessment AI tagged an incident at a diner outside the city, so we tasked a satellite with scanning for exotic energy signatures. Imagine my surprise when we found one that matched the signature at your lab in this building. If it's any consolation, I'll kill your friend quickly." She tilted her head. "Probably."

I went cold. *Vee.*

"She's not part of this!" A thrill of fear and adrenaline crystalized into focus, and my vision started to clear.

Lynx flicked a switch on the side of her weapon. "I might be the one carrying out the sentence, but you signed your death warrants when you turned on your machine."

Concentrating, I fought to regain control of my new abilities. *Help!* I thought to Bowie.

"Goodbye, Mr. Carter," Lynx purred, adjusting her aim slightly as Bowie growled.

Got it!

With Bowie's help, I **grabbed** her rifle with a flicker of energy and **squeezed**, just as Lynx pulled the trigger. The railgun exploded, battering me with a thunderous blast that picked me up and threw me into a wall.

I was dazed for a few seconds, ears ringing. As I opened my eyes, I wondered if I should get checked for tinnitus.

Acrid smoke filled the remains of the living room, and the floor where Lynx had been standing was cracked and blackened. The drapes, and one of the few walls still standing, were on fire, along with some of the furniture.

I was on fire too.

The shredded remnants of my shirt smoldered, along with my jeans. While the rain falling through the jagged remains of the roof put out the fire in the living room, I had to clumsily pat myself out. The flames didn't hurt, but I was dimly aware of the heat.

Staggering to my feet, I looked for Lynx and found her sprawled face up across the smoking wreck of Vee's couch, her head against the floor and a leg tossed over the back. Her armor was battered and cracked, but still intact.

I stumbled toward her. With a shock, I noticed that Lynx's faceplate was missing a chunk the size of my hand where it had rested against her weapon's sight, exposing the woman below.

Something about what I could see of her features was profoundly familiar. Shaved dark-chestnut hair surrounded a face that was unhealthily pale despite its coppery-olive complexion, with deep eyes, prominent cheekbones, and the hint of a full mouth. She might have been in her late thirties or early forties.

Seeing flesh and blood under the featureless mask brought Lynx's humanity into stunning detail. Unconscious, the woman was transformed from a ruthless killer into a person. But as soon as she woke up, she would keep coming after me. Whoever Lynx was, she'd killed at least a hundred people. People I knew.

I had a chance to end her, and I needed to take it. Or she'd go after Vee.

And Mom.

I swallowed, trying to harden my resolve, and effortlessly lifted her with one hand.

Lynx's visible eye slowly opened. It was startlingly

green and filled with confusion. Her gaze flickered, shock visible through the hole in her mask. "What's . . . ?" She blinked rapidly, looking around. Trembling, her gaze filled with horror before returning to me.

I faltered, disarmed by the flood of emotion on Lynx's face.

A tear formed at the corner of her eye, mixing with the rain that ran down her cheek. With an effort of will, she composed herself, her gaze boring into mine. "Who are you? It doesn't matter. Listen to me, you nee—"

She froze midsentence, twitching, her visible eye flitting from side to side, before she went limp like a puppet with her strings cut.

A thrill of danger cut through the fog of fatigue and pain clouding my brain.

Lynx's eye shot open again, her confusion gone. Viper quick, she reached over her shoulder.

I threw my head to the side, and a blade sliced through the space where my eye had been a fraction of a second before. A line of fire erupted along the side of my head. The stench of burnt blood filled my nostrils, and my left eye went blind. As Lynx pulled her arm back for another cut, I hurled her toward the kitchen.

Flying through the air, she turned over like a cat and hit the wall feet first. The brick cracked, absorbing the impact, and Lynx sprang back at me, covering the distance between us nearly too fast for me to register.

Until it wasn't.

Bowie growled, and time seemed to slow again, giving me my first clear view of the blade Lynx had pulled from the sheath on her back. It was nearly four feet long, straight, and single edged. An energy field surrounded the blade, distorting it.

While everything might have been moving slowly, *Lynx* was *fast* and I was off-balance. She slashed down, a diagonal cut aimed at my neck. I felt it coming and threw an arm up, staggering to the side.

The blade sliced into my forearm with a spray of blood, leaving a line of cold fire that numbed me to the bone. Lynx's visible eye narrowed with lethal focus. There was nothing playful there now, only murderous intent.

She flowed from one attack to the next, blending superlative skill with supernatural speed, strength, and agility as her blade flickered toward my blind side.

As I had when I fought the mercenaries, I sensed where the blow was going to land, but she was too fast.

The shriek of metal shearing metal accompanied the stench of burning flesh as the sword bit just below my ribs. My side exploded with agony.

I screamed and stumbled. Lynx lunged forward, feinting toward my side again, before scything toward my head when I threw myself back.

My world went white again.

When I opened my working eye, Lynx loomed over me. Rain dripped through the crack in her helmet, mixing with blood and the tears that still ran down her cheek.

I could barely lift my limbs. Distantly, I noted that two concussions in as many days probably wasn't good for me. I chuckled, coughing up blood.

Bowie pounded on my mind, his alien thoughts a desperate jumble, but he felt muffled. Distant.

I coughed weakly and struggled to stand.

"You're surprisingly hard to kill," Lynx spat, her voice a mechanical growl as she pointed the tip of her blade toward my good eye. "I think I'll aim somewhere a little *softer.*"

Bowie reached out, distress and fear flowing through our link. He seemed to focus as he shared impressions and memories. At first, I couldn't understand, but then, just as I had at the diner, I saw the meaning in the noise.

My eyes glowed, bathing the assassin in violet light, as I poured energy into a point behind me, stretching and then tearing space.

Lynx's visible eye narrowed, and her blade plunged downward. However, the tip seemed to slow, taking an eternity to descend. With a crackling eruption of violet energy, I fell backward out of space-time.

SEVENTEEN

GRYPHON

I was falling.

My limbs flailed as I tumbled through the air. I caught a glimpse of what looked like a roof rushing up to meet me a moment before I crashed into it, landing hard on my head and shoulders. Disoriented, I lay there panting until cold rain and a vibrating pocket brought me back to myself. Rolling over onto my stomach, I dry heaved until I was too exhausted to continue.

It was still night, and the roof I'd landed on was punctuated by ventilation, air-conditioning units, and an access door. The rain had grown into a storm that drenched the city. Bolts of lightning occasionally cracked the sky, illuminating the clouds above. What little remained of my clothes were soaked through.

Somehow, I was still alive, but the side of my head where I'd been shot was numb, my vision was blurry, and I still couldn't see out of my left eye. My new sense flickered in and out, and my thoughts were muddled, as if my head were filled with greased cinder blocks.

162

Struggling up to a seated position, I leaned against the cool metal of an air conditioner and looked down. I expected to see blood flowing from deep lacerations covering my arms and torso, but the rain had washed away most of the blood. Impossibly, the cuts weren't deep, as if my flesh was too hard to slice, and somehow, the wounds were already reknitting, forming silvery scabs.

Wincing, I carefully touched the left side of my face. A rent in my skin ran from the corner of my eye to the back of my skull. I probed the socket. It didn't hurt much, and everything seemed to be intact, just swollen and crusted with blood. Cupping some rainwater in my hands, I washed the eye out and slowly opened it. Relief rushed through me; I could still see.

Bowie touched my mind gently, letting his exhaustion flow through me. Then he retreated into the background noise of my mind, as if to rest.

Figuring I should find out where the hell I was, I looked around. I found myself looking west over the UCU campus. Beyond it, the skyscrapers of Union City pierced the night, murky towers of concrete, glass, and steel lit by signs and massive holographic displays still visible despite the rain.

After a second, I realized I was on the roof of Galden Hall. It was one of the best views on campus and one of my favorite spots in the city. Vee and I had spent many nights up here. We'd get high or bring food and beer, along with a portable speaker, and hang out, enjoying the view and each other's company.

How the hell . . . ?

Confusion filled my trauma-muddled brain. Somehow, I—or we, considering Bowie still shared my skull— had transported myself miles across the city in an instant.

The Rakkari manipulated gravity to create temporary wormholes that allowed them to travel vast distances. Some had theorized that voidrium was the key to whatever method they used . . .

"No way . . ." I breathed. The explanation was only slightly less outlandish than the reality of my circumstances. I'd have been fascinated if I weren't exhausted and in so much pain.

Thank you, I thought to Bowie. He didn't respond, prompting worry to flicker through me.

My phone vibrated again. Vee.

I dragged the phone out of my pocket. There was a massive crack in the case, but the screen had been pressed against my leg, so the phone still worked. I had several missed calls from Vee's number, the last of which was just a few seconds ago. Hands trembling, I hit the call back button, terrified she wouldn't answer.

"Brandon!" The relief in Vee's voice was palpable. "Are you okay?"

I grunted out a chuckle that turned into a cough. I was only okay if we were *very* generous with the definition. "Yeah . . ." I paused. "I—"

Her voice hardened. "I saw the camera feeds. Are you okay physically, at least?"

"I think so. Somehow." I stared at the cuts on my arms, silvery scabs bisecting tattooed skin, and then the gouge in my side, which no longer oozed blood. "Where are you?"

"I can't tell you that, and don't tell me where you are either. I don't want to take the chance that someone might be listening."

"Listening?" I asked. "How?"

"Dude, that apartment was buried, but they found it.

I don't know who these people are, but we need to be very, *very* careful. There are maybe ten companies, militaries, and organizations in the world with gear like that."

I grunted again. I could think of one person who might have the resources. *Nate Chambers or his billionaire industrialist father.* "What about Mom?"

Vee paused for a second. "Do you trust me?"

"Of course," I answered without hesitation.

"I'll take care of Mom. Whoever's behind this cares about flying under the radar. We can use that." She took a deep breath. "Hey, do you remember where we were the first time we met Sydney Icious?"

I blinked, momentarily caught off guard. "Huh?"

"Brandon, think. Sydney Icious."

I drew a blank, my thoughts muddled, but then it hit me. Ben had been a friend from high school. He'd paid for a fake ID with the name Sydney V. Icious. He'd been so proud of the stupid thing, he hadn't shut up about it. The name became a running joke for years, but the first time Ben had used it was to rent a hotel room on one of Vee's stolen credit cards. We'd thrown a party there.

The Union Arms?

"I remember Syd, yeah."

"Good," Vee said, relieved. "Can you get there?"

"Yeah, I think so." The hotel was only a mile and a half from the university, just off Vanguard Square near the Cultural District, surrounded by museums, galleries, and performance halls. I was bone-tired and injured, but I was pretty sure I could make it on foot. I was more concerned about getting stopped along the way.

"Ask for Sydney's friend, okay?" Vee said, pulling me back.

"Are you going to meet me there?"

She paused again. "I'm not sure. We talked about a meeting. Make sure you go. I'll get you the details and meet you there if I can."

"I will." I took a ragged breath. "Vee, I—"

"Destroy your phone after you hang up." Then she disconnected.

I checked the time. It was 10:32 p.m. Sighing, I pulled the SIM card out of the phone and snapped it. Then I pulled out the battery too, just in case.

I sat there for a second and closed my eyes, letting the rain wash over me as it let up.

"Rough night?" asked a deep voice from above.

Startled, I opened my eyes and looked up.

The speaker was a burly guy in white spandex and a bird mask with a beak that covered his nose, leaving the lower half of a broad, stubbly jaw exposed. He was built like a powerlifter; his leotard stretched over broad shoulders and a wide belly that mushroomed over the front and sides of his belt. The costume was accessorized with blue leather gloves, matching boots, and a codpiece. A cloak of soggy feathers hung from his back, and a massive *G* was emblazoned on the middle of his chest.

He floated about five feet above the roof.

Great, a mask. Wariness fought through my fatigue.

I didn't recognize the guy, but that didn't mean much. The city was lousy with wannabe heroes. There were hundreds of costumed vigilantes in Union City, maybe even thousands. Most were independents trying to make a name for themselves by harassing people, stirring up shit with each other, and generally causing more problems than they solved.

"What would give you that impression?" I managed.

"Well, you're near naked and beat to hell in a

puddle of your own sick, for one." The mask scratched his head. "And it looks like you were on *fire*, which isn't usually a good sign. Oh, and you appeared in a flash of purple light and fell ten feet onto a roof, which is how I caught sight of you in the first place."

The mask floated down until his boots touched the roof and then walked slowly toward me, holding his hands up. "Look, kid, whatever's happening, you're safe now. The Gryphon is here." He paused expectantly.

I shook my head. "I don't . . ."

"The Gryphon . . . ?" he said again.

"Uh, I'm sorry. I'm not really up on *superheroes*."

"Come on, man. You've *definitely* heard of me. Founding member of Chimera Squad, with Hippogryph and Manticore?"

I shrugged slightly. "Still doesn't ring a bell."

Gryphon sighed, exasperated. "I helped stop the time-traveling robots that attacked Union Field last year?"

I shook my head again.

"Oh, hey, I teamed up with Dr. Furious to fight the giant amoeba that tried to eat Pittsburgh last fall."

I winced. "I'm sorry . . ."

"What about the swamp monster in Louisiana last month? C'mon, man, the goddamn thing was forty feet tall."

I shook my head a third time.

"I'm going to fire my publicist." He sighed, deflating. "No worries, I guess. There *are* a lot of us these days."

I nodded. *Too many.*

Gryphon puffed up a little, sticking his chest out. "Well, whether you know who I am or not, I'm here to help. What can I do?"

"Do you have a shirt?"

He squinted at me, his eyes scanning my wounds. "Jesus Christ, kid, you don't need a shirt; you need a hospital. What the hell happened to you?"

"That's kind of a long story . . ." I needed a cover. I struggled to think of one, but my thoughts were still sluggish.

"You can tell me on the way." Gryphon leaned down to pick me up.

"No, please!" I pulled away as much as I could. "I can't go to a hospital. Besides, it looks a lot worse than it is."

"Kid, you look like you got gangbanged by a knife collection." Gryphon's deep voice was skeptical, and he crossed his arms, daring me to disagree, while he looked me over again. "I guess you're not bleeding. Anymore. If you won't let me take you to the hospital, at least tell me what happened."

Reaching into a utility belt pocket, he pulled out a pack of cigarettes and a lighter. He took a cigarette out, lit it, and then offered me the pack. I shook my head, and he put the pack and the lighter back in his pouch.

"Did you just get your powers?"

"Uh, powers?"

He snorted and took a drag on his cigarette. "I've been doing this for a while. You appeared in a flash of light, but more than that—I mean seriously, just look at you. Your skin, the eyes, those scars—not to mention you've clearly been in a fight or two you probably shouldn't have survived."

"Uh, yeah. I just got my powers."

Gryphon exhaled smoke and shook his head. "That's always a shit show. I was in Greece, on vacation with my ex-wife, when I got mine. We were hiking in the mountains north of Athens when we found this old shrine, and I got possessed by the gryphon spirit inside it. I spent a week flying around, hunting goats with my bare hands, and eating them raw before I got control of myself. Not a great week, and I still don't like the taste of goat, but it was worth it in the end." He pointed to the *G* on his chest and looked at me expectantly.

I just blinked.

Gryphon raised an eyebrow. "Want to tell me what's going on?"

"Honestly? I'd rather not."

"I get that." He shrugged. "I can respect a man's right to privacy. Still, you look like you've been through some shit. Unless you can give me a good reason not to, I'm going to have to report this to *somebody*. I can't just leave you up here."

I sighed, closing my eyes. My head still felt like it was filled with cement.

"I was attacked, uh, bitten."

Ugh. I wasn't off to a great start.

"Bitten?" Gryphon frowned. "By what?"

I blanked, eyes flicking out onto the campus, searching for inspiration. The first thing I saw was an ad for the robotics team. "Uh, a robot," I replied, immediately berating myself.

"Wait, you got bitten by a *robot*?" Gryphon asked, incredulous.

"Yeah?" I couldn't imagine how I wasn't going to end up in a cell.

Gryphon shook his head and sighed. "Was it about seven feet tall? One big blue eye in the middle of its head?"

I blinked. "Uh, yeah, that's it."

"Sounds like the Telarian collective." He nodded knowingly. "Biosynthetics from an alternate dimension." He rolled his eyes and took another long puff of his cigarette. "I heard they replicate by injecting people with a nanovirus that transforms them. Doesn't always take. You're the second guy this month. First person I've heard of that got powers, though. Lucky you!"

For a second, I couldn't process what he was saying. "Yeah, lucky."

"Hey, offhand, you weren't on Washington Island earlier tonight, were you?" Gryphon asked, sending a chill down my spine. I most definitely had been on Washington Island earlier. I'd destroyed two buildings and nearly died there less than fifteen minutes ago.

"Uh, no. Why? Did something go down?"

Gryphon snorted. "You could say that, yeah. Someone, probably a new supervillain, leveled a city block in about ten seconds. A Vanguard team is already picking through the rubble. Anyway, about that shirt . . ."

He reached under his soggy feathered cloak and pulled out a small messenger bag. Unzipping it, he pulled out a hoodie. It was white and blue, like his uniform, with a big *G* in the middle.

"I keep them for the people I rescue," he said, a little embarrassed. Taking a hit of his cigarette, he held the shirt out to me. "It's yours. Just do me a favor: follow me on Vwitter and like me on Instabook, okay? I could use the subscribers."

He stared at me for another second. "Hey, if you need anything . . ."

The mask's large fingers reached into a small pouch on his belt, and he handed me a card with a phone number, an email address, and various social media tags around a big *G*.

"It can be a hard transition. Hit me up. If you decide to put on a mask, maybe you can join the team. Most of us are mythological, but maybe a half robot would be good. Expand the brand."

I nodded. "I'll, uh, give that some thought. Thanks."

Gryphon finished his smoke and tossed the butt on the roof, rubbing it out with his boot. "No *problemo*, kid. You take care of yourself." With that, he nodded at me and leaped into the air, vanishing into the night sky.

EIGHTEEN

VANGUARD

I sat for a few minutes gazing at the skyscrapers across the water. Behind a veil of rain, they were a dream painted in glass, steel, and pastel neon. An artist's vision of a city washed clean.

Eventually, the storm passed.

Dragging myself up, I grunted in agony as my injuries protested. The door to the roof was locked, so I ripped it off its hinges and tossed it aside, too tired to be amazed by my newfound strength.

When I got down to the street, I tried to blend into the crowds of students, pedestrians, and tourists pouring onto the Boulevard of Heroes after the rain.

At this time of night, the boulevard was always filled with crowds, and with the memorial celebration only a few days away, it was *packed*. The week before Resistance Day always saw tourists and travelers coming into Union City from around the world, and the street performers, panhandlers, and impersonators were out in force.

I slid around people too distracted, drunk, or inconsiderate to make space.

My face had been on the news, so I pulled my hood up and kept my eyes down, stealing a medical mask and a pair of sunglasses from a kitschy souvenir shop at the edge of campus. Dr. Pestilence's latest pandemic was still making the rounds, so wearing face masks had become pretty normal.

A theater on the next block had *Requiem for a Supervillain* on the marquee. From the poster, the show appeared to be a play about Crimson Specter, one of the most notorious supervillains of all time, and his fatal attack on Initiative Headquarters.

A group of people all dressed in the same blood-red skull mask, cloak, and armor—Crimson Specter's signature attire—had formed a loose ring around paramedics who were treating a similarly dressed guy lying on the ground.

Nearby, cops talked with a wild-eyed woman in a leotard with pointed ears, fur, and a lashing tail who gestured helplessly at the man on the sidewalk. A couple other costumed metas I didn't recognize watched uncomfortably.

It looked like another guerilla marketing campaign gone awry. At least no one had died this time.

Proselytizers from a dozen different religious groups were out too, stuffing literature into the hands of anyone they could hassle into taking it. A group of what looked like Mormons glared across the street at blue-clad monks with static-covered screens over their faces. I couldn't remember what the monks called themselves, but they were from one of the alien religions that had started cropping up a few years earlier and were currently all the rage. The group claimed that if you looked deeply into the static, you could see the shape of your soul in the noise.

Above the crowd, a digital billboard bathed the street in light, advertising the induction ceremony for a new Vanguard team. It highlighted a bronze-skinned alien woman and a guy in a hulking power suit, along with a couple other metas.

After I'd walked a ways, Bowie flowed out of the recesses of my mind to take in the scene. He seemed unsettled and off-balance, radiating anxiety and wariness. As if sensing my awareness, Bowie shifted his attention to me. He seemed to grunt, almost like he couldn't decide whether he was glad I'd survived.

Happy to see you too. I sighed, dodging around a group of laughing college girls. *I guess I should thank you,* I added, trying to convey gratitude on an emotional level.

Bowie seemed to consider that, as if he understood. Grudging acceptance came through our link, followed by another blast of incomprehensible thoughts and impressions.

Disoriented by the flood, I missed a step and staggered into a street performer dressed like a statue. Muttering an apology, I hurried away before he could get a good look at me.

I don't understand, I thought once I'd caught my balance, a tinge of frustration creeping into my thoughts.

Bowie responded with annoyance, before shifting his attention back to the street.

Good talk.

Eventually, we made it to Vanguard Square. Like the Boulevard of Heroes, it was filled to bursting. A K-pop boy band dressed like zombie presidents was performing for tips, while street vendors sold cheap masks and other junk to drunk revelers and kids. Imitators and D-list metas were out in force as well, trying to make money by harassing people into paying for pictures.

An anthropomorphic hippo in chainmail knelt next to a weeping child, while the kid's father took a picture with his phone.

I kept my head down and slipped through a small group of college kids protesting the Vanguard expansion who were being ignored or mocked by the rest of the crowd.

I needed to get off the street, but I found myself falling onto a bench instead. With a shock, I realized it was the same bench I'd sat on after leaving Claire's office the day of the experiment. It had been just a couple of days ago, but it felt like another lifetime.

In front of me, the Vanguard's bronze statues stared down as if in judgment. My eyes stopped on Aegis. It was hard to believe I'd just met the guy. Hard to believe the meeting had happened to me and not another person.

Reaching into my wallet, I pulled out the card Vaydan's bodyguard had given me, turning it over in my hands. I could still call him or walk up to the Watchtower and tell Vanguard what was going on. But I wasn't sure they'd believe me. I had powers, sure, but there was no way I could prove I wasn't responsible for the accident, and any proof I'd been attacked was pretty circumstantial. Given that I didn't want to get locked in Blackstone, or any other metahuman detention facility, putting my life in Vaydan's hands didn't seem worth the risk.

For some reason, my eyes were drawn to Fennec's statue. Before I could figure out why, a couple of teenagers dropped, giggling, onto the bench beside me, so oblivious, I might as well have been invisible. Given my appearance, that was probably for the best. One of the girls pulled her phone out and took a couple of selfies while they chattered about dinner plans.

Ugh. I leaned away from the picture, not wanting teenage narcissism to be the reason I got caught, and stuffed my hands into the hoodie pocket. There was still some blood on them—maybe mine, maybe someone else's—and I didn't want to have any more awkward conversations.

A few feet away, a woman dressed as Arachnia, an A-list mask with spider powers, leaned down, posing with a grinning toddler as the mom took a picture. A wave of unsteadiness washed over me. I couldn't reconcile their perfectly mundane evening with the nightmare my life had become.

But that was just how it was. We were all contained within the threads of our own lives, oblivious to the tragedy and pain of the people around us.

How else could we function?

I dragged myself up, relinquishing the bench to the giggling teens, and forced myself toward the hotel, tossing Vaydan's card into a trash can along the way.

The Union Arms was located on the opposite side of Vanguard Square. The hotel was one of the few buildings that had survived the Rakkari attack, a large nineteenth-century stone structure with an air of faded grandeur. The lobby was an oval with a bar on one side and a piano on the other. A giant chandelier hung above a marble floor filled with plush seats and tables, all occupied by well-dressed guests enjoying cocktails.

I made my way up to the front desk, trying not to let

the pain of each step show in my gait. A well-manicured young woman with dark hair and a black dress looked me up and down, her eyes tightening.

"I'm sorry, but our bathroom is only for guests." She glanced past me to a tall guy in a suit, who I guessed was security.

I was too tired to be annoyed.

"I *am* a guest. I think someone checked me in already. The name's Ben Rigulo." As I gave her the name Vee had referenced, avoided eye contact. I was already memorable enough without her catching a glimpse of my new eyes.

The desk attendant almost managed to hide her surprise when the reservation came up in her system. "Ah, yes. We have you right here. You're in room 917. It looks like your packages have arrived. Would you like me to have them sent up to the room?"

"That'd be great, thank you," I replied, also too tired to be curious.

She handed me a key card, and I made my way into the elevator. I rode up with a well-dressed older couple who stayed as far away from me as they could, not bothering to hide their disdain.

My room was on the top floor, at the end of the hall. When I opened the door, I was surprised to find a suite with a living room, a dining area, two bedrooms, and a large balcony. The whole place had a strong neoclassical vibe, with lots of marble.

Jesus, Vee.

I went to the sliding glass door that opened onto the balcony. Driven by an entirely rational desire to block any lines of sight into the room, I closed the drapes and then collapsed onto the couch.

Just as I did, there was a knock on the door. I jolted upright, a thrill of fear banishing some of my fatigue. Making my way to the door, I looked through the peephole. Relief washed over me when I saw a younger guy in a bellhop uniform with a cart full of packages. I opened the door, trying not to meet his eyes.

His practiced smile faltered when he saw me. "Mr. Rigulo! We have some deliveries for you. They got here a few minutes before you did. Can I bring them inside?"

"Sure," I muttered, stepping out of the way

The bellhop rolled the cart in and turned to me. "Just push the cart back out into the hall when you're done." He paused for a second.

"I'm sorry, I don't have any cash."

His smile turned wooden. "Not a problem, sir. Have a great night."

The cart was filled with rapid-delivery packages from an online retailer. Digging through them, I found new clothes, a phone, a computer, and a first aid kit. There was also a bag with some takeout from a nearby Thai restaurant. Gratitude flooded me. My stomach clenched with hunger as soon as I smelled the food.

I forced myself to take a shower before I ate, wanting to clean off the gore. My hands shook, but when my thoughts turned back to the attack, I was too tired to feel anything. I suspected the trauma would come—shock and horror couldn't just be tossed aside—but it wouldn't be tonight. The trauma would leak out over days and weeks as it always did.

Besides, Vee was right. The mercenaries hadn't exactly given me a choice, and neither had Lynx. Whoever those people were, they hadn't come in reading me my Miranda rights.

My self-assurances didn't help clean the blood off, but a shower did. Afterward, I devoured my food at the table while Bowie looked on in disgust.

What's your problem? I growled mentally.

Bowie bristled, berating me with thoughts and images. The barrage was hard to understand, but I had the impression Bowie found corporeal biology revolting, which left a lot of questions. I knew there were metas that existed as pure energy. If Bowie *had* been trapped in the voidrium, maybe he'd been similar.

Yeah, well, organic life is messy. Get used to it.

Bowie lapsed back into silence, so I made the mistake of checking the news again.

"In a shocking turn of events," the news anchor pronounced, "Dr. Nathan Chambers, son of wealthy tech mogul Jerimiah Chambers, was found dead in his apartment earlier today. While the details have not yet been released, we do know that medical examiners have already labeled the death a homicide. Further complicating the matter, Dr. Nathan Chambers was one of the researchers working on the disastrous project that resulted in the deaths of more than a hundred people on the UCU campus earlier this week. Notably, Dr. Chambers was last seen in an altercation with Brandon Carter, a fellow researcher whose whereabouts are still unknown. Anyone with information is being urged to speak to the police."

The news hit me like a fist in the gut, quenching my anger. Nate might have been an entitled prick, but I'd known him for years and he probably didn't deserve whatever had been done to him. Particularly because Vee had been right; he was likely a victim too.

I shut off the TV and mechanically ate as much food

as I could. When I was finished, I stumbled into one of the bedrooms and fell onto the bed. I was asleep seconds after my head hit the pillow.

And then I dreamed, my mind filled with alien vistas as I swam through the stars.

NINETEEN

RICTOR

The van rumbled to a halt and turned off as a sliding door shut behind it. The garage we'd pulled into didn't look like much. Rack lighting flickered erratically overhead, a few workbenches sat in corners, and some rusted shelves lined the drab concrete walls. A couple of reinforced security doors were the only exits, other than the steel sliding doors in front of the vehicle bays.

A tall, improbably beautiful woman dressed in a tight, black sleeveless blouse and olive miniskirt that showed off a sculpted physique waited a few feet away. An ebony pixie cut surrounded a pale face with electric-blue eyes and features so accentuated, they didn't seem real. Everything was perfectly, eerily symmetrical.

"Hello, Brandon! I'm Alice, Rictor's operations manager. It's nice to meet you." Alice's tone was warm, bordering on bubbly. She gestured to the van. "Apologies for the subterfuge. If the wrong individuals were to learn of our operation, the results would be unfortunate." The van's windows had been blocked with screens that displayed various images, everything from outer space scenes to aquatic vistas, making it impossible for me to see where I'd been going.

"No apologies necessary." I hadn't been thrilled about riding around for two hours with no idea of where I was, but at least no one had tried to kill me, which felt like a step in the right direction.

It was also nice to be out of the hotel, given that I'd spent the last twenty-four hours in the suite. I'd fallen asleep immediately and woken twelve hours later with silvery scabs over my new collection of cuts and scrapes, but I had been far, *far* from healed. My head, ribs, and arm throbbed with a bone-deep ache that made *existing* painful, and I still felt fuzzy.

When I woke up, I'd also been floating above the bed, along with most of the furniture, which was an exciting new development.

Once I'd fallen back to the bed, I'd spent the rest of the day distracting myself, hoping to avoid memories of the night before, though there wasn't a lot to do. I worried experimenting with my new abilities might bring more unwanted guests, and my gravitational sight brought on a pounding headache.

Bowie had also seemed particularly grumpy, alternating between barraging me with incomprehensible thoughts and ignoring me. I'd spent a couple of hours tentatively trying to communicate with him, wondering again if I was losing my mind, but it was no good.

Even worse, I'd started noticing gravitational distortions around me when I wasn't trying to use my abilities. They got stronger as the day went on, and each time one occurred, I listened for an engine like the one I'd heard above Vee's safe house.

I wasn't sure if my new powers were fundamentally unstable, if I'd "sprained" something by overusing them, or if the instability was the result of repeated head trauma. Regardless, I needed to figure out what to do about it, and I needed to figure it out soon.

It had been a relief when Vee confirmed that the text from a restricted number with instructions on where to meet my ride wasn't a trap.

"Thank you for meeting me."

Alice beamed. "Of course! Any friend of Vee's is a friend of ours."

I nodded, still on edge. I'd been worn ragged by the last few days, and I wasn't the only one. Bowie mentally glowered at Alice, radiating suspicion. At least it was aimed at someone else for a change. *Progress.*

Alice tilted her head slightly, her expression shifting to concern. "Your respiratory and pupillary responses suggest discomfort. I assure you, Brandon, you're safe here."

Respiratory and pupillary responses? I boggled. *How the hell . . . ?* I studied her too-perfect features, and realization hit me.

She's an android.

Artificial intelligence wasn't science fiction anymore. Alien tech, nazi research, and rogue geniuses had produced a long list of synthetic intelligences with goals and motives as varied as their creators. There were even a few androids on various mask teams. Some were like Alice— so close to human, they were nearly indistinguishable from their organic counterparts—but not all. News stories had circulated a few weeks before about a vending machine that had become self-aware and attacked some college students in Seattle by shooting cans at them. A month before that, a cell phone that had somehow gained sapience had launched her own line of cases.

Strange times.

Controlling my breathing, I nodded. "Yeah, okay," I managed with as much sincerity as I could muster.

Alice's eyes scanned my body. "You seem to have sustained injuries. Do you require immediate medical attention?"

I shook my head, fighting the urge to wince as pain radiated from my ribs.

"Good!" Alice beamed again. "Rictor will be here in a few moments. While you wait, is there anything I can get for you? We have coffee, tea, and a variety of narcotics."

I blinked. "No, thank you."

"You're welcome!"

The security door at the end of the garage opened, and a bedraggled figure emerged.

Vee had said her friend was eccentric, but whatever I had been expecting, Rictor wasn't it.

He was short, with a mop of brown hair over a thin, haggard face partially covered by a pair of Aviator sunglasses. A battered Ramone's shirt and a pair of boxers were visible underneath a leopard-print faux-fur bathrobe that seemed to swallow his thin frame. The whole look was completed by a pair of fluffy slippers and the cigarette dangling from his lips. I put him in his midforties, but it was hard to tell.

He was hungover. Still drunk, maybe.

The whole look gave the effect of a cross between Hunter S. Thompson and Nikola Tesla, with a dash of Sam Rockwell thrown in.

I liked him already.

Rictor's sunglasses slid down his nose, revealing electric-blue eyes. He squinted, blurry confusion on his haggard face, and then yawned. "Are you here about the fridge? I didn't think I'd called anyone yet."

"No. I'm Brandon, Vee's friend?"

Rictor squinted again and then lit up with excitement. "Oh, right!" His arms opened wide. "The physicist!" Bringing his hands in, he made finger guns. "Yeah, sorry, man." He chuckled. "It's still early, you know? It's hard to keep my head straight before I've had my smoothie."

I glanced at my phone. It was two in the afternoon.

Rictor's expression shifted to concern. "Hey, you're the voidrium guy, right?" He crossed his arms and took a drag on his smoke. "The whole explosion thing—I'm sorry to hear about it. This isn't a customer complaint, is it? I don't think I've sold any voidrium, but if I did, it was good stuff."

I stared at him, at a loss. "Uh, no."

"Great!" His arms shot out again, leopard-print robe flapping as his excitement returned. "Come in, come in, come in." Rictor beckoned me toward the steel security door behind him. "*Mi casa, su casa.*"

"I'll be here to show you out," Alice said, before stepping through the other door.

Rictor watched Alice leave, a wistful look on his face. "Isn't she something? She was a prototype an old client stole and offered up as payment when he was short on cash. I gave her some upgrades and set her free. She chose to stick around.

"Hey, want some breakfast?" He turned back to me, a twinkle at the corners of his eyes. "You can tell me what's going on. Vee didn't give me a lot of details."

I felt the clock ticking. I'd been attacked twice in nearly as many days, and my powers were quickly becoming a danger to myself and others, not to mention that I could be having an extended psychotic episode.

Still, I hadn't eaten this morning. "Food would be great, thanks."

He smiled widely and then yawned. "Follow me!"

Rictor led me through a security door and down a long hallway, before turning up a flight of stairs that ended in a well-appointed home with an open floor plan. The walls were covered with rock paraphernalia and sci-fi movie posters.

The biggest dog I'd ever seen sat on a couch in the living room, intently watching a baking show on a flat-screen mounted above a fireplace. He had to be at least three hundred pounds, some sort of pit bull or mastiff, with a massive head and thickly muscled body covered in a brindled coat.

As big as the dog was, though, his size wasn't his most distinctive feature.

The right side of the dog's head bore a chrome plate that extended from his snout to the base of his neck. His right eye had been replaced by a solid blue lens that glowed slightly in its steel housing, and his front left leg and shoulder had been replaced with a cybernetic prosthesis.

When we entered, the dog craned his massive head toward us. His tail thumped the couch a couple of times at the sight of Rictor, but the dog fixed me with a flat stare, a low rumble I felt more than heard emanating from his chest.

Radiating what seemed like indignation, Bowie mentally growled back.

I waited by the door, raising an eyebrow. "He friendly?"

"Of course he is!" Rictor walked over to the dog and scratched his neck. "Of course you're friendly! Hey, T-Rex!" Rictor looked back at me. "Brandon, meet T-Rex. T-Rex, this is Brandon. He's Vee's friend."

T-Rex's ears went up, and he straightened, excited. The dog looked past me, hopeful, and then back to Rictor, whining slightly and bumping Rictor with his head.

"She's not here now, buddy. I'm sorry. Soon."

T-rex sighed explosively and flopped back onto the couch, which squeaked in protest. His disappointment palpable, the cyborg dog turned back to his baking show.

"Don't worry about him." Rictor smiled apologetically. "It takes T-Rex a while to warm up to people, but he'll get there. He *loves* Vee. She brings him pizza.

"Come on." Rictor gave T-Rex a couple of neck scratches before leading me into a big kitchen. He started pulling containers of fruit out of the fridge and tossing them on a counter.

"Where'd you get T-Rex?" I asked.

"Do you remember the dogfighting ring with genetically modified hybrids that got busted a few years ago?" Rictor gestured back to the living room with a half-peeled banana. "One of them fished T-Rex out of a dumpster and figured I might give him a few bucks for parts." Rictor's expression hardened. "If T-Rex hadn't been enhanced, the little guy would have been dead before he ever made it to me. As it was, he was scratching at death's doggy door."

I looked at T-Rex and then back at Rictor. "Didn't the people running that ring get caught when all their cell phones sent confessions to the cops?"

Rictor's smile returned, and he went back to making his smoothie. "It was the Federal Genetic Manipulation Task Force, actually. They never did find out who sent them. I bet you could guess, though."

"Vee?"

"Bingo!" Rictor shoved fruit into a blender, following it with orange juice. "Damn smart, that girl. Good heart."

Rictor opened a cabinet and pulled out several small square tins in a carrier. "Ground lion's mane mushroom, ginkgo biloba, powdered ashwagandha, and fresh *Bacopa monnieri*." He pointed to each as he scooped a spoonful of the powder. "Nootropics. Good for the brain! I mean, the nanites do most of the heavy lifting in terms of my cognitive enhancements, but the herbal supplements don't hurt!"

"Nanites?" I asked, just before he hit the power button on the blender. The scream of the motor took my headache up another notch.

"Yep!" Rictor said over the blender. Reaching into another cabinet, he pulled out a small jar with an eye-dropper lid and lifted it so I could see it. "Psilocybin!" he yelled. "It's the active ingredient in magic mushrooms. Really takes the edge off! Want some?"

"I'm good, thanks." I didn't think psychedelics and erratic gravitational distortions would be a great mix.

"Suit yourself!" Rictor poured me a smoothie and then put a few drops from the jar into the blender. After running the blender for a few more seconds, he poured himself a glass.

In the span of about ten minutes, Rictor bounced from topic to topic while he made waffles. Setting a heaping stack on a plate, he covered it in fruit and set it in front of me. "Protein infused, my boy!" Smiling, he sat on the other side of the kitchen island.

"So, what's your deal?" He speared a waffle with his fork, while Bowie looked on with his typical distaste. "Vee didn't want to say much over the phone. She was worried about the line being tapped." He tapped the side of his head. "She did say you were her best friend, which is why I agreed to meet so early."

I hesitated.

"Look, I get it," Rictor said softly, his expression comforting. "A lot of the people who come my way—they have stories, and they aren't good ones. Usually, people are out to hurt them. And sure, I'm a little, uh, *eccentric*, I guess, but all the great ones are, believe me. I get that you're scared and you don't know who to trust. But you have to tell me what's going on for me to help."

Rictor paused to take a bite.

"And have some of my clients done some bad things with the work I do for them? Sure. Have some of them blown up some buildings? Maybe, but they were *empty*. Did one of them try to conquer the moon? Yeah, okay, but his *motives* were good, and the only people who got hurt were the capes who showed up and tried to throw his ass into the sun. Do you get me?"

I nodded, at a loss for words.

Even Bowie seemed mystified.

Rictor sighed, glancing out the window. Outside, the early fall sky was a crisp blue. Beyond what looked like an old barn, a forest of trees rustling gently in the wind stretched down to the lakeshore.

Vee trusted Rictor. She'd said he was "good people," which was high praise from her, and I didn't have a lot of other options.

I took a deep breath. *Here goes nothing.* "How much do you know about voidrium?"

"It's exotic matter that the Rakkari used as a power source for their ships. Supposedly psychoactive and interacts with gravity. *Very* dangerous."

Bowie snarled at the mention of the Rakkari, hatred and fear flowing through the link between us. I tried to send calm back through the link, and his anger dwindled, replaced by a mournful longing. A pang of sympathy shot through me as he settled into the background of my mind.

I kept going, talking around bites of waffle, suddenly ravenous. "The interest for most researchers revolved around voidrium's potential to generate power and artificial gravity. My advisor was provided with data from some classified studies, which she shared. Something about it clicked, and I realized that voidrium was the perfect material to test Colville's hypothesis."

Rictor leaned forward, a glimmer of excitement in his eyes.

"I came up with a model using a Nyserian exception to sidestep Sabri's paradox, breaching the Colville membrane at a frequency of three hundred seventy-one melvilles." I paused long enough to gulp my smoothie. "My first proposal was designed for the transport of non-quantum-scale matter, but it was too risky, so I went for something smaller: a machine that made stable quantum-scale singularities that could break through the Colville membrane and pick up electromagnetic activity from other multiversal strands. We called it MICSy."

"Wow," Rictor breathed.

Words spilled out faster and faster. "We submitted a proposal to the Vaydan Foundation's Extradimensional

Threat Detection program. They were intrigued and offered us all the funding we needed and more, as well as helping us get access to a voidrium sample."

I kept going, telling him everything. The attack, the aftermath. Bowie.

Afterward, Rictor sat quietly for a moment, reflecting. "That's a hell of a few days," he said eventually. "For what it's worth, you're holding yourself together pretty well."

"I need to figure out what's happening and try to find a way to control it. Can you help?"

Rictor finished his smoothie and grinned, wiping a juice mustache from his upper lip. "I think maybe I can help a little. Want to see my workspace?"

TWENTY

REVELATIONS

Holy shit."

Rictor's workshop was underground. It was huge, but the sheer quantity of tech turned it into a labyrinth of fabricators, high-tech polymer printers, robotic assembly systems, and a massive iterative manufacturing chamber nearly two stories tall. Most of it looked scavenged, cus-tom built, or cobbled together, but some of it was *defi-nitely* beyond the scope of human technology. And it all *worked*, threaded through with cables and wires that led back to an ominous black obelisk the size of a small tour bus in the middle of the cavernous room.

The tech left a near-constant hum in the background that cut through the cool air.

I must have been rubbernecking, because Rictor paused and looked back. When he saw my expression, he beamed proudly. "Quite the setup, isn't it? My own little slice of heaven!"

"It's amazing," I said, in awe despite the circumstances.

Clearly, crime does pay. Very, very well.

My eyes widened as they caught on something I hadn't noticed yet. "Is that a bespoke xenotech reactor?"

Rictor grinned. "Sure is!" He patted it as we passed.

"Here we are!" he said as we turned a final corner in the maze of tech. We stood in front of another massive machine, this one surrounded by a workstation and monitoring devices.

The machine had two major moving parts: a horizontal padded table large enough for a person to lie on, and a massive vertical ring, the interior diameter of which was easily five feet. Both were connected to the main body of the machine via robotic support arms—one set into the head of the table, holding it aloft, and the other set into the outer casing of the ring, leaving the interior free to spin. Once the machine was turned on, the spinning ring would encircle the table, moving parallel to the ground along its length.

Rictor gestured at the machine and smiled. "She's a beauty, ain't she? A brand-new full-spectrum scanning suite, courtesy of Holt Medical Technologies by way of a stolen shipping container. She cost me a pretty penny, but she's worth it. This baby does it all: magnetic resonance, tissue-penetrating light tomography, photoacoustics, neurosynaptic electrographic mapping, and more."

Rictor floated around the machine and spun with a flourish, his robe billowing out. He pointed his thumb at a nearby tabletop holographic display. "She'll generate a virtual model of you that's realer than you are!"

I took a ragged breath as a spike of anxiety roiled up within me. I needed answers, even if I suddenly wasn't sure I wanted them. *Ready?* I thought to Bowie, who seemed to study the scanning suite suspiciously.

"Well? What are you waiting for?" Rictor drummed on the bench. "Get up there! Let's see what's going on inside. Oh, hey, want some tunes?"

I nodded. "Uh, sure."

Rictor slid himself in front of a workstation, cracked his fingers, and began typing.

Iggy Pop's "The Passenger" filled the workshop as I kicked off my shoes and climbed up on the table.

Rictor hit a key, and the machine started up with an energetic hum. "Here we go." The massive ring began to spin. "Please keep your arms and legs inside the ride at all times!"

The ring spun, faster and faster. The interior was composed of curved sections of smoky glass, each three inches wide. There were lights inside, and as the ring accelerated, the lights blurred, making the whole ring seem to glow. Abruptly, the table rose farther off the ground, and the spinning ring slid over the foot of the table. My skin tingled as it traveled the length of my body.

The first pass was slow and smooth, but after that, the ring's pattern became erratic, moving at different speeds and concentrating on different parts of my body for different lengths of time. Rictor stayed at the workstation, typing in commands and guiding the system as he muttered to himself.

Out of the corner of my eye, I saw an image forming above the holo table. It began with a simple outline, but with each pass, the image got more detailed, adding biological systems and processes. Holographic muscle tissue grafted onto holographic bone and then threaded through with blood vessels, arteries, and veins. My nerves were threaded in next, followed by the sparkling constellation of neurons in my brain.

The process was fascinating, and if the situation had been different, I'd have had a lot of questions. As it was, I spent the whole time worrying that something in the sensor ring was going to cause a reaction with whatever was wrong with me. I focused on my breathing, counting to seven, holding it for a beat, and then exhaling.

It helped, a little.

After what felt like an hour—but was probably less than five minutes—the ring stopped spinning and retracted as the table lowered so I could stand.

"That's it." Rictor slid out of his chair and moved over to the holo table. Using gestures and a holographic keypad, he began manipulating the scan, expanding it and filtering out various layers of information.

My stomach churned, and my heart beat against my ribs. "Well?" I asked, both impatient and terrified.

"One sec." Rictor split the scan into two images, separating the holographic representation of my brain and nervous system from the rest of me. He took a step back to regard it.

"Would you look at that," he said after a minute or so, a touch of wonder in his voice.

"What?"

"This." Rictor gestured to the holographic image on the right, which displayed my body. "This is your body, right? We've got muscles, bone, skin, organs, and a circulatory system, right? All the good stuff."

"And?" I tried not to let my impatience show.

With a wave of his hand, my body vanished from the holographic image, leaving a faint outline of every structure and organ, all glimmering with a metallic sheen.

"You said your machine, MICSy, used a xibrantium housing for the voidrium, right?"

I nodded.

"Well, my friend, what you're looking at is xibrantium." Rictor shook his head. "Every cell in your body has been saturated with it, with higher concentrations in your skin and skeletal tissue. The radiation released by the voidrium must have fused the xibrantium with your body on a cellular level and in a highly energetic form."

He gestured to spots on the hologram where the silvery hue was concentrated. "For some reason, whenever your body is damaged, the tissue created by the healing process has even *higher* concentrations of xibrantium."

"So what does that mean?" I asked, stunned.

Rictor blinked. "What does it mean? This should have killed you! It means you survived the impossible. Metas created through this sort of biometallic fusion— assuming they don't die—develop increased strength and toughness, usually proportional to the metal in question. In your case? To the best of my knowledge, there's never been a meta whose body was saturated with xibrantium."

Rictor grabbed another cigarette and lit it, taking a long puff.

"Now, the quantity matters. You're *mostly* organic, unlike Cast Iron or Goldenboy, whose bodies are basically living metal. Don't ask me how *that* works. Bottom line? Enhanced strength and durability, maybe a *lot* of it. Hell, you might eventually be damn near invulnerable."

"Not quite," I muttered, thinking back to Lynx's gigantic sniper rifle.

"Xibrantium also has a bunch of weird qualities that might interact with your nervous and biochemical systems," Rictor continued. "It looks like you've been healing more quickly than normal for a baseline, which is partially a result of the fusion."

I remained silent, considering.

"I know, I know." He patted me on the shoulder. "Hey, it's okay. It's a lot to take in." Rictor took another long hit on his cigarette. "I'm going to give you a minute to sit with that, and then we're going to talk about the *really* interesting stuff."

"Wait, what?" I said, my head spinning. "That's *not* the interesting stuff?"

Rictor smiled and shook his head. "Oh no, my friend. There are a lot of metas who've had their bodies transformed by lab experiments. That shit's been happening since the 1930s. This would be cool, sure, but on its own? Biometallic fusion is nothing mind-blowing. Now *this*." He gestured at the holo image of my nervous system. "I've never seen *anything* like *this* before."

I looked at the hologram. Rictor expanded it, and suddenly, I could see staggering amounts of detail. My brain was suffused with strands of a glowing violet substance interwoven among neurons and synapses across all the structures of my brain. The realization hit me like a thunderbolt. "Is that . . . ?"

"Yes, sir." Rictor's maniacal grin was nearly too large for his face. "Voidrium! Your central nervous system is bursting with the stuff, but it's in your peripheral nervous system too. Look here!" He used his hands to expand the image again. "Every nerve in your body seems to have been infused with it. The electrochemical energy of your brain is stimulating the voidrium, and vice versa. Your brain is changing, maybe even restructuring itself to accommodate the new material. Like with the xibrantium, this should have killed you. And yet." Rictor stuck his hands out and slowly raised them, wiggling his fingers. "Voila! Here you are!"

I gestured to the display, thinking about my new abilities. "Did the scanner detect gravitons?"

"Not just gravitons, my boy. Do you see this?" Rictor vibrated with excitement as he pointed to an indicator on the display. "That's a *cosmic* energy signature, the same stuff Polaris and Empyrean have coursing through their bodies."

"So my abilities . . ."

"Your abilities are the result of the voidrium and your brain interfacing! It's like a new sense or a new limb. A new faculty, if you will. Right now, your brain is trying to integrate the new material and is just coming to terms with it. The process is probably a little rocky, but it seems like you're already most of the way there, which is amazing. It can take people years to figure this stuff out."

"I felt like I was starting to figure it out, but then I was . . . shot. My control's been worse. Erratic."

Rictor nodded, gesturing to the holographic image of my brain. "There does seem to be a bit of swelling near your temporal and parietal lobes." He switched to the skeletal scan. "I'm also seeing evidence of a fracture on your temporal bone. What did she shoot you with again?"

"It looked like a rail gun about six feet long." I winced. "It didn't feel great."

"Didn't feel great?" Rictor's eyes widened, and he blew out a cloud of smoke. "That's the sort of thing that puts holes in tanks. It would have left most metas spattered all over the wall, and all it did was crack your skull." Rictor gestured to the holographic lacerations. "What about those cuts?"

"Uh, it was a sword with some sort of energy field around it."

Rictor whistled. "Sounds like a disruption field. They weaken molecular bonds. Make things easier to cut. Very expensive, *very* dangerous. Death Merchant used a blade with a disruption field to kill Ironhide, the guy that had, well, an iron hide. It went through him like he wasn't even there."

He shook his head, a mixture of wonder and disbelief on his face. "And you're still *changing*. Sapient creatures, organic or synthetic, exposed to cosmic energy are transformed on a cellular level. This process makes them better able to contain and channel the cosmic energy, making them stronger and more resilient as a by-product. Interestingly, the process is continuous over the course of the being's life, after a rapid period of reconfiguration immediately following exposure." Rictor paused, taking a drag on his cigarette. "Assuming they survive."

I blinked. "Assuming they *survive*? What does that mean?" The monitor beeped as my heart rate increased.

Rictor winced. "The thing is, most beings exposed to cosmic energy don't handle it well. In the least severe cases? Total instantaneous cellular collapse. I've seen pictures; it's *messy*. Like a Jackson Pollock painting. More commonly, saturation results in cellular combustion, usually in a highly energetic fashion."

I gaped at him. "Wait, 'highly energetic'? Are you saying most people catch fire or fucking *explode*?" The monitor beeped again.

"Yeah, but don't worry, buddy!" Rictor said hastily. "You made it through the hard part. No spontaneous combustion for you! The xibrantium lattice in your cells, the voidrium in your brain—somehow it allowed you to survive the process. It's also part of the reason you're so tough. We aren't entirely sure how, but cosmic energy seems to reinforce the corporeal forms of the metas that channel it.

"In fact,"—Rictor gestured to the display—"the xibrantium seems to be sustaining and magnifying the effect. Assuming you continue to change at the same rate, assuming you're able to regain control of your abilities, with cosmic energy supercharging you . . . there's a good chance you could end up *very* powerful. Like Vanguard-level strong."

I shook my head, unable to process what Rictor was telling me. It was too big. Like being told I'd won the lottery and been diagnosed with a terminal illness in the same breath. I felt like I was floating or falling, disconnected from my body.

"Will I get control of it?" I managed eventually.

Rictor mulled it over for a second. "You're still integrating the voidrium into your system, so I'm not surprised things are a little wonky, especially given the brain trauma. Over time, you'll regain the ability to decipher what you're seeing and take control of what you're doing. Probably."

"Probably?" I nearly shouted, my pulse quickening. The scanner started to shake, along with other nearby equipment. An alarm sounded as the scanner detected graviton emissions spiking.

"Hey." Rictor put his cigarette down, slowly resting a hand on my shoulder. His expression shifted to concern. "We're in uncharted territory here. A barely understood form of psychoactive alien matter has merged with your nervous system. I wish I could tell you how this is all going to play out, but I can't. All I can do is tell you that I'll do whatever I can to help, okay?"

Sympathy and sincerity glimmered in Rictor's eyes. I thought about Alice and T-Rex. I could see why Vee trusted him, and despite my reservations, I realized I trusted him too.

I nodded, and things stopped shaking.

Rictor scratched his chin. "In the interim, we should be able to cobble together a dampening field to negate the uncontrolled manifestations. We might even be able to rig up some sort of regulator to give you back some control. Given how quickly you heal, you probably won't need it long."

A rush of genuine gratitude cut through my foreboding. "Thank you."

After a minute, I added, "What about the consciousness sharing my skull? Is it an alien life form?"

As if sensing he was the topic of conversation, Bowie shifted forward, listening.

"Honestly?" Rictor blew some air through his lips and pondered. "No idea." He took another drag on his cigarette. "Voidrium is psychoactive, right? It also interacts strangely with space-time." He shrugged. "It could be an alien. Or maybe the presence you're feeling is a manifestation of your subconscious. Or an echo of your future or past self. Or a version of you from an alternate dimension.

"Hell," Rictor mused after another puff. "Maybe it's Elvis! The best thing we could do for that would be to find a telepath, but that might take some time."

Alien thoughts flowed from Bowie, along with indignation and what felt like a mental eye roll.

Christopher Lee Rippee

Rictor's phone beeped. Annoyed, he pulled it out of his pocket, fumbling for a second. When he opened the screen, his face lit up. "T-Rex is going to be thrilled!"

"Why's that?"

"Vee's here, and she brought pizza!"

TWENTY-ONE

GANG'S ALL HERE

We sat around the kitchen island with a couple of empty pizza boxes and some beer. Rictor and Alice were on one side, Vee and I on the other, sitting so close we were touching. T-Rex hunkered behind us, staring at me happily. He'd warmed up to me after I'd given him a couple of slices, a small price to pay for his love.

Vee hadn't been able to meet me at the hotel because she'd been getting Mom to another safe house operated by her contacts. I'd been worried sick about both of them, so it was great news, even if I was starting to have questions about who Vee's contacts were.

The less great news came when Vee showed me recent news coverage.

I was all over it.

Someone had recorded the attack on Vee's safe house with a camera drone, and the footage had circulated through the internet and onto the news. The people trying to kill me were invisible, so it didn't paint a sympathetic picture.

My face was plastered on articles across the internet, with titles like "Troubled Grad Student Turned Super-villain?," "Deranged Researcher Destroys City Block," and my least favorite, "Broken Homes to Broken Laws: Brandon Carter."

Most of the articles included my Vaydan Institute badge photo, which wasn't exactly flattering. One website had managed to dig up my ninth-grade yearbook photo, which seemed unnecessarily cruel. If I *were* a deranged supervillain emerging from the chrysalis of my former life, that was the sort of insult that might make me pay someone a visit.

Reporters also went after the people I cared about.

Vee's friends had planted enough evidence to make it look like Mom had gone on a trip, but the longer she was gone, the more news outlets were speculating that I'd done something to her.

Claire was out of the country, but her lawyer had issued a statement saying she'd resigned from her po-sition at both the Vaydan Institute and the university, and asked that all inquiries be directed to her counsel. The news hit like a hammer, and I couldn't help but feel responsible for costing my mentor and friend her career and reputation.

I was also the prime suspect in Nate's murder, which wasn't surprising. Our last encounter had been *very* public.

Fearing what I might do, the police had taken Abby, Itzel, and Harvey into protective custody. A group of re-porters had struck gold when they'd ambushed the three of them outside the police station. "I don't understand," Itzel sobbed. "Brandon's a good person."

It made me sick to think about what this was doing

to the people I cared about, but I told myself it wasn't my fault. I hoped I'd eventually have the opportunity to explain—to Itzel and Harvey, to Claire.

The news also covered the cops raiding my apartment. The sight of my meager possessions being carted away left me feeling strangely hollow.

Unfortunately, the coverage of my life being torn apart wasn't the only surprise the news had to offer.

Vincent Vaydan had held a press conference to address the disaster at the university. At the end of it, he'd looked directly into the cameras and spoken to me. Personally. "Brandon, if you can hear this, you need to turn yourself in. Whatever has happened, we can help you. All you have to do is let us."

He oozed sincerity, but I didn't *quite* trust him.

After Vee and I had caught up, the four of us—or five, if you counted T-Rex—ate pizza and talked. Alice and Rictor entertained us with a story about a rogue AI that had escaped from captivity by hiding itself in a Bluetooth-enabled sex toy. It felt good to laugh. It was the first time since I was attacked in the lab that I had come close to feeling safe.

Even Bowie seemed to relax a little, the indecipherable noise of his thoughts tinged with something that felt a little like amused curiosity.

By the time we were done with dinner, it was nearly seven. We all quieted, sensing a shift in the conversation.

I needed a plan.

Taking a deep breath, I let it out explosively. "The way I see it, we know of one person who knows what's going on."

Vee pushed the hair out of her face and looked at me skeptically. "Who's that?"

"Lynx."

Vee took a sip of her beer. "We don't know anything about her."

Alice glanced at Rictor, leaning forward. "That's not *entirely* true. While you and Rictor were in the lab, I searched the databases of several law enforcement and intelligence agencies for anything matching your description of her. I got a hit from a redacted file at the FBI's Office of Metahuman Threat Assessment."

Alice moved a pizza box, and a holographic display embedded in the center of the island flared to life, projecting a grainy image that appeared to have been taken from a webcam. The subject of the image, a lithe woman in form-fitting armor with a featureless and vaguely feline mask, was unmistakable. It depicted her in an alley, her blade in hand, standing among three corpses in costumes.

A tremor passed through me, and my pulse quickened. "That's her." I fought to keep my voice steady, clenching my hands as the memory of her standing over me flashed through my mind.

Vee glanced at me, concern in her eyes, and put her hand on mine.

"This image came from a motion-activated pet cam that happened to catch part of her attack on a trio of villains in Manhattan," Alice continued. "It was the only one I found, suggesting someone has been scrubbing any evidence of her presence. The pet cam that took this footage was offline at the time, and the owner didn't discover the footage until months after the attack."

I took a deep breath. "Who is she?"

A second holographic window containing lines of text opened. Alice gestured at it. "She's been connected to the murders of dozens of metahumans, on both sides of the law, and black-market tech dealers in the last few years. Despite the obvious attempt to scrub any evidence of her existence, there was enough trace evidence remaining for me to reconstruct some files."

"Boy, oh boy." Rictor leaned forward, frowning, and gestured at the victim list. "Can you expand that?" The list of names became the focus of the holo projection. Using the tip of his cigarette, he scrolled through them. "I know a lot of those names."

"How?" I asked.

Rictor looked up. "These guys specialized in the sale of some pretty dangerous stuff. Nuclear material, alien smart alloys, mutagenic compounds . . ."

Vee and I glanced at each other. She leaned forward. "What?"

"Jose Perra, or Lucky Jose, and Uri Sartova." Rictor gestured to a couple of names on the list. "They reached out to me last year. Said they'd just acquired some new merchandise." His voice was quiet. "Voidrium."

I sucked in a breath, the image of the smoking pit where my lab had been flashing through my mind. "Fucking hell."

Sensing my thoughts, Bowie thrashed in my head, his anger, fear, and longing so strong, it opened a little hollow of grief in my own chest, causing an idea to crash into me like a bus. Above and beyond the danger, if my suspicion was correct and Bowie was an alien being that had been trapped in the voidrium, there was a chance others of his kind were trapped in other voidrium samples.

Vee glanced at Alice. "Can you check the crime scene records for an evidence inventory?"

Alice's eyes unfocused. "Several highly dangerous materials were found, but no voidrium."

I leaned back, a flutter of disquiet in my chest. "How much voidrium did they say they had?"

Rictor shrugged, an uncomfortable expression crossing his face as he took a drag on his cigarette. "A few kilograms." He paused. "Each."

"A few *kilograms?*" I nearly shouted. "A gram blew through a bomb shelter and destroyed part of the campus. The Department of Energy doesn't even have that much."

Rictor snickered, a rueful grin crossing his face. "Buddy, the Department of Energy doesn't have a clue. The demand for stuff like this? It's through the roof." I narrowed my eyes, and Rictor held up his hands. "Hey, before you get your panties in a bunch, it's not just techs like me or my clients, supervillain or otherwise. Hero types need this stuff too, along with crime syndicates and corporations. Even academics. You name it!"

I shook my head, horrified by the revelation that so much dangerous material was floating around unregulated. "How did it get to the black market?"

"The old entrepreneurial spirit!" Rictor grinned. "The Rakkari invasion didn't do the global economy a lot of favors, but for the black market?" He whistled. "*Thousands* of ships went down all over the world. In a lot of cases, it took *weeks* for teams to get out to them. Scavengers were on the ships as soon as the dust cleared. Hell, from what I heard, a lot of the investigators made *fortunes* selling salvage on the side. The stuff that ended up in storage? It was nothing compared to what's in circulation."

Vee sighed, absently scratching T-Rex's head. "The

other dealers on here, do you think they had voidrium too?"

Rictor nodded. "Odds are good."

I frowned. "But Lynx didn't *want* the voidrium."

Rictor frowned, scratching his head, and then chuckled ruefully. "Maybe she had enough."

"Then why—"

The realization hit me like a sledgehammer.

"Oh, shit," Vee said at the same time.

We turned, locking eyes, while Vee voiced what we were both thinking. "They blew up the lab to hide the evidence. Lynx and whoever she's working with—they didn't want anyone to know it *worked.*"

"Motherfucker," I cursed quietly. "They didn't just want to derail our experiment. They wanted to steal it, and they did. They had access to everything, and with that much voidrium in their possession, they could rebuild MICSy. Maybe more than one of her."

Bowie roiled in on himself in his corner of my mind, radiating panic, and now I understood why. If I was right, they were going to use others of his kind to fuel copies of my machine.

I sat quietly for a second, stunned by the implications. "Any chance you found out who or where Lynx is? Anything that could help us find her?"

Alice shook her head. "I'm sorry, Brandon. There were some notes about the powers she's displayed, all largely in line with your description, but nothing about her identity. The FBI seems to think she works for the Cabal."

"The Cabal?" I raised an eyebrow. "Does that even exist?"

There were thousands of supervillain organizations.

Some were small-time operations with a few members that confined their activities to a particular location or goal. Others numbered in the hundreds and operated across the planet. Most were motivated by money or power; others had aims that ranged from the esoteric to the inscrutable.

The Digital Liberation Front was a coterie of synthetics bent on destroying organic civilization. Baise Mianju was a cult of undead assassins looking to resurrect their demon lords. Singularity was a cybernetic hive mind seeking to network the whole of humanity. Superpowered Nazis looking to restore the Reich. Confederate ghosts. Mad scientists. Would-be alien conquerors. Pantheons of gods.

Irate libertarians.

Some supervillain groups were so ineffectual, they bordered on comical. Others were filled with monsters who paved the road to infamy with corpses, baseline and metahuman.

The most infamous supervillain groups, like Darktide, Legio Tyrannus, and Total Kaos, had terrifyingly powerful members who had committed countless atrocities, killing masks and going toe to toe with Vanguard, along with some of the other most powerful superheroes.

Thankfully, most supervillain teams didn't last long, collapsing under the collective weight of their members' psychopathy and narcissism in explosive displays of infighting that could be as bad as their schemes.

The Cabal was different, a legend that had supposedly operated in the shadows for decades. Some speculated their founder was none other than Crimson Specter, the most infamous supervillain of all time, portrayed as a madman responsible for the deaths of hundreds, including nearly a dozen masks. He was one of a handful of beings who had fought Empyrean and walked away.

Some painted him as an anti-hero. A lot of angry teens had T-shirts with the image of his skull mask.

Crimson Specter's background was a mystery despite dozens of books, biographies, movies, and more than one porn parody. His motives were equally inscrutable, attacking governments and corporations in a reign of terror that had lasted half a century. Each theory that tried to make sense of his actions was more outrageous than the last.

The only thing nearly everyone agreed on was that he had finally been put down in 2015, when he attacked the headquarters of the Initiative, the intergovernmental agency responsible for overseeing metahuman threats.

Vee and Rictor shared a troubled look at the mention of the Cabal.

Huh. I filed that away for later.

"Look, regardless of who she works for, she's the one lead we have. If we don't do something, she'll eventually find me."

Vee snorted. "Brandon, she's nearly killed you whenever you've come within arm's reach of her, and now you want to, what? Interview her? Take a deposition?"

"No, I want to capture her."

Everyone stared at me. Even T-Rex.

"Look, there's something wrong with her. There was a moment when she seemed like another person, like she was trying to tell me something. I know it sounds crazy, but—"

"It doesn't sound crazy," Vee interrupted. "It *is* crazy. It *sounds* stupid. Don't be an idiot."

"What's the alternative?" I shot back. "I stay here forever? Hide for the rest of my life? What about Mom? Is she going to spend the rest of her life in a safe house operated by your *friends*?"

Vee's jaw hardened. She looked away, shaking her head.

"I'm sick of running," I said eventually. "Right now, I'm putting everyone in danger, and we don't even know who or what we're dealing with. We can only guess as to their motives. If I can get Lynx out in the open, I might be able to take her."

"Bork!" T-Rex added, contributing enthusiastically to the conversation.

"Okay, walk me through it." Vee's tone dripped skepticism. "How do we get her to show her face?"

"What if we approached Jeremiah Chambers? I'm sure he'd like to know who murdered his son, and I'm betting whoever is behind this is watching him. When she shows up, we get her."

"We '*get*' her'? Are you for real? So, what? We just waltz into Chambers's $200 million luxury apartment and wait around for the woman who's trying to kill you to show up with her hit squad?" Vee turned to Rictor. "How damaged did you say his brain was?"

"No," I nearly growled. "You get his number, and I text him. I make it sound desperate. I tell him someone's trying to kill me, that I think he's in danger too. We pick a place and a time, and then I ambush her."

"Alone?" Vee rolled her eyes. "Jesus fucking Christ, Brandon. There are easier ways to kill yourself. Assuming you *can* subdue Lynx, what then? Are you going to throw her over your shoulder and *walk* back? What about the interrogation?" Vee crossed her arms and leaned back. "Dude, I love you, but this is the worst idea you've *ever* had, by far."

"Apologies, Brandon," Alice cut in. "You're still recovering from the assassin's last attack, and you've just started to understand your powers. There's a high probability that you wouldn't survive another encounter. At the very least, you would need *significant* assistance."

I sighed. "The two of you have already done *more* than enough. I couldn't ask you to risk any more than you already have, and I don't see any other backup. I'm going to have to do this on my own."

Rictor was quiet for a second, his eyes flickering from Alice to Vee. "What about our mutual friends?"

I looked back at Vee. She didn't meet my eyes. "Are these the same people who have Mom? They've been coming up more and more often. Who are they?"

Vee chugged the remainder of her beer and opened another. "For the last few years, I've, uh, done some work for some enhanced individuals who occasionally break the law."

"Wait, what?" My eyes widened. "'Enhanced individuals who occasionally break the law'? It sounds like you're saying you're working with supervillains."

"You could call them that." She sipped her beer.

I blinked. "How did *that* happen?"

"They approached me after my mom's hearing." She leaned forward, resting her elbows on the countertop. "I was a mess, looking for anything that could help me get the assholes at Raxxil. A woman found me one night at the Downlow. She said she worked with a group who shared my goals and could help with funding and information. Then she said there might be the opportunity to make some cash on the side too."

Vee sighed, still not meeting my eyes. "I told her to piss off, but when I got home that night, there was an envelope on my desk. It had a note and a flash drive inside. The note said *A good faith gesture* or something, and it had a phone number at the bottom. I'd been working for a lawyer on a class action lawsuit against Veritech Pharmaceuticals, and the flash drive had all the evidence I'd been looking for and more. After looking at the data, I called the number on the note."

"Who's your contact?" I asked skeptically.

Vee took another sip of her beer. "I call her Inara, but it's *definitely* a fake name. Given our relationship, neither of us is sharing intimate details."

"What sort of work are we talking about?"

"Electronic intrusion, mostly. Sometimes, I locate items through less than legal means. Other times, I delete records or security footage. I've created false entries in corporate personnel databases and hacked traffic control systems."

"These are the people you left *Mom* with?"

Vee shook her head, her jaw tightening. "They were the only people capable of keeping her safe, and I'm paying them. Besides . . ." She trailed off.

"What?"

A shadow crossed Vee's face, and she wrapped her arms around herself. She still wasn't looking at me.

Something was wrong.

"What aren't you telling me?"

Vee shook her head slowly and pushed her hair back, a nervous gesture she'd had since we were young. She glanced at Alice and Rictor.

"Do you mind if we take a walk?"

TWENTY-TWO

BETRAYAL

We stepped out of what I realized was a lakeside compound east of the city and into a beautiful fall day. The sun was setting, casting a halo around the skyscrapers that ran together with the holographic lights, before turning the lake into a sea of rippling gold.

Most of Rictor's compound was concealed underground. Only the living space was visible, disguised as an old farmhouse with a shed and a barn, surrounded by dense woods. It looked quaint, if slightly dilapidated. One of the few homes in the desolate strip around Union City.

The evening was quiet, suffused with a stillness that would have been impossible among the frantic activity of the city. Part of me found it comforting. Another part of me got a little anxious surrounded by wilderness. Mom and I had spent some time in rural areas while we were moving around, but most of my life had been spent in New York and Union City. I was a city kid at heart.

The change in scenery affected Bowie too. He

rushed to the forefront of my mind. Instead of assailing me with inexplicable thoughts and images, he seemed to take in the landscape, radiating something like surprise tinged with wonder.

Vee pulled out a cigarette and lit it as she led me onto a small trail that carved through the dense woods surrounding the house. Still wet from the storm, the ground sucked at our boots as we tromped over it. The scent of damp earth filled the air.

We walked without speaking, just listening to bird-song and the gentle rustle of the trees. T-Rex followed us, lumbering through the underbrush and woofing at chip-munks, squirrels, and any other adorable creatures un-fortunate enough to cross the giant cyberdog's path.

After a few minutes, the babble of water flowing over rocks greeted us. We turned a corner a minute later to find a small wooden bridge spanning a creek that wound through the tree line. The water was high and fast, splash-ing over rocks and against the banks.

Stopping halfway across the bridge, Vee leaned on the railing and watching the water. "I love it out here," she said with a sigh. "It's beautiful."

I nodded, studying her.

Vee wore the same clothes I'd seen her in last, a cut-up black band shirt and black jeans tucked into combat boots, and she looked exhausted, pushed beyond her limits as she ran herself ragged to help me. The hollows of her eyes were covered with deep purple bruises that stood out against the sepia-brown tones of her skin, and she had the glassy stare she got when she'd been pushing herself too hard. Black fuzz, normally shaved, obscured the tattoos on the side of her head.

I knew Vee was also worried. Her body language

screamed it. Worried about the situation, but more than that, she was worried about how I was going to react to whatever she was about to tell me.

Her nerves were contagious, and a chill ran through me.

I waited, watching the water splash along the creek as worry churned my stomach.

Finally, Vee took a ragged breath, resignation settling over her face. "A couple years ago, six months after I started working with my new associates, my contact started asking me for information about your project." She took a long hit of her cigarette and crossed her arms. "I refused at first. Told her to go fuck herself, actually, but they had information on Raxxil. Information that helped my mom's case. At first, they didn't ask for much. Schedules, grant funders, innocuous stuff that wasn't much more than what they'd get from an internet search. As it went on, the asks got bigger."

Maybe I'd had too many shocks already, because this one landed with a soft thump instead of a bang. I nodded. "What did they want?"

"Information on the research team and the oversight committee. Stuff about Vaydan Industries. Copies of the mathematical models, the schematics for MICSy." Vee paused for a second. "The control system code."

"How did you get it?" I knew the answer, but I wanted to hear it, as if it wouldn't be real until she said it out loud. Anger, despair, and confusion pulled me off-balance as they swirled and shifted like uneven weights in a centrifuge.

Vee's shoulders slumped. "I broke into your laptop and used it to access the university servers. They should probably update their security."

I turned, leaning against the railing beside her, while T-Rex jumped into the creek, barking at currents and splashing wildly with a grin that nearly split his massive jowly head.

"Did it ever occur to you that they might be the people who sabotaged the experiment? Did you think that maybe whoever you're working with are the people trying to kill me?"

Vee snorted, rolling her eyes. "I'm not an idiot. My contact was the first person I called. I was furious. Told her I'd fucking kill her if she, or any of her people, had anything to do with what happened."

I grinned despite the situation. "Threatening super-villains, huh?"

"Yeah, well, I thought you were dead." Vee took another, longer hit from her cigarette, a tremor running through her. She sniffled and wiped her eyes. "I wasn't exactly thinking clearly. My contact denied responsibility, and for what it's worth, I believed her."

"She doesn't exactly seem like a poster child for trustworthiness."

Vee shook her head. "These people—they're not what you think, at least not entirely. Don't get me wrong, they're dangerous, ruthless even, but they aren't mon-sters. They don't go for civilians, and they don't do col-lateral damage, definitely not on the scale of the lab. At least, not on any of the jobs I've assisted with. Besides, Inara's poker face slipped when I told her. She was *pissed.* They weren't behind this."

I closed my eyes, taking a beat to process what I'd just heard.

Vee was one of the pillars of my life, a fixed point of support and stability, even when the rest of my life was burning down around me. The idea that I couldn't trust her shook my very foundation, as if the ground were turning to sand and blowing away from beneath my feet. However, I shook it off. Vee had *always* been there, and in the last week, she'd saved my life, putting herself in the crosshairs of whatever conspiracy I'd stumbled into.

Still, an ember of anger threatened to catch in the tinder of my hurt and confusion. Not because of some perceived betrayal, though I didn't love that she'd given my life's work to whoever the hell her associates were. It wasn't even that her associates might have been responsible for everything. Vee had good instincts.

She didn't trust me enough to just ask.

It hurt more than any perceived betrayal.

But what else could she have done? Would I have done anything differently?

I took a breath and opened my eyes.

Vee was staring at me, her lip quivering, as she waited for a response. Her arms were crossed, her expression a mixture of stubbornness and brittle vulnerability.

After a few seconds, she sagged. "I get it. I'd be fucking furious too. I betrayed you and broke your trust. Maybe even put your life in danger, but—"

I shrugged. "Whatever."

Vee's jaw dropped. She turned toward me, her eyes widening in surprise. "*Whatever?*" she sputtered. "That's what you've got for me after an admission like that? *Whatever?*"

"Yep." I shrugged again. "Whatever."

Vee started to speak, but I cut her off. "I don't love it, but it was for your mom. You were doing what you had to do. The only thing that irritates me is that you didn't just *ask*." I took her cigarette from her, stealing a puff and leaning beside her on the railing. "I'd have given you anything you needed."

A pained expression crossed Vee's face. "I thought about it. Agonized over it. I guess I didn't want to put you in that position, force you to choose between your project and me."

"It wouldn't have been a choice. You'll *always* come first."

Her expression slowly shifted from worry to relief by way of surprise. Reclaiming her cigarette, she took a long drag, which she exhaled with a shuddering breath.

"I also don't love that you left Mom with whoever the hell your friends are, but I trust you. If you think it's the right move, it probably is."

"You're not furious? Ready to cut me out of your life?"

"Vee, with what we are to each other, with what you've done in the last week alone?" I smiled, feeling lighter than I had in a while. "What's a little academic espionage?"

"What are we to each other?" Vee asked, her voice softening.

T-Rex scampered back up the bank and scrambled up to us, his paws slipping on the muddy earth. Tail wagging, he stared at us.

"I'm in love with you." My voice shook, as if the truth were almost too much for mere words to contain. "After the last time we tried *us*, I was too afraid to risk losing you. But now? I know you said you wanted to wait until all of this was over to figure us out, but whatever happens, it'll always be you."

Tears welled in Vee's eyes, and she threw her arms

around me, squeezing. Pulling my head down, she kissed me suddenly, frantically, her mouth tasting like beer and cigarettes.

The world around us faded. The horror, fear, and uncertainty washed away as everything collapsed into a single moment in which Vee was my entire universe.

Eventually, she pulled away, sniffling and wiping her eyes again as she rested her head against my chest. "I love you too." I hugged her gently, suddenly aware of how terribly fragile she was.

T-Rex was still staring up at us, his happy expression shifting to confusion. His eyes crossed, as if looking at his nose.

Vee suddenly pushed away from me, eyes wide with horror. "T-Rex, n—"

It was too late. With a thunderous explosion of snot and spittle, the giant mastiff sneezed on us.

"Ugh," I muttered. "Gross."

Not finished, he began to shake, spraying us with mud, creek water, and more spittle. When he was done, he sat down in front of us and smiled again, letting out a happy bark. The bridge creaked.

Vee and I looked at each other. "You've got some . . ." I used my finger to wipe a massive glob of snot off Vee's cheek.

"Yeah, you too." She wiped something off my neck.

"So, what do we do now?" I scratched T-Rex behind one of his ears.

Vee gestured to the snot and river muck T-Rex had deposited on her pants. "Burn these clothes?"

"After that."

"I can make a call and try to set up a meeting with my associates, but their help—it'll come with strings."

I nodded. "Might as well hear them out. Any idea how long it'll take?"

"Inara's usually fast. A couple of days, maybe?"

"Good. You could probably use some sleep."

Vee nodded. "I'm going on thirty-six hours without it. Caffeine will only take you so far." Reaching out, she gently traced the cut on my face. It was healing shockingly quickly, but it wasn't gone yet. "You could use a few more days to recuperate."

"That's probably a good idea." My hand drifted reflexively to the wound on my side. It still ached. "Rictor thinks we can build a dampening field generator. They found a way to track me, and I want to make sure they can't do it again. Maybe we can throw something together before Inara wants to meet."

Vee tilted her head, thinking. "Rictor and Alice have helped other people who developed powers on the wrong side of the law. If he thinks he can do it, he can."

I took a breath and let it out slowly. After the damage I'd caused and the people I'd hurt, I wasn't exactly eager to meddle with my powers again.

"We'll get through this." Vee's eyes flashed, filling with resolve. "In the meantime, let's see what we can do about arranging a meeting with a group of supervillains."

I nodded.

She took my hand and squeezed it, gently pulling me as she started back toward the farmhouse.

Vee glanced back at me when we reached the end of the bridge. "Hey." Her expression was deceptively mild, but her eyes glittered mischievously. "I could do with a shower. Want to join?"

I grinned back. "Absolutely."

TWENTY-THREE

DANGEROUS FRIENDS

We exited the autotaxi at the corner of Lexington and Ninth in Aeon Square, at the heart of Union City's nightlife. It was dark, and the street was a riot of people chatting and laughing as they made their way in and out of bars, nightclubs, and concert venues and through streets bathed in the light of the buildings above.

Vee had called her contacts after our shower. They'd agreed to meet us the following evening, which hadn't left me a lot of time to second-guess my decision. After Vee fell asleep and I called and spoke with Mom, Rictor had invited me back to his lab with a six pack of beer, offering to get started on the wearable dampening field.

It hadn't taken me long to realize a couple of things.

First, the guy redefined genius. Rictor must have been brilliant before the nanites, but whatever they'd done to him had taken him way beyond anyone I'd ever met—and I'd spent most of my adult life surrounded by some of the best theoretical physicists and xenotech engineers on the planet.

Second, Rictor's facility put our lab—and any other I'd ever seen the inside of—to shame. He operated on a different level. In his workshop, he could design, model, and fabricate prototypes in shockingly little time. In other circumstances, I could have happily spent weeks there.

By the time Vee woke up around two the following afternoon, Rictor and I had mild hangovers and a working prototype.

Bowie had seemed to understand what we were doing and was *not* thrilled. I'd done what I could to make sure the dampening field wasn't *hurting* him, and then using images and simple concepts, I'd tried to explain that it was necessary to keep us safe. He hadn't cared. All the wariness and distrust that had eroded over the last few days flared back to life.

Despite Bowie's sulking and my own exhaustion, Rictor and I spent the afternoon debugging the dampener and had an early dinner. Then Vee and I climbed into the Danger Van—Vee's nickname for Rictor's ride—to get into the city limits. From there, Vee hacked an autotaxi, which took us the rest of the way, careful to avoid routes with lots of camera coverage.

Standing on the curb, I looked around as I rubbed the field dampener under my coat. Intellectually, I knew the dampening field was working—my gravity sense was gone and Bowie was silent—but I was still wary. It didn't help that my face had been all over the news. I couldn't shake the entirely rational fear that someone would recognize me. I had a medical mask on, and the crisp fall evening meant that having my hood pulled up wasn't out of the ordinary. I'd finished my fugitive ensemble with a pair of tinted glasses, hoping to hide my eyes, which had fully changed to a striking, slightly luminescent violet.

Figuring that whoever was after me was also looking for her, Vee also wore a mask and had her hood up.

"Come on." Vee gestured to the entryway of one of the nightclubs lining the block. It occupied the top three floors of a building on the corner. Massive glowing letters spelled out *Inferno.*

"Seriously?" I didn't move. "A nightclub named Inferno? Why don't they just call it Supervillains?"

"They don't own the building—at least I don't think so. This is only the second time I've met Inara here."

"Seems a little cliché, don't you think?"

Vee shrugged, gesturing to the line of people waiting to be let in. "It's new, and it's popular, but not with metas. The crowds reduce the risk of a super team throwing a cement truck through the ceiling. Now, will you come the fuck on? We need to get off the street." She put her arm through mine and pulled me forward. "The last thing we need is for some rando to recognize you and call Vanguard."

We walked past the line of people and slipped down a side alley. There was a door at the end guarded by a couple of bored-looking bouncers. Vee slipped one of them a card, and they opened the door for us, revealing a short hallway that ended in an elevator.

"What, no secret handshake?" I asked when the door was closed behind us.

"I'm pretty sure they work for the club." Vee rolled her eyes. "They probably think we're celebrities trying to avoid paparazzi."

We stepped into the elevator, and Vee hit the button for the top floor.

I was jittery. I didn't know what I was walking into, and I still didn't love the idea of turning to people I didn't know, particularly given their vocation, but I didn't have a lot of options. And I trusted Vee.

Besides, they were already helping Mom.

I slowed my breathing, which helped.

A little.

Noise and light poured in when the elevator doors opened, a pounding bassline and a crimson light display that dominated the club's ceiling. We stepped out onto a balcony that encircled the club, overlooking a dance floor filled with writhing bodies. The balcony looked like a VIP area, with tables and chairs occupied by small groups being waited on by attractive drink runners.

Vee led me to a bar being tended by a pale woman in her thirties with a mane of red curls and tattoo sleeves. Leaning over, she said something to the bartender, who nodded and gestured to a hallway across from the elevator. It was guarded by two more well-dressed bouncers who seemed more alert than the ones outside. Thanking her, Vee slipped her a twenty that disappeared as the bartender turned to another customer.

I followed as Vee made her way to the hall and said something to the bouncers, who nodded and stepped aside. We walked down the corridor, which turned abruptly, ending at a red door.

Vee glanced at me. "Ready?"

I shrugged. "Is anyone *ever* ready for something like this?"

Snorting, Vee let a lopsided smile spread across her lips. "Probably not."

The door opened to a private room. It was dimly lit but bigger than I'd expected, with its own bar to the right of the door and a few tables. The music from outside cut off abruptly as the door shut behind us.

There was only one person inside—or at least that I could see—sitting at a table in the back with a drink. She looked up as we entered, a smile spreading easily across her face.

Inara appeared to be a strikingly attractive woman in her early forties. Her hair was long, straight, and inky black, framing an olive face with angular features. She seemed underdressed for a supervillain, with a charcoal blazer and matching skirt over a deep-blue blouse and tights, but I wasn't exactly an expert.

I considered the woman for a moment. Inara didn't look dangerous, but there was something about her that unsettled me. Made me wary.

Standing smoothly, Inara made her way over to us. "Vee." Her voice had the hint of an accent I couldn't place. "Always a pleasure."

Vee nodded, removing her mask and lowering her hood. "Inara. You too." She gestured my way. "This is Brandon."

Following Vee's lead, I lowered my hood and removed my mask and sunglasses, nodding in greeting. "Thanks for meeting with me."

Amusement sparkled in Inara's eyes. "Of course. We're glad Vee reached out." She gestured behind her to the table she'd been sitting at. "Shall we?"

I glanced at Vee. There was tension in her shoulders and a tightness around her eyes, but she nodded.

I looked back at Inara. Her smile widened. "I take it I'm not what you expected."

"Not really," I admitted. "I guess I didn't know what to expect. I figured you'd be wearing a mask or something."

Inara's eyes glittered. In the dark, she looked almost

predatory. "Why, Brandon, what makes you think I'm not?"

We made our way to the table. Inara returned to her original seat, while Vee and I sat down across from her.

"You've had quite a week," Inara said. "Why don't you tell me about it?"

"Don't you already know? Vee told me you've been spying on my research, keeping tabs on me."

Inara glanced at Vee, raising an eyebrow.

Vee bristled. "He needed to know."

Inara just nodded.

I didn't quite glare. "Why?"

"Is that really what you're here to ask me? Given the circumstances, I'd think you'd have more pressing questions." Inara picked up her wineglass and took a sip of liquid so dark, it was nearly black. "As I told Vee, regardless of our interest, we had nothing to do with what happened to you or your project."

I grunted. "It would be nice to know that for sure."

Inara's expression hardened, and without any other visible changes, she seemed to radiate menace. "You've had a difficult week, so let me be clear. As I already told our mutual friend, despite our line of work, we aren't in the habit of committing mass murder and had nothing to do with either the attack or the preceding sabotage."

She shrugged, taking another sip. "If you can't accept that, we'll have your mother returned to you within the hour and you can go on your way. However, you should know the people who are after you won't stop. They've already demonstrated the lengths to which they're willing to go. There's a good chance they'll kill anyone who even *might* know something, a list that now includes your mother and Vee, along with Rictor and Alice."

Inara's expression softened along with her tone, and the nearly palpable aura of danger receded. "If you want to survive this, you're going to need help, which means you'll have to trust *someone*. And as they say,"—she smiled slightly, her eyes glittering with amusement again— "Better the devil you know. Vee and I have worked together for years. She's seen how we operate."

I studied her, looking for any sign of deception, and then looked at Vee.

Vee's eyes were fixed on Inara. "Your call. If you don't like this, we'll find another way."

Finally, I nodded reluctantly. "You're right. We need help."

Inara leaned back, her posture relaxing. "Believe it or not, I'm sympathetic."

She must have seen the skepticism on my face. "We're not all monsters, Brandon, even those of us who are *literally* monsters. Law and morality occasionally intersect, but there's less overlap than many believe. Not everyone who lives on the wrong side of the law is a sociopath, metahuman or otherwise. You'd be surprised how many people have stories similar to yours."

That struck a nerve.

I'd grown up around career criminals. Most were just people trying to get by. Uncle Mike used to say that many laws were made by the rich and powerful to make them richer and more powerful.

Besides, Nightfang called himself a *hero*, and he'd murdered my dad.

I was quiet for a moment, studying Inara. Something about her still unsettled me. She seemed sincere, but I wasn't stupid enough to think I could judge the intentions of someone I'd just met, particularly given what she did for a living. And just because I agreed with what she was saying didn't mean she was trustworthy.

Still, I didn't have a lot of options.

"Someone's trying to kill me. She calls herself Lynx, and she's not working alone. I need to know why, and I need to stop her." I went on to tell Inara about the attacks, how I'd changed, and the things I could do.

Inara listened, nodding and asking a few clarifying questions. When I finished, she silently considered me for a few moments, wineglass in hand.

"You're asking for more than you understand," she said eventually. "We're willing to help, but we'll need something from you."

Vee snorted. "What does that mean? What aren't you telling us?"

"Quite a lot, of course." Inara laughed softly and glanced at Vee, before turning back to me. "We have suspicions about who might be trying to kill you."

"Because you've been watching whoever's behind all this, right?" If Inara's people weren't behind the attack, it was the only answer that made sense. "*That's* why you were spying on the project."

Inara leaned forward. "Very good, Brandon." Her dark eyes gleamed in the dim light, and I suddenly realized what had been nagging me. Inara's shadow didn't match the woman in front of me. It was too big and strangely shaped. Its movements were slightly out of sync.

And it had horns.

"Why not just help us, then?" I asked, trying to ignore her shadow.

Inara took another sip of her wine. "We have our own plans, and we could be exposing ourselves. We need to make sure our help's worth the risk."

I glanced at Vee, who gave my leg a comforting squeeze under the table. "What do you want?"

"One of my associates is putting together a job, a simple bank robbery complicated by a short time window. Most of the team are external assets, individuals who aren't part of our organization, and she could use some help."

"Wait." My eyes widened. "You want me to rob a *bank?*"

"That's right." Inara's eyes glittered with amusement. "What did you think we were going to ask for?"

"Money?"

Inara nodded. "Do you have any money, Brandon?"

I sighed. "Don't you have people for this kind of thing?"

"Of course." She laughed lightly. "But our organization doesn't want to advertise our involvement, which is why we aren't using them."

"I'm not asking for a favor," I grunted. "We have a mutual problem. Why can't we work together?"

"We can. Once you do this for us."

Frowning, I looked at Vee. Her brow was furrowed as our eyes met. The look on her face told me she didn't buy Inara's explanation either, but she shrugged slightly. "I mean, it could be worse."

I sighed, closing my eyes and racking my brain for other options. I was already a criminal. Short of walking into Vanguard HQ and turning myself in, which would almost certainly result in me spending the rest of my life in Blackstone or some other ultramax metahuman detention facility, I couldn't think of any alternatives.

I glanced from Vee to Inara. "I don't suppose I could take some time to think about it?"

Inara shrugged slightly. "You have as long as it takes for me to finish my wine." She raised her nearly empty glass in a mock salute and took another sip.

"You'll continue to keep my mom safe?"

Inara nodded. "Of course. We've already been paid for that service. And from what I've heard, Laura is a lovely woman."

"And you'll help me deal with Lynx or whoever the hell she is?"

Inara's smile shifted, becoming predatory. "We'll help you deal with her, one way or another."

What the hell, I thought. Crime was a family tradition.

"I'll do it."

"Excellent. We need to move fast, so expect us to be in contact soon. I would practice with your powers as much as you can between now and then. I suspect your friend Rictor can facilitate that without you risking exposure."

I took a breath. "Will do."

"Oh, and Brandon?" Inara said, a hint of mischief in her eyes. "You'll need a costume."

TWENTY-FOUR

OLD WOUNDS

Rictor flicked on the lights, revealing yet another room full of machines. Unlike the main workshop, which was mostly filled with manufacturing equipment, this room looked like a giant's physical therapy lab. It was packed with biometric screening devices and industrial versions of workout equipment.

I shook my head. "Man, I didn't realize there'd be *more*."

Rictor smiled deprecatingly. "You know how it is. Never enough space!" Leopard-print robe flapping, he gestured to a workstation near the door. "Come on, let's get you set up!"

After meeting with Inara, Vee and I had gotten a ride back in the Danger Van and told Rictor and Alice about the meeting. Not wanting to put them in any more danger, Vee and I had offered to leave, but Alice and Rictor wouldn't hear of it. Even T-Rex had protested, flopping all three-hundred-plus pounds of himself onto Vee's lap.

Once that was settled, everyone had piled into the

living room to watch old monster movies and drink beer. Despite the stress and residual pain from my injuries, I'd almost felt at ease.

Eventually, Vee and I had gone to bed. Not that we'd gone right to sleep. When we did finally pass out, I was exhausted, but that didn't stopped the dreams from coming. Despite the dampening field, I once again found myself swimming through stellar vistas as alien thoughts permeated my mind.

Vee had been draped over me when I woke up, snoring softly and drooling on my chest. I'd studied the soft lines of her face, the subtle way the morning light painted the warm-brown tones of her skin, and tried to burn the moment into my memory. Even after all the horror and stress of the last week, I was overwhelmed by profound gratitude. We'd been given another chance, and I had a feeling we were going to make it work.

Assuming I survived.

When we finally untangled ourselves from the sheets and each other, we took a long shower and had breakfast with Rictor and Alice.

Putting off some of his other projects, Rictor had offered to spend the morning working with me to assess my physical changes, while Alice and Vee investigated Lynx and other instances of missing voidrium. After I'd checked in with Mom, Rictor and I went to the lab.

Rictor gestured to a small platform with an opaque glass disk set into it, next to a workstation against the wall. He slid into a chair, set his smoothie down, and started typing. "Jump on that, pretty please."

I gingerly stepped on the disk, which began to glow. Meanwhile, four tiny drones left a charging stand nearby and flew in a circle around me.

"We already have a baseline, so we're just going to run a quick scan to see what's changed. Then we'll slap on some sensors, get everything calibrated, and see what you can do."

After a minute or so, the scanner generated a holographic representation of my body.

"Well, I wasn't wrong!" Eyes wide with amused disbelief, Rictor gestured to the display. "Your body's still integrating the xibrantium, and your brain's still merging with the voidrium." He turned to me, tapping his temple. "Is your friend still around?"

I nodded, and shifted my attention to Bowie, who seemed to be watching Rictor warily. "Yeah, he's still here."

When I'd been wearing the dampener, I hadn't been able to hear Bowie. If I'd focused, I'd still been able to **feel** him, but it had been tenuous, like knowing I wasn't the only person home in a massive house. It had been a relief, but I'd also found myself missing him, as if there were an empty space in my head where Bowie had been. When I'd removed the dampener so we could calibrate it, Bowie had berated me with a tirade of incomprehensible thoughts, before sulking in a corner of my mind.

"Speaking of!" Rictor grinned and hit a button. "Ziggy Stardust" started playing from speakers in the corners of the room. He hummed along as he worked.

"Hey, can I ask you a question?"

Rictor looked over. "Having second thoughts?" He smiled comfortingly. "Hey, I get it. Robbing a bank isn't for everyone. In fact—"

"No, that's not it. I don't *love* the idea, but I don't really have a choice." I might not trust Inara's motives, but she was right about that.

Rictor took another sip of his smoothie before swiveling his chair to face me, a hint of concern in his expression. "What's up?"

"You and Alice—you're risking a *lot* to help us. I'm grateful; I just . . ."

"Hey, no, I get it." Rictor waved off my concern. "You're putting a lot of trust in us at a time when you don't have a lot to go around, and you want to understand why we're doing this." Sighing, he fumbled through his leopard-print robe for a pack of cigarettes.

"Like you, I was a pretty smart kid." As he fished out a cigarette and lit it, a self-deprecating smile played across his thin face. "Finished high school at fourteen. My first PhD at MIT by eighteen. My second too."

I nodded, impressed but unsurprised.

"I was captivated by the complexity, the beauty, in *everything*, you know?" Rictor leaned back, smiling wistfully. "From the beginning, though, I was fascinated with robotics and cognition. The pulleys and levers of thought. Synthetic, organic—it didn't matter."

Nostalgia filled his expression. "A paper I'd written on nanorobotic life cycles in biological systems got me an invite to a project funded by DARPA—the Pentagon branch that handles all the weird science—developing nanites housed in implants designed to restructure and augment the human brain. In addition to the military applications, the tech had the potential to treat a ton of different neurological conditions, but DARPA didn't care about that."

A hint of bitterness broke through Rictor's smile. "Neither did I, really." He sighed, looking away. "Man, it was a dream, you know? My first *real* project. All the funding, all the toys! Real recognition."

I knew the feeling. I'd felt like I was floating for days after we got the grant for MICSy.

"This was less than a decade after the Rakkari attack. We'd had breakthroughs in every field you could think of, and the hits just kept coming. I was going to change the world, get my name up there with Einstein, Hawking, and Tesla."

Rictor was silent for a moment, taking a long drag on his cigarette. "The project coordinator was this guy Suresh. A few years older than me. Suresh was damn smart and great at his job. He listened, gave credit where it was due, and didn't bully the research assistants. By department standards, the guy was a saint. We got along fine at first, but he got tired of me doing whatever the hell I wanted, and I got tired of him telling me what to do, even though it was his job. I figured he was jealous. Insecure, maybe."

Rictor leaned back, stretching his arms over his head and crossing his bunny-slippered feet. "Looking back, he was just trying to help me. Trying to grind down my edges a little. A lot of kid-genius types don't do well in real labs. They spend so much of their lives getting told how brilliant they are that they can't listen to anyone else."

I nodded again. I'd met *plenty* of insufferable baby geniuses.

"But, boy, I *hated* that he didn't worship me like everyone else did. Instead, he was always on me, making sure I was following protocols." Another rueful smile flickered across his face. "I had a problem with rules. Big surprise."

I could sympathize.

Rictor took another drag on his cigarette. "About six months into the project, I got stuck with inventory duty and noticed a defective prototype never arrived at the disposal company. When I mentioned it to Suresh, for a second, he looked guilty as hell. Told me he'd take care of it. I figured he'd taken it home to work on. Sold it, maybe."

Taking research materials from a lab was a massive protocol breach, especially on a government project. I knew a guy who had been threatened with jail time for taking his own lab notes home.

"The next week, I removed some stress tests from the schedule without his permission. Oh boy, did we have it out. Suresh called me a reckless prima donna and told me I had no business being in a lab. I told *him* he was an incompetent nobody who had more business cleaning bathrooms than running a research project in front of everyone." Rictor chuckled. "He kicked me off the team on the spot. I didn't leave him much of a choice."

I tried to imagine how Claire would have responded to me saying something like that. It wouldn't have been pretty.

"The next day, I marched right into the principal investigator's office and told her about the missing implant. I figured he'd get yelled at. Fired, at the worst." Rictor shook his head, his shoulders slumping. "Some men in black from the Bureau of Human Enhancement, the guys who investigate illegal human augmentation, showed up the next day and arrested him."

I winced, leaning back against the wall. Stealing research data from federal projects rarely ended well.

"It turned out Suresh had a daughter. Bindia. He'd failed to disclose that the poor kid had early-onset Harden-Klein syndrome. The stuff we were working on was her only chance of seeing her tenth birthday. He hadn't stolen the implant to sell. He'd taken it for her."

Rictor bowed his head, his leopard-print robe enveloping his thin frame. "When the feds found out, they made his daughter get a blood test and then injected the poor kid with an agent that neutralized the nanites that were saving her life, before extracting the implant."

My jaw hardened. "Motherfuckers." There were stories about nanite treatments for HKS that had never gone public. Thinking about Mom and all the other people whose lives could have been changed, I wanted to hurt whoever was responsible.

Rictor nodded, a flash of old pain in his eyes. "I hadn't just gotten this poor guy arrested or destroyed his career. I'd killed his daughter."

"Man, that's not on you. You couldn't have—"

"No!" Rictor's voice was sharper than I'd ever heard it. "It *was* my fault. Suresh was right. I *was* a reckless prima donna, and I *didn't* have any business being in a lab. I didn't report him because he was violating protocols. I wanted to get back at him for embarrassing me."

Rictor sighed and took a hit of his cigarette. "His wife, Naomi, called me afterward, sobbing." He looked up at me. "Have you ever felt like you're stuck in a nightmare? Like nothing's real?"

"I think so," I said quietly.

"I had the sort of epiphany that only happens when you've messed up so badly, it changes the way you see yourself. My work, my hopes, whatever bullshit *legacy* I thought I'd leave, it was nothing compared to that girl's life. The guilt filled me so full, there wasn't room for anything else. Suffice to say, I wasn't exactly thinking rationally, but I knew I couldn't let that girl die.

Rictor paused, his eyes widening with the echo of old excitement. "The lab was being guarded by BHE agents, so I swiped a wireless taser prototype from another project. Long story short, I assaulted some federal agents, took the implants and our stock of nanites, and hauled ass to Suresh's house. It took a while to convince Naomi, but she was desperate. I also had some money from a few patents, which I gave them—after I implanted another nanite hive—and put them on a red-eye to Toronto, where they had some family.

"It turns out tasing a federal agent, even a *little*, is a crime." Rictor shrugged helplessly, raising his hands. "Who knew? Anyway, I went on the run—to my dealer, actually. Jerry. Nice guy. He put me in contact with a lady, who had me meet with a guy, et cetera. Eventually . . ." He gestured around us, his robe flapping. "Voila."

Rictor ashed his cigarette in a petri dish he'd been using as an ashtray. "It made me realize a lot of people make bad choices for good reasons, or find themselves breaking rules because their conscience or their heart won't let them do anything else. I figured if I could help those people out, I'd be making up for being such a shit."

"I'm sorry. I didn't mean to—"

Rictor waved me off. "No *problemo*, buddy. They are old wounds, and it all worked out. Suresh got released after six months due to a totally-not-hacked bug in the prisoner database and reunited with his family. He started his own company a year later. Naomi's a florist. Hell, Bindia just finished art school. *I* was lonely at first, but I found Alice and T-Rex and great people like you." He smiled widely. "I'm right where I'm supposed to be."

A rush of affection for Rictor and Alice flooded me. "We're lucky to have you."

He took one last drag on his cigarette and put it out. "Now, come on. Let's finish up so we can move on to the *real* fun!"

After covering me in electrodes, Rictor led me to what looked like a massively reinforced bench between two large pillars, each about two feet thick, that stretched nearly to the ceiling. A bar extended from a vertical track on one pillar to a vertical track on the other, resting about two feet above the bench, like a press machine.

Rictor puffed up, curling his thin arms into a body-builder pose. "I'm going to pump." He clapped and pointed at me. "You up." His voice dropped a few octaves as he adopted the worst fake German accent I'd ever heard.

He looked at me expectantly and sighed when I only stared back blankly. "Kids these days."

I looked at the machine. "What's *that?*"

"This bad boy?" Rictor patted the machine, a proud smile expanding across his thin face. "This right here is the Hercules 3. It uses electromagnets to generate resistance. Vanguard techs use it as part of their initial physical assessment. *Very* expensive. It *may* have fallen out of a train car en route to one of Vanguard's Watchtowers. Slide right in there."

I slipped underneath the massive bar, wrapping my hands around it. "How much does the bar weigh?"

Rictor scratched his head. "Uh, four hundred and fifty pounds, give or take? Don't worry, though. It goes a *lot* higher."

Uh-oh. That was a *lot* more than I'd *ever* been able to bench, and I kept myself in shape. "Are you—"

"Don't worry, *mi amigo.*" Rictor took a long sip of his mushroom-enhanced smoothie. "I know you're still injured. We'll start light. How does eight hundred sound?"

"Will it shatter my skull if I drop it?"

"Nope!"

"Then it sounds fine, I guess." I settled myself onto the bench. "Here goes."

The pillars on either end of the bar hummed with electricity. I took a breath, let it out slowly, and then breathed in again, pushing against the bar as I exhaled. To my surprise, it moved easily, sliding to the top of my extension, where I held it, before returning it to the resting position. It wasn't quite weightless, but it felt *much* lighter than it should have.

"Not bad!"

I blinked. "Not bad?"

Rictor smiled indulgently. "I know it seems like a lot, but it's nothing on the metahuman enhanced strength scale. This thing can generate about a hundred metric tons of resistance—about as much weight as a train engine. I have it on good authority that Polaris, Empyrean, and the other strong guys in Vanguard can put the machine's max load up all day without even breaking a sweat. All the metas in the top strength quintile can. Hell, the metas in the middle quintile average about fifty."

I shook my head. *So much power, given out at random.* "Damn."

"I know, right?" Rictor laughed ruefully. "I can't even open the peanut butter jar. I make Alice or T-Rex help, and T-Rex makes me give him some."

I took a breath. "Let's try again."

"There's my guy!" Rictor grinned and made finger guns. "Let's double it!"

To my absolute astonishment, I managed to lift

almost forty-five metric *tons* before we stopped. It was like my whole range had expanded profoundly. I felt like I could have done more, but Rictor didn't want to push it with my injuries.

After the Hercules, Rictor put me through dozens of other tests, following Vanguard's assessment. I sprinted on a reinforced treadmill and dodged stinging projectiles from a swarm of small drones. He tested the tensile strength of my skin and my resistance to various forms of energy, extreme environments, and pathogens.

Ultimately, I was stabbed, shot, electrocuted, and poisoned. Frozen and burned. Irradiated and exposed to vacuum.

He tried to drown me.

And crush me under extreme pressure.

Asphyxiate me.

The whole time, Rictor maintained a sort of manic cheer as he bounced around from one test to the next, intermixing anecdotes with explanations.

Once Bowie realized we weren't being attacked, he seemed amused by the process. *I'm glad one of us is enjoying this,* I thought to him.

It was a strange three hours.

After reviewing the data, Rictor flopped into a chair across from me. "Well, my friend, you're one tough *hombre.* Like I said before, beings that survive cosmic energy saturation undergo a period of rapid transformation, which you seem to be right in the middle of. Even after, they continue to change. Why don't we start with a look at your ambient energy radiation before we—"

"Can you bottom line it for me?" I cut in quietly.

"Bottom line?" Rictor slid down in his seat and scratched his head. "Even injured, you're in the lower-middle quintile for metahuman strength. The upper-middle quintile for resilience. You're *fast*, and your reflexes are enhanced, on top of some sort of predictive ability. I'll need more readings, but it looks like you perceive time differently in stressful situations, which is why things seem to slow down. You also heal rapidly. Not as fast as someone with a healing factor, but much faster than a baseline. Beyond that, you'll never catch a cold again. You'll age slowly. Hell, you could be functionally immortal, but it's too soon to say. You can almost certainly survive in the vacuum of space or a host of other inhospitable environments. You probably don't need to eat, drink, or *breathe*. And that's not even touching your *powers*."

I blinked, leaning back slowly, filled to bursting with a mix of euphoria and horror that left me reeling.

"This is just the beginning. As your body becomes a better conduit, you'll get stronger, in terms of both raw physical abilities and your powers, and more resilient, like Empyrean, Polaris, and the other metas that channel cosmic energy."

Rictor paused for a moment. "Buddy, with time, you could end up one of the most powerful beings on the planet."

"No pressure, though, right?" I shook my head. The sheer enormity of the statement settled in. It was as if the tapestry of my life were being rewritten, made glorious and horrible.

Rictor gave me a sympathetic look. "At least you won't have to ask your dog to help you open jars of peanut butter."

"I don't want this," I whispered. "I don't deserve it."

"Good, bad—nobody gets what they deserve, pal."

Rictor's voice was quiet, his expression almost apologetic. "They get what they get." Reaching out, he put a hand on my shoulder. "Now." His eyes twinkled mischievously, and a grin split his face. "Wanna go have some *real* fun?"

TWENTY-FIVE

PRACTICE MAKES IMPERFECT

You ready?" Rictor's voice echoed from the top of an old yellow school bus, where he reclined in a folding chair next to Alice, a smoothie in one hand and a tablet in the other.

I glanced at Vee, who sat on the edge of the bus's roof, her legs dangling over the side. Leaning back, she grabbed another beer from the cooler, beside which sat a portable speaker blasting NOFX. "You've got this!"

T-Rex looked from her to me and then barked thunderously in support, his tail wagging.

"Don't worry, Brandon," Alice said through the earpiece she'd given me. "I can activate the dampener remotely, in the event something goes awry."

"Awry," I muttered, trying not to think about all the horrible possibilities contained in such a small word.

After our morning tests, we'd had lunch and then piled into the Danger Van to make our way out to what Rictor had referred to as Test Site Alpha. Rictor had sworn Test Sight Alpha was a cutting-edge facility where

I could safely test my powers without attracting unwanted attention.

When we arrived, Vee had looked at Rictor with a mixture of bemusement and resignation after surveying it. "Dude, this is a *junkyard*."

He'd nodded. "Yeah, but Test Site Alpha *sounds* really cool."

Taking a breath, I looked around.

About ten minutes from Rictor's compound, the junkyard was nestled in a small wooded valley in the no-man's-land that surrounded the city. It was a huge maze of rusting vehicles, dead appliances, industrial equipment, and other heavy refuse that sprawled for more than five acres. Dirt pathways ran through hills and valleys of tetanus-inducing hazards, from piles of vehicles stacked three or four high to mounds of old washing machines and other appliances.

The school bus everyone was using as a perch was on the northern side of the clearing in the junkyard's heart, a barren space walled in by stacked vehicles. It was mostly empty, aside from a few wrecks, a collection of scattered appliances, large tires, and some other junk.

"You're sure no one will notice?" Lynx had mentioned that she'd found me using a satellite. Despite the mild fall weather, the open sky made me nervous.

Rictor laughed and shook his head. "Like I said before, this isn't the first time I've conducted illicit tests with wanted supervillains." He gestured around. "It's not *just* a junkyard. I've made some improvements. This place is hidden from external sensors, and we have drones outside keeping watch for energy emissions. In the unlikely event that you're too much for the screens to handle, we'll know immediately and shut down."

"What about all of you?" I asked, trying to ignore memories of the night I was attacked. "Are you sure it's safe?"

"This isn't my first rodeo, buddy." Rictor tapped on the roof with his foot. "We have an emergency force field built into the top of this thing. Don't *worry*."

I was worried. *Very* worried, in fact.

"Here we go." Taking a breath, I held it in and turned off the dampening field. The power crackling at my core returned instantly, along with the barely perceptible violet shimmer that subtly overlay everything.

Bowie returned too, greeting me with his usual sullen silence.

"Look at that!" Rictor shouted, standing as he waved his tablet in front of Vee. Grabbing it to hold it steady, Vee pulled her sunglasses down to look at the display.

"Anything?" I yelled, trying to ignore Bowie, which only seemed to piss him off more.

Look, I thought to him. *We're stuck with each other. Can you please at least* try *to work with me?*

He seemed to consider me warily. After a few moments, I got the faintest acknowledgment, underpinned by morose annoyance.

"Thank you," I muttered.

"For what, Brandon?" Alice said in my ear.

"Just talking to myself," I replied. "Kinda."

"Oh, yeah!" Rictor yelled. "Your brain activity and radiant energy levels just spiked."

"What do you want me to do?" I yelled back.

"Do your thing!" Rictor smiled and gestured around with his smoothie, spilling some, his robe flapping in the light breeze. "Move some shit around. We need readings from that big, beautiful brain."

Closing my eyes, I extended my gravitational sense outward. Like before, my new sense transformed the infinitesimal gravity fields generated by the mass of everything around me into a shimmering violet representation of the world. Unlike last time, it was both instantaneous and mostly clear, likely the result of the voidrium integrating more fully with my brain.

My head throbbed dully, but not as much as the previous day. Rictor's scans had shown that the intracranial swelling had gone down.

"Okay," I grunted. "You got this."

A battered refrigerator, overgrown with weeds, sat on its side about twenty feet away. I concentrated on it, feeling its mass, contours, and texture. Then, with a thought and a flicker of power, I slowly **lifted** it about five feet off the ground. It floated, shifting ever so slightly in the wind.

"Holy shit." Vee slowly climbed to her feet. Beside her, Rictor whooped.

Like before, using my power was intuitive, if awkward, as if I'd developed an extra set of hands I was learning to use for the first time. I didn't think about the configurations of the gravity fields I was manipulating or the rotational force or speed of the objects I moved.

I just did it.

"Very good, Brandon," Alice said supportively through the earpiece. "Try turning it."

Concentrating, I drew on what little insights I'd managed during my previous practice session, along with Bowie's help. I also tapped into what I'd begun to suspect were Bowie's memories of a time before he was trapped, which I'd been experiencing as dreams. Carefully, I rotated the refrigerator parallel to the ground.

The refrigerator shuddered and shook as I started to

lose control. My headache redoubled, and with a shriek of tortured metal, the fridge crumpled like someone twisting a tin can, before spinning off and embedding itself in the ground more than thirty feet away.

Bowie radiated amusement.

Alien Schadenfreude, I thought. *Awesome.*

Leaping to his feet, Rictor danced a small jig in his fuzzy slippers. "That was great!"

I stared at him and then at Vee, who shrugged. "Were we watching the same thing?"

Rictor grinned. "The practice matters, but anything you do gives us data, helps us see how your brain interacts with the voidrium when you use your powers. The hiccups are important too!

"You know what they say." Rictor scratched T-Rex on the head. "Practice makes imperfect!"

Thanks for the help, I thought, sending sarcasm to Bowie, who gave me the mental equivalent of the middle finger.

During the attack on Vee's safe house, Bowie had helped me, but not since. At least he could be bothered to help when my life was in danger. Our lives, maybe.

"Hey." Vee leaned down, gesturing to the tablet. "Did you see that?"

"See what?" Rictor asked. "Holy cannoli," he muttered after a moment, glancing from the tablet to me. "Did you try to . . . ?" He wiggled his fingers.

I shook my head. "No. I was having what passes for a conversation with Bowie."

Rictor glanced at Vee and Alice.

"What?" I asked.

"Talk to him some more." Rictor glanced up, almost vibrating with excitement. "Ask him if he knows Elvis."

"Hey!" Vee shouted down, a smile playing across her face. "Do you remember the Police State show where the lead singer dressed up like zombie Elvis?"

I grinned. "Didn't the stage catch fire when his amp shorted out?"

Vee sighed with relish. "Good times."

I concentrated, trying to share an image of a heavy-set punk dressed like Elvis—complete with white pleather jumpsuit—with Bowie, who responded with a mixture of bewilderment and disdain, as if stunned by the sheer, inexplicable stupidity of my entire species.

Vee was looking at Alice when I glanced back at them. "What do you think?"

Alice's eyes unfocused for a second, and then she nodded. "We need more data."

Vee looked down at me. "Keep going!"

With a sigh, I looked for more garbage to move.

I spent the next hour picking up, rotating, and moving junk. I kept things small, not moving anything larger than a battered Volkswagen Beetle, but each attempt ended in an uncontrollable spasm of power that destroyed the object and damaged its surroundings. Still, it seemed like the spasms got *slightly* less intense as I progressed.

My control improved as well. It got easier to pick up, move, and manipulate objects with my power, requiring a *little* less concentration.

Eventually, Rictor stopped me. "All right, buddy. That was good. Let's move on. Try going big!"

"What about that?" Vee pointed to the rusting hulk of an old cement truck near the edge of the clearing.

I blinked. "Are you for real?" Extending my perception, I could feel the truck's mass. The rusting cement truck was *much* larger than anything I'd tried to manipulate so far. "That thing has to weigh at least ten tons."

"More like thirteen." Rictor smiled sunnily. "Perfect!"

Taking a breath, I focused on the massive vehicle in front of me. It was farther away than anything I'd moved yet, easily sixty feet away, but I didn't think distance would make a difference.

In my mind, I could feel Bowie observing curiously.

I reached out and, with a flicker of power, **grabbed** the cement truck. It groaned ominously as it lifted off the ground, a shower of dirt and debris falling from underneath.

"Mother bitch," Vee swore, taking off her sunglasses.

Despite its mass, **lifting** the cement truck and holding it aloft wasn't much more taxing than a smaller object. I couldn't be sure, but I suspected it was because I wasn't moving the *object* so much as manipulating gravitational forces in its immediate area. The implications were stunning.

I was also pretty sure I could go much, *much* bigger.

"How does it feel?" Rictor called. "Any fatigue or strain?"

I shook my head. "No, it's fine."

But it wasn't fine. It was euphoric. Transcendent and terrifying. With the primordial energy of the cosmos, electrifying every molecule in my body, I could imagine how metas, hero or villain, could see themselves as more than human. Godlike.

How could anyone be trusted with this much power?

How could I trust myself?

The ground rumbled and dirt started to fall upward as the cement truck squealed, before tearing apart.

Wheels and pieces of the frame erupted outward like shrapnel from a blast. A shard of metal sliced through my shirt and deflected off my stomach. The cab sailed southward, tumbling end over end, before crashing into the piled-up cars that formed the clearing's southern wall.

The massive concrete drum, ripped free of its housing, shot toward the school bus where Rictor, Vee, Alice, and T-Rex sat.

Time slowed as Bowie surged to the front of my mind. With a flicker of alien instinct, I **caught** the drum in midair, holding it for a second before allowing it to crash to the ground.

Thank you, I thought through the link Bowie and I shared. Annoyed disbelief flowed back to me before Bowie lapsed back into silence.

"Fucking hell," Vee breathed. Her face slack with shock, she finished her beer in a single long gulp.

"Guys." Rictor laughed. "I told you, we have nothing to worry about. See? Force field!" He tossed a beer can off the edge of the truck. Vee and I watched in growing horror as it arced to the ground, before shifting our shocked gazes to Rictor.

He chuckled nervously, scratching the back of his head. "Uh, I might have forgotten to turn it on."

After I finished hyperventilating and Rictor made sure the emergency force field was in place, we continued.

Despite my reservations, there was something else I wanted to try.

My vision tunneled, and a wave of dizziness washed over me. I staggered a step but caught myself.

"Brandon!" Vee's tone was sharp. "What the fuck just happened? Are you okay?"

"Yeah." I took a few steadying breaths.

"You sure?" Rictor scrolled quickly through data. "Your brain activity, your power signature, and your vitals—they all just spiked, and we got a *massive* burst of energy. Gravitons too. *Way* bigger than anything we've seen so far. What did you do?"

I gestured to a fist-sized lump of twisted metal about ten feet away. "Tried to crush a toaster."

Rictor blinked. "What?" He started looking through the sensor data. After a minute or so, he whistled. "I don't think you're squeezing it. You're exponentially increasing the force of gravity at a point inside it, causing it to collapse under its own weight. Almost like—"

"A tiny black hole," I finished, filled with a mixture of awe and disbelief.

Rictor nodded. "For a fraction of a second, yeah."

"The amount of energy required . . ."

"I told you, buddy. You're powerful." Rictor chuckled again, scratching his head. "But maybe don't do that, at least until we can learn more about it."

I nodded. Both times I'd done the move previously, Bowie had helped me. I hadn't been sure I could manage it on my own. Given the results, I wasn't sure I wanted to.

"Hey, I know!" Rictor said after a moment, excitement filling his tone. "Have you tried to fly yet?"

It turned out I could fly.

Kind of.

It wasn't a great start.

With just a trickle of energy, I was able to lift myself off the ground and move in three dimensions. Unfortunately, if manipulating objects was like learning to use a new pair of hands, flying was like learning to use an entirely new appendage altogether.

On my first attempt, I managed to float for a few terror-inducing moments, before landing face-first in a pile of old bicycles. I dragged myself off the ground and wiped my face, spitting dirt and weeds.

Reaching into the cooler, Vee pulled out a bottle of water, which she tossed down to me after momentarily deactivating the force field. "I'm not an expert, but I'm pretty sure it's not really flying if you're just smashing your face off the dirt."

Bowie was also amused. *I don't suppose you have anything to offer?* I thought to him. His response suggested he was just fine watching me drag my face through the dirt.

Eventually, I was able to hover and move in different directions, but the uncontrollable spasms of power almost invariably resulted in me crashing into the ground, the rusted cars around Rictor's practice field, or even the force field around the bus. Vee laughed so hard, she nearly fell off the bus's roof.

Despite the hiccups, attempting to fly was exhilarating, a rush of wild freedom beyond anything I'd ever experienced. Every fiber of my being thrummed with excitement, sharpening my senses and my reflexes. It was like being fully awake after a lifetime of sleep. After another hour of practice, I was pretty sure I'd gotten the hang of the basics, assuming I could get control of my powers.

My first halting attempts at flying also had another effect. For the first time, Bowie's alien thoughts radiated something like joy, even if it was tinged with bittersweet sadness.

Despite needing a shower after my clumsy practice— and maybe a tetanus shot—we kept going. Rictor needed more data, and moving junk around was the best way we had for him to get it. As frustrating as the process was, by the time the sun was drifting toward the horizon, I'd improved. Larger uses still resulted in spasms of power with uncontrollable effects, but I got a better handle on smaller stuff. With a bit of concentration, I could even move a few objects at once.

I wanted to try recreating the way I'd **jumped** from the safe house to the university rooftop, but as soon as I started, Rictor's energy alarms screamed and I nearly blacked out. We decided to save that for another day.

Finally, Vee waved me over as she deactivated the force field. "We're done. Come here."

Rictor, Alice, and Vee were examining data on Rictor's tablet as I climbed the rusted ladder to the roof of the yellow school bus and grabbed a beer, joining them. Rictor and Alice looked excited, but Vee radiated tightly controlled worry.

"What is it?"

Rictor chuckled, shaking his head. "We may have some news." He turned the tablet toward me and brought up two real-time displays. He pointed at one. "These are your brain waves, right?"

I nodded. "Okay."

"And *this* is the energy field surrounding you." He pointed at the other display.

I nodded again.

"When you're thinking, feeling, trying to activate your power, your brain activates along these pathways, which in turn interacts with the voidrium, which impacts your energy field, et cetera, et cetera."

I frowned. "We talked about this. I get the concept, but I'm not a neuroscientist."

"Just bear with me, buddy." Rictor swiped the screen, and a couple of graphs appeared. "These are some overlays of what that looks like."

More graphs. "And *these* are some readouts of you talking to Bowie. If Bowie was just a hallucination or some sort of psychotic episode, it would only show up as brain activity, right?"

"And . . . ?"

"And if he were just some weird echo of your power, it would look like this." Rictor gestured back to the display. "But it doesn't. It has its own energy signature. Highly complex." He swiped up, overlaying a different readout.

Vee nudged me. "*Think* about it."

Their meaning hit me like a hammer, the last bit of information confirming what I'd known for a while. "Oh shit."

"Oh shit, indeed, my friend!" Rictor grinned like a madman. "You're having a *very* close encounter of the third kind."

Bowie gave the mental equivalent of a grunt, as if to say he'd been trying to tell me that the whole time.

When we returned to the compound, Rictor patted me on the shoulder. "Hey, I know that was frustrating, scary even, but it was worth it." He tapped the tablet in his hand. "We got some great data. I'm pretty sure your power fluctuations are a by-product of your injury and the integration process. As you heal and the integration process continues, we should see the fluctuations lessen and maybe disappear altogether."

I nodded. "Can we do anything before then?"

He squinted, thinking. "It'll be close, but with the brain activity and the power readings, I *should* be able to rig up something that'll give you a little more control over your powers."

"Thank you." I closed my eyes for a second, relief washing over me in a wave. "What about Bowie?"

Rictor smiled ruefully. "That might take some time. We don't even know what he is, let alone how he communicates. But we'll work on it. I promise."

After that, Rictor and Alice disappeared into his workshop to get a jump on designing a device that would help me control my abilities. He also mentioned whipping up "a little something special," but with Rictor, it was hard to guess what that might be.

Vee went for a walk with T-Rex, more shaken by her near-death experience than she let on and wanting some time to decompress.

I took a long shower.

Vee came back while I was getting dressed. "That was fast," I said, but her expression stifled the grin spreading across my face.

"Inara reached out."

I nodded, fighting down a sudden spike of anxiety. "What'd she say?"

Vee pushed her black-and-red mane back and took a breath, a hint of worry in her large eyes. "It's happening. Tomorrow."

TWENTY-SIX

BREAKING THE LAW

I sat in the back of a battered minivan, dressed in the featureless black helmet and matching suit of hard-shell composite armor Rictor had printed for me, his "special surprise." He'd also included a floor-length *cape*, insisting it was a classic part of the look. I'd already gotten it stuck twice. The whole effect was "evil space wizard meets witch king."

I didn't love the armor, but Rictor had said I needed to look the part. Plus, he had argued it would conceal my identity, which was probably for the best, given I was a suspect in several active investigations and on my way to commit a slew of felonies.

Rictor had also taken it upon himself to engrave a black hole on the chest piece, the swirling lines of the accretion disk surrounding the singularity.

That, at least, I liked.

The Dead Kennedys' "Police Truck" blasted from the van's speakers while the driver, a deranged mime caked in dried blood, screamed about the death of

humanity's artistic soul. I didn't think mimes were supposed to talk, but it didn't seem to bother him. His
copilot, a woman made of smoke and shadow in a black
cloak lined with arcane symbols, took a drag on her
cigarette and did her best to ignore him.

In the back with me, an anthropomorphic lizard in
a scarlet mankini and a high-collared cloak ranted about
mammalian oppression to a man-shaped swarm of cockroaches in a trench coat, while a middle-aged pirate
checked his AK-47, throwing the occasional glare my
way.

It was definitely in the running for the strangest ride
of my life.

Reaching into a battered backpack, the pirate tossed
out a couple of empty beer cans in the process of fishing
for a spare clip. He stuffed the clip into his bandolier,
next to a trio of hand grenades spray-painted black and
finished with a white skull and crossbones stencil, giving
me a toothy smile that would have given a dentist nightmares.

"You heard of me?" Pulling a pendant out of his
ruffly shirt, the pirate unscrewed the top and snorted the
contents. His eyes widened, and his nostrils flared.

Like most pirates, he had a thick New Jersey accent.
I tried to ignore him, hoping my helmet prevented him
from making eye contact.

"Hey, new guy!" he yelled over the din of music and
deranged ranting. "I asked you a fucking question! You
heard of me?" He slid over and kicked my boot.

I looked down at his foot and then back. "No," I
grunted, my voice a deep growl thanks to the voice-
distortion system Rictor had installed in my helmet, along
with a bunch of other gadgets, and turned away.

Despite my response, I had heard of him.

Captain Jack was a lifelong D-list criminal who had gone over the edge after buying a haunted cutlass at a yard sale outside Trenton. He occasionally made the news with a signature blend of absurdity and violence.

Over the years, he'd robbed banks and worked as a hired gun for other criminals. He'd even tried to assassinate an Illinois state legislator who'd attempted to ban Talk Like a Pirate Day. He didn't have any powers I was aware of, unless you counted his terror-inducing dentition, but he was handy in a fight and happy to hurt people, qualities that counted for a lot in the small-time villainy and henchmen circles.

Captain Jack's smile curdled. "When we get out of this van, you listen to *me*. I've been doing this for years, and I won't let some first timer fuck up a good score."

I sighed.

Captain Jack scrambled toward me, putting his face close to mine and dropping a hand to the cutlass in his sash. His fetid breath steamed my visor. "And you better pray you can get that vault open." The pirate's voice was low and dangerous.

I thought about grabbing his jaw and squeezing. I was pretty sure I could crush his head like a tomato. However, the suit was new, and I'd already had enough blood on me in the past week to last a lifetime.

"Two minutes," announced Shade, the cloaked spectral woman in the front seat. "Jack, put your dick away." She turned around. I could see the shape of a frowning face, but it was painted in shifting smoke, translucent and shadowy. "I vouched for him, and besides, you're not in charge. I am. He'll get the vault door. Worry about yourself."

Captain Jack sneered at me and slumped back into his seat. "Sure, Shade. Don't worry about me." He took another bump from his pendant, dusting his mustache with cocaine, and grabbed his AK. "I'm a fucking *professional.*"

A minute passed. We made a couple of turns. A roiling ball of excited anxiety expanded in my stomach as we got closer.

"Mime, Lizard Prince, shut up!" Shade yelled. Their diatribes interrupted, the mime and anthropomorphic lizard lapsed into sullen silence. "We have three minutes until the police arrive once we're inside. We get in and subdue any security. New guy gets the vault open, while Mime and Lizard Prince keep a handle on the employees and customers."

Shade gestured to the mound of cockroaches in a trench coat. "Human Swarm will pop the safety deposit boxes and transfer the cash and any other valuables to the escape vehicle through the back passage, at which point we'll blow this van. Captain and I handle any police or heroes who show up. If a mask we can't handle arrives on scene, we abort and get the hell out of there."

"And remember,"—Shade shot a warning look at Lizard Prince, who sulked—"no bodies."

The van screeched to a halt in front of the Union City Commonwealth Bank in Chessbrook, an upscale shopping district near the water on Franklin Island. It was a sunny fall afternoon. The street was filled with pedestrians enjoying the early autumn weather as they made their way between the boutiques, coffee shops, and restaurants that lined the block.

I glanced at a café on the other side of the street. I'd written a paper there. They made a mean cold brew.

Lizard Prince was the first out, leaping through the minivan's wood-paneled side door and onto the side-walk. "Behold your doom, primate oppressors!" he screeched into the face of a middle-aged woman, his tail lashing furiously. The woman squawked and staggered back in shock, tripping over her puffy suede boots as Lizard Prince charged toward the bank entrance.

Shade was out of the passenger seat after him, her shadowy silhouette expanding into a cloud of smoke that billowed from her magical cloak and roiled through the air. She was still tangible, and as she expanded, she pushed the pedestrians out of our way, sending them stumbling from the door and clearing a path for us.

Mime somersaulted across the hood of the van, two cleavers appearing in his hands with a flourish.

"Ahoy, fuckers!" Captain Jack yelled, laughing and firing into the air. The pedestrians who weren't already fleeing started to scatter as terror rippled down the block.

The pirate looked back at me as he fumbled for another bump. "What the hell are you waiting for?" he yelled, before turning to follow the rest of the crew.

I paused for a beat, tallying the number of crimes we'd already committed, before jumping out and bring-ing up the rear.

Lizard Prince didn't bother with the door. Crashing through the glass and into the bank's marble-appointed lobby, he unleashed an ululating scream. An overweight security guard, easily sixty, who'd been leaning on a podium right inside stumbled back a step when he saw Lizard Prince and fumbled for the gun at his hip.

Lizard Prince pounced, sinking all four sets of claws into the guard's torso as he drove the man to the ground. The guard's shout was cut off with a wet sound of meat tearing as Lizard Prince ripped the aging rent-a-cop's throat out with his fang-filled maw. With blood pouring down his muzzle and soaking his mankini, Lizard Prince reared up, chewed twice, and swallowed, while the guard spasmed beneath him and died.

Screams erupted. Employees and customers scattered—except for a skinny teen in a red hoodie, too shocked by the sudden violence to move.

I was horrified, too, and probably in shock. I stared at the security guard, whose blood-spattered face was carved into lines of surprise. His neck was all but gone, a ruin of torn meat, gristle, and sinew pouring blood onto the faux-marble floor. My pulse pounded in my ears.

"God*damn* it!" Shade cursed, flowing in right behind Lizard Prince.

Another security guard, young, clean-cut, and brawny, came out of a back room, smoothly drawing a massive chrome pistol. He scanned the room and saw Lizard Prince, who was already up and moving toward him, screeching.

The guard's eyes widened.

His gun roared, the shots impossibly loud inside the high-ceilinged bank.

The first two missed Lizard Prince, who loped toward him like a cheetah. I felt something clip my shoulder, and the glass shattered behind me as a bullet tore through Mime's gut. He staggered and fell, mewling, while his cleavers clattered to the floor.

"My pain is a canvas, you philistines!" he screamed, before passing out.

The guard was still firing. Lizard Prince covered most of the ground between them in the blink of an eye. He was six feet away, his taloned hands reaching out and his bloody muzzle open in orgiastic battle lust, when the guard's next shots tore through his chest. Lizard Prince's own momentum sent him crashing to the ground, cape and mankini tangled.

Eyes wide and nostrils flaring, the guard reoriented to his next target as Shade flowed across the bank. He aimed at the cloak and began to squeeze the trigger, but Shade was already on him, swallowing him in coils of strangling smoke. The guard vanished under the cloud, reappearing only when Shade dropped his unconscious form to the ground.

"Jesus Christ," Captain Jack spat, staring disgustedly at Lizard Prince and tracking with his rifle for more threats. He stepped over Mime, boots squelching in blood. "What a shit show."

I tried not to hyperventilate, but my breath was fogging up the inside of my helmet.

Expanding again, Shade enveloped the remaining customers and employees, asphyxiating them into unconsciousness with her tenebrous form. She reformed by the vault door.

"New guy. New guy!" she hissed. "The vault door."

Captain Jack looked back at me in disgust. "Hey, asshole, snap out of it," he growled. "Do your fucking job."

I looked at him, uncomprehending, and then back at the corpse of the aging guard in front of me. A few roaches had slipped out of Human Swarm's coat as they came in and were lapping at the pool of blood as it spread toward my boots.

Stepping in front of me, Captain Jack raised his rifle and pressed the barrel to the front of my helmet. "Open the vault, or I'll open up your skull."

As the rifle filled my vision, my pulse raced and panic clawed at the edges of my mind. Intellectually, I knew it probably wouldn't even scratch me, but my animal brain was freaking out.

Something in my head flipped like a switch. The part of me capable of feeling terror—the part screaming with horror—shut off, overloaded. It would all be for nothing if I didn't finish this. Vee and Mom, Rictor and Alice—they were all in danger, and this was the path through it.

"Get out of my face," I snapped, the voice modulator turning the words into an electronic snarl. Captain Jack grunted, glaring, and shifted his gun. I stepped past him and over the dead guard. I didn't let myself look down, tried not to think about grandkids sobbing at his funeral, and headed toward the vault door.

It was massive, a circular disk more than six feet in diameter and a foot and a half thick, made of titanium alloy with trace bits of exotic metals. All but impenetrable.

I stopped about fifteen feet from it and flipped open the cover on the pad strapped to my arm. I fumbled with the interface, as my gloves made it hard to press the buttons.

Here goes nothing.

I toggled off the dampener and activated the stabilization field. Rictor and I had worked quickly to build it, and we were both almost certain it would work.

Almost.

Energy surged through me, welling up from within, an electric thrill coursing through every nerve in my body. Bowie came flooding back as well, a sulky presence brooding in a corner of my mind.

It was *working.*

A rush of exaltation flowed through me as my gravity sense expanded. Like the first time I'd used it, my other senses were nearly overwhelmed, but I focused. With the voidrium bonded to my nervous system, I could feel gravity—could **see** it. Something within me registered gravity in the same way eyes registered light. I could see the subtle waves connecting everything—a trillion, trillion microgravity fields overlapping and enveloping everything, from grains of sand to vast celestial bodies, all bound together in an impossibly intricate dance.

More than that, with the stabilization field, I could manipulate those fields or create new ones.

Rictor, you goddamn genius.

"You might want to get back," I said.

Focusing on the vault door, I extended a hand, took hold of it with my power, and **pulled**.

Nothing happened.

"A fucking shit show," Captain Jack said again, disgusted. "Let's just get the tills and—"

I **pulled** harder, channeling more energy. The walls and floors around the vault cracked thunderously, and the building shook as squeals of twisting steel echoed through the interior. Pieces of concrete and plaster erupted from the wall, pelting me with debris. Captain Jack cursed when something cut open his face.

Around me, things began to float, untethered from earth's gravity by the energy pouring from me.

It was intoxicating.

It was beautiful.

The vault door whined, the surface beginning to twist as the metal deformed. The rumbling increased. Objects fell off desks or began levitating as glass broke and light bulbs exploded overhead.

I raised another hand, modulating the gravity field. The vault door screamed again, and the lock tore. The whole door bent further and further, swinging ever so slightly, jarring and shuddering as it did.

Sirens wailed in the distance.

Focus.

If I wasn't careful, I could rip the door off its hinges. I didn't want to crush anyone with it if I lost control.

Nearly there.

A chunk of concrete the size of a fist erupted from the wall like a gunshot, directly at my head. I threw up another field, a reflex I didn't know I had, and its trajectory changed, glancing off my helmet.

I staggered, but I kept hold of the vault door.

An alarm screeched in my helmet, and the heads-up display threw up an alert as the field generator in my helmet shut off abruptly.

Uh-oh.

The steady, precise force I'd been exerting became an uncontrollable spasm of power. The door exploded off its hinges and spiraled through the air. I threw myself down just before it sailed overhead.

Oh shit.

One of the customers was lying right where the vault door was going to land. With a thought, I altered its path, and the backwash of power sent more cracks through the walls.

Lizard Prince spasmed and sat up, having apparently regenerated. He threw his blood-spattered cape back, uncovering his head just in time to see the vault door come crashing down atop him, spattering me with a spray of gore.

I stabbed at the control panel on my arm, trying to

reactivate the dampener, but it wouldn't respond. Frantically, I wiped some of Lizard Prince off the panel. The building began to rumble violently, my control slipping further the more I panicked.

Got it! The dampener kicked in and my power cut off, taking an annoyed Bowie with it.

I staggered to my feet, wiping more of Lizard Prince off my faceplate.

Human Swarm released their human form, roaches spilling out of their trench coat and scuttling into the vault. They flowed up the walls and onto the shelves, picking up bales of money and wiggling into security deposit boxes, filling the vault with insects. The doors of various safe deposit boxes began to hiss as Human Swarm's acid melted through them with ease.

Captain Jack dragged himself to his feet. He was bleeding from a gash that ran from his scalp to just above his left eye. Unsteady, he turned toward me and took a step. He looked drunk on amphetamines and head trauma, his eyes glassy, but his face split into a grin.

"Fucking hell, new guy," he yelled. "That wasn't half bad! *And* we reduced the split!" He glanced at the liquid mess that was Lizard Prince. "Let's get the loot and get out of here."

"The back passageway is blocked," Human Swarm chittered. "The structural damage collapsed it. We can get out, of course, but the loot will not fit.

"Neither will you," they added as an afterthought.

Near the teller window, Shade regarded me from beneath the cowl of her cloak with eyes of swirling smoke and shadow. "Great," she muttered. "Just fucking great." Her frustration manifested as roils and billows within her smoky form.

The sirens had gotten louder. Cops didn't usually fare well against metas, but they were still an issue. Shade was probably immune to conventional attacks, and I suspected Human Swarm would need to lose a lot of their component bugs before they suffered, but Captain Jack didn't seem bulletproof. Unless they brought an antitank weapon, I figured I'd probably be fine, but just because bullets wouldn't injure me didn't stop them from *hurting*.

I also couldn't shake the thought that masks were probably on their way too.

Outside, the street was empty. Cars lined the curb, but it would take more time than we had to hack or hotwire one, assuming any of us had the skill. The only vehicle running was the same battered minivan we had arrived in. It sputtered and coughed black exhaust, shuddering a little.

It was also wired with incendiaries to burn away any traces of us.

Great.

Shade had the same idea. "The van—it's our only option. I can try to cloak it. Swarm, get the cash. I'll take care of the cops. Jack, you're driving. New guy, get Mime to the van. I'll deactivate the incendiaries."

Jack gestured at the puddle of gore that used to be Lizard Prince. "Any chance he'll heal from that?"

I hoped not.

"No idea." Shade shrugged. "But unless you have a Shop-Vac in your sash, we don't have time to find out."

Dragging myself away from the spectacle, I made my way past the dead guard to Mime, whom I grabbed. Despite being tall and sinewy, he was nearly weightless.

Shade moved into the vault and pointed at one of the safety deposit boxes. "There!" she hissed. Reaching out, her hand shifted into a swirling column that poured through the lock and tore the door off, before coming out with what looked like an amulet. "Yes!" The shifting smoke of her face made it hard to read her, but her satisfaction was clear.

Huh.

Turning, I started jogging toward the van, Jack and some of Human Swarm a few steps ahead of me. Captain Jack whooped with savage joy, firing another burst into the air.

"God*damn*!" he shouted, a toothy yellow grin splitting his beard. "I *love* this shit!"

The scream of guided munitions split the air, and the van exploded.

TWENTY-SEVEN

HEROES

Jack was blasted off his feet, landing hard, his poet shirt smoldering. A chittering screech erupted from Human Swarm as dozens of their constituent insects were immolated; the rest swarmed for cover.

I turned, instinctually shielding Mime's unconscious form with my body when a wave of force, heat, and roiling flame washed over me. I looked back, expecting to see my cape ablaze, but it was fine, made of nonconductive, flame-retardant material.

I grunted. Maybe the cape wasn't such a bad idea.

Through the smoke, figures descended from above and emerged from alleyways around the bank, sending a thrill of fear down my spine. *Shit.*

The first was a massive gunmetal-gray humanoid. It was nine feet tall, a bulky mix of curves, radar-defeating angles, and ablative plates that bristled with weapons, including a rack of missiles over its right shoulder, some sort of railgun over its left, and what looked like rotary cannons mounted on its forearms. An elongated head sat slightly forward between its massive shoulders, a trio of lenses on one end. Thrusters built into its back and feet strained to slow its descent as it dropped to the street. One of the metal behemoth's shoulder plates had an American flag spray painted on it.

The other had what looked like an ad for a car dealership.

Android or exosuit, I guessed.

Either way, the giant mechanical figure was orbited by three floating drones covered in weapons of their own.

At the same time, a muscular woman in a sleeveless, crimson bodysuit floated down, radiating power and danger. Her hair was black and close-cropped, and her skin seemed to ripple and shift like liquid bronze. Fans of energy extended like wings from her back, and she glowed slightly with warm golden-white light.

Near the north end of the block, a pale girl in a pink uniform with a short skirt and high boots pirouetted and struck a pose. Her palms emitted a piercing radiance too bright to look at.

The fourth member of the mask team, assuming no one was invisible or hiding, was a blond guy in a Japanese demon mask, a sleeveless black ninja tunic, and a pair of puffy pants covered in a variety of martial arts weapons. He was bouncing on the balls of his feet like a boxer, but he was moving too quickly, as if he'd been sped up somehow.

"Shit," Shade cursed. "We're screwed. Run for it."

She started to disperse into a swirl of smoke, and Human Swarm began to scatter as well.

"Wait!" My mind raced. I didn't think I had a chance in hell of running, and there was too much at stake—too many people in danger—for me to get caught.

I ran through scenarios as I set Mime down behind a newspaper vending machine.

"We can't take them," Shade hissed. "They're the Union City Defenders, one of the Vanguard expansion teams. The douchebag in the power suit is Arsenal, an MIT dropout with some car dealerships and too much disposable income. The metal chick is Warhawk, an alien bounty hunter with enhanced strength, resilience, and a *massive* stick up her ass. The wannabe popstar is Spotlight; she's got laser hands and a raging case of narcissism. The last one is Speed Demon, an internet martial artist with a magic mask that gives him super speed."

"Jesus fucking Christ," I grunted, "who names these people?"

"They're out of our league, new guy."

I studied the masks. Arsenal looked big but slow, and a human being was inside. "Swarm, if I can knock that thing over, can you get inside? Shut it down or disable the pilot?"

Human Swarm chittered in thought. "Probably."

The wannabe ninja was a problem. I was faster than I'd been, and with the dampener off, I had an instinct for what was going to happen, but against a real speedster, I might as well be asleep. "Shade, can you deal with the ninja? I'm guessing he still has to breathe."

Shade's swirling eyes pierced mine, her mind working. "I think so."

"Great." To my surprise, Jack's eyes were open, and he was moving. "Jack's still alive. He can deal with the popstar. His hygiene alone should do the trick. I'll take the alien."

Taking a breath, I opened my control panel and shut off the dampening field. Immediately, power crackled within me, time slowed, and my gravity sense returned. Bowie rushed back, and he was more than grumpy; he was *pissed*.

Maybe being shoved repeatedly into a back crevice of my brain and pulled out when our lives were in danger had something to do with it.

I didn't have the stabilizing field, so I couldn't control my powers. If Bowie fought me every step of the way, we were dead. I tried to communicate regret, appreciation, need, and danger to him, but Bowie retorted with what I was pretty sure was a mental *Go fuck yourself.*

I pushed through his anger, shoving the ideas of incarceration and imprisonment toward him as I begged him to help. Bowie recoiled, and I got a sense of grudging agreement.

If we lived through this, Bowie and I were going to need a couple's therapist.

"Well, if it isn't Captain Jackass," boomed Arsenal's voice from speakers as his thrusters cut out. He dropped the last few feet to the ground, cracking the pavement as he landed. His armored head turned to Captain Jack, who was staggering to his feet while beating out the flames spreading up his sweat-stained poet shirt. "Goddamn, Jack. An AK? Can't you at least buy American?"

Jack spat out a bloody tooth and glared, one eye already swollen shut. He raised his rifle. "Suck my dick, Arsenal!" he bellowed, opening fire.

"No thanks," Arsenal replied as bullets bounced off his armor. "If I wanted syphilis, I'd pay your mom a visit." Raising an armored gauntlet, he aimed at Jack, servos whining as the built-in rotary cannon started to spin. "What do you think, Warhawk? Does this constitute resisting detainment with lethal force?"

The bronze woman looked down, disgust plain on her too-perfect features. "End him."

Jack spat, ejected the magazine from his rifle, and reloaded. Not that it would matter.

"Hey, dickwad," I called out, striding through the smoke. Arsenal's armored head shifted to me, along with the rotary cannon.

I was glad my face was covered by my helmet, because I was terrified.

Arsenal's head tilted. "Who the fuck are you?"

With Bowie's help, I reached out with my gravity sense and **grabbed** the three heaviest vehicles in the area: a giant pickup truck, an overloaded delivery van, and an ancient luxury sedan.

Power crackling, I **pushed**, shifting the vehicles' "down" and increasing their relative gravity by many times that of the Earth's. Five tons of groaning metal turned into fifty and accelerated to several times terminal velocity in under a second.

The pickup and the delivery van hit Arsenal like artillery shells from different angles, metal shrieking as the gas tanks exploded. The force of the impact tossed him a few feet, burying him under automotive wreckage.

The sedan crashed into Warhawk, who'd still been in the air, and smashed most of the way into the fourth floor of an office building in a spray of glass and masonry, leaving the rear of the car dangling out.

"Now! Jack, get the girl!" I urged, glancing at Shade and the Human Swarm. Jack looked up, eyes glassy, but nodded.

Shocked by the ferocity of my automotive assault, Spotlight took a step back as Jack whirled on her. "Avast, fucker!" he yelled, charging toward her with his rifle up.

The discount demon ninja blurred, nearly disappearing as he covered the sixty feet or so between us in a fraction of a second. I caught the hint of motion over his shoulder and let my expanded instincts guide me, twisting to the side and barely avoiding a slash that flashed a hair's width from my eye.

Thankfully, his blade looked mundane, but I didn't want to risk getting hit. Energy equals mass times acceleration squared, and he was moving *fast*. I threw a cross, but he was already gone, a blur of cultural appropriation speeding away.

A roiling cloud of smoke and shadow raced after him, almost as fast. Half a beat later, a scuttling wave of insects flowed around pockets of burning oil and smoldering wreckage, swarming toward Arsenal, who was struggling under the weight of wrecked cars on his back.

Instinct screamed again, and I leaped to the side a split second before the sedan I'd thrown at Warhawk crashed into the ground where I'd been standing.

She floated in the air, ablaze with power, her liquid-bronze features twisted with rage. "You. Hit. Me. With. A. Car!" she roared. Diving at me, she turned to deliver a stomping kick at the last second.

I threw myself out of the way, and the pavement cracked beneath her as she landed.

Without missing a beat, Warhawk launched a blistering combination. I slipped her first punch, ducked her second, and covered up for the third. She must have expected it, because she caught my arms and wrenched herself forward, using every muscle in her body to drive her knee into my gut. It hit like a cannonball, cracking my armor and blasting the air from my lungs.

I tried to pull away, but she stepped with me, turning

my momentum into a throw that launched me into the building she'd just come from. I smashed into the entry-way twenty feet from where I'd been standing, shattering stone.

Pain shot through my back and side. *Ouch.*

She was *very* strong, probably stronger than me, and fast. Maybe more resilient too. If that weren't enough, she was definitely a better fighter.

Great. I was outclassed. Again.

Pushing myself up, I leaned against the shattered wall and sucked air into my lungs. My helmet was cracked nearly in two from the impact. Pulling it off, I tossed it aside, coughing as I inhaled the stench of burning fuel and melting rubber.

I glanced around at my coconspirators.

Human Swarm washed over Arsenal, assaulting joints and seals with their acidic bite, while Arsenal roared and batted at his armor. His drones bathed him in flame, but Human Swarm quickly scuttled away, using the suit as cover.

Shade and the bargain-basement ninja were a swirl-ing blur of smoke and shadow, bouncing from rooftop to rooftop as she tried to ensnare him.

Jack was cackling madly, throwing stenciled grenade after stenciled grenade at Spotlight, who was doing all she could to blast them out of the air with bursts of focused light from her hands.

I was the weak link.

My heart pounded, fear roiling in my stomach. What the fuck had I been thinking?

"I am considered a master of unarmed combat, you filthy primate. Even Empyrean has complimented my skill," Warhawk sneered, stalking toward me, ablaze with golden energy. "I've killed beings you couldn't conceive of on worlds you couldn't imagine."

Her contempt transmuted my fear and doubt into anger, sharpening my focus. Alien rage mirrored my own; Bowie might not have understood the words, but he was infuriated by the implications.

I smiled savagely, cracked my neck, and pushed myself off the wall. "Yo, daytime Emmy. That all you got?"

Warhawk growled. "Be glad I don't understand what that means."

Her lips peeled back, and she charged, clearing the twenty feet between us in an eyeblink, turning her last step into a leaping kick that sent her foot spearing toward my gut.

A glimmer of forewarning allowed me to bat the attack aside. Warhawk flicked out a jab as her foot touched the ground, but I expected it and slipped to the side, her fist missing my head by a fraction of an inch.

I came up with a hook that crashed into her jaw. She rolled with it, rotating into a scything hook kick. Foreknowledge, inhuman reflexes, and speed saved me. Ducking underneath, I kicked her planted leg, tearing it out from under her.

She hit the ground hard but rolled to her feet, an involuntary grunt of pain leaking out when she put weight on the leg I'd kicked.

"I'm sorry." I wiped some of the blood off my nose with a thumb. "You were saying?"

Eyes narrowed, Warhawk came forward again, more cautious this time. I slapped aside a probing jab and retaliated with a kick at her ribs. She stepped into it, robbing the kick of its force, and caught my leg, crushing it to her body. Her wings flared, launching us both at a stone pillar behind me. I struggled to turn her, but I had no leverage and no time.

We crashed through the pillar and the stone behind it, emerging into the women's clothing boutique on the ground floor of the building, destroying displays and sending mannequins flying as we crashed into the far wall.

The impact was tremendous. Pain exploded through my back, and I sagged, my vision tunneling, but Warhawk didn't let up. She grabbed a handful of my hair and dragged me to my feet, chopping at my temple with the back of her elbow.

I threw up an arm, but the force of her attack sent up a spray of masonry from the brick behind me. She threw another and another, battering my guard and smashing me into the stone.

I shoved out, creating space. Grabbing her biceps in a vice grip, I stepped past her and twisted, trading places with her as hunks of masonry rained down on us. Our snarling faces inches apart, we struggled for position, straining against each other.

Lifting a leg, I smashed my knee into her ribs. She absorbed it with a grunt and used a surge of strength to break my grip, slipping her arms inside mine and behind my head. I expected a knee, but a flash of foresight showed me my mistake just before her forehead smashed into my nose, staggering me with an explosion of pain.

I pushed back, anticipating another headbutt, but I was wrong again, and the flash of forewarning wasn't enough to make up for my mistake. Warhawk drove three hooks into my lower ribs and liver, each punch ringing like an anvil. The last hit right where Lynx's blade had stuck. Something in my side snapped, and blood shot from my mouth, spattering her bronze face with crimson.

Trying to cover my ribs, I dropped my arm, opening my chin to the hook that was already coming.

A flash of white filled my vision, and then nothing.

When I opened my eyes, I was on the ground looking up at Warhawk. She was breathing hard and favoring one leg, but her eyes, alight with bloodlust, told me she was only getting started.

She wiped some of my blood from her face with a finger and licked it. "Get up," she hissed. "I can't kill you in front of the cameras if you're lying on the ground, and I want your head for my trophy room."

I spat blood. "Not what I'd expect from a *hero*."

Reaching down, she grabbed me by the jaw and lifted me with one hand, pulling my face close to hers. "I don't care for your nonsensical designations, human. I'm content to serve Vanguard because they let me hunt miscreants like you."

"I take it back," I grunted. "You're *just* what I'd expect."

Warhawk contemptuously tossed me back through the hole we'd made in the building. I flew twenty feet before hitting the street and rolled a little farther.

Glancing around again, I saw my accomplices, still engaged in their own fights. One of Arsenal's limbs hung limp, acidic smoke coiling off it, while his drones still tried to burn Human Swarm away by bathing him in flame. The smoldering husks of insects scattered around their melee suggested it was working.

Shade and Speed Demon were a whirling blur. The speedster had shifted tactics, attempting to destroy her cloak, which left blood leaking from rents in the fabric.

Captain Jack had a smoking hole in his chest large enough to see through, but he was still cackling like a madman and returning fire.

Huh. Maybe Jack was more than a deranged cosplayer after all.

Dragging myself up again, I tried to shake the grogginess away and bounced a little, struggling not to topple over as I looked at Warhawk. A predatory smile crossed her face as she emerged from the damaged building.

It didn't take a genius to realize I couldn't take her, given that she'd been beating me like a drum. We were roughly equal, in terms of strength and resilience, and I might have been a bit faster, but she was more experienced, this being my first rodeo. Even my foresight, instincts, and speed weren't enough to offset the ocean of training and combat experience that separated us.

In a fair fight, I was dead.

Uncle Mike said fighting fair was a sucker's game, particularly if you couldn't win.

It was time to cheat.

I exaggerated my swaying and lowered my guard, doing my best to look dead on my feet. It wasn't hard; I was almost there.

"You want my head?" I said, slurring a little. "Come and take it."

She stepped **up**, her wings igniting, and shot toward me, a murderous angel cast in gleaming, blood-spattered bronze.

My eyes crackled with violet light as Bowie and I worked in unison to **catch** her, freezing her in the air ten feet from me. Her eyes widened. She tried to move, but she was frozen in place with unbreakable shackles of gravity.

"Catch," I spat as a delivery truck crashed down on her at nearly the speed of sound. It hit Warhawk with the force of a meteor strike, and the impact caused a roaring blast wave that shattered windows for blocks and left a smoldering crater in the pavement.

Squinting, I eventually caught a flicker of bronze beneath the twisted wreck of the delivery truck in the middle of the crater. I wasn't sure if she was dead. I wasn't sure I cared.

Bowie roared in triumph inside my head, but instead of victory, a pit of horror opened in my gut.

I staggered back a couple of steps, looking around. The devastation we'd unleashed was stunning. Oily smoke poured from the burning wreckage of cars along a street strewn with glass, pits gouged out of it as if it had been hit by artillery shells. Most of the buildings on the block were partially ablaze, their stone facades chipped by bullets or shattered by impossible strength.

Car alarms and shouts echoed on the wind, along with the sound of rapidly approaching sirens.

Yet to my utter surprise, we'd won. Shade finished suffocating Speed Demon, dropping his limp form from coils of shadowy smoke before she reformed and landed. Her cloak was tattered, but still whole.

Arsenal lay still, other than the occasional spark from the small electrical fires that burned across his suit. Smoking holes the size of quarters were visible near joints, seams, and access ports. The drones hovered in what appeared to be standby mode.

Human Swarm reassembled themselves, but they'd lost a lot of mass and looked more like a chittering child made of insects in an adult's trench coat.

Spotlight was gone, probably driven off by Captain

Jack's charm. The pirate listed to one side as he turned, an expression of shocked surprise on his face. He barked a laugh.

"Jesus Christ, new guy," he bellowed across the ruined street, where acrid smoke poured from pools of burning fuel. I could see through the hole in his chest, and his beard was on fire. "Why didn't you fucking lead with that?"

TWENTY-EIGHT

FRIENDS IN NEED

Ow," I grunted as pain shot through my side.

"Quit whining." Vee grinned, taking the sting out of her words, as she shifted in bed beside me.

"Sorry." I smirked. "I'll try to keep my pain to myself."

"Good. T-Rex doesn't have time for your shit."

We both glanced at the giant cyborg mastiff, who snored thunderously in the corner of the bedroom I'd been stuck in for the last thirty-six hours, barring trips to the bathroom and a few medical scans. "He's a real workaholic, that dog."

After Warhawk had dropped, we'd fled down a manhole, stumbling through sewer tunnels for blocks before eventually reemerging. Jack hotwired a battered hatchback that was older than I was and drove us to the abandoned warehouse Shade had chosen as our fallback point. The back-alley doc Shade had had waiting gave Mime even odds of survival but promised to take care of him.

We'd been forced to leave most of the money behind, but from the way Shade clutched the necklace she'd pulled out of the safety deposit box, I suspected it had been the real target anyway. When we finally split up, she told me our "mutual friends" would be in touch, and I waited with a battered grocery bag full of nearly twenty grand for the Danger Van to pick me up.

I hadn't expected a payout, but Shade had insisted. When I got back to Rictor's place, I handed him the bag, minus the few thousand I kept. "Call it rent," I muttered as I stumbled past.

Unable to shake the memory of the dead security guard's sightless expression or the devastation we'd unleashed, I didn't want the money. The whole experience left me feeling sick and shaken.

The next day, Inara reached out, extending her appreciation and letting us know she and her people were already looking for Lynx. She told us to lie low and expect a call in a week or so.

Lying low sounded great.

Despite my superhuman toughness, Warhawk had broken three ribs, my nose, and one of my orbitals, in addition to battering me with bruises, cuts, and contusions. With this new set of injuries, on top of the wounds from my second encounter with Lynx, I planned to spend the next several days convalescing in bed, rapid healing or not.

My injuries, though, weren't the only reason to keep my head down.

Footage of the bank robbery, including the fight with Warhawk and her team, had been posted on the internet almost instantly, and it already had more than three million views. Both local and national news sites had picked it up. Apparently, there were a lot of people who wanted to watch some of Vanguard's newest members get their asses handed to them by a group of unknown villains stupid enough to rob a bank in broad daylight.

Since I'd made the mistake of taking my helmet off after Warhawk cracked it, I'd been identified seconds after the video hit the internet. Thanks to the waitress at Dellah's, I'd also been connected to the incident at the diner.

Between the explosion, Nate's murder, the diner, my brawl on Washington Island, and now a bank robbery, the press had all but branded me the next Dr. Catastrophe. I couldn't exactly blame them. The sequence of events didn't paint a sympathetic picture, particularly given how short a span of time it had all happened in.

Just like that, I was a supervillain.

What can I say? It was a busy week.

Articles like "Physics Student Robs Bank" and "Mass Murderer Trounces Vanguard" were everywhere. There were also profiles of me, some more accurate than others. Most took the "budding psychopath with a history of trauma and violence" angle.

Despite thousands of other targets, most of whom were *actual* supervillains, dozens of masks, both individuals and teams, had issued statements promising to bring me in. Some were no-name D-listers hoping to capitalize on the latest hot thing for a ratings bump, but others even I recognized.

Gryphon and his team got in on the action too, posting a video online. Gryphon seemed pretty pissed, which made sense. I'd slipped right through his meaty fingers.

Even the Vanguard public liaison, a well-coiffed woman in her thirties, had mentioned me by name in a press conference about the robbery. She promised that Vanguard would devote resources to my capture, though only after confirming that none of the Union City Defenders had died in "the incident."

Nate's father had held a press conference too, stating that he was fully cooperating with the police and would use any and all of his considerable resources to bring whoever was responsible to justice. As I was now the prime suspect, I guessed he was talking about me. The idea of a billionaire industrialist with a company focused on advanced weapons tech bent on my destruction didn't exactly fill me with rainbows, but it was a problem for future Brandon.

Current Brandon had plenty of his own issues.

At least Bowie and I had reached an uneasy peace. I could still feel him watching, but the raw animosity and ire were gone, replaced by confusion, irritation at the dampener, and what I interpreted as weariness.

Knowing Bowie wasn't just a complex hallucination, I spent some of my time in bed trying to communicate with him, starting with simple concepts and words. It might have been my imagination, but we seemed better able to understand each other. Maybe it was all the head trauma, but his incomprehensible thoughts and impressions were starting to make sense.

Vee leaned down and kissed me lightly before smelling herself. "I stink. I need a shower. Want anything?"

I winced at another jolt of pain. "New ribs?"

Vee tilted her head, pretending to think. "My rib guy is out of the country. I could probably get you a spleen. You can never have too many of those."

"I'm good on spleens, but some water would be nice."

"Your loss." She shrugged, her lips turning up at the corners. "One water, coming up."

Hearing the door shut, T-Rex opened an eye, surveyed the room, and then dragged himself to his feet and lumbered onto the bed. It squealed in protest as the massive dog settled in the spot Vee had just vacated. Pausing just long enough to lick the side of my face, he closed his eyes again.

I gave him some pets, then reached for the remote and turned on the TV.

It was Resistance Day, and the crowds gathering for the celebrations in Union City, and across the world, occupied most of the press. A lot of it was focused on Vanguard, who was using Resistance Day as the official launch of its new teams. I guess I'd kicked a little dirt on that one.

I settled on some more *D-List* reruns.

Vee eventually came back in nothing but a towel, which she pulled off and used to dry her hair as soon as the door shut. I whistled appreciatively, my eyes playing across her tattooed brown skin, marveling at the lines and curves of her slim form.

Vee snorted, but her eyes glittered mischievously. "You're too fragile for physical activity, remember? Let's give it a couple of days."

I smiled widely as I started to reply, but the expression curdled and died on my face when something caught my eye on the TV behind Vee.

Itzel, Harvey, and Abby were on a breaking news alert.

I hit the volume, dread filling my stomach.

"In a startling attack that left more than twelve police officers and two local heroes dead, four individuals in protective custody were taken by a masked assailant," the news anchor began. "Brandon Carter, the researcher linked to the recent explosion on the Union City University campus and several other incidents, is the prime suspect."

Following my gaze to the screen, Vee sat heavily, her expression a mixture of disbelief and shock.

"We have footage of the attack, though some viewers may find the following content disturbing."

The news feed cut to security footage from a hotel lobby. Five cops, part of the guard detail, were sitting inside when someone wearing a near-perfect copy of the armor Rictor had made for me burst through the door. The armored figure was about my height but more heavily muscled, not that people who weren't me would be able to tell.

The cop by the door, a doughy guy with a thick mustache, drew his weapon and opened fire immediately, but the bullets didn't penetrate the imposter's armor. Without pausing, he drove his fist *through* the cop's chest as he advanced, making short, messy work of the rest of the security detail before going up the stairs.

Another security camera outside showed the imposter marching Abby, Itzel, and Harvey, along with a mystery guy I didn't recognize, toward a waiting van.

A couple of street-level metas—a bulky kid with dark skin in a domino mask and a kung fu uniform and a pasty girl on rollerblades carrying a baseball bat—tried to stop whoever he was. They were young, still in their teens maybe.

They didn't stand a chance.

After a brief exchange, they attacked. The girl on rollerblades darted in, pirouetting and launching a kick at the imposter's head. An invisible force caught the kick, holding her for a second before another unseen attack hit her in the chest with enough force to send her crashing through the windshield of a car down the block.

The other kid roared, launching what looked like *snakes* out of his hands. The imposter caught one behind the head, glancing curiously at the hissing reptile. Another invisible force struck the kid like a wrecking ball and left him broken on the pavement dozens of feet away.

"Fucking hell," Vee breathed. Her phone beeped, and she glanced at it. "Huh."

"What is it?"

"I just got a notification from KoVault, a secure mail service I haven't used in years."

A knife of dread slipped between my ribs. "That's a hell of a coincidence. Do you think it's Lynx?"

Vee chewed her lip. "Maybe" Grabbing her laptop, she flipped it open and pulled up KoVault. Sure enough, a new email from an unknown sender waited in her inbox. After checking to make sure it didn't have any nasty surprises, she opened it.

The email contained a single phone number.

Vee and I turned to each other. "Damn it!" she cursed again, loud enough to wake T-Rex, who barked ferociously as he shot up, looking around. "I thought they'd be safe in protective custody. I underestimated them. *Again.*"

My warm sense of safety collapsed in on itself, crushed beneath sudden worry and guilt, which was then eclipsed by a cold rage that left me shaking.

"We both did. Can you secure a line?" I asked quietly. "I have a phone call to make."

Vee closed her eyes and forced herself to breathe. "Give me a minute." Reaching into her backpack, she pulled out a phone. "Here, this should be good for at least five minutes. We'll toss it when you're done."

I nodded, took the phone, and dialed the number.

"Mr. Carter," Lynx purred, her voice filled with malevolent satisfaction. "I see you got my message."

Hatred and rage flowed like lava in my mind. I fought the urge to scream. Bowie roared in my head, adding his fury to mine.

"What do you want?" I asked, my voice shaking.

"You, of course. We want you."

"So you can kill me?"

"On the contrary. You're much more *interesting* than we could have imagined. It's been decided that you could still be useful. If you turn yourself over, your friends might walk away from this in one piece."

"What guarantee do I have that you'll let them go?"

Lynx laughed. "The only guarantee you get is that if you *don't* turn yourself over, I'll take them apart slowly and record it. And when I eventually catch you, I'll make you watch it."

Numbness radiated from my core outward, horror dousing the rage.

"Do you understand?" Lynx demanded.

"I understand."

"Good," Lynx purred again. "Come to the warehouse at the corner of Ninth and Morrow in Southbrook at eleven p.m."

"Ninth and Morrow in Southbrook at eleven," I confirmed, dread crushing my chest like a vice.

"If you tell anyone—the police, the media, or any masks—we'll know, and I'll make your friends pay in pain for your inability to follow instructions. Are we clear?"

"Got it."

The line went dead.

"Brandon!" Vee's voice was sharp. "If you walk in there, she'll fucking kill you, maybe worse. Then she'll kill Abby, Harvey, and Itzel, before hunting down me, your mom, Rictor and Alice, and anyone else who might know *anything*."

I nodded, battered by waves of helpless rage and despair. "I know, but if there's even a *chance* they'll let Abby, Harvey, and Itzel go, I don't have a choice."

"There isn't." Vee put her hands on either side of my face, forcing me to meet her eyes. "She said if we told the cops, the press, or any masks, they'd know, right? But we have some friends she probably doesn't know about."

"What if she's already connected me to Inara and her associates?"

Vee's voice was surprisingly calm. "If you go to that warehouse alone, everyone dies."

She was right. There was only one chance that any of us had to get out of this alive, and I had to take it.

"Call Inara."

We met Inara in the same private room in the Inferno. She smiled faintly when we entered, but there was an edge of wariness about her that hadn't been there at our last meeting.

"Brandon, Vee, it's good to see you both again. We haven't found anything yet, but—"

I cut her off. "They've taken my friends."

Inara frowned. "Tell me what happened. From the beginning."

We told her about the abductions, the message, the email, and the phone call.

Inara's frown deepened, and she checked her watch. "Brandon, it's nearly six. If you're going to meet them at eleven, that leaves very little time. You're asking us to take a *very* significant risk."

"One way or the other, I'm going. With your help, I have a chance of getting out alive. Without it . . ." I chuckled mirthlessly. "The alternative wouldn't be good for any of us."

Inara's eyes narrowed as the shadows around the room thickened, drinking in the light. "I'd be careful who you threaten, Brandon."

"It's not a fucking *threat*," I snapped, overcome with stress and worry. "But I can't do this alone. Before they kill me, they might want to know who else I've told, and I don't think they'll ask nicely."

"Whatever your angle is, you need us," Vee cut in. "Whoever the fuck these people are, they're good at covering their tracks. Do you want to know who they are and what they're doing? This is your best chance."

Inara regarded us silently.

"Please," I begged, my voice shaking.

Inara's gaze softened. "As I said before, we're not monsters." She took a sip of her wine and slowly swirled the glass, gazing pensively into the deep crimson liquid. "I won't promise anything, but I'll confer with a colleague."

I blinked. "Aren't you in charge?"

A hint of amusement glittered in her eyes. "Not *quite*. Wait here."

As soon as the door shut behind Inara, Vee reached across the table and squeezed my hand. We waited in silence for a few minutes that felt like an hour, dread and guilt crushing me like a weighted blanket.

When Inara returned, she spoke briskly. "I've spoken with my associate. We feel the opportunity this presents outweighs the risks. We'll do what we can, but we don't have a lot of time. We have to go."

I closed my eyes, nearly sagging with relief. "Thank you." I sat for a moment, fighting the sudden wave of emotion, and then stood, moving toward the door.

Inara smiled faintly.

Her eyes shifted, becoming inky pools of utter darkness. Her skin darkened to midnight blue as two slightly curved horns erupted from the crown of her head. Her ears lengthened, tapering to points that emerged from hair so dark, it seemed to drink in the light. Behind her, a tail appeared, lashing back and forth.

"Fucking hell," Vee breathed.

"Almost." Inara grinned, displaying teeth that were pointed and sharp. "There's no need for the door. We'll be taking a different route."

The shadows thickened again, swallowing the light in the room before they started moving, flowing into Inara's monstrous shadow, which seemed to grow.

"A warning," Inara said, her voice more ominous than before. "Mortals have told me that this can be uncomfortable."

Vee's eyes widened. "*Mortals?* What can be unc—"

The shadows reached up and pulled us down, swallowing us whole, too fast for us to scream.

TWENTY-NINE

AN ASSEMBLY OF VILLAINS

We fell, enveloped in darkness. Other than Vee's hand clutched in mine, the shadowy abyss was completely absent of sensation, as if my physical body had ceased to exist, leaving my psyche howling in an endless void. It could've been a second or a century.

Bowie wasn't thrilled either, alarm and agitation flowing through our link.

Abruptly, we stumbled into a well-appointed sitting room. I sucked in a lungful of air, nearly overwhelmed by the sudden rush of sensory stimuli, and leaned against a wall as vertigo crashed over me. "Do you have a trash can? I think I'm going to be sick."

"What the *fuck* was *that*?" Vee gasped, bent over.

"Apologies," Inara replied, not quite smirking. "As I said, it can be uncomfortable."

"That's a word for it," I muttered. Forcing myself to take slow, deep breaths, I looked around.

The sitting room had a Victorian feel, with dark wood paneling, a fireplace, and heavy antique couches.

Paintings covered the walls, and two large windows looked out onto a wooded expanse beyond.

I shivered, fighting more nausea. "Where are we?"

"Think of it as a field office." Inara opened the door and gestured for us to follow. "Come on."

She led us out into a mansion with the same late-Victorian vibe. By the time I'd stopped feeling nauseous, we'd made our way to a set of double doors on the second floor that opened into a library with a heavy wooden table surrounded by chairs, two of which were occupied.

A woman in yoga pants, a sweatshirt, and a familiar cloak sat facing the window, looking up when we entered. In her late twenties, she had shoulder-length dark-brown hair that framed an olive face with prominent cheekbones and an aquiline nose. She inclined her head to Inara before shifting her gaze to me, smirking. "Hey, boss. New Guy."

The guy beside her looked up as well, nodding to Inara. "Hello, Nyx."

The guy was nondescript, possibly early forties, with a strangely flat expression, but I recognized the trench coat. "Shade? Human Swarm?"

Shade nodded to Human Swarm. "Told you he'd recognize us."

Vee grunted, raising an eyebrow. "Nyx?"

Inara shrugged slightly, her tail swishing through the air behind her. "My actual name. Wait here." She slid back through the door, leaving us with two supervillains.

Shade looked me over. "It's good to see you up and about. You weren't doing so hot the last time I saw you."

"Getting beaten within an inch of your life will do that."

Shade glanced at Vee. "Who are you?"

"Vee."

"The hacker." Shade nodded, recognition in her eyes. "You did some work for me a few months back. Solid stuff."

Vee shrugged. "Customer satisfaction is my number-one goal."

A pained expression crossed Shade's face when she shifted her gaze back to me. "Hey, apologies. That whole job was a mess. Especially the guard. That shouldn't have happened. The Old Man has rules against killing baselines." Her expression twisted in disgust. "Fucking Lizard Prince."

I winced. "Are all your jobs like that?"

"No. We got a tip right beforehand that left us less than twenty-four hours to get what we needed, so it was amateur hour. If we'd had more time, we'd have planned better, gone at night . . ." She shrugged. "Anyway, you pulled our asses out of the fire back there. Thanks."

Swarm nodded as well. "Yes," they buzzed. "We are grateful."

"If you ever need anyone to take a beating, call me. I'll try not to bring the building down next time."

Shade chuckled, but Human Swarm's head tilted and then slowly swiveled to look at Shade.

Shade rolled her eyes. "It's a joke, Swarm."

"Ah." Human Swarm's expression didn't change.

I noticed a flash around Shade's neck. It was the pendant from the bank.

"Was that what the robbery was really about?" I gestured at the pendant. "Seems like a lot of trouble to go through for some bling."

Shade touched the necklace reflexively. "It's a little more than bling. This is a charm of anchoring. Without it, I'm stuck in my other form. I was trapped that way for years, unable to eat or sleep. Get laid. This allows me to change back."

"Damn." My eyes widened as I tried to imagine what that sort of existence must have been like. "How did you get stuck like that?"

Shade raised an eyebrow. "That's awfully personal, New Guy. You hitting on me?"

I glanced at Vee, who smirked. "Hey, I'm sorry. I didn't realize—"

"I'm messing with you." Shade chuckled. "My mom was a witch. My aunt killed her, usurped her coven, and trapped my soul in my cloak so she could siphon power from me. I got free, kind of, and I've been trying to stop my aunt ever since."

I glanced at Human Swarm. After a second, Shade nudged them. "Your turn."

Human Swarm leaned forward, and a roach fell from their chin to the table, before scuttling into their sleeve. "We are a hive of psychic, genetically enhanced insects that had the personality of our creator partially imprinted upon us when he was murdered by his partner, who stole his research, his startup, and his family."

My eyes widened. "Wow." I glanced at Vee, who looked pained.

"How do you look like that?" she asked.

"A holographic projector is installed in our coat. We can turn it off if you—"

"No, that's okay," Vee cut in, a hint of panic in her expression. She didn't love bugs and had been horrified when she'd seen footage of Human Swarm.

"Most of us have stories like ours." Shade shrugged. "Or yours. Not everyone's as willing to share, though."

The door opened. The first in was a muscular guy in his midforties in a black armor-weave tactical suit who moved with predatory grace. A shaggy mane of salt-and-pepper hair and matching beard did nothing to soften his severe features or hide the spade tattoo under his right eye. Blades were sheathed across his body, along with a pair of massive pistols at his hips. He slipped into the room and slid into a chair.

"Hey, kid. Hey, Swarm," he grunted, nodding to Shade and Human Swarm before shooting me an appraising glance. His voice was rough, deep, and tinged with a Spanish accent.

A lean woman in her late twenties with dark-brown skin and a shaved head strode in after him. A sleeveless leather vest showed off the tattoos covering her chiseled arms, but her most distinguishing feature by far was her eyes.

They were ablaze, like two molten orbs.

She radiated heat and fierce intensity, and the temperature climbed when she entered the room. Dropping into a chair, she gave Shade and Human Swarm a slight nod before her gaze swiveled to me, suspicion and skepticism on her face.

The last new arrival was, by far, the strangest. A slender humanoid robot with a slightly antiquated, almost steampunk aesthetic, wearing a top hat and greatcoat, sauntered in. A thrill of horrified fascination filled me when I noticed the back of its head was transparent, revealing a fluid-encased brain covered in electrodes that connected it to the robotic body.

It paused on the threshold, head tilting as it looked at me. *It's not polite to stare,* a male voice, deep and resonant, echoed in my head, tinged with amusement.

Sorry, I thought, slightly embarrassed.

He bowed slightly, revealing more of the brain behind the robotic face as he tipped his hat, and then glided to a chair, spinning it with a flourish before sitting.

Nyx came in last, having changed into a black, form-fitting armored suit. She shut the door and made her way to the head of the table, the shadows thickening and flowing around her as she moved. She sat at a slight angle to accommodate her tail.

I gawked for a moment, stunned by her transformation from business casual to demon chic, taking in her midnight-blue skin, horns, taloned hands, and tail. Even more unsettling, she was cloaked in otherworldly power that felt primordial and *hungry.*

I glanced at Vee. Her eyes were wide, and she slowly shook her head in astonishment.

The heavy-set guy surveyed the group before turning to Nyx. "This everyone?"

"Everyone available on short notice." Nyx nodded. "Thank you all for coming." She gestured to us. "This is Brandon Carter and Vee Devi. Brandon and Vee, this is Solitario, Pyre, and Professor Cerebrian." She motioned to the guy with the spade tattoo, the woman with blazing eyes, and the brain-in-a-bot in turn. "Aifa will be joining us remotely."

As she spoke, the holographic image of a woman composed entirely of flowing metal appeared in another chair, nearly indistinguishable from the rest of the villains present. "Correction," the hologram announced. "Aifa *has* joined you remotely."

Nyx paused, glancing at Pyre. "Where's Alyrea?"

Pyre shrugged. "Dealing with whalers near the Arctic Circle. Is the Old Man coming?"

Nyx smiled slightly, her gaze flickering to us. "He's been apprised of the situation. As usual, he'll show up when he's needed. We can begin."

Who the hell is the Old Man? I glanced at Vee. From her expression, she was wondering the same thing.

Nyx surveyed the assembled supervillains, her tail weaving through the air behind her. "You have all been briefed on the background, Vee and Brandon's involvement, and our primary target, but the situation has evolved. The target's agents have abducted four civilians, killing twelve police and two masks in the process. Earlier this evening, Lynx, his main field asset, reached out to Brandon, demanding that he surrender himself."

The atmosphere grew tense, and I glanced at Vee again. "Your primary target? Who the hell is *that?*"

Nyx looked at me, her ink-dark eyes meeting mine. "There are things we can't tell you, Brandon, but I promise we'll do everything we can to get your friends back. Now, can we continue?"

I took a breath and nodded, hoping they were as good as their word.

Nyx nodded back before looking around at the assembled villains. "The Old Man thinks there's a high probability that our quarry will be present tonight, which makes this too good an opportunity to pass up."

Drawing a knife from a sheath on the chest, Solitario started trimming his fingernails. "We weren't planning to move on him yet. Is the package ready?"

Nyx glanced at Aifa, who nodded. "Forgemaster and I are working out a few last-minute bugs. No offense." The hologram smirked at Human Swarm, who looked confused. "It'll be done."

Solitario nodded. "Good. We'll need it if we're

going to have a chance in hell, and I don't feel like dying tonight. What do we know about this Lynx?"

Nyx shrugged. "Very little, except that she's dangerous. She appeared out of nowhere a few years ago and has been linked to dozens of killings, many of whom were metahuman. The Old Man wants her captured. Under no circumstances are we to kill her."

Nyx and Solitario shared a significant glance. "Any idea why?" he asked. "It'd be easier to just put her down."

Nyx's tail flicked behind her. "Nothing I can share, but it's nonnegotiable."

Great, more secrets. I hoped I wasn't making a mistake my friends would pay for by trusting these people.

"Whoever she is, she can't be that good." Pyre's molten eyes shifted to me. "He's still breathing."

"The first time we met, Lynx beat me until she got bored and then left me to bleed out while she rigged my machine to explode. I should have died. Did die, maybe." I stood up, slowly lifting my shirt to show them the scar right below my ribs.

"Goddamn," Shade muttered, taking in the lattice of silvery scars that covered my torso.

"The second time, she shot me in the head and almost cut me in half." I gestured to the scars on my temple, my brow, and the vicious scar along the side of my ribs. "I managed to get away, but only because something happened to her. She was confused, as if she'd forgotten why she was there. I'd have been dead otherwise."

"If her encounters with Brandon aren't convincing, take a look at some of her other victims." Nyx pulled up a list of names, displaying them via a holoprojector built into the table.

"She killed Karnivore and TermiGator?" Solitario raised an eyebrow. "Damn."

Shade leaned forward. "Isn't TermiGator the guy who had his DNA fused with that of an alligator in a lab accident in South Florida? I thought he was a joke."

Solitario shook his head. "That's Mangator. He *is* a joke. Ripped off a liquor store, went on a bender, and passed out on the hood of Inquisitor's cruiser. Termi-Gator's the reptiloid cyborg from an alternate future timeline, the one always putting lasers on reptiles and trying to take over the world. Real bastard."

"And Attila the Nun," Pyre grunted, a hint of grudging respect in her tone. "That bitch was crazy, but she was tough."

She killed Dr. Radioactique as well? Professor Cerebrian's mental voice sounded almost sad. *He had panache.*

Solitario turned to me, reassessing. "You must be tough as shit or lucky as hell."

I shrugged. "I don't really feel like either."

Do we know anything about him? Professor Cerebrian's voice echoed in my head as he pulled up an image of my doppelgänger from the abduction video.

Nyx shook her head. "Only what's on the footage."

"I ran them both through the database," Aifa offered. "But we didn't have enough for a match."

"There's more." Nyx's eyes narrowed. "We have evidence to suggest our target has acquired significantly more of the voidrium used in Brandon's experiment."

Pyre turned to me. "How much of that shit detonated in your lab?"

"A little more than two grams."

"And how much do they have now?"

I took a breath. "A hundred kilograms, give or take."

The villains at the table shared concerned glances.

"It's worse than it looks," I said quietly. "Voidrium's exotic matter. It generates power in excess of whatever it's fed. With that much going off simultaneously, the reaction would be *very* bad."

Solitario leaned forward. "How bad are we talking?"

I did some quick mental math and then wished I hadn't. "We'd need a lot of new maps."

Pyre leaned back into her seat, her eyes blazing as she rubbed a hand over her shaved head. "There are easier ways to blow something up. What does your machine do?"

"It uses a Nyserian exception to sidestep Sabri's paradox, breaching the Colville membrane at a frequency near—"

Solitario snorted, amusement spreading across his bearded face. "Maybe dumb it down for the kids in the back, eh, Professor?"

"Sorry." I took a breath. "It uses the voidrium to manipulate gravity and punch a microscopic hole from our multiversal thread to another to transmit and receive electromagnetic waves, like a radio that picks up signals from parallel Earths. The thing is, the design's scalable. With more voidrium, they could open a bigger hole."

"How big?"

I did some more mental math. "The statue of liberty could walk through it without ducking. Assuming the puncture in the multiversal thread were stable, they could keep it open as long as they had power."

Solitario chuckled humorlessly. "You're just full of good news, aren't you?"

"There's something else," I said, regarding Bowie,

who seemed to be listening. "The voidrium isn't just matter. There are alien beings inside it. Alien beings the Rakkari enslaved and trapped to use as faster-than-light drives."

Nyx considered. "We'll do what we can to retrieve it," she said after a moment, glancing around at the assembled villains. "Our target wants Brandon badly enough to expose himself. It might be a long time before we get another chance like this. The Old Man thinks it's too good an opportunity to pass up, and I agree, but you know who we might be going up against. Any of you are free to walk."

Everyone seemed to consider, but no one moved.

Nyx regarded me for a moment, black eyes unblinking. "As it stands, our target instructed Brandon to meet a pickup team at a warehouse in Southbrook at eleven tonight, at which point they'll almost certainly transfer him to another location."

Solitario flashed a razor-sharp grin at Nyx. "So we have three hours to plan an assault on an unknown number of hostiles, at least three of whom are metahuman, with unknown capabilities and motivations at an unknown location, while extracting four noncombatants. Not to mention, trying to capture the person we're *actually* after, which isn't exactly trivial, particularly considering our ace in the hole is untested."

Nyx smiled faintly. "If you wanted easy, you'd have found another line of work."

"The Old Man gave this a green light?"

Nyx nodded. "He did, assuming we can come up with a plan that won't get us all killed." She paused for a second. "What do your instincts say?"

Solitario considered for a moment. "It's risky but not

Anti-Hero Blues

impossible." He glanced at me. "If they're picking him up in Southbrook, they'll take him to the port by ground transport. To one of the private docks, probably. It's only ten minutes from there, and the Resistance Day celebration means there are a *lot* of eyes on the sky tonight. Even with stealth technology, it's too risky to fly. Better to take a circuitous route and blend in with the traffic."

Nyx nodded. "That was my read too."

Solitario's brow furrowed. "If he has a teleporter, we're fucked."

Shade frowned pensively. "Can we put a tracker on Brandon?"

Solitario shook his head. "They'll check him for bugs. We'll have to follow the pickup team, assess the target, and then improvise. With more time, we could try and infiltrate beforehand, but that's not on the table."

Aifa leaned forward, excitement on the quicksilver metal of her holographic features. "I'll get eyes on the docks. We should be able to reduce the number of potential targets."

Solitario nodded. "That'll help."

Even from here, I can start scanning the docks for hostile intentions, projected Professor Cerebrian.

"They'll be wearing psi dampeners," Pyre grunted.

I'd say that's still rather telling, wouldn't you?

Solitario nodded. "They're probably operating out of a cargo ship. It's bigger than a warehouse, easier to shield, and mobile. Given who we're dealing with, we should assume they've taken precautions, but it won't be too hard to crack. We need a few of us on the inside to get New Guy's friends out before shit pops off, or they'll be dead before we make it in. Any ideas?"

Pyre made a fist that erupted into flame, gazing

307

thoughtfully into the firelight. "Can we come up from underneath?"

Solitario twirled a knife while he considered it. "We don't have the time to get the gear we'd need."

Nyx's eyes widened. A predatory smile spread across her face as her eyes settled on Human Swarm. "How about a *matryoshka*?"

Everyone slowly looked at Human Swarm. A smirk crossed Shade's face as Pyre's frown deepened.

Solitario snorted in amusement, flashing Nyx another razor-sharp grin. "It's been years since we did one of those." He considered for a moment. "It could work."

Human Swarm slowly swiveled his head to Shade. "What is a *matryoshka*?"

Nyx and Solitario spent the next hour planning, with everyone else adding suggestions drawn from their own expertise. Despite being rough around the edges, they were professionals who had obviously worked together before. None of them seemed like the narcissistic sociopaths I'd expected. They seemed to respect, trust, and even like each other. They were also surprisingly calm, planning an assault on a fortified target held by dangerous enemies the way I'd plan a camping trip.

For a group of supervillains, they seemed surprisingly functional.

I, on the other hand, was about as far from calm as it was possible to be without screaming. I had questions—about who their leader, the Old Man, was and who they were after—but they weren't providing answers, and I had no choice but to trust them. Whoever their target was, they'd been after him for a while, and he seemed *very* dangerous. I hoped I wasn't about to get my friends killed.

When they were done, Nyx looked at Solitario. "Well?"

"There's a lot riding on him." Solitario pointed at me with his knife. "If he can't handle it . . ." He turned to Shade. "You've worked with him. What do you think?"

Shade considered me and then nodded. "New Guy's solid. He'll get it done."

I nodded to her in thanks, trying my best to keep the worry curdling my stomach off my face.

"Good enough for me." Solitario slammed his knife back into the sheath on his chest. "Try not to fuck this up, *cabrón.*"

The rest of the assembled villains turned to me. Aifa and Human Swarm stared at me unblinkingly. Shade nodded in encouragement as the furrow in Pyre's brow deepened. The glittering voids that were Nyx's eyes regarded me expectantly, while Professor Cerebrian tilted his head.

I took a breath and looked around. "Let's do this."

Nyx and the rest of her people left to prepare, leaving Vee and me alone.

"Hey," Vee said, her dark eyes fierce. "We'll get them back."

I looked at Vee, seeing her with startling clarity. I absorbed the way the light reflected in her eyes. How her lips shifted subtly. The way her muscles moved under her skin.

Despite the horror of the last week, we'd found our

way back to each other. Fear constricted my chest, along with gratitude for the time, however fleeting, we'd had.

"Vee." I sighed. "Look, I don't know what's going to happen tonight, but yo—"

Her eyes widened and then narrowed, flashing with anger as her nostrils flared. "Don't!"

I blinked. "What?"

"I don't want to hear your bullshit self-sacrificial speech," she growled, pinning me in place with the ferocity of her gaze. "That's just you giving yourself an out. Fuck that. Fight."

I stared into Vee's eyes. Determination burned in them as she grabbed my hand and squeezed. "Just look at the shit you've been through. Most people wouldn't have survived it, powers or not, but you've *never* given up. Don't start now."

She was right. I'd lost a parent, spent years homeless and on the run, never feeling safe. Nearly been killed. Watched as Mom was devoured from within by illness. I'd been fighting my whole life. Sure, it all left scars, but scars were just a record of what we'd survived.

None of it had broken me.

In the last week alone, I'd survived the impossible. I didn't know what was going to happen, but there was no way I was giving up.

Abby needed me. So did Itzel and Harvey. They were in this because of me, and I couldn't let them down. Lynx, and whoever else was behind this, had hurt or killed hundreds of people in pursuit of their goals, and I had no doubt they'd hurt a lot more before they were done.

I nodded slowly. The resolve in her eyes lit a spark within me.

"Whoever the hell these people are, whatever they want, it doesn't matter." Vee leaned in, her voice quivering with intensity. "They have no *idea* who they've fucked with, but they're about to find out."

As if he'd understood, Bowie roared in agreement.

THIRTY

MISTAKEN IDENTITY

I was nauseous with stress by eleven, when a hacked autocab dropped me in Southbrook at the address Lynx had given me. The meeting point was a derelict two-story warehouse with broken and boarded-up windows. A single lightbulb flickered over a door in a side alley.

I took a breath and let it out slowly, wincing as one of the many souvenirs from Warhawk twinged with pain. Despite superhuman toughness and accelerated healing, I'd been pushed beyond my limits. I needed to be in bed with Vee, not walking into an ambush.

The nagging questions about Nyx and her people didn't make me feel any better about the situation either. They were obviously after whoever Lynx was working with, or for, not that they'd told me who it was. Or who their boss, the Old Man, was, for that matter.

All I could do was hope Nyx was as good as her word. People I cared about were in danger, and given the amount of voidrium in Lynx's possession, the city—hell, the entire eastern seaboard—could be as well.

Bowie radiated wariness, growling at the edge of my consciousness.

Once more into the breach, I thought to him, hardening my resolve.

I'd tried to explain what was happening to Bowie on the cab ride, that we were going to do what we could to help the rest of his kind trapped in the voidrium. When I was done, Bowie had seemed to understand, but I could feel his uncertainty and lingering suspicion. I just hoped he'd help when the time came.

Crossing the street, I made my way to the side door and gently tried the handle. It was open. I waited a moment, scanning the area, and then stepped inside. Despite the darkness, I **saw** the violet outlines of six armored figures in cover. I raised my hands when they emerged from the shadows, training their weapons on my head.

One of them stepped in front of me, shoving the massive barrel of a bulky weapon against my forehead. "Freeze, motherfucker," he snapped, his voice a distorted growl as he gestured at his rifle with his chin. "You know what this is?"

My eyes widened. From the configuration, it looked like a particle cannon. Highly experimental and *extremely* illegal, it packed more of a punch than most tanks. The last I'd read, a working prototype the size of a rifle was still a decade away.

I'd have been fascinated if the cannon hadn't been aimed at me.

I nodded slowly.

"Cuff him," the man snapped.

Another faceless armored figure whom I could only guess was a mercenary slid behind me, attaching binders to my wrists. Bowie and the fountain of energy at the core of my being vanished as the binders snapped into place, replaced by cold dread.

Shit.

I'd suspected Lynx might come up with something to nullify my powers. She had access to MICSy's schematics and what seemed like endless resources. It turned out I had been right.

As soon as the binders were on, the mercenary behind me patted me down. "Nothing."

"Scan him," barked the guy I assumed was in charge. A third armored figure pulled out a wand-like device and carefully waved it over me.

This was it.

I forced myself to breathe normally, worrying irrationally that they could hear the thunderous pounding of my heart. If they found our surprise, my friends and I were fucked. The scan felt like an hour, but it probably took less than a minute. "He's clean," the mercenary with the wand finally grunted, stepping back. "Bag him."

One of them dragged a black canvas bag over my head, cinching it around my neck. We'd expected this, but a spike of panic still burrowed into my chest.

"Forward," snapped the guy in charge, jabbing me with his weapon. I felt the rest of the mercenaries close in around me before leading me down a short hallway and into what sounded like a large room. An electric engine hummed over the clatter of the mercenaries' steps as they marched me toward it.

What sounded like a van door opened in front of me. Two of my escorts grunted and shoved me in, and my ribs screamed in protest as I fell to the floor. "Heavy bastard," one of them, a woman, muttered, while other doors opened and shut.

The vehicle started to move. I tried to sit up, but a boot crashed into my shoulder, knocking me back to the floor. "You killed some friends of mine," the leader growled, suddenly close to my ear, his tone thick with malice. "I'm gonna enjoy watching that psycho cut your fucking head off."

We drove for what felt like twenty minutes, taking turns and passing through what sounded like tunnels before we finally rolled to a stop. The side door opened, and hands grabbed me, dragging me out onto concrete.

I lay there for a moment. The scent of salt water carried on the cool night air filled my nostrils as traffic echoed in the distance. Eventually, two of my captors pulled me to my feet and pushed me forward. I stumbled across the concrete, the mercenaries shoving me whenever I wandered off course, and then onto a metal ramp that echoed strangely. *A gangplank.* The dull echo of deck plating rang out when we stepped inside what I guessed was a cargo ship.

Looks like Solitario was right. The thought wasn't particularly comforting in the moment.

They marched me into what could only be the bowels of the ship. As quiet as it had been on the outside, the interior bustled with activity. Conversation mixed with the hum of electronics and the noise of construction.

A few times during the walk, I felt the faintest sense of movement in my hood, followed by the deeply unpleasant sensation of something skittering down my leg. I forced myself not to react, fighting the urge to shudder.

I stumbled down yet another flight of stairs before the shriek of an old metal door echoed, and one of my escorts prodded me inside.

Abruptly, someone ripped the bag off my head.

We were in a cavernous cargo hold, easily a hundred feet long and sixty feet wide. Its rusted walls vanished into the darkness above, but a hint of light emanated from a massive freight hatch. Stacked shipping containers created pathways and open spaces.

Oh, shit. The pit of dread in my stomach expanded as I stared at the man standing before me.

Unlike the last time we'd met, he wasn't in a tux. Instead, he wore the armor that turned him from a man into a force capable of killing monsters, alien armadas, and gods.

The Aegis Mark XIII exosuit, white with touches of silver and blue, was a blend of smooth lines and soft angles, the repulsors, flight surfaces, and weapon systems integrated so well, they were barely visible. The whole effect was both agile and imposing, a lethal masterpiece invented by one of the greatest minds of his age. Only the raised faceplate softened the effect, revealing the familiar features underneath.

Vincent Vaydan, I thought, momentarily numb with shock. *Of course.* Who else had the resources, the tech, or the knowledge?

"Hey, Carter. Glad you could make it." Vaydan's voice was deceptively casual. He grinned, a quick twitch that never touched his eyes. "You really should have taken that job."

Lynx stood beside Vaydan. She tilted her head, regarding me through the eyeless faceplate of her helmet and radiating menace. The armor covering her lithe form had been repaired or replaced, and the long blade that had nearly ended me twice was visible over her shoulder.

To make matters worse, Vaydan and Lynx weren't

alone. Instead of the single other meta we'd expected, there were *two.*

The first was a tall, athletically built guy floating a foot off the ground and dressed in a gray-and-black suit patterned off a raging storm. His long cape flowed and snapped as the air around him roiled and writhed, howling like a barely contained hurricane.

He's the one, I thought, comparing him to the mental image of my doppelgänger.

The other was a monster of iron and steel that loomed behind Vaydan. He was easily seven feet tall, impossibly muscled, and covered completely in spiked plates fused into a nightmarish armored sheath. Even his face was covered, the rusted iron and steel shaped into a malevolent snarl. His right arm was disproportionately large and made of bars, cables, and plates, ending in a massive claw tipped with serrated metal talons.

Some of the deck plating flowed off the floor and up his leg, filling in a pockmark on one of his leg plates before rehardening.

In addition to Lynx, Vaydan, and the two metas, mercenaries stood on either side of the door I'd entered by and flanked another on the far side of the hold, the only ways in or out other than the hatch above. Two more aimed rifles down at me from a catwalk that ran along the hold's perimeter. With the six that had escorted me, I counted twelve mercenaries altogether.

It was quite the party.

Lynx's eyeless gaze switched to the mercenary leader. "Were you followed?"

He shook his armored head. "Negative, ma'am. Our follow vehicle didn't pick up any tails or aerial spotters, and the dock's clear."

Vaydan took a couple of steps toward me, his boots clicking on the metal deck. "What's the matter? Surprised to see me?"

I shook my head, my face twisting with revulsion. "Arrogant narcissist is only a short hop away from mass-murdering sociopath. I should have known."

Vaydan shrugged. "You know what they say. Never meet your heroes."

I glanced back at the meta wreathed in wind and then the metal monster. Vaydan followed my gaze.

"Don't mind them. They're part of my little off-the-books metahuman work release program from Blackstone. I have them on hand, along with a few others, in case you made the tragically stupid mistake of attempting a rescue with your D-list bank robber friends. They don't play well with others, but the neural implants make sure they follow orders."

The memory of Lynx confused and trying to warn me flashed through my mind. I gestured to her with my chin. "Is that how you keep *her* on a leash?"

Vaydan glanced at Lynx. For a second, his smug confidence faltered, but then his sarcastic mask settled back into place. "She's more of a partner than a subordinate. A little too in love with her work, but I can't argue with the results."

Lynx regarded me through her featureless mask. Shooting forward, she grabbed the back of my neck, producing with her other hand a dagger with the same disruption field that covered her sword. She pressed herself against me as the tip of the dagger flashed forward, stopping less than a fraction of an inch from my eye.

"Your eyes are truly remarkable. Would you mind if I kept one . . . ?"

A tremor of panic rippled through me as the point of her blade loomed in my vision. I pulled back involuntarily, struggling against the binders, but Lynx's iron grip kept her pressed against me as the tip of the blade drew ever closer.

Vaydan sighed. "Unharmed, remember?"

Lynx quivered, her whole body tense. Sighing, she stepped back and sheathed her dagger. "Pity."

I slumped, drawing in a ragged breath as my heart pounded against my ribs. Taking a shuddering breath, I fought the reply that boiled up. We had a plan.

Focus.

"My friends. Where are they?"

"They're here, safe and sound, as promised. We were going to leave them out of this, but you surprised us with your bank stunt." Vaydan turned away from me and took a couple of steps, his armored boots thudding on the deck as he stepped around the metal giant. "I saw your robbery, by the way. Nice costume. A little too 'sci-fi convention' for me, but still, lots of style. You and your band of no-names really beat the brakes off my new team." He chuckled. "I guess that's what I get for hiring a used-car salesman and a couple of internet celebrities. Warhawk had promise, though."

I grunted. "She's a real gem."

Vaydan paused, raising a metal-encased finger as a hint of curiosity flitted across his face. "Given your daddy issues, I didn't really peg you for the mask type. Our algorithms said you'd go to your friend Vee—which you did—and we figured she'd take you to that small-time tech, Rictor—which *she* did—before the two of you attempted to flee the country."

I stiffened, a thrill of fear shooting down my spine.

Vaydan rolled his eyes. "Give me a little credit, Carter. I'm *Aegis*, not to mention a genius, *and* one of the richest men on the planet. Of *course* I know about your girlfriend and the land of misfit toys her friend calls a workshop. Your little tech friend's slippery, but we'd have tracked him down eventually. We'll find them in the next few days, and then we'll round them up. If you cooperate, you might even get to see them again."

Good thing they aren't home, asshole, I thought, trying to keep the relief from my face.

"After you went to Rictor, you really threw my predictive algorithms for a loop. How'd you hook up with the other bank robbers, anyway?" Vaydan turned, his eyes narrowing. "What was your endgame?"

"Rictor said he could get us out of the country, but we couldn't afford to pay him," I lied, just as I'd practiced. "So he set me up with a crew in exchange for a finder's fee and a percentage of my cut." It wasn't exactly an Oscar-worthy performance, but given the situation, I hoped Vaydan, Lynx, and the two metas chalked my shaking hands and excessive sweating up to stress.

Vaydan studied me silently for a moment before snorting. "Still. Captain Jack? Where's your dignity, Carter?"

I fought the nearly overpowering urge to sag with relief. "My friends. Let them go."

"Yeah . . ." Vaydan winced. "The thing is, you don't respond well to authority, so we're going to keep them on hand to make sure you behave. Unless . . ." He paused, raising an eyebrow. "I know the lab might be a sticking point, not to mention my overly enthusiastic partner nearly killing you twice, but I don't suppose there's any chance you'd reconsider my offer? You ended up being so much more *interesting* than I would've thought possible. We'd have to take precautions to make sure you were playing ball, but believe me,"—he glanced at the two metas again—"it beats the alternative."

I shook my head, stunned. "Why do you need me? If this is about the machine, why not just build it yourself?"

Vaydan shrugged. "Don't sell yourself short. You did what some of the best minds in the *world* couldn't. What *I* couldn't, at least not in the time I had. Considering the source,"—he touched his armored chest—"that's high praise. And now, with your powers?" He whistled. "We might not even *need* your machine."

"You destroyed your own research center and killed *hundreds* of people. Why?" Anger wormed through my shock and dread. "What could be worth all this?"

Vaydan chuckled, rolling his eyes, but a hint of annoyance crept into his tone. "Careful. You wouldn't want to insult me by thinking I'm stupid enough to reveal my plan. I've been on the other side of this." He flashed a grin that never touched his eyes. "Except I was the hero. You're the villain in this little drama, remember?"

"A hero?" I shook my head, a tremor of revulsion flowing through me. "You're a fucking monster."

Vaydan's eyes hardened, and his gauntleted hands tightened into fists, his glib mask slipping again. "I get the optics, but I'm on the right side of the equation here. You have no *idea* what sorts of things are out there. Things that make the Rakkari look like schoolyard bullies. Make their invasion look like a tea party." His expression faltered again, filling with pain. "Believe me."

I shook my head. I was missing something. I could *feel* it.

Why fund our project and then sabotage it? He wanted MICSy, or at least the tech, and with the amount of voidrium he'd gathered, Vaydan could bring macro-scale objects—*people*—through and in large quantities. But why would he want the tech to open gates to other worlds if he was worried about something dangerous?

Unless . . .

I studied Vaydan. His expression was haunted, and for a moment, he looked like a different person. Like a man indelibly scarred by trauma, instead of the cavalier hero whose face was plastered around the world.

Holy hell, a different person.

My eyes widened as the puzzle pieces fell into place. "You're not Vincent Vaydan, are you? At least, not the one from *this* Earth."

His head snapped up, but his surprise was quickly replaced by a rueful smile that spread slowly across his face. He looked at Lynx. "I told you the kid was brilliant."

THIRTY-ONE

MATRYOSHKA

I was silent, stunned by the enormity of the revelation. "Something happened to your Earth, didn't it?" I managed eventually.

Vaydan stared at me for a moment before looking away with a sigh. "Ever heard of Black Sun? They were a cabal of occultists and sorcerers. Powerful, immortal, and not even remotely sane. Here, on *this* Earth, they were wiped out. On mine, they succeeded in summoning their alien god from some dark recesses of the multiverse in 2015."

The quiet horror in his tone, bleak and barren, shook me, silencing my reply.

Vaydan's face went slack as he stared into the rusting darkness of the cargo hold. "They called it the Devourer. It appeared in low orbit above Washington, DC, a sphere of writhing flesh and chitin five *miles* across. The Devourer unfurled tentacles as thick as skyscrapers that burrowed into the planet's crust, while pods the size of mountains crashed into cities and disgorged monsters that consumed the planet's biomass, starting with humanity."

He turned back to me, his eyes a bottomless pit of grief and horror. "We assembled every mask who could fight—hero, villain, it didn't matter—and attacked. We lost half our number fighting through the shoals of predatory symbiotes that lived on its surface. The Devourer barely noticed us until our Starwind rammed it with his starcruiser, detonating the ship's energy core in a blast that would've killed a small moon.

"That got its attention." Vaydan grunted a ragged and desolate laugh. "It started killing us. My friends. Allies. Enemies, even. The most powerful beings on the planet, dozens at a time, snuffed out like candles by its psychic attacks. Out of *thousands*, barely two hundred masks survived."

A sudden pang of empathy for the man in front of me cut through the hatred and disgust.

Closing his eyes for a second, Vaydan bowed his head. "When the Devourer and its feeders were done gorging on the planet, it reabsorbed them and just . . . left. A few survivors of our counterattack, heroes *and* villains, managed to save just over three million people, but all we'd really done was prolong the inevitable."

Vaydan's expression twisted into a ragged wound of loss and bitterness. "We were rats living underground in barely habitable shelters, using failing hydroponics and faulty recyclers. Not to mention, trying to survive raids from other metas or attacks from monsters that hadn't made it back to the Devourer before it departed. Hundreds of thousands died in the first six months. We tried everything we could think of. *Everything*. Tech, magic, miracles, you name it, but our Earth was *dead*, incapable of sustaining life. Most of us lost hope. At least until your Vincent Vaydan appeared."

"How did he get there?" I asked quietly.

"He arrived a few years after the Devourer, tumbling through the multiverse after a duel with a sorcerer called the Vizier. Which was ironic, considering the Vizier from *my* Earth had died fighting at my side." Vaydan shook his head, a bitter smile flashing across his features. "We picked up his distress beacon and brought him back to the tunnels we were using as a shelter. When your Vaydan regained consciousness, we *begged* him to help evacuate the survivors to his Earth."

"What happened?" I asked in the same quiet tone, suspecting I already knew the answer.

"This is a waste of time," Lynx hissed.

Vaydan ignored her. "He promised to organize a rescue when he got back to his Earth, *this* Earth, but I could tell he was lying. Who knew what contaminants we might have brought with us? Or what might notice? It was too dangerous, and that's not even talking about the political or logistical challenges." He grunted in sour amusement again. "I couldn't blame him. I'd have made the same call. The multiverse is filled with dead worlds. Infinite echoes of dark futures averted. We might as well have been ghosts."

I recoiled internally, sickened by the thought of having to choose between the lives of millions and the safety of billions.

"Your Vaydan's armor had a device, a sort of dimensional tether, capable of pulling him back to his Earth—*this* Earth—for just that sort of an emergency. I knew because I'd been designing one before our world ended. But it was a one-way trip, and it only worked for him."

"Or someone with his DNA," I guessed.

"And retinal scan." Vaydan tapped the side of his helmet with an armored finger. "We locked him up. I took his suit and used the dimensional tether. It deposited me in his lab at the top of Vaydan Industries Tower." He shook his head slowly, his voice filling with quiet wonder. "It was like stepping into a dream. I stared out the window at the living, breathing city and sobbed until an android assistant tried to summon medical help."

"What did you do?"

"I started working the problem, but it wasn't exactly trivial, mostly because of the scope, and the time frame didn't help either. Every day that went by meant more people dead. I managed to bring a few individuals over, but even with your Vaydan's resources and influence, I couldn't do it on the scale I needed." Vaydan turned to me, a smile creeping across his features. "Until Claire sent me your research proposal."

"So all of this . . ."

"Is a multiversal rescue operation." Vaydan shook his head, chuckling. "Congratulations, Carter. You got me to lay it all out, after all. You're only the second person I've told, and I've got to say, it feels good. Is it strange that I feel a rush of sympathy for all the supervillains I've mocked for monologuing their plans?" He flashed me another grin. "Besides, it's for the best. You get the stakes now. With your abilities, I'm betting you can help us save *millions* of people who were just like the ones out there, before their world was destroyed. What do you say?"

I reeled inwardly. My anger and resolve had kept me going, but they'd been quenched by a nightmare on a scale I could barely imagine. *Focus,* I thought. *There are people depending on you.*

I took a ragged breath. "My friends. Let me see them."

Vaydan considered and eventually shrugged. "Why not? Trust is the foundation of a good working relationship. Bring one of them out." He gestured at one of the mercenaries, who vanished into the far door.

The cold band of living darkness wrapped around my torso shifted, and a chill rushed down my leg. For a moment, my shadow seemed to elongate, pouring itself toward a pocket of darkness near a cargo crate before following the mercenary.

I held my breath, studying Vaydan, Lynx, and the others, but nothing in their body language suggested they'd noticed.

"Get the fuck off me!" a familiar voice echoed, before the far door opened and a mercenary stepped through, dragging Abby behind him.

Abby was in her pj's. Worry and fatigue were etched into the freckled brown skin of her face, but she didn't seem hurt. She looked around, eyes wide and nostrils flaring. Her jaw dropped in surprise and confusion when she saw me. "Brandon? What the hell is going on? Who are—"

"It's going to be okay," I cut in. "Itzel and Harvey, are they here too?"

She nodded.

"Good. Don't worry, I've got this."

Abby's eyes widened as she finally seemed to notice Vaydan. "Wait, what the—"

Vaydan gestured. "That's enough."

The mercenary grabbed Abby and picked her up, carrying her struggling form back through the hatch they'd come from.

"Brandon! Brando—" Abby's voice cut off suddenly as the door shut.

Vaydan looked back at me. "Like I said, safe and sound. Once I trust you and other safeguards are in place, we can see about letting them go." He extended a gauntleted hand to me. "Together, we can save everyone. All you have to do is say yes."

Part of me wanted to say yes, like when he'd offered me a job at the party, which felt like a lifetime ago. Despite my reservations, I believed him, and as much as I still hated the guy for all the horrible things he'd done, I couldn't punish the people he was trying to rescue just because of him. I had a moral obligation to help them.

"Come on, Carter." Vaydan's smile widened. "Don't leave me hanging."

Still, something felt wrong. I was missing a piece of the puzzle. Despite his grin, Vaydan's eyes burned with raw intensity. I'd glimpsed the oceans of grief and pain within. I'd seen the lengths to which he was willing to go, the price he was willing to pay.

"You're expanding Vanguard. The Sentinel program. Why?"

Vaydan's smile wavered. "We tried being glorified public servants on our Earth. It didn't end well. We need more control if we want to make sure what happened to our Earth doesn't happen here."

"Control? So you're planning, what, a worldwide coup?"

"Let's just call it a rebalancing of the global distribution of power. If all goes according to plan, it'll be nearly bloodless."

"*Nearly* bloodless?" I snorted, not hiding the bitterness in my voice. "Is that how my project ended? What happens when the rest of Vanguard finds out? Other masks?"

Vaydan frowned. "I have contingencies."

I shook my head. "And how many lives will that cost?"

"Excuse me?" Vaydan's expression hardened. He dropped the hand he'd extended.

"How many people need to die for you to seize power?"

"We're talking about the fate of the *planet* here, Carter, not some high-minded ideal."

"You can't justify murder by claiming to be a savior, particularly when you're plotting a global takeover."

"Why not? People do it all the time." Vaydan's eyes narrowed with annoyance. "Besides, if I'd had my way, your project would've ended with lots of pats on the back for everyone and you'd be gainfully employed, making more money than you could have imagined, while putting your brilliant mind to use for the betterment of humanity. No loss of life whatsoever. *You* went back. *You* reran the experiment and left me with no other choice."

You didn't do this, Vee's voice echoed in my head. "I didn't make you kill anyone." My hands clenched, my knuckles whitening as my voice hardened. "Those deaths are on you. You could've just asked for help."

"Don't be naive, Carter." Vaydan rolled his eyes. "Humans are selfish at the best of times. There was no way your Earth's leaders would agree to resettle *millions* of people from a different Earth that had been exposed to alien pathogens. And even if they *did*, it would take *years*, during which time the survivors on my Earth could all die anyway."

"If I said yes, would you agree to tell people what

happened to your world? To *warn* them and then help them prepare instead of trying to stage a planetary coup?"

Vaydan's eyes were coldly calculating. "And trust the fate of yet another world to politicians and petty tyrants? That's a risk I'm not willing to take."

I grunted a laugh. "There it is."

"There *what* is?" Vaydan snapped.

"Despite everything you've been through, you're still a billionaire narcissist who thinks he knows better than *everyone* else."

Vaydan's face twisted into a snarl of frustration. "I *do* know better than everyone else, you arrogant little shit. I'm *Aegis*. I've seen and done things you can't *imagine*."

"I want to help your people, but I've seen how you treat your *partners*." I gestured at Lynx, the flying meta, and the metal giant. "And given how this plan turned out, I think you're going to end up killing more people than you're trying to save. No deal."

Vaydan shook his head, anger flashing in his eyes. "I had high hopes for you, Carter, but don't worry. I'll have plenty of time to figure out how your powers work once I've installed a control rig in your brain."

We glared at each other for a moment.

"My friends," I asked eventually. "Would you have let them go if I'd said yes?"

He looked away with a sigh. "Probably not."

I nodded. "Didn't think so."

I found Brandon's friends and have gotten them out. They're safe, Nyx's voice announced in my head via Professor Cerebrian's telepathic link.

Do we happen to have any idea who the other metas are? Professor Cerebrian asked.

I recognize them, Nyx grunted, her mental voice tense. *The one in the air is Stormherald. Enhanced physical abilities and aerokinesis. The other is Iron Curtain. He's extremely strong, with a limited form of ferrokinesis tied to his armor. They were part of Red Dawn, a Soviet-era metahuman kill team. Very nasty.*

I thought they were dead, Pyre replied through the link.

Nyx is right, Solitario's mental voice echoed in response. *Cold War—radioactive ice powers—is on deck with twenty more mercenaries, give or take.*

Pyre, leave the deck to Solitario and Shade, Nyx responded. *We're going to need you down here.*

Just give me the word. Pyre's thoughts were tinged with anticipation.

Swarm, if you'd be so kind . . . ? Nyx asked.

I held myself still as more roaches scuttled out of a concealed pocket inside my hoodie. They rustled down my sleeves, and a faint hiss emanated from my bindings a second later, along with the slightest whiff of acid eating through metal. Out of the corner of my eye, I saw small curls of smoke coming from the backs of a few of the mercenaries behind Vaydan and Lynx. I held my breath, terrified that Vaydan, Lynx, or one of the metas would notice, but they didn't respond.

Done, Swarm chittered.

Go, Nyx echoed.

"Sir." The mercenary standing beside Lynx stiffened suddenly and leaned over, his voice tense. "The prisoner team's gone dark. Comms are down!"

Gunfire and screams echoed from elsewhere in the ship, followed by a massive explosion that rocked the superstructure.

Around us, six of the guards shuddered and jerked as Human Swarm's component roaches finished melting their psi dampeners, allowing Professor Cerebrian to take control of them from his hiding place at the edge of the docks, hundreds of meters away.

"Ah, perfect," said the mercenaries as one, the pitch and inflection of their voices perfectly matching Professor Cerebrian's. "I was afraid you'd start without me."

Hissing, Lynx drew her blade and vanished as the stealth technology in her armor activated. However, I could still see her as a shimmering violet figure with my reactivated gravity sense, thanks to Human Swarm having melted through most of the binders.

"What's happening, Carter?" Vaydan's faceplate snapped shut and sealed as he leaped into the air, thrusters burning blue white as he hovered a few feet above the deck. Weapon ports opened across his armor.

I tore my hands apart, snapping what was left of the binders. Bowie flowed back, bristling. *It's now or never, buddy.*

Bowie didn't hesitate. He rushed to the forefront of my mind, ready, his strength and resolve rushing into me. We were united by the fact that we both had people to fight for.

Together, we opened the floodgate inside me, and power poured through, saturating every atom of my body as violet arcs of energy crackled around me. I floated into the air, rising to Aegis's level, about ten feet away from him. The world slowed to a crawl as time dilated.

Meeting Vaydan's gaze, I smiled slightly, while Bowie roared a challenge in my head. "It's called a *matryoshka*."

THIRTY-TWO

RESISTANCE DAY

The six mercenaries under Professor Cerebrian's control spun and opened fire, their weapons deafening in the confines of the cargo hold.

Lynx dove behind a shipping container as high-velocity rounds tore through the air where she'd been, while more rounds shattered against Vaydan's suit as micro turrets emerged from his armored shoulders. "Take the kid alive," he snapped, unleashing needle-thin beams of energy that scythed through the armor, bone, and steel of four of Professor Cerebrian's puppets.

Stormherald shot up, protected from the barrage of automatic fire by a wall of hardened air, and extended a hand. Blades of wind screamed across the hold, shredding armor like paper and cutting one of Cerebrian's mercenaries to pieces in a shower of gore.

Pops erupted from the helmets of the other six mercenaries as Human Swarm burned out their psi dampeners. They twitched and spasmed as Professor Cerebrian instantly took control, adding their fire to the others'.

Roaring like a locomotive, Iron Curtain charged two of the puppetized mercenaries in leaping strides. He lashed out with his oversized claw, shattering armor and rending flesh.

Brandon, now! Nyx's voice shouted in my head.

Channeling a torrent of power, I **grabbed** Vaydan, freezing him in place with a gravity field, as Nyx erupted out of a shadow above, holding a rectangular metallic device. Vaydan reacted instantly, flares of blue white erupting from his thrusters as he attempted to dodge, without effect. In a blur of midnight blue and inky darkness, Nyx slammed the device onto the back of Vaydan's armor, before vanishing into Vaydan's shadow on the floor.

Adhesive held the device in place for a fraction of a second, long enough for it to unleash a crackling blast that seemed to split the world, nearly blinding me.

Vaydan crashed to the deck, arcs of electricity playing across his smoking armor. He twitched for a moment and then lay still.

Surprise, asshole.

Bowie radiated savage satisfaction, which shifted to a warning as Lynx emerged from behind a shipping container. Her sword sheared through three of Professor Cerebrian's puppets in two quick slashes, before she pivoted and sprinted toward me.

I **caught** her with a gravity field before she made it halfway, slamming her into the wall of the hold with enough force to dent metal. As she had at the safe house, Lynx turned in the air to land feet first. She tried to spring off the wall, but this time, I knew the move was coming, so I poured more energy into the gravity field. She collapsed against the steel wall, which deformed under the massively increased weight of her body.

My eyes blazed with violet light as the power of the cosmos coursed through me, singing in every cell of my body. I raised a hand, the urge to **crush** Lynx nearly over-powering, but hesitated. Killing her wouldn't undo the lives she'd taken, and I'd seen the face behind her mask. The horror in her eyes during the moment she'd managed to regain control of herself. Whoever she was, Lynx was a victim of Vaydan's machinations. Like the people who'd died at the Vaydan Institute and my friends.

Even Nate.

Bowie growled, confused. His rage and his desire to destroy the being that had hunted and nearly killed us battered against my consciousness.

She didn't have a choice, I thought to him, sharing concepts, memories, and impressions.

Bowie thrashed in my head, frustrated, but seemed to understand.

I kept Lynx pinned in place as I turned my attention to the rest of the hold.

Finishing two more of Professor Cerebrian's puppets, Iron Curtain took a step in my direction—and fell into a shadow that opened beneath his feet. He wrapped his metal claw around a nearby support beam, catching himself before the shadowy pit could swallow him whole. Cursing in Russian, he plunged his other hand into the shadow and dragged Nyx out by the throat, hoisting her into the air as he pulled himself out of the void.

Before I could help Nyx, Bowie growled a warning as Stormherald unleashed another scything blast of air, this time at me.

Instinct took over. I spun toward the meta in the air and **grabbed** a cargo crate with a flicker of power, throwing it into the path of Stormherald's attack. The torrent of air sheared the steel crate in half, and Stormherald fired more wind blasts, forcing me on the defensive. I threw more crates in the way, but Stormherald's screaming winds tore them apart as well, depriving me of shields faster than I could grab them.

A line of pain erupted across my shoulder when one of his attacks slipped through, breaking my concentration. The field holding Lynx in place vanished, and she dropped to the deck, unmoving.

Nyx struggled against Iron Curtain in the corner of my vision, snarling, her claws tearing deep gouges out of his armored hide. Metal flowed like liquid from the deck plating, repairing the damage as fast as Nyx could inflict it. Iron Curtain's mask grinned as his hand closed like a pneumatic press.

Shit.

My world was a storm of razor-sharp wind, but Nyx was dead if I couldn't help her. Gritting my teeth, I **hurled** all five tons of a shipping container at Stormherald with a spasm of power, leaving myself open to his counterattack. Another line of fire erupted across my forehead, filling my eyes with a sudden sheet of blood, as the container slammed my opponent into the wall, rocking the hold with a deafening crash.

As I wiped the blood out of my eyes, the Russian giant raised his claw for a killing blow. Before the claw could descend, something scuttled across his cheek and dove into his right eye with an acidic hiss. Iron Curtain bellowed in pain and crushed the insect, distracted.

With a flicker of power, I **tore** the sword from Lynx's limp hand and **launched** it at Iron Curtain. Its disruption field parted armor and flesh, and the blade sank to the hilt in the giant meta's lower back.

Bellowing again, he tossed Nyx aside. As she flipped over in the air and vanished into another patch of darkness, the metal giant turned to me, his mask twisted in rage, and charged, streaking across the deck like a speeding train.

Despite his size and my dilated perception of time, he was *fast.*

I threw myself to the side as the monstrous meta's fist punched *through* the ship's hull. Foresight and speed saved me from a direct hit, but even the glancing blow hit like an artillery blast. My world flashed white, and I went spinning through the air.

Pain erupted in my back as my spine dented a support pillar, before I crashed to the ground, gasping.

Taking a step toward me, Iron Curtain stumbled as his leg plunged through another shadow. Grunting, he tried to pull himself out, but something held him, and this time, the portal was too small for him to reach into.

Overhead, Stormherald reappeared. Blood oozed across his face, and one arm hung limply at his side. "They can dissect your corpse," he hissed. A roiling ball of razor-sharp air appeared in his remaining hand.

My foresight showed me a glimpse of his attack as alarm radiated from Bowie. I tried to stand, but dizziness sent me tumbling back to the deck.

Suddenly, one of the walls blew inward in a spray of molten steel, through which Pyre exploded, wreathed in nuclear fire. She leaped at Stormherald, who knocked her aside with a blast of wind and floated up to the ceiling, nearly vanishing into the darkness above.

Pyre hit the ground rolling and came to her feet with a grin as the intense heat of her fiery aura buckled the plates beneath her. "He's all yours."

Taloned hands reached out from the darkness of the ceiling and wrenched Stormherald upward. His shout of alarm cut off abruptly as his head vanished into a portal to Inara's shadowy abyss. He spasmed, and a sheet of blood poured from the portal, followed a second later by his decapitated body.

Iron Curtain roared as Stormherald's corpse hit the deck, finally wrenching the blade out of his spine. With a burst of strength, he tore his foot out of the shadow portal beneath him and leaped at Pyre.

I staggered to my feet and floated up, ready to help Pyre with the rampaging giant, but Bowie growled another warning. Turning, I saw Lynx running unsteadily toward me, invisible but outlined in violet unlight. Her hands flashed as she hurled a trio of throwing knives.

Raising a hand, I **caught** the blades with a gravity field. As I tossed them aside, Lynx leaped at me, locking her legs behind my back like a vice, and plunged her knife toward my eye. I caught her wrist with both hands, and we grappled in the air, struggling for position. This time, I was ready for her, my greater strength and foreknowledge offsetting her skill and speed.

"I'm going to find your friends and cut them apart," she growled. Arching her back, she used every muscle in her augmented body trying to drive the point of her blade toward my eye.

"I hope you weren't this awful before Vaydan got his hands on you," I grunted, grinning into her featureless faceplate as I held her immobile.

A little help?

The last of Human Swarm's roaches that had hidden in my hoodie scuttled up my sleeve and onto Lynx. The downward pressure on the knife pointed at my eye disappeared abruptly. She tried to struggle free, but I held on as roaches swarmed down her arms to the base of her neck, their acidic bite burning through her armor.

With the crackling pop of damaged electronics, she screamed, spasmed, and went limp in my grasp.

One of the roaches turned to me and raised its fore-leg, giving me what I was pretty sure was a thumbs-up.

Lungs heaving, I set Lynx down, careful of Human Swarm's roaches, and glanced around.

Pyre and Nyx were still locked in combat with Iron Curtain, whose leg and oversize metal claw were stuck in patches of shadow, pinning him in place.

Eyes blazing, Pyre snapped her hand out and closed it like a vice around the giant's throat. Her flames inten-sified, the fury of a blast furnace radiating from her in waves. Iron Curtain's metal sheath melted, flowing in rivulets down his body. Some of the molten droplets rolled back up, but Pyre's flames were undeniable. The Russian meta shrieked like a steam engine as the last layer of metal ran like rain to the deck below, revealing the twisted form beneath for a fraction of a second before it was seared to ash.

Pyre's fiery aura flickered and died, except for the twin flames of her eyes. She bled freely from a laceration in her shoulder and a hole in her hand, but her wounds didn't dim the satisfaction in her expression.

Nyx leaped down from a shadow above. Her mouth and talons were covered in blood, and her throat was covered in bruises, visible despite her blue skin. She had a hand pressed over a puncture in her side that bled blood so dark, it looked black. Despite her injuries, Nyx's eyes were clear and she was steady on her feet, which was more than I had going for me.

Pyre held out a fist, which Nyx bumped with her own, a predatory grin playing across her blood-covered lips.

Looking down at Vaydan, Nyx reaching for another device on her belt. "We need to secure him befo—"

The lights on Vaydan's armor flickered to life. His thrusters fired a split second later, sputtering unsteadily as he launched himself off the deck and through the hatch in the ceiling before we could react.

"Shit!" Nyx hissed. *Aegis is in the air!* Her voice echoed in my head. *Solitario, do you see him?*

He's heading across the water in the direction of downtown and Vanguard HQ. His suit looks damaged, but I don't have anything capable of punching through that armor.

What do you think? I thought to Bowie. *Can we catch him?*

Determination flowed from Bowie, followed by memories. Finally, I understood fully, and in them, we soared. It was like flying was a dance for which I'd just remembered the steps. "We're on it," I announced, leaping up as I took flight.

Nyx turned toward me, her eyebrow shooting up. "'We'? Brandon, what are you—" The rest of her sentence was swallowed by the wind as I emerged from the cargo hold into the night above, looking toward downtown as I scanned for Vaydan.

The Resistance Day fireworks were underway, scintillating blasts of color detonating over the water, joining the holographic displays on the buildings in a dazzling tapestry of light. Distant music carried across the black water, which was painted with the ghostly reflections of the fireworks.

There! I thought, catching a glimpse of blue-white thrusters heading toward the distinctive shape of the Vanguard Watchtower in the distance. Undamaged, the Aegis suit was capable of breaking the sound barrier a few times over, but Vaydan seemed to be limping along, juddering and shaking. *Nyx's surprise must have royally damaged his suit.*

Violet energy crackled around me as I shot forward, streaking across the night sky after him, closing the distance rapidly. With a final burst of speed, I slammed into Vaydan, sending us both tumbling through the air. He recovered a second before I did, climbing slightly and then hovering a dozen feet away.

Our pursuit had taken us across the threshold of the fireworks show. Detonations filled the air with joyous light and thunder against the backdrop of Union City's glowing downtown skyline. The lights from helicopters and drones winked in the distance, while party barges and other pleasure boats filled the water below.

We watched each other as we circled warily, blasts of multicolored light exploding in the night around us as the city spread out below. Vaydan's armor was charred and blackened. His thrusters still sputtered, struggling to hold him aloft, while the lights on his suit flickered unsteadily.

I wasn't exactly at my best either, battered and bleeding and held up by cosmic power, adrenaline, and pure resolve.

Besides, a damaged suit didn't mean Vaydan wasn't a threat. He'd beaten some of the most dangerous enemies imaginable in worse circumstances. One of the turrets on his shoulders was fried, but the other was still intact. As tough as I was, I didn't want to gamble on whether it could slice through me, and I had no idea how many of the other weapon systems built into his suit were still online.

Any ideas? I thought to Bowie. His mind raced as he shared memories in which he seemed to shape something fluid, bending and shifting it with a gravity field more complex than anything I'd managed. My eyes widened when I understood what he intended for our defense, but I nodded mentally.

"The pulse charge was a neat trick. Fried most of my systems. Nearly got the backup power too. Took me a minute to get it back online," Vaydan said finally, the speakers in his armor projecting his voice over the rushing wind. "I'm guessing your new friends whipped that up. I recognized the demon and the pyromaniac. I don't suppose you know who you're working with?"

I shrugged, wincing as pain shot through me. "Whoever they are, they can't be any worse than you."

"I'm working to save lives. Can you say the same about them?"

I thought about my friends, rescued by people who society had labeled villains, and the other creatures like Bowie trapped in the voidrium. "Yeah, I can."

Vaydan grunted, looking me over. "You know, you're not looking so hot. Sure you don't want to surrender?"

"Funny," I grunted in return, wiping blood and snot from my face. "I was going to say the same thing. Now co—"

A blast of light and color detonated about twenty feet away.

Forewarning brushed my mind and time dilated just before the micro turret on Vaydan's shoulder swiveled toward me, unleashing a needle-thin beam of energy just as the firework went off. I raised my hand, alien instinct flowing from Bowie as we **bent** space itself, the beam appearing to curve away from us, and **crushed** the turret in its housing with another gravity field.

At the same time, Vaydan raised his gauntlets, aiming their built-in blasters at me. The emitters in his palms flashed and then exploded in a spray of sparks. Vaydan glanced down for a second before turning back to me. "Well, that's embarrassing. I don't suppose you'd let me do some repairs before we finish this up? It's the least you—"

Another flash of foresight warned me as Vaydan surged forward with a burst from his thrusters, a blade springing from the top of his gauntlet.

I **caught** him with a thought and a flicker of power, pinning him in place with a gravity field before he'd covered half the distance and **tore** the blade off his gauntlet with another flicker of power.

Another flash of foresight brushed my mind as two small compartments opened along Vaydan's ribs, launching a salvo of micro missiles that screamed toward me, devouring the distance in a fraction of a second.

Bowie and I worked in unison, acting simultaneously to **catch** and **crush** the missiles just before they hit, their warheads detonating in a blast of fire and heat that washed over me. Another flash in a night full of lights.

"Anything else?" I growled.

Vaydan shook his head. "Impressive, Carter." His thrusters burned more brightly as he pushed them to their limits, trying to escape from my grasp.

I held him in place until the thrusters sputtered and died.

"So, what's your plan now?" he asked. "Some of those helicopters and drones already have us on camera, and your friends can only scrub so much footage. You going to kill me in front of the whole world? Try to make me confess? You're not that stupid. We can still—"

"Do you *ever* shut up?" My fists clenched as a spike of annoyance and rage flashed through me. Before I could think about it, I **ripped** him toward me with a flicker of power and drove my fist into his faceplate once he was within arm's reach. The hit rang like a bell and sent Vaydan spinning end over end in my gravity field.

Oh, shit. I sucked in a breath, worried I'd just killed him. When a soft groan emerged from behind Vaydan's faceplate, I sagged with relief.

Bowie grunted, as if to say he'd have been happy, either way.

Brandon, Nyx's voice echoed in my head. *What the hell is happening?*

I've got him. We're heading back to you now.

I flew back down to the ship, carrying Vaydan's unconscious body in a gravity field behind me.

The cargo hold smelled like a slaughterhouse and looked worse. The fight had only taken a few minutes, but the damage we'd inflicted bordered on apocalyptic.

Mercenary corpses were strewn about, shredded by weapons fire, sliced in half, or torn apart. Stormherald's headless corpse oozed blood on the deck, near the droplets of cooling slag and ash that were all that remained of Iron Curtain.

The hold wasn't in great shape either. The walls were dented and punctured; the deck plating warped and melted. Alarms rang over the groans of metal, echoing throughout the ship.

Realizing I was shaking, I fought the urge to vomit.

Nyx pulled another metallic device from her belt and slapped it on Vaydan's armor. "That should be sufficient until we can get him back." A tight smile spread across her midnight-blue features, and her horns dipped as she nodded at me. "Excellent job, Brandon."

Pyre looked me over, raising an eyebrow. "You all right?"

I snorted, which turned into laughter that nearly overwhelmed me, despite the pain.

A flicker of amusement flowed from Bowie as well.

Pyre's eyes narrowed. She glanced back at Nyx, who shrugged slightly.

"I'm sorry," I managed after a few seconds. "I'm fine. Thanks."

Pyre shook her head and rolled her eyes, but her lips twitched.

Mighty fine scrap overall, wouldn't you say? Professor Cerebrian's voice cut in brightly.

We need to get out of here. What's the status topside? Nyx asked via Professor Cerebrian's mental link.

Deck's clear, Solitario responded. *We're making our way to you.*

We found something, buzzed Human Swarm's voice in our heads. *Most concerning. Nyx, Brandon, you should take a look.*

Hissing, Nyx checked the black blood oozing from the wound on her side. "Where?"

In another hold nearby. We will guide you.

Her horns dipped as she nodded and picked up Lynx. "Pyre, get Aegis." *Solitario, Shade, meet us there.*

We raced through the ship. The roaches Human Swarm had sent to scout rejoined the whole as we followed them to a door that opened into a control room filled with workstations and holographic displays.

Solitario and Shade were waiting when we arrived. Solitario's hair and beard were filled with frost, and there were holes in his armor, but no wounds were visible underneath. Shade's cloak had bullet holes in it, but her roiling smoky form was otherwise unharmed.

A broken glass window at the front of the room looked out onto the ship's main cargo hold, revealing a massive machine against the far wall, which was connected to a web of hoses and cables.

Harsh violet light poured from an open containment bottle the size of an industrial garbage can.

I recognized the design immediately, and Bowie recognized the energy coming out of the containment bottle; he radiated anguish. Within the torrent of pain, he interspersed alien thoughts and emotions with my own. Images of Mom, Claire, and Vee flickered unbidden through my mind, and I understood.

As I'd suspected, others of his kind were trapped within the voidrium cluster.

Nyx's tail lashed in annoyance. "Someone tell me what I'm looking at."

"It's MICSy," I said breathlessly. "Vaydan built my machine."

THIRTY-THREE

TECHNICAL ISSUES

Something was very, *very* wrong. The machine looked like MICSy's much bigger, *much* angrier sister. She was growling so intensely, the entire hold shook.

Worse, the giant containment bottle appeared to be stuck open. The voidrium at her heart, a cluster of crystals the size of my torso, radiated harsh violet light almost too bright to look at. To my gravity sense, it burned like a star, pulling, twisting, and tearing the fabric of space-time so violently, it made me nauseous.

Heart pounding, I scanned the control room. Most of the staff was gone, but I caught a hint of white pressed against the side of a console in the corner. Reaching around the console, I dragged out a terrified tech with a shock of receding blond hair and thick glasses.

"What the fuck is happening?" I demanded.

The tech flinched away, shaking. "The p-p-power grid was damaged when something hit the ship during a systems test. A couple of the generators blew and sent a s-s-surge to the voidrium cluster."

Human Swarm and Shade glanced at Pyre.

"What?" She crossed her arms and shrugged. "No one told me to be gentle."

A thrill of fear shot down my spine, and I spun the tech to face the computer in front of us. "Unlock the workstation!"

Hands shaking, he typed in his login information. "There!" he squealed, stumbling back.

Stepping up to the console, I looked at the interface. It was nearly identical to the one Harvey and I had written. My fingers flew across the keyboard, déjà vu hitting me as I looked at the diagnostics panel, which was throwing up alarms—too many alarms.

"Oh, shit." I fought a wave of panic. *Focus.*

"That doesn't sound good," Solitario grunted behind me, impossibly calm.

Nyx leaned over my shoulder. "Can you shut it down?"

"No." I shook my head. "The voidrium's entered the autocatalytic phase of its life cycle."

"Meaning?"

The voidrium cluster's gravity was increasing. Dread washed over me as the horrid realization hit. The voidrium was going to *implode*, collapsing in on itself.

Sensing it as well, Bowie radiated panic, barraging me with thoughts of something like family.

Space around the machine swirled and crashed like a maelstrom, tugging at my gravity sense. Out of the corner of my eye, I saw a few strands of Nyx's ink-dark hair begin to rise. A second later, a pen on the console tumbled toward the machine.

Nyx's tail thrashed. "Brandon!"

I turned to her, my heart crashing against my ribs.

"The voidrium crystals in the cluster are interacting with one another, feeding each other power and strengthening the gravitational field it's generating. When the reaction hits critical mass, the voidrium will collapse, devouring us, the docks, and probably the city. If we're lucky, it'll explode afterward, taking out a good chunk of the state."

"Damn." Pyre's blazing eyes widened. "What if we aren't lucky?"

"The collapse will create a small black hole that'll consume the planet."

Nyx's eyes narrowed, her tail lashing. "Can we fix the power system?"

"It wouldn't matter. The field generators are fucked."

"What if we break the machine?"

I shook my head. "Then it'll happen faster."

Shade glanced at Nyx, her smoky form billowing. "Time to go?"

It doesn't sound like there's anywhere to *go,* Professor Cerebrian cut in, his infuriatingly chipper tone undercut by near-palpable tension.

Nyx looked from the crackling heart of the machine in front of us to me. "Is there any way to contain it?"

"Maybe." I turned back to the machine, concentrating on my gravity sense. It was like standing in the heart of a tornado that was spinning faster and faster. I closed my eyes and reached out. The gravity field twisted and pulsated, too complicated for me to grasp in real time. Reaching within myself, I drew as much power as I could channel. My eyes blazed with violet light as I reached out, **grabbing** the gravity field around the voidrium and trying to stabilize it through sheer, brute force.

Even with Bowie's help, it was like trying to hold back the tide, like compressing a hurricane in my hands.

I staggered back and shook my head. "No."

"We need to get rid of it." Nyx thought for a second, her expression a mask of concentration, before coming to a decision. "I might be able to drag it into the abyss with me before it detonates."

The machine is rather large, Professor Cerebrian thought to us. *Are you sure you can take it with you?*

"We'll find out shortly."

Nyx turned, but Solitario grabbed her shoulder. "Will you survive that? I'm not telling the Old Man we lost you."

Nyx shrugged. "Probably? It's the only play."

Solitario's jaw clenched, but he let go.

Nyx put her hand on the wall, the shadows pooling around it as she started to step into the abyss beyond.

The shadows below MICSy 2.0 thickened, congealing into an oil slick of utter darkness. Something groaned as the machine started to shift, and a cable snapped.

Bowie roared, battering me with waves of grief and fear.

"Wait!"

Nyx looked at me, her expression tense. "There's no time. What is it?"

"There are *living beings* inside the voidrium."

Nyx hissed, frustration filling her midnight-blue features. "I'm sorry, but—"

"Besides," I interrupted, gesturing to the trunk cables that were stretched nearly to breaking. "If the machine moves another inch, those cables will tear, the generators will shut off, and it'll explode before it goes all the way through."

Solitario sighed behind us, running a hand through his dark mane. "Did anyone have a black hole in the death pool?"

Pyre shrugged. "Ironborn, maybe?"

Solitario sighed. "He's always right."

"He's an android. Stop gambling with synthetics."

I'd say we're all *about to lose, wouldn't you?* Professor Cerebrian cut in.

My mind raced. There *had* to be a solution. The energy from the reaction was the problem. If we could find a way to channel it away, ground it out, or discharge it somehow, the reaction would fizzle, but we needed a way to direct it. To do that, we'd need a conduit that had a chance in hell of surviving the cataclysmic forces.

Any ideas? I thought to Bowie.

A flash of my first conversation with Rictor came to mind, and it hit me. The explosion had transformed me, allowing me to serve as a conduit to the energy that now coursed through me, energy the voidrium in my brain allowed me to control.

We couldn't hold back the gravitational forces, but Bowie and I *might* have a chance of redirecting the cosmic energy being released by the voidrium crystals. We could *be* the conduit. Bowie flooded me with thoughts and concepts, as if agreeing and trying to show me how.

"Nyx, can you open a small portal beside that glowing metal garbage can? Something just large enough for me to put my hand through?"

She nodded. "Why?"

"I'm going to try channeling the energy so the reaction cascades into the void."

Her eyes narrowed. "How is that possible?"

"I'm willing to bet I can channel the energy in the crystal matrix, using myself as a conduit."

"Can you survive that?"

"Probably?" I shrugged, grinning nervously as I mirrored her previous tone. "It's the only play."

She looked at the other villains.

Solitario grunted. "How much worse can it get?"

Nyx nodded. "Do it."

I leaped through the broken window and landed on a deck. Gravity fluctuations battered me like waves. As Bowie and I got closer, they'd get exponentially stronger, thanks to the magic of the inverse-square law, and near the voidrium, the waves looked strong enough to rip us apart. Eyes crackling, I wreathed myself in a gravity field and pushed through the distortions, like the prow of a ship turning into a swell.

Bowie bent what felt like every fiber of his being to the task, our wills merging as we pushed through the swirling maelstrom, until we stood beside the machine.

This close to the voidrium cluster, gravitational distortions tore at us. Together, though, we maintained the gravity field that insulated us from the worst of the effects.

Gritting my teeth against the grinding in my injured shoulder, I drove my right hand into the shadowy void Nyx created on the side of the containment bottle. Reaching out with my left, I pushed through the gravity distortions to touch the voidrium cluster at the machine's heart.

Pain exploded in my hand and radiated down my arm, before spreading throughout my body. I did my best to ignore it, concentrating on the font of power beneath my fingertips instead.

Primordial power flowed through me, setting every

atom of my body ablaze as it responded to my will. It was intoxicating, godlike, as if I held raw creation in my hands, saturated in the quintessence that had forged the universe and burned in the heart of every star.

But even working together, the power was too much for Bowie and me.

Crackling lines of violet energy erupted from me, slicing through the deck plating and the walls and sending sprays of water into the chamber. I screamed, every nerve in my body shrieking with white-hot agony, as I fought for control, but even transformed, I was an insufficient vessel.

Patches of skin on my arms started to glow and smolder, before burning with violet fire. The pain was transcendent, searing my body and mind, so much that nonexistence was preferable to another second. All I needed to do was let go. With just a momentary lapse of control, the torrent of energy would utterly unmake me.

I concentrated on Vee and Mom and all the people who would die if I failed. I screamed, fighting to exert enough control over the energy coursing through me to hold myself together.

Suddenly, I felt them. Dozens of alien minds—more—contained within the voidrium matrix. Despite the agony, I could tell Bowie was communicating with the howling chorus. They were confused, muddled by agony and torment, but he reached them and beckoned them outward.

The entities flowed from the voidrium and into me, adding their strength to mine and Bowie's.

We merged and *understood.*

For the first time, I comprehended Bowie as he truly was: a sinuous, coruscating pattern of violet energy with the impression of structure—a head attached to a serpentine body, with rippling patterns of light like wings on its sides.

A dragon of cosmic fire.

My sense of scale was insufficient. In the face of such a being, I was less than a mote of dust.

My mind expanded to encapsulate him, but where I was a drop of consciousness, he was an ocean, his mind a vast alien landscape that was now my own.

In Bowie's memories, I lived for eons in the rich oceans of space, moving through space-time with others of my kind. I swam through layers of reality, winding through the threads that connected an infinite, ever-expanding multiverse, on a level with the ancient powers and alien gods of the cosmos. I watched as galaxies came into existence and died, an integral part of both creation and destruction.

Bowie was a wellspring of cosmic power, an embodiment of the primordial forces of the universe. Manipulating gravity and space-time as easily as I breathed, he was capable of more than I could have ever dreamed.

In his memories, I existed above crude physical reality, the layer of muck on the bottom of the multiverse. Some of the rocks that drifted around stars contained the rotting film of life, some with simple minds, but they were less than nothing, and I ignored them.

Until the Rakkari came.

Their energy fields tore at me like hooks as the Synod, their guiding intelligence, crushed me with its impossible will. I lashed out, my rage tearing space-time and shattering their ships, but always there were more. They exhausted me, dragged me down, and bound me, rendering me into crude matter. An agony and a violation.

I was as alien to Bowie as he was to me, and as I experienced the cosmos, Bowie experienced a human life. His awareness expanded to understand a complex world that he had barely been able to perceive as he lived every moment of my life at once. He felt the loss of my father, the terror and uncertainty of being on the run, of struggling to survive.

He experienced my love for Mom.

For Vee.

A second that felt like centuries passed between us as power roared through us. Slowly, bolstered by the other entities that had been trapped in the voidrium, we bent the torrent of power to our wills, channeling it through us into the shadowy void beyond Nyx's portal. Robbed of its catalyst, the voidrium matrix began to dim, and the gravity distortions lessened.

Bowie cut through the deluge of power and agony with a plea that was echoed by the chorus inside us. A plea for freedom.

At the last instant, I ripped my hand out of the void, sending a column of cosmic fire skyward that disintegrated the ship above before erupting into the night. With a thought, I let them go.

From the crackling pillar of power, sinuous shapes of violet-white energy emerged, spreading wings of cosmic fire as they were freed from their crude physical prisons. Even weakened, they were glorious to behold, vast and beautiful, roiling across the sky. At last, only Bowie remained. His yearning poured through our bond, and with an effort of will, he began to follow the rest of his kind back into the cosmos.

Another spasm of agony racked my entire body, as if something were trying to tear me apart from the inside out. The horrible realization that we were too intertwined for me to survive being separated from Bowie crashed into me like a bus. Bowie paused, fury and sadness flowing through the pain as he came to the same realization. He wavered at the precipice, torn with indecision.

It's okay, I thought to him, exhaustion closing around me. We'd saved my friends and the city. The thought of leaving Vee and Mom plunged a blade of regret into my chest. *I don't want to be your prison. You deserve to be free.*

Bowie snarled, radiating grief and longing as he pulled back from the brink, settling into the familiar space in my mind.

Thank you. Relief and regret flowed through me as the column of energy exploding from my hand cut off, just before the voidrium crystals, utterly dark, crumbled to dust. The cosmic beings above us sang joyously, a chorus that echoed through my mind, and then they were gone, sliding through the layers of space-time. Bowie watched them go, emanating mournful resignation.

I staggered a step and then collapsed to my knees. My skin smoked, and my clothing was gone. I was covered in burns. My whole body hurt, but compared to the agony of the cosmic fire that had nearly turned me to ash, it was bearable.

I turned back to the villains in the control booth, who looked on with a mixture of surprise and relief.

Shade was the first to find her voice. "See?" she said, turning to Solitario. "I *told* you New Guy was solid."

THIRTY-FOUR

REUNION

MICSy 2.0 was destroyed, along with the rest of the hold, torn apart by violent gravity distortions. Debris and machine parts were strewn about or embedded in the buckled walls. The deck plating was warped and torn, and the rest of the ship wasn't in much better condition. It listed badly to one side, and water rushed in as the groans and squeals of overstressed metal echoed all around.

"We need to go," Nyx said, glancing around. She gestured to the tech as she threw Lynx's unconscious form over her shoulder. "Pyre, get him. Let's move, people."

The tech struggled weakly before wilting under Pyre's glare, made all the more terrifying by the fact she was already carrying Vaydan's unconscious form.

I couldn't stand, so Solitario came down and slipped an arm under my shoulders, helping me to my feet. "Don't worry, kid. I've got you," he said as we made our way up the stairs to the control center, where everyone else waited. Each step was agonizing, but I made it without needing to be carried, which felt like something.

As soon as we were back with the group, Nyx's shadows thickened and swallowed us. I fell through darkness, and then stumbled with everyone else into the abandoned warehouse Nyx had chosen as our fallback point.

We stepped into the windowless back room, where Alice, Rictor, Professor Cerebrian, and Aifa waited for us. It had probably been a big break room at one point, with some chairs, a round table next to a microwave, a coffee maker, and a mini fridge by the door to the main warehouse, but we'd stuffed it with supply bags and had a medical station set up in the corner.

"Hey, buddy!" Rictor smiled brightly. "Where'd your clothes go?" His smile faded to concern as he looked me over.

We'd needed a support team in place, and since they were already involved and Nyx's people had worked with them before, Rictor, Alice, and Vee had been the obvious choice. We'd called Rictor and Alice after finalizing the plan.

"Hey, man," I managed through gritted teeth as Solitario half carried me to the medical station.

Solitario set me down, flashing a razor-sharp grin. "Not bad." He patted me on the shoulder, before making his way to the table, where he started checking his weapons.

Pyre set a still-unconscious Vaydan onto a designated part of the floor and activated a restraint field. Then she zip-tied the green-looking tech to a chair.

Alice made her way over to me, concern on her too-perfect face. "You have sustained injuries. Would you like me to provide first aid?"

"Please," I replied, and Alice started looking me over. When she was sure I had no life-threatening injuries, she applied a cool spray that numbed the burns, before wrapping them.

With nothing else to do, Human Swarm and Shade grabbed a couple of beers from the mini fridge and sat down at the table with Solitario.

Still carrying Lynx, Nyx stepped through a moment after the rest of us, dropping lightly onto the concrete as the void behind her returned to normal shadow. She set the assassin's unconscious body on the concrete beside Vaydan.

Aifa, our holographic tech expert, looked over. "Welcome back, boss. Don't worry, Vee and I kept their comms on lockdown. Nothing got in or out, and we've already wiped you from every camera within three blocks of the ship. I'll do the same thing when we're done here." Aifa glanced at me. "His little performance might be harder to scrub, though. It's already on the internet."

I sighed. *Great.*

Nyx nodded, her tail swishing behind her. "Do what you can. Rictor." She pointed to Lynx. "Check her over. Make sure she's not sending a distress call or about to self-destruct."

"Will do!" Rictor grabbed a tool kit and made his way to the unconscious assassin. He paused, gesturing at Vaydan. "What about him?"

"Don't touch him. The inhibitor we attached is based on some fairly recent schematics of his armor and should keep him locked down long enough for us to transport him. Aifa, check radio chatter and keep an eye out. Brandon's light show wasn't subtle. I want to know if anyone so much as twitches in our direction."

Christopher Lee Rippee

Aifa's hologram flickered in the corner of the room. "On it, boss."

Nyx looked around, hissing as she put her hand to the wound oozing black blood from her side.

The door flew open as Vee rushed into the back room from the main warehouse. "Brandon!" She made her way to me, weaving through the activity. Her eyes widened when she got close. "What the hell happened?"

I winced as Alice applied more spray to my burns. "We won."

"Given his injuries and the energy readings, it appears Brandon sustained significant internal and external damage as a result of overexposure to cosmic energy."

Vee slowly shook her head. "If that's what winning looks like, fuck losing." She paused, her eyes widening when she caught a glimpse of Vaydan. "Holy hell. Is that . . . ?"

"Yeah." A shadow crossed my face, and I took a shuddering breath. There was no way to tell her how close I'd come to letting go. How close we'd all come to death. "I'll tell you about it, but maybe not right now."

She reached out and carefully took my hand. Glancing around, she noticed Nyx's and Pyre's wounds as well. "That bad?"

I shivered, closing my eyes. "Yeah, but we made it. How are Abby, Itzel, and Harvey?"

"They're shaken up, especially Harvey, but they're okay. They want to know what's happening. I haven't told them shit, other than they're safe."

"Good news!" Alice smiled brightly, wrapping the last of the burns on my arm. "I see no indication that your life is in imminent danger. We will need to perform a more thorough examination when we return home,

360

however. Your vitals suggest you are in significant pain. Would you like me to induce a coma?"

She wasn't wrong. Just existing bordered on excruciating. I was pretty sure shock was the only reason I wasn't screaming, and the idea of a long nap was *very* appealing, but I shook my head. "Can you give me something for the pain?" I turned to Vee. "Any chance we have some spare clothes?"

After giving me some meds, Alice moved on to Nyx, while Vee dug into one of the supply bags in the corner, pulling out a sweatshirt and matching pants that she helped me get on. It didn't feel great, but whatever Alice had sprayed on my wounds had sealed and numbed them enough to make dressing tolerable.

Once I was dressed, Vee helped me stand. "Let's go talk to them."

Rictor looked from Lynx to Nyx as we slowly made our way to the door. A quartet of small drones were scanning the assassin, while he examined the readout on his tablet.

"I'm not detecting any outgoing signals. I *am* getting some power readings, but they're from cybernetic augmentations, and there are a *lot* of those. No bombs, though. We'll have to get her out of the armor to be sure, but I don't see anything that would indicate any chemical or solid-state explosives either."

I paused, leaning on Vee as I looked over. "Any chance she'll wake up?"

Rictor shook his head. "She's lucky to be alive. Her brain signals are all over the place. I'll have to get her out of the armor and into a lab to be sure, but it looks like she has a neural-regulator implant. Some of the best work I've seen, actually. Your little roach buddies fried it."

I sighed, unsurprised. "Can we do anything?"

"We'll give her a thorough exam when we get her back." Nyx considered Lynx for a second. "In the meantime, try to get that helmet off. Brandon, go talk to your friends. Keep them calm. We don't want them trying to escape their own rescue."

When I stepped out of the back room leaning on Vee, Abby, Itzel, and Harvey were clumped together in a small waiting area to one side of the main warehouse. Water bottles and a couple of protein bar wrappers sat on the table in front of them.

Like Abby, Itzel and Harvey were in their pj's. The mystery guy too. He was about my age and good-looking, despite the massive purple-yellow bruise on the side of his face. When he saw me, he took a step closer to Abby, not quite stepping in front of her.

A tired smile crossed my face as Vee helped me to sit on an old file cabinet. *Mystery solved.*

Harvey was shivering with his arms wrapped around himself, rocking slightly back and forth, but he looked at me, nodding slightly. Itzel wiped her eyes and tried to disappear into her space-patterned house robe. Abby's hands trembled, but she was holding herself together.

"Brandon?" Abby's eyes widened, her expression a mixture of fear and confusion. She pulled back slightly as she took in the physical changes my transformation had wrought. "Jesus, your eyes, your skin . . ."

I smiled, trying to keep the hurt off my face. "Hey."

Abby stepped back, glancing around. "The *thing* that brought us here, is it—"

"*She's* a friend," I said gently. "She helped rescue you."

"Told you." Vee shrugged.

"That's about the only thing you told us," Abby snapped before turning back to me. "What the fuck is going *on*?"

I paused, trying to find the words, but Harvey spoke up before I could.

"This was about the experiment, wasn't it?" His voice was quiet as he rubbed his arms.

"Yeah. I'm so sorry."

"The lab explosion, was it you?"

"No." I shook my head. "It was one of the people who took you. She attacked me and rigged MICSy to explode, to hide the fact that it worked."

Harvey considered that for a second. "They killed Nate too, didn't they?"

I nodded again.

"Why? What were they after?"

I sighed, shrugging. Harvey didn't need to know that Nate had probably been murdered to conceal Vaydan's role in the sabotage. "It's better you don't know."

Darting forward, Itzel hugged me and sniffled into my hoodie. It hurt, but the drugs and spray were doing their work. "I *knew* you would never hurt anyone. The guy at the bank robbery didn't even look like you."

I gently hugged Itzel back and glanced at Vee, who rolled her eyes, her lips twitching up at the corners.

Eventually, Itzel pulled away, wiped her nose, and looked up at me, her face puffy from crying.

Harvey closed his eyes and took a few breaths, his arms falling to his sides.

The guy with Abby stepped forward. "What about the assholes who kidnapped us?"

Intertwining her arm with his, Abby pulled him closer. "This is Jameel."

I looked back at Jameel. "They won't be a problem for you anymore, and we'll do what we can to make sure no one bothers you again."

Jameel took a breath, some of the tension leaving his shoulders, and he nodded.

"What happens now?" Abby asked softly.

I traded glances with Vee. "One of my associates will wipe your minds." I held up my hands when Abby stiffened in surprise. "He'll only remove everything that's happened since your abduction. It's for your own good. Don't worry, he's, uh . . . a professor."

Itzel sniffled, dismay filling her expression. "But then we won't know you're innocent!"

Understanding filled Abby's eyes. "If we don't know anything, then whoever was behind this won't have as much reason to come after us."

The only alternative we'd come up with was for them to tell everyone everything, but Nyx and her people valued their anonymity too much.

I nodded. "Short of going into hiding for the rest of your lives, it's the only way to keep you safe."

"And after that?"

"Someone's coming. He'll stay with you until the cops and Vanguard arrive. When you complain about lost memory, a Vanguard telepath will confirm it, which should be enough to get you out of the line of fire."

Concern softened the frustrated anger and worry in Abby's expression. "What about you two?"

"That's complicated, and we don't have a lot of time. I just wanted to see you all, I guess, and let you know how sorry I am."

"You shouldn't be." Harvey looked at me. "This wasn't your fault. We owe you our lives."

"Your feathered friend is almost here," Aifa announced over the intercom. "ETA: one minute."

I nodded. "I better head outside." I looked around at my friends. There was so much more I wanted to say to all of them. To Abby. "Wait here, okay? This will be over soon."

Abby frowned, her eyes brimming with unasked questions, but nodded.

I started to drag myself up, but I couldn't quite make it, overburdened by pain and exhaustion.

Vee helped me up again, grunting under my weight. "I got you."

I grinned through the pain. "I know."

Helping me outside, Vee deposited me on a crate beside the exterior door. "Try not to pass out, okay?"

"No promises."

I glanced at the sky as Vee made her way back inside. Ripples of violet light, an aftereffect of the energy pillar, shimmered overhead, mixing with the lights of the city and the holographic displays that painted the sky.

The column of energy must have been visible across the city and beyond. I could only imagine what people had thought when they'd looked up. Masks were already streaking overhead toward the rapidly sinking ship.

A few seconds later, a familiar figure dropped from above, wobbling slightly as he didn't quite stick a superhero landing. He was big and burly, with a bird mask, a feathered cape, and a white spandex suit that was just a little too small for him, his gut spilling out over his belt. A *G* was emblazoned on his chest.

I waved. "Hey, Gryphon."

Taking Abby, Itzel, and Harvey with us hadn't been an option, so we'd needed someone who could get them into custody. There hadn't exactly been a lot of options, so I'd suggested Gryphon.

"The pudgy guy in the bird mask?" Shade had asked, her skepticism plain. It had taken a few minutes, but I'd brought them all around.

As soon as we'd returned, Aifa had sent Gryphon a message saying I was ready to turn myself in on the condition he came alone. She'd monitored his phone to make sure he didn't tell anyone and had also taken the precaution of freezing his social media accounts, just in case.

"Holy shit, kid." Gryphon frowned as he looked me up and down. "You look even worse than the last time I saw you."

I looked at the burns and other wounds that covered my arms. "It's been a rough week."

"Well, that's all over now." Gryphon puffed up. "You made the right decision. I can guarantee you'll be treated humanely. You'll get the help you—"

"Yeah, about that." I grimaced slightly. "I'm not here to surrender."

"Why the fuck did you call me, then?" Gryphon asked incredulously. His eyes narrowed a second later. "This isn't a trap, is it? I will whup your charred, scrawny ass if I have to."

I held up a hand. "Slow your roll, big guy. I was actually hoping you could do me a favor."

Gryphon grunted. "I don't do favors for villains, especially when they lie to me and take my merch. I want that hoodie back."

"Look, there are some people here who could use your help." I grinned slightly. "And I figured this would be good for your Vwitter and Instabook presence."

Gryphon glanced past me to Abby and the others, who looked on anxiously from the open warehouse door. Everyone else was out of sight.

Doubt crept into his expression, but he shook his head. "Kid, as far as I know, you blew up a lab, murdered someone, leveled a city block, and robbed a fucking *bank*. In less than a *week*!" Gryphon's jaw hardened. "Hell, my gut says you had something to do with that ship in the harbor too." He cracked his neck and slammed a fist into his open hand. "I don't have a choice. I'm taking you in."

Nyx and Pyre emerged from the gloom behind him. Pyre glared, eyes blazing. "You can try."

Nyx smiled, a predatory twist on the face of a demon goddess of darkness and ruin. "But you really shouldn't."

Gryphon's eyes narrowed. "Three on one, eh? I like those odds."

Nyx rolled her eyes in disbelief.

Shade flowed out of the warehouse, her billowing form coalescing as Human Swarm scuttled into view beside her.

I'm afraid it's closer to nine on one, old chap, Professor Cerebrian's voice cut in brightly, though he was nowhere in sight. *How do you feel about* those *odds?*

Gryphon's eyes widened in alarm. "You, uh, made some friends since I saw you last."

"It looks that way." I nodded. "But it's been a long night. We're not looking for more trouble."

"So, what exactly is it you want? Some sort of hero-villain team up? I'm not robbing any banks." He paused, his eyes narrowing again. "It's not a sex thing, is it?"

Pyre shook her head. "This fucking guy."

I blinked and then gestured to my friends. "They got

caught up in some trouble, and now they need someone to watch over them and make sure they're safe. A hero."

"That's it?" Gryphon eyed me suspiciously.

I winced. "Not quite. We're going to need to alter your memory. It's for their safety, and yours."

Gryphon's expression soured. He pulled a cigarette out of his utility belt and lit it. "Do I have a choice?"

"Not really?" I shrugged helplessly. "My friends are pretty private."

"These people I'm guarding—none of them are robotic infiltrators or clone assassins or anything weird?"

I blinked. "Nothing like that."

"All right, fuck it. Sure." Gryphon sighed heavily, his shoulders slumping. "What do you need me to do?"

I nodded to Nyx. After one last look at Gryphon, she led everyone else back into the warehouse.

"As far as you'll know, you were patrolling when you heard a cry for help and found them tied up in the warehouse, at which point you felt compelled to call the press, the cops, and Vanguard."

"Fine," he grunted. "But you should know, I meant what I said in our weekly blast video. I *will* bring you in."

I nodded, not quite smirking. "Sure, buddy."

I beckoned Abby, Harvey, Itzel, and Jameel out of the warehouse and into the courtyard. "This is Gryphon. He's going to keep you safe until help arrives."

Gryphon glowered at me before nodding to them. "You can count on it."

Abby frowned. "What happens now?"

Professor Cerebrian sauntered outside, whistling. Everyone recoiled as he bowed and tipped his hat.

"Goddamn," Gryphon muttered. "Why is your skull *transparent?*"

"My friend will modify your memories, and we'll go. You'll return to your lives."

"Will we be safe?" Itzel's voice was quiet.

I slowly forced myself to my feet. "You won't know anything, and I think I have a way to make sure someone will be looking out for you. You'll be safe." I had a couple of ideas I needed to discuss with Nyx.

Itzel nodded as I turned around.

"Hey, Brandon," Abby called out as my hand hit the door to the back room. "You take care of yourself, all right?"

I looked back, smiling. "You too."

Don't worry, ladies and gents. This will be quick and painless. Gather 'round. You too, birdman.

I took one last look at the group and smiled before opening the door. There was a near-palpable aura of shock as I stepped into the back room.

Everyone was staring at Lynx, who was still on the floor. Rictor leaned over her, a cigarette in one hand and her faceplate in the other.

I glanced at Nyx. Resignation filled her face, along with what might have been relief.

Even Pyre's eyes were wide.

Glancing down, I finally saw the face of the woman who'd hunted me.

I recognized her instantly. Anyone on the planet would.

It was Isabella Ruiz, better known as Fennec, one of Vanguard's founding members, who had supposedly been murdered three years ago.

Oh, shit.

THIRTY-FIVE

THE OLD MAN

When the shock of Lynx's identity wore off enough for us to function again, we finished removing any traces of our presence. Aifa scrubbed our digital evidence, somehow finding and altering, or wiping, camera footage across a huge portion of the city in a shockingly small amount of time.

We might as well have been ghosts.

When that was done, we said our goodbyes.

Nyx had placed a taloned hand on my arm, a tired smile on her midnight-blue features. "You were excellent tonight, Brandon. They might not know it, but millions of people owe you their lives. Perhaps more."

If anything, I felt like I had more questions than answers, but Nyx had assured me she'd be in touch soon. "Go rest. *Heal.*"

"Not bad." Solitario had grinned at me, his eyes flashing with amusement. "Try not to die, eh?"

Shade, back in her corporeal form, and Human Swarm, with his holo mask on, had come up to me as

370

well. "Later, New Guy. Let us know if you're ever looking for work."

Even Pyre had given me a nod of grudging respect.

Aifa had even pulled Vee aside too. "For an organic, you're pretty good. I'll be sure to send the work I don't want to bother with your way."

Vee had rolled her eyes and given the hologram a lopsided grin. "Thanks, I guess?" On the way home, Alice assured us it was high praise from a synthetic consciousness.

Be seeing you, chaps, Professor Cerebrian had offered brightly as Nyx's shadows swallowed them, along with Fennec, Vaydan, and the whimpering tech.

Afterward, Vee and I returned with Rictor and Alice to their compound. When we got back, Rictor and Alice administered more medical scans. The results weren't good.

Despite my transformation, the raw power of the combined voidrium crystals in MICSy 2.0 had nearly killed me. Burns covered nearly forty percent of my body, and I'd suffered extensive internal injuries as well, including nerve and organ damage.

In what was becoming a familiar pattern, I spent most of the next week in bed recovering, closely monitored by Alice and Rictor.

Vee was with me the whole time. We watched old horror movies or episodes of *D-List* with T-Rex, and when I felt up to it, we walked through the woods, enjoying the beautiful surroundings and each other.

Despite having wanted him gone, I was glad Bowie was still with me, even if he'd withdrawn into the recesses of our shared mental space. We still couldn't *speak* exactly, but we understood each other. We'd lived each other's lives and could communicate without words. I could feel his constant longing to be with his own kind again, his desire to return to the stars. I'd promised him we'd do everything we could to find the rest of his kind and free them, and I meant it.

He'd responded with hope and something like trust.

Bowie was still around, as was my gravity sense, but my powers weren't. The torrent of cosmic energy we'd channeled had come perilously close to killing us. I was still strong and tough, but the first time I tried to access our wellspring of power after Resistance Day, it felt empty. Depleted. I worried that I'd burned out like a blown circuit, but Rictor was optimistic, already planning a new battery of tests.

Mom had arrived the second day, transported by Nyx's people. With the immediate danger over, keeping her at a safe house had seemed unnecessary, and in yet another display of endless generosity, Alice and Rictor had offered to let her stay with us while we figured out our next move.

We'd had a tearful reunion. Given that she wouldn't be able to return to her normal life either, Vee and I had told her as much as we could.

I'd worried she might not be able to handle it, but Mom had been on the run before. She'd listened calmly, asked questions, and then did her best to comfort *us*.

She'd always been kind of badass.

When Mom noticed the way Vee and I sat together, she'd smiled in a self-satisfied way. "Took you long enough."

Not long after Mom arrived, Rictor found out she had HKS and offered a refined version of the regenerative nanotherapy he'd worked on years before. After just a few days, Mom's scans were better, and her energy and focus had improved. Her eyes were alert.

We all cried.

I told Rictor and Alice yet again how grateful I was, and that our family had grown by two—or three, counting T-Rex.

Despite my injuries, being surrounded by Vee, Mom, Rictor, Alice, T-Rex, and Bowie was the happiest I'd been in a long time. I knew it wouldn't last, so I made the most of it.

While we might not have made the news, the coruscating pillar of energy that had released dragons made of fire certainly had. For the first twenty-four hours, the footage had been on nearly every news channel in the world, before it got edged out by the onslaught of other inexplicable and astonishing events.

News outlets also picked up the story of a local superhero who'd rescued a group of hostages taken by yours truly, the recently minted supervillain who was still wanted by law enforcement and various super teams across Union City and beyond, but no one said anything about Vaydan's disappearance. There were some eyewitness accounts of two figures fighting amid the fireworks, but with no corroborating footage, they'd faded into the background of the news cycle.

Nyx called two days after the rescue to let me know her associate wanted to meet. Which is how I found myself pushing through a rusted gate a little more than a week after the rescue, the metal squealing as I stepped into the gloom of an old subway station.

Stale air assaulted my nostrils, and safety lights stuck to the wall cast just enough ruddy yellow light for me to see, not that I needed them.

Passing an old wooden ticketing booth, I slipped over one of the turnstiles and went down to the platform, my footsteps loud in the thick silence. Old handbills from before the Rakkari attack were still plastered to the tile of the stairway tunnel, most too damaged by water and time to read.

At the bottom of the stairway, the platform opened up. It was about a hundred feet long, a soft curve with a few access tunnels visible on either side. Concrete walls punctuated by blue mosaic-tile designs arched gently up to a ceiling nearly twenty feet above.

A trio of old subway cars rotted on a track that ran about two feet below the platform in front of me.

I couldn't see anyone, even with my gravity sense, but the animal awareness of being observed was strong. Coming alone to an abandoned subway station deep underground to meet an unknown supervillain made me a touch uncomfortable, and unease gnawed at my gut.

Bowie growled warily in my mind, just as unsettled.

I took a step onto the platform. "Hello?" My voice reverberated through the shadowy station.

"Mr. Carter."

A voice, distorted and deep, pierced the gloom as a figure stepped out of the shadows, utterly silent, about ten feet away.

He was tall, though still a little shorter than me, and heavily muscled. A helmet shaped like a skull obscured his face, beneath a hooded cloak that fell over form-fitting body armor composed of hard plates and soft material. All of it was the deep crimson of nearly dried blood.

His mask was an icon of terror, a death's head that haunted the nightmares of billions. Recognition brought a wave of dread and awe.

"Holy shit."

"I'm guessing I don't have to introduce myself?"

I knew who he was. Everyone did. He was the most infamous supervillain of all time.

"You're Crimson Specter," I breathed, a flutter of panic in my chest.

He nodded. "Good, that will save us time."

"Aren't you supposed to be dead?" I blurted.

"Don't believe everything you read," Crimson Specter replied, a hint of amusement in his tone. He waited patiently, letting me work through the shock.

"You're Nyx's associate," I said, rocked by the near-tangible force of the realization. "The Old Man."

"Our relationship is complicated, but that's close enough for our purposes."

But if Nyx worked for Crimson Specter . . .

"She's Cabal. It's real."

Crimson Specter nodded. "Hopefully, given recent events, you might be open to the idea that we aren't what we're portrayed to be."

I looked around, taking in the abandoned station. "I'm guessing you didn't bring me here to kill me?"

"I was hoping we could have a conversation, actually." He gestured toward a tunnel at the north end of the platform. "If you'll indulge me."

Completely still, he radiated menace, and I wondered how many people had spent their last moments staring into the black lenses of his skull mask. But he was right. His people had risked their lives to save Abby, Itzel, and Harvey, not to mention the city.

What do you think?

Bowie radiated wariness, but there was an undercurrent of curiosity as well.

After a couple of moments, I nodded.

"Excellent." Crimson Specter took a couple of silent steps and dropped down onto the track. "Walk with me."

We followed the rusted tracks into the north tunnel. It was dark, but he didn't seem to need light to see. With my gravity sense, I didn't either. For a few minutes, my footsteps were the only sound, other than the occasional drip of water.

"I should begin by apologizing," Crimson Specter said eventually. "I used you, and by extension, your friends. For what little it's worth, it was necessary."

I nodded, unsurprised. Vee and I had spent a lot of time discussing everything that had happened. "The bank robbery. That was just a way for you to provoke Vaydan, wasn't it?"

He shrugged. "Sometimes, the best way to expose your target is to push them into making a mistake. Aegis expected you to run and hide. We confused him. Forced him to act."

"So you made me rob a *bank*?"

"Nyx believes in efficiency," he replied, amused. "Shade needed help with the vault door, and you were well-suited to the task. We gambled on them taking a risk to avoid losing you, and it paid off."

"*Paid off?*" I stopped, anger bubbling up. "You *knew* they'd go after my friends."

"As your lab team and former partner were in protective custody, I suspected Vaydan would make a play for Dr Wright, and had a team in London on standby." Crimson Specter paused, the black lenses of his mask inscrutable. "If I'd had another option, I'd have taken it. Keep in mind, my people did get all your friends out safely, which was always my intent."

"Why didn't you just *tell* me that Vaydan was behind everything?"

"Nyx wanted to. Ultimately, I decided the risk was too great. For you and everyone else involved." He raised a hand to stall my angry retort. "Despite being an arrogant narcissist, Aegis is a canny opponent. We needed your shock and surprise to be genuine. Besides, there was a good chance you wouldn't have believed us."

I shook my head. "How are *you* involved in all of this, anyway?"

Crimson Specter turned away, gazing into the darkness. "The night before she was supposedly murdered, Fennec contacted me, asking to talk. The next morning, I discovered a file in a secure drop box only she and I knew about. It was corrupted, but I was able to salvage a list of research projects, all funded by Vaydan, all focused on accessing parallel Earths. One of them was yours. My working theory is that Fennec discovered that this Vaydan was an impostor, and sent the file before either confronting him or being found out." His fists tightened with the creak of leather. "At which point, Vaydan overpowered her and took measures to ensure he could control her."

I blinked. "Fennec, a member of *Vanguard*, reached out to *you*, one of the most infamous villains of all time?"

He shrugged again. "We were friends."

"*Friends?*" I snorted, shaking my head. "I'm sorry, I'm going to need a little more than that."

"I wasn't born the Crimson Specter, Mr. Carter. In another life, I was a member of the Initiative during World War II, a part of the super-soldier program that produced Knightblade. She and I served side by side for years, protecting the world from Nazi occultists, mad scientists, and other, stranger threats. It's how I met Fennec in the first place."

"What happened?" I asked, not bothering to hide my skepticism.

"That's a long story." Crimson Specter sighed as he started walking again, giving me a moment to catch up. "The short version is that I stumbled onto a cabal of alien sorcerers trying to infiltrate the United States after World War II, who tried to kill me. When that didn't work, they framed me for murders I didn't commit." He paused, tilting his head to me. "I suspect you can relate."

We turned down a side passage that turned into a stairway with a door at the top. I racked my brain as we walked up the stairs. Most theories about Crimson Specter's origin agreed that he'd been an Initiative agent who'd had a psychotic break, killing his family and the agents sent to capture him, but I'd never paid enough attention to memorize details.

Crimson Specter opened the old door, revealing a long-abandoned control station lit by more adhesive emergency lights. Old cathode-tube displays sat above banks of levers and switches that had been left to rot on counters. He stepped inside, and I followed.

The infamous supervillain turned, leaning against one of the counters. "I hunted the creatures responsible for decades—alone at first, but others joined me along the way. There were distractions—the Rakkari attack, for example—but my mission never wavered."

I frowned, slipping into an old metal folding chair. "You fought the Rakkari?"

Crimson Specter nodded. "The Rakkari. The Lord of Winter. The Gorod Imperium. Every planet-level threat the Earth faced."

"Why have I never heard this before?"

He shrugged. "Inconvenient facts are often forgotten. In 2015, after nearly a century, we finally succeeded in exposing and destroying our quarry, after which I went into retirement, of a sort. Nyx took control of our day-to-day operations."

"You supposedly died in 2015, after your attack on the Initiative . . ."

"The cabal I was after had so thoroughly infiltrated the Initiative by that point that they were using it as their primary ritual site. We had no choice but to attack, and my death was a necessary fiction."

"Ritual site? The other Vaydan said the cult that summoned the thing that devoured his Earth arrived in 2015 . . ."

"Black Sun, yes. They were successful on his Earth. I was able to stop them on ours, but it was a near thing."

"But that means you saved . . . *everyone.*" I shook my head, stunned. "What about all the assassinations? The crimes? The dead masks and terrorist activities?"

"Black Sun liked to replace key figures with their shape-shifting puppets. They also liked to hide their operations within legitimate activities." He sighed, and a note of exhaustion crept into his voice. "Some of the masks I supposedly killed were wrongfully attributed to me or murdered by copycats. Others hoped to use me to boost their reputation and left me no choice."

"Even if I wanted to believe you, how could I verify *any* of what you just told me?"

Crimson Specter regarded me, ominous and inscrutable. Then, slowly, as if he were afraid to spook me, he lowered his hood and removed his helmet, the seal hissing as it opened.

Crimson Specter was more than a hundred years old, but the man behind the mask looked to be in his forties. He was pale and clean-shaven, with close-cropped white hair. A heavy brow sat above deep-set blue eyes like chips of ice and a strong jaw.

Something about his face was familiar.

Without taking his eyes off me, Crimson Specter set his helmet down and reached into a pocket, pulling out a couple of black-and-white photos, their corners creased with age, and held them out to me.

Taking them, I held them close so I could see in the dim light.

I recognized the first one immediately. It was famous, a picture of Knightblade and the other super-soldier program volunteers. After the war, each participant had been honored at a memorial in Washington, DC, their faces immortalized in stone.

With a shock, I realized the man beside Claudia Winston, the woman who would become Knightblade, was the same man standing before me now, only younger.

The second picture was the same man in his twenties, smiling happily with Isabella Ruiz, or Fennec, as they stood under an umbrella in front of the Eiffel Tower.

Crimson Specter smiled, the corners of his eyes crinkling. "Other than what you've already seen of us, I'm afraid that's the most compelling evidence I can offer. Although I do hope Fennec will eventually be able to corroborate my story." Without his helmet, his voice was rough, with a slightly antiquated American accent.

"Why am I here?" I asked eventually.

"I want you to join us."

I shook my head in disbelief. "This is a *recruitment* pitch?"

"You've been gifted with power, power you've already used on the behalf of others despite the risks to yourself. You're smart, and you're a fighter. You care about doing the right thing, have a significant distrust for authority, and aren't motivated by wealth or status. You also impressed my people, which is *very* hard to do."

I hesitated, looking away.

"I started our organization to fight Black Sun, but our mission has grown. We work from the shadows against threats conventional authorities can do nothing about: Criminal syndicates and human traffickers. Corrupt governments. Ruthless corporations. Masks on both sides of the line. I suspect you'd find it all very fulfilling, but regardless of what you choose, you should know that your old life is over." Regret tinged his words. "What you need to decide now is what the rest of it will look like."

He was right, even if I hadn't been willing to confront the harsh reality. Part of me had hoped that when I'd exposed whoever was hunting me and been vindicated, I'd be able to go back.

But there was no going back. My old life was ash and memories. It had burned along with my lab.

I'd been transformed and had an alien hitching a ride in my head. I was hunted, wanted for crimes I both had and hadn't committed, by authorities and masks alike. There was no path back to my old life.

Part of me wanted to vanish with Mom and Vee, but Vee would never run, and I couldn't stand by while I had the power to prevent what happened to me from happening to others. I had an obligation to use my powers for the benefit of others, regardless of what side of the law I ended up on, and Crimson Specter was offering me a chance to do just that.

I took a shuddering breath as a wave of grief for the life I was about to leave behind washed over me. "I didn't want any of this," I said quietly.

"We don't choose the cards we're dealt. We can only decide what to do with the hand we've been given."

"I'm not going anywhere without Vee. She's the only reason I survived this."

"Ms. Devi has proven herself an extremely capable and formidable woman. We're planning to make her a similar offer, regardless of your answer."

What about you?

Bowie considered the man in front of us for a moment before acceptance flowed through the link.

Okay.

"I'm in." I took a deep breath and nodded at the door. "Let's go."

Crimson Specter retrieved his helmet, slipping it back on. It sealed with a slight hiss as he pulled his cloak up, transforming him from a man out of time into a legendary villain.

Making his way over to another door, he opened it, revealing a second access tunnel that stretched into the yawning dark. I took a step forward, but he raised a hand. "We won't be going that way," he said, his voice once again heavily distorted.

He made an intricate gesture and muttered a string of impossible words that didn't belong to any human language. The air crackled with power, and a line of fire erupted in the doorway, spreading open to reveal a hole in reality, bound in a ring of fire. An unworked stone room with a black granite floor lay beyond.

I stared for a second, astonished.

"What the *fuck* is that?" I finally managed.

"It's a door, Mr. Carter," Crimson Specter replied, a hint of amusement in his voice. "Of a kind."

I looked from the tear in space-time to Crimson Specter and then back. "Are you fucking kidding me?"

"I spent nearly a century hunting a cabal of alien occultists. I picked up a few tricks along the way. I assure you, it's no worse than public transportation." He stepped through, ducking slightly. "Watch your head."

What had I expected? Whatever else happened, I was positive that things were about to get *weird*.

Taking a breath, I followed him. Other than a tingle on my skin and a noticeable drop in the temperature, I didn't feel anything as I crossed over.

The room on the other side was circular and about twenty feet in diameter. Lights were embedded in the ceiling, and a heavily reinforced security door was set into one of the walls. Crimson Specter's portal deposited us above some sort of mystical diagram that had been carved into the stone and filled with what looked like silver.

As soon as I was through, he muttered a word, and the gate collapsed in on itself, disappearing.

"Where are we?" I asked, trying unsuccessfully to keep the unease from my voice.

"Home," he said simply.

I looked at the exposed stone walls. I wasn't a geologist, but it looked like natural stone. "Is this an underground layer? Are we in a volcano or something?"

"Or something," he replied with another hint of amusement.

The door opened with a beep and the clatter of sliding bolts, and a woman stepped through. Two slightly curved horns jutted through an inky mane that fell straight down to her waist, framing an angular face with midnight-blue skin, large eyes like twin pools of night, and a wide mouth. She was dressed in a form-fitting armored suit, a black leather jacket, and a pair of tall boots. A tail emerged from the uniform near the base of her spine. Shadows, ominous and predatory, shifted and writhed around her.

"Welcome back, old man," Nyx teased, before turning to me. "Brandon. I told you we'd see you again."

I smiled. "Hey, Nyx."

"There are some things I need to check on, Mr. Carter, and I suspect you need to digest what I've just told you, but we'll talk soon." Crimson Specter looked at Nyx. "In the interim, allow me to leave you in the capable hands of my associate. Nyx, I trust you'll show our guest around."

She raised an eyebrow. "The full tour?"

"The full tour. Introduce him around and find him some quarters, something suitable for both Mr. Carter and Ms. Devi. I think they may be staying awhile." He nodded to both of us and left.

Nyx looked at me after the door shut. "Take a breath. The next hour is going to be *interesting.*"

"I bet. I've never been in a *lair,* unless you count Vee's first apartment. Are we still in the States?"

Nyx's black eyes glittered with amusement, her tail twitching slightly. "Why, Brandon, what makes you think you're still on *Earth?*"

EPILOGUE

AFTERMATH

Falling silent, Brandon leaned back in the battered wooden booth and took a sip of his beer. He gestured to the untouched pint in front of Polaris, a flicker of amusement in his striking violet eyes. "I'm guessing you're not a beer guy?"

Polaris glanced around the tiny dive Brandon had insisted they meet at, his brow furrowing with annoyance. The bar was loud, crass, and filled with too many young people in too much black listening to bad music and making worse decisions. It wasn't the sort of place he'd have frequented even when he was young, and now, as a respectably dressed black man who looked to be nearing sixty, Polaris stood out even in his street clothes. Being nearly six and a half feet tall and built like a professional football player didn't help the matter.

Turning back to Brandon, Polaris studied him. He'd been suspicious at the beginning, only agreeing to hear him out at the urging of a dear friend. But as he'd listened, Polaris's mistrust had shifted to disquiet.

There was something compelling about Brandon's story, and however much of it was true, he barely resembled the photos taken before the explosion at the Vaydan Institute. His skin had a metallic sheen, and his face was crisscrossed with silvery scars. Even Brandon's hair had turned a metallic silver gray, but his eyes were by far his most distinctive feature: a violet so bright, they glimmered in the darkened bar.

He's dangerous, Polaris thought. Not only had he watched the footage of Brandon in action, Polaris had spent a lifetime around dangerous people. There was something hard and unyielding in the young man's eyes. He was also *powerful.* Polaris could feel the same cosmic power at the center of his own being radiating from Brandon like heat.

Dangerous and a fighter, but not a killer. Polaris had stared into the eyes of too many monsters over the long decades, and he liked to think he could tell the difference. But his assessment didn't verify anything he'd just heard, as much as he wanted to believe some of it.

"You're telling me Isabella is *alive?*" Polaris said finally, managing to keep the rush of shock, hope, and horror out of his voice with self-control cultivated over a lifetime. Isabella had been more than a teammate; she'd been a dear friend for decades, and her death had torn a hole in his heart he'd thought would never heal. "Why isn't she here?"

"She's still recovering." Brandon pulled a flash drive out of his pocket and slid it across the table. "She asked me to give you that. It should corroborate everything."

Polaris gestured at the flash drive without taking it. "How am I supposed to trust that whatever's on there is real? Or anything you've told me, for that matter."

"Isabella and the Old Man said you'd say that." Brandon snorted, a flicker of weary amusement in his eyes. "She told me to ask you how the azaleas she planted with your wife in your backyard were doing and whether you ever made her muffin recipe."

Polaris closed his eyes as a tremor ran through him. He took the flash drive. "Why are you telling me this?"

"Both Isabella and the Old Man thought they could trust you." Brandon grunted. "You need to get your house in order. Vaydan said he'd brought a few others from his world across. They're likely in Vanguard and might try to continue what he started."

Polaris had lived and worked with Aegis, and the rest of his team, for decades, long enough to know them well. He couldn't deny that he'd noticed some irregularities in their behavior, but he'd assumed they were the result of grief over Isabella. But now . . .

Weariness and foreboding, bone deep and heavy as a star, settled within him. "I'll look into it."

Brandon nodded. "I was also hoping you could keep an eye on my friends. You've met Abby, and the rest are good people too. If you're watching over them, they might have a chance to live something like normal lives."

Polaris nodded. "Of course."

The back door opened, revealing a pretty young woman with rich-brown skin and a partially shaved head. She looked at Brandon. "Time to go."

"Ms. Devi, I presume," Polaris said, nodding.

"Holy shit," Vee muttered, her eyes widening. "It's really him."

"The way to contact us is on the flash drive too." Brandon nodded, sliding out of the booth. "Take care of yourself."

Brandon and Vee left through the back door, leaving Polaris to his thoughts. If even some of what Brandon had told him was true, he'd shown bravery, resilience, and a willingness to sacrifice himself for the well-being of others. Those were the principles that Vanguard had been founded on, whatever had happened to it.

"Damn it." Polaris sighed and slid out of the booth, following after them. The door opened into a trash-strewn alley covered in graffiti and lined with dumpsters filled to the brim with garbage. "Mr. Carter, wait."

Brandon and Vee paused, glancing back.

"If the evidence you gave me verifies your story, it would go a long way toward clearing your name. With your powers, you could make a difference. Come with me, let me help you. You don't need to go down the same path Crimson Specter did. We can deal with whatever this is together." Polaris paused. "Who knows? You could end up wearing the *V* yourself someday."

Brandon and Vee glanced at each other and then looked back at Polaris. "I appreciate the offer, but after everything that's happened, my institutional trust is at an all-time low. Besides,"—his lip twitched into a half smile—"I'm no hero."

Brandon's eyes flashed with violet light, and a mote of utter darkness appeared him and Polaris, ringed with more violet energy. Expanding quickly, it swallowed Brandon and Vee and vanished.

And they were gone.

ACKNOWLEDGMENTS

Anti-Hero Blues is more than just my debut novel; it's my first book. In a sense, what you're holding is my proof of concept, and you reading it means it's already exceeded my wildest expectations. But it didn't happen by magic. Like all books, *Anti-Hero Blues* is the result of an iterative and, more importantly, collaborative process, and I'm profoundly grateful to everyone who played a role in bringing this novel to you.

First, I'd like to thank the amazing human beings in my writers group. Writing your first novel is a lonely road, and without Amanda, Leela, Jodie, Joel, and Nicole, *Anti-Hero Blues* would never have made it to publication. Not only did your feedback and ideas make the book better in a thousand different ways, your constant support and commiseration helped me claw my way toward what often felt like an unattainable goal.

I look forward to spending many, many more Monday nights with you all.

Similarly, the feedback from my alpha readers, Kaitlyn, Amul, Jon, and Ed, helped polish the many rough spots while convincing me I'd written a book worth reading, instead of four hundred pages of gibberish.

You all rock.

I also want to thank Leo Otherland, my editor and advocate on *Anti-Hero Blues*, who became a friend,

Acknowledgments

along with Tod Tinker and Charlene Templeman from Balance of Seven. Not only did you take a chance on a then-unpublished author, your tireless hard work and dedication brought *Anti-Hero Blues* from a rough draft to the book we've released into the wild.

I'd also like to thank Eric Smith and Kat Howard. Eric is an extraordinarily talented writer and literary agent who does a lot for the writing community as a whole, and his insight and advice helped get me on the right track at a critical time in the process. Kat Howard, the truly fantastic writer and developmental editor, also played a pivotal role in bringing *Anti-Hero Blues* to life, and her skill, experience, and instinct helped make the book's ending a real banger.

Last but certainly not least, I'd like to thank my wife, Nicole, who tolerated my excited rambling and my endless handwringing and read two complete versions while providing me copious amounts of encouragement and support.

ABOUT THE AUTHOR

Christopher Lee Rippee won a young authors contest in third grade, which was the day he officially decided to become a writer. He prepared by reading comics, playing too much Dungeons & Dragons, and devouring every sci-fi and fantasy novel he could get his hands on.

Along the way, thanks to some great people and a lifelong love of punk rock, Chris found his way to social work and currently works at a Pittsburgh-based non-profit. He's also a certified mental-health first-aid trainer, has worked as a neurodiversity consultant for several Pittsburgh-based tech startups, and has contributed to several tabletop RPG products.

When not writing, Chris reads, plays games, and spends time with his lovely wife, Nicole, and their adorable rescue dog, Belle.